YOUR TV TWINS

Also by Gregory G. Young, M.D.

YOUR PERSONALITY AND HOW TO LIVE WITH IT

YOUR TV TWINS

Gregory G. Young, M.D.

FAWCETT COLUMBINE
NEW YORK

A Fawcett Columbine Book
Published by Ballantine Books
 Published in the United States by Ballantine Books, a division of Random House, Inc., New York, and simultaneously in Canada by Random House of Canada Limited, Toronto.

Library of Congress Catalog Card Number: 86-92115

ISBN: 0-449-90231-5

Cover design by Sheryl Kagan
Book design by Beth Tondreau

Manufactured in the United States of America
First Edition: October 1987
10 9 8 7 6 5 4 3 2 1

CONTENTS

YOUR TV TWINS

INTRODUCTION

Your yacht has sprung a leak. An environmental group is marching on your front lawn demanding to know why you keep "polluting the scenery" with your oil wells. Your teenage daughter has locked herself in the bathroom because you refuse to let her date a professional wrestler. Hollywood is on the phone and wants to do an intimate and revealing TV movie based on your first two marriages. Meanwhile, your present spouse suddenly announces at the breakfast table that he "needs more space" to find himself. And you've just discovered that there's a family of squirrels living in the trunk of your car.

Time to change the channel? Not so fast. It's true that the problems mentioned above—with the possible exception of the last two—are the kind you would be likely to encounter only on the TV screen. But even though those types of problems may be far removed from our everyday experience, the way those folks in videoland *deal* with their dilemmas can make a big impact on the way we live our lives on this side of the screen.

Consider the fact that we are witness to the lives of hundreds of TV characters, as well as actors, artists, sports stars, business moguls, and celebrities of every other sort whose lives are chronicled on the tube through interviews, talk shows, and the nightly news. We watch our favorite TV friends and families grow up, fall in love, marry, raise children, deal with the boss, handle a blind date, dent a fender, or blow a business deal, all from the safety of our easy chairs. We watch Barbara Walters, Johnny Carson, and Phil Donahue ask those questions we'd love to pose to find out what makes a celebrity tick. Interestingly enough, it is often just what makes us tick.

Granted, the predicaments and pleasures of videoland are occasionally a bit different in size and scope from ours. Vacations take place in exotic paradises; stress arises from trying to prevent the takeover of a giant corporation, needing to hit a home run to win the World Series, or solving the fourth spectacular crime of the evening. Even everyday problems seem to be magically resolved in a weekly, half-hour time slot (commercials not included).

But TV friends, on screen or off, face the same basic wants and needs, the same strengths and weaknesses that we do. We are all part of the same human family and we live under the same human conditions: a situation occurs, we react to it in a certain way (depending on our particular Personality Style), and our reaction affects those around us.

As individuals, we all have thoughts, feelings, and attitudes that are unique to us, but as human beings, we respond to pleasure, stress, opportunity, and disappointment in predictable ways. Over time, a recognizable pattern develops. People come to recognize and know us by that pattern, and we come to know ourselves. Well, it's no different in videoland. So for every big promotion, marital snag, wayward child, or empty toothpaste tube we face, we begin to notice that there is someone on the TV screen who seems to be facing similar situations in a similar manner. If we watch these TV friends carefully, see them working through their problems, challenges, triumphs, and failures closely enough, we might just begin to see some of those patterns develop. The spark of recognition begins to flicker. Some start to look and sound awfully familiar. And if we study certain TV friends long enough, the screen becomes a magic mirror. At that point we feel as if we are watching ourselves. In a sense we are: We have found our TV Twin.

Imagine a TV character who acts, reacts, behaves, and feels much the same way you do—someone who shares your strengths and weaknesses, who handles joy, stress, disappointment, and frustration in a manner that you can relate to. Once a week, your "Twin" sets out on a wide variety of excursions into the sometimes perplexing tangle of modern existence and social intercourse, meeting and resolving all sorts of situations, while allowing you to profit vicariously from the same experience without ever having to give up the best spot on the sofa.

Of course, it's going to take a little time and effort, a little honest evaluation of yourself, to determine just who your TV Twins are. But once you've gotten acquainted, the possibilities are endless. While you watch your TV Twins go through the same situations you find yourself dealing with, you'll discover which of those actions and responses net positive results and which cause problems. You can decide what the strengths and weaknesses of your shared Personality Style are. And, best of all, you can gain some useful insights from this dress rehearsal without having to suffer the consequences.

So don't touch that dial. You are about to discover how you share an intimate relationship with some of the most famous, talented, admired, and successful people on TV. You will also discover how to be the best you can be, the "star" in your own life. Just sit back, read, learn, and enjoy. You are about to meet your TV Twins.

Chapter One

WHO ARE THESE TV TWINS AND HOW DID THEY GET INTO MY LIVING ROOM?

What if I told you that I've discovered a fantastic window through which you can watch certain people who are consistently acting and reacting to love, pain, joy, stress, opportunity, failure, and success in much the same ways that you do? And what if I told you that the way these people function in situations comes incredibly close to mirroring the way you might function in similar situations? And that by acquainting yourself with these "Twins" and watching them closely you can learn to channel your own personality effectively and purposefully, both in your attitude toward yourself and in your relationships with others?

"Fantastic window? Personality Twin? You must be watching too much TV," I hear you say.

Well, watching TV is exactly what I *have* been doing. And I have discovered some new, very exciting, and interesting uses for "the tube" beyond basic entertainment. But I have to give credit where it's due; originally it was other people's TV watching that led me from my own recognition of the twelve Personality Styles to the discovery of TV Twins. I never used to be much of a TV watcher. I felt, like a lot of other people did, that watching TV was just a way to pass the hours or "tune out" when I needed a break. But then . . . Well, let me start at the beginning.

WHAT ARE PERSONALITY STYLES?

In over twenty years of psychiatric practice here in the United States and throughout the world, I have met thousands of people from all walks of life. In speaking with all of those people in a variety of situations I began to hear many similar expressions of attitudes, fears, wishes, and ways of dealing with life. I certainly did not set out originally to match people to any sort of preconceived notion, but throughout the years, and all that communication, I couldn't help but notice the similarities. Gradually, through much painstaking research and observation, my staff and I concluded that these similarities were not the result of mere coincidence.

We sifted and sorted through data, testing people on all levels of mental health, and began to plot first one Personality Style and then another as they became apparent. We refined, amended, corrected, and clarified until we finally determined that there are twelve identifiable Personality Styles. Those twelve include

- the Ambitious,
- the Perceptive,
- the Anticipating,
- the Conscientious,
- the Accomplishing,
- the Persistent,
- the Influencing,
- the Patient,
- the Idealistic,
- the Sensitive,
- the Determined,
- the Adaptable.

Although each person creates his or her own life to a varying extent, each of us does it in a way that can be positively and accurately identified by one of these twelve Personality Styles, and in a way that is common to all people who share that particular Style.

Throughout the years I have seen these same Personality Styles occur again and again in people of both sexes and of all ages, races, and ethnic, economic, and educational backgrounds. The common aspects of each Style give us a way to recognize people who share those Styles and give those people a way to recognize themselves and each other. For example, the people who share the Ambitious Personality Style are typically competitive, hard-driving, and goal-oriented. They like nothing better than to accept a challenge and keep the action going. On the other hand, people who share the Sensitive Personality listen a lot but say very little. They are very much in tune with the nuances of life and they like a low-key approach. There are differences between each style; some are subtle, some not so subtle. *But each of us fits one and only one Personality Style.*

"But how can you say there are people in the world who are that much like me?" you may ask. Good question, and you're justified in asking it. After all, in a world that has given us all a number and a label, it's natural for us to resist being further classified and compartmentalized. But we should also consider that, before we can begin to talk about how we are all different, we first have to discover how we are the same. If anything, a clear understanding of the concept of Personality Styles can be liberating. It can help us understand what makes us tick and what allows us to be the unique persons that we are. We no longer have to be all things to all people. We are free to be ourselves.

What Does Personality Style Really Mean?

Here I should make the distinction between Personality Style and the personal traits and patterns of behavior that are unique to the individual, such things as how you fix your breakfast in the morning or how you style your hair. When we speak of Personality Style, we are examining *why* you style your hair the way you do. Do you try to draw attention to yourself, or to be inconspicuous? Do you always go along with the latest fashion, or do you strive to create your own? Is your hair a social statement, or is it just the way your spouse, family, or friends like it?

It's your Personality Style that causes you to feel that competitive urge every time you step to the starting line, or to feel that protective compulsion when you see an animal injured in the street, or that strong sense of worry that seems to accompany any change in plans. Each of the twelve Styles displays different skills and coping strategies and opportunities for investment of emotional energies. Your Personality Style presents you with an outline for life that you, in turn, can fill in with your own choice of colors, depending on your interests, abilities, values, tastes, and personal experiences. The better you understand yourself and your Personality Style, the clearer and more beautiful your individual picture will be.

Why Does It Help to Know Your Personality Style?

The more we discover about our sameness, the more we seem to be attracted by what we share in common with others. Our sense of community, so necessary to the human condition, is solidified and intensified by common experiences and shared feelings. It's nice to know that in Miami, Moscow, and Madrid, there are other human beings who share our strengths and weaknesses and our feelings, who tend to react under stress as we do, and who behave, in like situations, in much the same way that we behave. The more we discover about our shared characteristic behavior, the more we understand each other.

One of the more interesting experiences I had in the course of discovering Personality Styles was seeing how sympathetic and empathetic persons of the same Personality Style are toward each other—without even being aware of sharing the same Style and what that means. They are simply tuned into each other. Empathy and concern always surface, as do basic insights into problems and ways to solve them.

How Do We Recognize Others with Our Personality Style?

Each Personality has its own currency. The Ambitious Personality, for example, places much emphasis on competing and winning. Another person sharing that Ambitious Personality will pick up on the sense of striving and aggressiveness and can offer appropriate advice. He may not quite know what the connection is, but there's definitely something there.

That experience of recognition can and does happen anywhere. It is no accident that we often hear such casual comments as "Bill is just like his father." Bill doesn't look a bit like his father; he looks like his mother. But Bill's expressed attitude and his actions very much resemble his father's characteristic way of looking at things and doing things. "Oh," you say, "Bill learned all that from his father." True, Bill did learn many things from his father, but more important, Bill shares a Personality Style with his father. His father may have been a particular influence but Bill and his father were both born with a comparable disposition to see things and do things in characteristically repeated ways consistent with their shared Personality Style.

You may have had an experience like this: You look at a new acquaintance and say, "I don't know why, but you remind me so much of a friend I had in college ten years ago." Or you may have said, "Alice's new husband is so much like her first husband—and come to think of it, her second husband too." Or someone may have said to you, "Oh, you're just like my Uncle Fred." Chances are, it's no coincidence that Alice's husbands are all so much alike, or that you are attracted to two very similar friends ten years apart. These casual comparisons and coincidental attractions illustrate the concept of Personality Styles at work.

Once you understand what a Personality Style is and what you can expect of a given Style, you can go beyond casual comparisons to a much deeper understanding of and appreciation for the behavior of others with whom you live and work. You might also begin to understand that mysterious bond between you and Uncle Fred.

WHO ARE THESE TV TWINS?

Through my years of treating patients, I began to notice that many of them frequently compared themselves to certain characters on TV who they felt exhibited behavior similar to their own. One patient confided to me, "My personality is just like Ralph Kramden on 'The Honeymooners.' " Another said, "My wife acts just like Miss Kitty on 'Gunsmoke.' " At the same time, I wasn't much of a TV viewer, but I was curious about who those characters were and about what was causing my patients and their families and friends to identify so closely with these characters. As I thought, and as I watched, the answers eventually became obvious: TV was simply a matter of art (or entertainment) imitating life. My patients were actually sharing Personality Styles with their TV Twins.

With that in mind, I began studying in earnest a number of TV stars and the characters they portrayed. I discovered three very interesting facts. First: Most of the successful TV stars portrayed characters who shared their own Personality Style. (I determined those star's Personality Styles through interviews, magazine and newspaper articles, books, and personal contact.) Second: Most shows that stayed on the air for any length of time did so because the character's parts and dialogue were written in a way that matched and enhanced that character's Personality Style. (Of course, the writers, producers, and directors of the shows were not consciously utilizing any direct knowledge of Personality Styles. But most of us are students of human nature, and they had simply found a formula for success.) And third: The manner in which a particular character met and dealt with situations often paralleled the experiences of my patients, family, and friends who shared that character's Personality Style.

I found that those patients who had inadvertently discovered their TV Twins felt a great deal of empathy for their video counterparts. They vibrated with them. When the TV Twin felt bruised, they felt bruised. When the TV Twin felt happy, they felt happy. Many times they knew what the TV Twin was going to say even before he or she said it. The space between the two sides of the screen dissolved. There was no ignoring the fascination, excitement, and reassurance that came with watching someone who shared one's own Personality Style act out his or her life in a consistent and predictable way.

The next logical step for me was to catalogue TV characters until I had enough to represent each of the twelve Personality Styles. With the advent of video recorders it became possible to study both programs and characters more closely and to preserve certain episodes that offer exceptionally accurate or interesting portrayals of a particular Personality Style. Then, when patients or friends came to me with problems or difficulties, I could prescribe that they watch the characters who shared their Personality Styles: their TV Twins. Better yet, if I had taped and shown a particular segment to patients that showed the TV Twin working through a situation similar to theirs, the patients could observe how their TV Twin resolved the conflict, learned and profited—or lost—from the occurrence in that particular show. For those patients, it was indeed art imitating life; the TV became a magic mirror that enabled them to work through some of their problems vicariously and then apply what they had seen to their own situations.

TV Twins in Pairs

In time, I began to find TV Twins helpful in a wide variety of situations. Not only could they help individual patients resolve conflicts and learn to accept themselves and their Personality Style, but they also could become a valuable tool in helping couples relate. For example, Jane, a Patient Personality, who was very soft-spoken, understanding, and forbearing, was having problems relating to her husband, an Influencing Personality and an exacting, forceful, take-charge guy. Knowing that this same Personality Style pairing existed between Patient Krystle and Influencing Blake Carrington on the TV show "Dynasty," I advised Jane to watch how Krystle successfully handled her needs in the relationship. Jane found that she, too, could be assertive, pursue some of her interests without having to rely on others for help, and became a more equal partner in the marriage without denying her Personality Style or alienating her husband. Jane recently reported to me that her husband enjoyed her new assurance and self-confidence—once he had recovered from his initial shock.

One of the major problems I see couples experiencing is the expectation by one party that the other will "change" Personality Styles to make things run more smoothly. But that is not going to happen, and forcing someone to deny his or her Personality Style can only result in a very unhappy arrangement. The alternative I found is to have the partners discover each other's TV Twin in order to see that other people share their view of life and to learn how best to negotiate and coexist. The ideal way, of course, is to find a TV Twin couple whose Personality Style combination matches the viewing couple's. But that isn't always possible.

Matches—and Mismatches

Sometimes, a patient will come to me and tell me that he or she is attracted to a certain person. When we determine what that potential partner's Personality Style is, I then advise my patient to watch the potential partner's TV Twin to see what a steady diet of that partner would be like, again with the understanding that who you see is who you get. Aside from a few cosmetic changes that might occur, the Personality Style you see on the screen, if it is accurately portrayed, will stay essentially the same through the transition from videoland to everyday life.

TV Twins in the Workplace

Knowing the TV Twins of friends, children, employees, or bosses can also be quite helpful. One man came to me because he was worried about his new boss. He described the new boss sufficiently for us to determine his Personality Style. I advised him to watch Frank Furillo on "Hill Street Blues," who just happened to share the new boss's Personality Style; he would see how his new chief was likely to think, act, and react, and what his own expectations might be. It proved to be a very valuable insight.

Know Yourself—Be Yourself

One of the best and most basic uses of TV Twins is to lead you to a greater recognition and acceptance of your own Personality Style. At times, though we try our best to be ourselves and to follow our inner voice, we still seem to suffer from criticism, misunderstanding, and a general lack of positive strokes. Some of our less understanding friends may even make us feel that our behavior, which feels natural to us, is somehow "weird." Self-doubt sets in. But a session or two with our TV Twins can show us that we're not alone, that we're not weird, and that well-known and successful people who share our Personality Style have made it to the top by emphasizing the strengths of our Personality Style and understanding the weaknesses: by being exactly who they are.

A woman came to me who was being criticized by friends and family for being a "cleaning nut." She discovered that she was an Influencing Personality, that one of the aspects she shared with her TV Twins was that they are absolute sticklers for neatness and order and that one of her TV Twins had mentioned that the best therapy for him after coming home from a hard day's work is cleaning out his refrigerator. She then realized that her own "cleanomania" was not so odd after all.

If You're Still Skeptical . . .

The idea that we all have "Twins" on television who mirror our Personality Style and behavior is not always met with immediate belief or acceptance. Some people say that TV watching in general is a waste of time. My answer to them is, "What could be better than to enjoy, be entertained, learn, and have your life enriched all at the same time while relaxing in front of the tube?" TV Twins can make your TV watching time worthwhile. I am not advocating that we all become couch potatoes, but I am suggesting that we not overlook a valuable tool that most of us already have in our homes. The TV simply becomes another option for understanding and feeling good about ourselves, our family and friends, and those around us.

Some people, watching their TV Twins for the first time, are put off by the fact that they do not live in videoland where the house is never dirty and no one ever goes to the bathroom. They also find it difficult to relate to a TV character whose problem is always solved in a neat half hour or hour time slot. But those who are initially skeptical soon come to realize that TV Twins are valuable not for *where* they solve their problems, or how quickly, but for *how* they solve them and how they interact with those around them during the process. Of course, we'll never live on the Ewing ranch or in Bill Cosby's house, but we can learn that, below the glossy surface, our own homes are not that different from those of our TV Twins.

Then there are those whose first reaction to meeting their TV Twins is, "I might act or feel that way at times, but never to that extreme or that blatantly." Others admit that it might be the way they'd act if their confidence were higher or if they didn't have to deal with possible repercussions. The important thing to remember, I tell them, is that the Personality Style of TV characters is often exaggerated for purposes of entertainment and to give the character a clear and readily definable identity. My study of TV and TV Twins has convinced me that most shows that stay on the air for any length of time do so because the character's actions and dialogue are created to match and enhance that character's (and the actor's) Personality Style. I have also noticed that if I can identify the Personality Style of a major character within three episodes, that show has a good chance of being a success. Otherwise, it's probably not going to catch on. The key to applying lessons you learn from your TV Twins is the recognition of consistency, the strengths and weaknesses of your shared Personality Style, and the ability to see past the apparent differences between life in your house and life in the penthouse or on the ranch.

Even though our TV Twins' pleasures and problems might be somewhat different in size and scope from our own, a common message comes through. We feel a tingle of excitement when we discover we're not alone in our feelings and actions, and a genuine feeling of empathy when we experience—albeit vicariously—our TV Twins' triumphs and tragedies. We feel a rush of relief when it's our Twins who have to pay the piper, not us.

Once we become familiar with our TV Twins and the TV Twins of our friends, family, and acquaintances, and begin watching programs in this new and exciting way, we also come to another important realization: As humans, we share a lot of the same basic needs—love, comfort, and understanding—but as individuals, who share some very different Personality Styles, we express and satisfy those needs in very different ways.

HOW DO I USE THIS BOOK?

Step One: Discover and Become Familiar with Your Personality Style

The first step in getting acquainted with your TV Twins is to determine which of the twelve Personality Styles is your own. That Style is the bridge between you and your Twins. It allows the communication and empathy to flow. Your Personality Style is also one of the most important factors in making you the unique person you are.

Each of us fits one of the twelve possible Personality Styles. You were born with that Personality Style. It was passed to you genetically, and that same basic Style will endure throughout your life. It is as much a part of you as the color of your eyes or the pattern of your fingerprint. And since your TV Twins share that same Style, the discovery of your Style will help you to know yourself better, and to discover your Twins—on TV and in "real life."

In the next chapter, you will take a short test that will reveal your Personality Style. Approach the test in an open and honest fashion, answering the questions quickly and truthfully. The results of that test will indicate which of the twelve Personality Styles fits you. Then you can move on to the next step: meeting your TV Twins.

Step Two: Meet Your TV Twins

The rest of the book is divided into twelve chapters, each describing one of the twelve Personality Styles. As you read each chapter, you will become further acquainted with that particular Style and will be introduced to the TV Twins who share that Style. You will find that there is one essential element that serves as a key to recognizing and understanding each Style. For example, the Accomplishing Personality is based on an overwhelming need to dazzle, to be "on stage," to be such a bundle of energy, exuberance, and enthusiasm that others can't help but be impressed and give their approval. You will read about the TV Twins who share the Accomplishing Personality Style and about scenes from TV shows that show those Twins and their Style in action. You also will read examples of how people on our side of the screen, who share the Accomplishing Style, have used the lessons they've learned from TV Twins to make changes in their own lives.

Step Three: Learn to Observe and Understand Your TV Twins

As you read your chapter and become better acquainted with your Personality Style and TV Twins, you will start noticing ways in which you share hopes, fears, and dreams with them. As you watch week after week, a consistent picture will begin to develop. You'll see what makes your Twins happy, anxious, comfortable, or uncomfortable; you'll see what sort of actions and responses are successful for them, and which aren't; you'll begin to experience their trials and errors and to take advantage of their imagination, energy, and resourcefulness while noting how they manage to avoid pitfalls. Then, with your increased self-awareness, you'll begin to apply what you have seen and learned to your own way of solving life's puzzles.

"It's the visual dimension that is really something special," one viewer commented after watching her TV Twins. "People can give you advice, tell you about their experiences, and try to communicate in that way. But when you can actually watch someone who shares your Personality Style acting out situations that you can in turn apply to your own life, the process of learning about yourself takes on a whole new meaning. As they say: 'One picture is worth a thousand words.' "

So, for example, if you are an Idealistic Personality, you'll discover that Clair Huxtable on "Cosby" is one of your TV Twins. You might watch her in one episode where she and daughter Denise, who is also Idealistic, are saying goodbye as Denise leaves home for college. You see that there is no gushy emotion, no physical clinging, just encouraging words and a love expressed by inner strength and independence. As you will discover from reading the Idealistic chapter and by examining your own feelings, that is the Idealistic way of dealing with an emotionally charged scene. By watching Clair and Denise, you have discovered that you are not alone in your feelings, and that your uncomfortable response to intimacy is not "weird," but normal for the Idealistic Personality.

That can be very reassuring.

Step Four: Learn to Recognize the Personality Styles of Others

As you read the remaining chapters in the book and become acquainted with the rest of the Personality Styles, you will begin to recognize friends, family, spouse, lover, boss, and co-workers. You'll be able to watch their TV Twins to get a better idea of how and why they act and react the way they do in various situations.

For example, let's suppose that you decide that your spouse is a Conscientious Personality. You then read that one of his or her TV Twins is Dick Loudon of "Newhart." You observe Dick, to see how well he illustrates the Conscientious Personality's dry, sly wit and the Conscientious tendency to doubt decisions he has made. With that knowledge, you begin to expect the low-keyed humor and learn that by offering fewer choices or options, you can make the decision-making process easier for your spouse. Instead of causing frustration and doubt by presenting ten choices of cereal at breakfast, you offer only one or two. The choice is simple. Your spouse is happy.

With more knowledge and experience, you can begin to predict how certain Personality Styles will respond to certain situations and, more important, how you can best get along with them by encouraging the positive aspects of their Personality and avoiding or downplaying the negative.

Your knowledge of Personality Styles and TV Twins can become a very valuable tool.

YOU'RE READY TO BEGIN

The combination of the short test in the following chapter and the twelve descriptive chapters will give you an accurate understanding of your Personality Style and how to relate to your TV Twins. But there are a few precautions you should keep in mind before you proceed.

As I said earlier, each Personality Style has an essential element that is the key to recognizing and understanding it. That essential element is explained at the beginning of each chapter and is the prime force behind all the other elements of that particular Style. So, even though you may find some elements that seem common to more than one Personality Style, don't be confused. For example, you might find that more than one Personality Style will mention the word *generous.* But as you read more closely you will notice that in one Style being generous is the prime moving force, while in another it might be a minor element, or perhaps might be tied up with trying to look good or trying to protect one's security. *Be careful not to decide your Personality Style too soon.* Even though you may think you recognize parts of yourself in many styles, *only one will emerge as a true composite picture of you.* You will recognize yourself as you read carefully.

Your next question might be, "Can I be part of more than one Personality Style?" The answer is no, and here's why. Each of us has one and only one Personality Style which is a unique and distinguishable part of our total being. The healthier we are, the more obvious our Style will be and the more we will be able to use it to our advantage.

Part of the significance of these twelve Personality Styles is that we don't have to be all things to all people. We learn who we are, why we act and react the way we do, and what we can and cannot share with each of the other Styles.

As you learn more about yourself and your TV Twins, you will find that you share a great deal with them. They will no longer be just images on the screen; they will become friends.

So tune in, discover, and enjoy. The show is about to begin.

Chapter Two

THE PERSONALITY TEST: WHO AM I?

A SHORTCUT TO YOUR TRUE SELF

There are times when I've found myself looking at another person, someone I was particularly impressed with at the moment, and thinking, "I wish I could be more like him." At other times, I've done something against my better instincts, and said to myself, "That was not really me doing that."

Well, this short test you are about to take will probably take care of both of those problems. It will help you to identify your Personality Style and it will also be your first step toward discovering people who are, in many ways, just like you: your TV Twins. Becoming better acquainted with your strengths and weaknesses, as well as discovering that you are not alone with your Personality Style, should make your life just a bit easier, if not a lot more exciting.

Since we are trying to determine your true Personality Style, you should be as open and honest as possible when you take the test. Your responses to the statements should be from the heart, should reflect the way you *really are,* not the way you wish you could be or the way family, friends, or spouse would like you to be. Your true self is, without a doubt, the best you can be.

You may find it helpful to complete the test in a quiet spot where you can concentrate on those distinctive elements that make up your Personality Style. Your first response is most likely to be your natural response, so trust your instincts. Also, you should always respond as you know yourself *now*.

The following statements are designed to help you describe yourself. Your natural personality, which you share with your TV Twins, will become evident as you complete the four-step test.

STEP 1: Take the test.
STEP 2: Score the test.
STEP 3: Read the short personality descriptions in the Personality Guide on p. 27.
STEP 4: Read the chapter that corresponds to your Personality Style.

Please rate each statement with:
1 = never
2 = occasionally
3 = frequently
4 = always

It is very important to rate each statement honestly, as you know yourself now. Do not respond as others might expect you to. After you have rated each statement, please refer to the scoring instructions that follow.

SCORING 1 = never 2 = occasionally 3 = frequently 4 = always

1. ___3___ wants to arrange and follow schedules
2. ___3___ seeks respect from others
3. ___2___ voices strong opinions
4. ___4___ needs and guards privacy
5. ___3___ needs to talk, share ideas
6. ___2___ creative daydreamer and schemer

7. ________ considered nice and nonthreatening
8. ________ needs many facts and figures to proceed
9. ________ ambitious to achieve high goals
10. ________ extremely loyal
11. ________ refuses to conform when it violates one's values
12. ________ tends to have a high level of doubt and uncertainty
13. ________ very compassionate with others
14. ________ has difficulty adapting to changes
15. ________ emphasis on giving and being helpful
16. ________ can communicate with people from all levels
17. ________ very imaginative, creative solutions
18. ________ viewed as liking to lead, sought out to do so
19. ________ tries hard to impress others
20. ________ great emphasis on financial gain
21. ________ avoids foolishness and nonsense
22. ________ very concerned and affected by others' opinions
23. ________ highly verbal, likes to debate
24. ________ very hard to say no to people
25. ________ looks for challenges to tackle
26. ________ experiences much searching and "wanting more"
27. ________ very protective with loved ones
28. ________ thinks and plans far in advance
29. ________ shy and guarded with strangers
30. ________ likes to be seen, noticed, receive approval
31. ________ has many varied interests and friends
32. ________ wants peace at all costs
33. ________ difficulty with being bossed by others
34. ________ tends to sit on fence and not take a stand
35. ________ very strongly believes in faith
36. ________ honest to the point of being outspoken
37. ________ encourages others to achieve
38. ________ tends to doubt decisions already made
39. ________ tries harder to do more
40. ________ appears confident, poised, self-assured
41. ________ good at taking charge, organizing
42. ________ very tolerant and accepting of others
43. ________ prone to worry a lot

44. ________ enjoys watching and studying people
45. ________ builds others up, bolsters their egos
46. ________ emphasizes fairness and equal treatment
47. ________ emphasizes being right and just
48. ________ high standards, principles, convictions
49. ________ many projects going at a time
50. ________ can't stop and enjoy successes
51. ________ dwells on pros and cons when deciding
52. ________ avoids sharing plans in the making
53. ________ has difficulty seeing own good points
54. ________ encourages and provokes general conversation
55. ________ great difficulty starting something new
56. ________ tends to be wishful, hopeful
57. ________ champion or defender of the underdog
58. ________ often speaks to strangers
59. ________ tends to be a creature of habit
60. ________ impatient when things aren't perfect
61. ________ marches to own drummer, individualistic
62. ________ strong need to feel included, be an important part
63. ________ pushes others to achieve
64. ________ won't force or be forced
65. ________ solicits opinions of others
66. ________ very curious and watchful
67. ________ full of optimism, avoids negatives
68. ________ stresses one-to-one relationship
69. ________ easygoing, calm, unflustered
70. ________ very hurt when rejection is perceived
71. ________ can be too detailed and precise
72. ________ has short fuse when impatient

Directions for Scoring

Each box below contains the crucial statement numbers and a space for the score of each of those items. Place the score for each statement on the line next to it. Add these numbers to find your total.

Box (1)	Box (2)	Box (3)	Box (4)
9. 2	13. 3	14. 2	8. 2
20. 2	27. 3	22. 2	12. 2
25. 2	36. 3	28. 2	38. 2
37. 3	46. 4	43. 2	51. 3
50. 2	57. 4	55. 2	59. 3
63. 2	70. 3	62. 3	71. 3
13 TOTAL	20 TOTAL	13 TOTAL	15 TOTAL

Box (5)	Box (6)	Box (7)	Box (8)
19. ____	6. ____	1. ____	7. ____
30. ____	17. ____	18. ____	15. ____
39. ____	26. ____	33. ____	24. ____
49. ____	35. ____	41. ____	32. ____
58. ____	56. ____	60. ____	42. ____
67. ____	68. ____	72. ____	69. ____
TOTAL	TOTAL	TOTAL	TOTAL

Box (9)	Box (10)	Box (11)	Box (12)
3. ____	4. ____	2. ____	5. ____
11. ____	10. ____	21. ____	16. ____
23. ____	29. ____	34. ____	31. ____
40. ____	44. ____	47. ____	45. ____
48. ____	53. ____	52. ____	54. ____
61. ____	66. ____	64. ____	65. ____
TOTAL	TOTAL	TOTAL	TOTAL

Record the numbers of the boxes with the three highest scores.
1. 2 2. 10 3. 12

2 5 9

Next, go to the following Personality Guide which provides a short description of each of the twelve Personality Styles. Match the box numbers with the numbers of the personalities. Then read the descriptions of the personalities and choose the one that *best* describes you. Record the name of your Personality Style in the space below.

Perceptive, Adaptable

I have a Sensitive Personality.
Know Yourself . . . Be Yourself!

Personality Guide

AMBITIOUS:

1

Competitive, hard driving, talks about goals and winning, accepts challenges, works well where there are many opportunities to succeed, good at getting things done, action-oriented, has difficulty enjoying successes, takes a "what's next" approach, works long hours, aggressive, likes to keep an eye on the competition.

PERCEPTIVE:

2

Compassionate, has much empathy for others, emotional, helpful, sympathizes with the underdog, needs to feel appreciated, can be jealous on occasion, animal lover, values honesty and fairness, protective of loved ones, outspoken especially when unfairly treated, romantic, the original Good Samaritan, wants and needs affection.

ANTICIPATING:

3

Planner, always thinking of the future, genuine, authentic, hates being phony, wants to feel that what is being done is important, does not like change, tendency to worry, thorough, does better when busy, organized, dislikes being rushed, needs to feel a part of things, takes gradual approach.

CONSCIENTIOUS: 4 — Logical, concerned with facts and figures, tends to procrastinate, compiles large amounts of data before making decisions, tends to be a creature of habit, has a wry/sly/dry sense of humor, practical joker—one liners, often doubts decisions, stores many facts, asks many questions.

ACCOMPLISHING: 5 — Energetic, always on the go, works fast, plays fast, laughs or smiles a lot, effervescence is contagious, wants approval and tries hard to get it, spontaneous, easily sidetracked, has good sense of humor, can exaggerate things, strives for recognition, the world is a stage.

PERSISTENT: 6 — Believable, soft, gentle, searching, persuasive, strong emphasis on hope and faith, often makes believer out of others, charismatic, does best in a one-to-one relationship and is persistent in building these relationships, dreams are important, creative thinker, late bloomer.

INFLUENCING: 7 — Emphasizes neatness and cleanliness, impatient when things aren't perfect, well dressed, well organized, emphasizes control, good storyteller, charming, often looked upon as a leader, time and schedules are important, very responsible, likes to go first class, strives for the grand and glorious in life—the ultimate, functions best when given choices.

PATIENT: 8 — Tolerant, often hints rather than asks directly, accepting of others, always cheerful and easygoing, puts others at ease, wants security for self and others, wants peace at all costs, has a difficult time saying no to others, uncomfortable expressing own needs, may tend to sweep problems under the rug.

IDEALISTIC: 9

Interested in image, independent, self-sufficient, poised, cool, marches to own drummer, sticks to strong standards and ideals, has a tendency to back off when people get too personal, verbal and lively conversationalist, likes to debate on intellectual level, free spirit, objective, uncomfortable with weaknesses.

SENSITIVE: 10

Curious, very watchful, listens a lot, says little, very aware, works well alone, takes job very seriously and is very responsible, lives by the Golden Rule, sensitive to others and their needs, tends to dwell on their own vulnerabilities rather than strengths, strong family orientation, very loyal, shy with strangers, open with close friends, privacy is important, affected by environment, nature lover.

DETERMINED: 11

Wants to be right and respected, sees self as responsible, would rather be right than popular, often indirect, does not like to argue or hassle, solves problems in a reasonable and strategized manner, will clam up under stress, often does not declare opinions until sure he or she is right, rules/regulations are very important, high morals, actions speak louder than words.

ADAPTABLE: 12

Life is an open book, flexible, able to fit into any situation, aware of whatever is current, avid listener, good in public relations, verbal and lively conversationalist, can play the role of devil's advocate, can be competitive but rarely threatening, different friends for different occasions.

Now you're ready to move on to the next step—the best part. Turn to the chapter that corresponds to your Personality Style. There you will meet your TV Twins and begin to see yourself in a brand new way.

Chapter 3

THE AMBITIOUS PERSONALITY

PROFILE

- Originator of the eighteen-hour work day.
- Always needs a challenge; needs to win.
- Very concerned with rating; one eye constantly on the scoreboard.
- Full of purpose and drive.

TV TWINS

- Alex Keaton—"Family Ties"
- Jennifer Keaton—"Family Ties"
- J. R. Ewing—"Dallas"
- Greg Sumner—"Knots Landing"
- Alexis—"Dynasty"
- Angela—"Who's the Boss?"
- Maddie—"Moonlighting"

THE AMBITIOUS PERSONALITY

The Ambitious Personality is just that: ambitious. Action is your life blood. You will never hesitate to accept a challenge and to compete willingly and willfully. You are sometimes openly aggressive but more often cautious as you move purposefully toward your goal. Achieving that goal—winning—is all important. You set your goal, plan how to get there and, before the plan is fully jelled, you are off and running, striving and striding toward your objective. If you run into a road block, you'll dig under it, climb over it, or detour around it. But you never stop moving, maneuvering, working, and you won't stop until you've achieved your goal.

The Ambitious Personality can be sociable and affable, but social moments are interludes; you are soon back to the task at hand. And while you work well within the group, you are forever urging others to move ahead toward whatever goals they are seeking. Those around you usually view you as a winner, and when they say so you are pleased.

You like to be told that you are getting the job done, that you do it well, that you are very good—perhaps the best—at what you do whether it is baking bread or teaching school, selling computers or playing golf. When you hear the compliments and experience the kudos, you can savor the good feeling of having done well. Then you move on to the next challenge. There is always another goal ahead.

Once you lock in on a project, you develop instant tunnel vision, eyes focused on the goal ahead. Nothing else seems to matter quite so much as achieving that goal. The sun could turn purple, a flood could roar through the center of town, your cat could have puppies, but you wouldn't notice. And that might be one of your greatest strengths: your ability to close everything else out of your mind but the task ahead.

Of course, setbacks are always possible. That's part of the challenge of the game, and certainly what makes the whole process so intriguing. But when setbacks come, the healthy Ambitious Personality can shrug them off, then move on to the next challenge—one that's perhaps a little more reasonable and attainable.

"No guts, no glory," is your motto. You're a survivor, and you always manage to find a way to come out on—or at least near—the top. If you find you can't win, you might compromise (a compromise is better than a loss) or change the rules, or even change the whole game. There's certainly no harm in trying.

The Ambitious achiever is always on the lookout for an opportunity, an edge, any kind of an edge. You might be tempted to stack the deck, bend the rules a little, or plant an extra set of eyes or ears if the stakes are high enough. After all, when the going gets tough, the tough get ambitious. At least that's how you may view the situation, assuming that everyone is just as competitive—and aggressive—as you: with an ace always up their sleeve. And, if you, the Ambitious challenger, find your opponent napping or overconfident, you love nothing more than pulling a "gotcha" to drive the point home. The Ambitious competitor relishes the thought of outfoxing and outmaneuvering an opponent, then at just the right moment: gotcha!!

Support often comes to the Ambitious Personality in the form of a confidante or sidekick, someone you can depend on for advice and reinforcement. If you choose marriage, and make it successful, it will be because of your supportive, understanding spouse. Your home and family become a sanctuary, a place free from the constant stress of competition, a place where the ratings come high from an appreciative family.

If you find you're being too aggressive, stepping on too many toes, or neglecting your closest supporters, you may begin to feel some guilt, along with a slip in your ratings. That situation calls for a transformation to Mr. Nice Guy. After all, nice guys finish first, not last.

MEET YOUR TV TWINS

"I live for challenges and competition, Dr. Young. There's not a whole lot of time in my busy life for TV watching."

That's what the Ambitious Personality might say to me when I mention TV Twins. Well, if it's action you want—along with a much better understanding of where all of that Ambitious energy comes from—then take a few minutes and meet your TV Twins. It just might put you one step ahead of the game.

Finding your TV Twins can be tremendously rewarding. They'll be easy to identify because they:

- Are aggressive and competitive.
- Look for opportunities and competitive edges in life.
- Are able to talk about wanting to be the winner.

- Assume that everyone is as aggressive and competitive as they, suspecting that "vultures" are everywhere.
- Are able to act and react immediately to a situation.
- Obviously enjoy continuous action.

You and your Twins are always on the move. The air around you crackles with energy and excitement. The pace is brisk, the action fast. The atmosphere is charged with challenge, competition, calculated odds, risks. You are like a race horse at a starting gate, unable to restrain yourself from getting on with the race. This action gets your adrenaline going, but the main thing that really counts is winning. Your life is a succession of goals, projects, plenty of hard work, and, in the end, the rich reward of putting it all together: sweet success.

As you follow your TV Twins' video lives, look carefully for examples of:

- Their enjoyment of their work and willingness to work long hours.
- Their need for a "first advisor" or sidekick.
- How bad they feel when they lose.
- The tunnel vision they show as they pursue success.
- Their readiness to move on to the next challenge immediately when they win.
- A tendency to feel guilty about being aggressive.

Alex, eldest son of the Keatons on TV's "Family Ties," is an enterprising, aggressive sort of a guy. Some might even call his self-assured manner cocky. But when opportunity knocks, he's always the first to answer the door even though he might have to cut in front of a few people to get there. Well, hey, a race is a race, right? Alex's younger sister **Jennifer**, shares his ambitious personality, although she appears, at times, a bit less aggressive.

On one episode, Mom and Dad Keaton go out of town during homecoming week at the local college. Alex, a student at the college, is quick to see the need for extra lodging for the huge influx of alumni. And he's just as quick to seize the opportunity when he sees Mom and Dad's empty bedroom. So out go the newspaper ads and flyers, and in come the potential lodgers. But the demand is bigger than Alex thought, and soon the entire house is full of paying customers, the living room has become a party room for postgame celebration, Alex has dollar signs floating in front of his eyes, and Mom and Dad arrive home early.

Well, needless to say, Mom and Dad aren't happy with the house full of strangers, much less with the billboard they passed on the highway advertising their "rooming house," or the flashing vacancy sign in the front yard. Alex is contrite but argues that the sound of money, and opportunity, calling out to him were too much to ignore.

On "Dallas," **J.R. Ewing** is the eldest son of a Texas oil family. When Ambitious J.R. is seen wheeling and dealing his interest in the family oil company, the air is charged with the electricity and intrigue of big-time competition.

When J.R. learns, in one episode, that the rest of the Ewing family is content to sell out some of their shares to a rival company which is attempting a takeover, his Ambitious fires are ignited. There is no way in the world that he would give in to a takeover attempt by a second-rate competitor; but at the same time he would like nothing better than to see that competitor try. His mother, Miss Ellie, reminds him that even though certain family members are giving up their shares, the Ewings will still keep a seventy percent interest. J.R. is clearly not impressed with those figures or satisfied with the outcome. Smashing the takeover attempt and retaining full control makes him a winner. Owning less just makes him a shareholder, and that's not the way he plays the game. He loves to play and he plays to win.

Joan Collins, who plays the scheming, slightly unscrupulous **Alexis** on "Dynasty," responds to an interviewer's question about how she sees life by observing, in typical Alexis fashion, "Life's a banquet and most poor suckers are starving to death."

The Ambitious Personality might watch these three segments and say, "That J.R. is kind of an underhanded, ruthless guy, but there's no backing away from a real, full-scale showdown," or "Alex does seem to get a little carried away with some of his schemes, but renting out rooms in his parents' house to homecoming alumni was one hell of an idea. My son's school has a yearly paper drive and parked outside is a forty-foot truck for collection. I suggested they put a big sign on the truck to get more papers and they looked at me like I was crazy." Or, "Alexis is a bit blunt, but I'd give anything to see her go up against J.R., one on one."

There can be no doubt that the Ambitious chord has been struck. It's the action, the call of the contest, the challenge, the pouncing on opportunity like the spider on the fly, the sweet smell of victory, that the Ambitious Personality is tuning in to. All that endeavor, enterprise, and adventure is music to your ears.

On "Knots Landing," **Greg Sumner** plays his Ambitious music, much as J.R. Ewing does, in the rough-and-tumble world of big business.

On "Moonlighting," **Maddie** answers the call of action and challenge as the head of her own private investigation firm.

Angela, on "Who's the Boss?", is a single mother who manages to raise a child and succeed in the highly competitive world of advertising. But she leaves the everyday routine tasks of housekeeping to her housekeeper Tony. Her time and energy are better focused on staying on top as head of an ad agency than on having the cleanest laundry on the block.

In one segment, Angela is beaten in competition for a prestigious advertising award by a newcomer to the field. Angela has worked very hard, focusing her energy on the work, but now she has to watch the award go to someone else, and she is not taking it well.

"You're right, I'm upset," she tells Tony after he tries to console her. "I'm upset because . . . because of that *L* word" (for all of you non-Ambitious readers, the "*L* word" is *lose*). Tony finally convinces her to attend the awards dinner and congratulate her victorious rival. He claims it will make her feel better and offers to go with her. Angela reluctantly agrees but gets so upset at seeing her rival that she sneaks outside during the dinner and lets the air out of her rival's car tires. Then she goes back inside only to have her rival call her to the stage and say, "I have to thank Angela. She is a wonderful professional and human being who has taught me so much. I couldn't have won without her, so this award is as much hers as it is mine."

Angela feels the rising tide of guilt. As that particular segment ends, Angela and Tony are standing outside the awards dinner in the parking lot. Angela is tempted to play Mr. Nice Guy. "Maybe I should go back in there and toast her with some champagne," Angela suggests. "No," says Tony, handing her a tire pump, "it's your turn to pump."

No one loves the thrill of competition more than the Ambitious Personality. But let's be honest, isn't there a little Angela and J.R. Ewing in all of us? Aren't most of us to some degree Ambitious? Aren't we all, at times, assertive? Don't most of us have goals that we strive to achieve? Of course. And we all like to win. Competing and achieving are prized virtues in our society—but not necessarily as the dominant, all defining style of behavior.

Most Personalities will rise to a challenge, given an appropriate challenge at an appropriate time, but some would happily settle for a four-day work week. And most of us enjoy relaxed moments away from the routine of challenge and competition. We like to pause to savor success, to polish the trophy, or to wander through the garden watching the clouds.

If you are an Ambitious Personality, you are probably gritting your teeth at this point. All of this unproductive contemplation is driving you up a wall. Let's get on with it!

TO BE AMBITIOUS IS TO COMPETE

You view life as a challenge. To be Ambitious is to compete, and the only way to play the game is to win. But ambitions come large and small, in low as well as in high places.

One Ambitious Personality might strive to be the president of the corporation. Another, captain of the bowling team. One Ambitious nurse may work toward being the best nurse on the floor, another toward becoming supervisor of nursing of the entire hospital. The Ambitious draftsman new to the engineering department prudently knows he is not equipped to challenge the chief of engineering for his position, but he might find it exhilarating to challenge him at chess. And useful. Given his skill at the game, the chess board might be his route to becoming head draftsman.

"I look on everything I do as a challenge, and I like to win," says one Ambitious Personality. "But my friends accuse me of being too competitive, of making everything into a contest, of not being able to 'just relax and play for the fun of it.' "

Does that sound familiar? Well, don't despair. Your Ambitious TV Twins are just as consistent in showing their desire to compete, and to be the best, no matter where or when the contest occurs.

In one episode of "Family Ties," Jennifer asks Alex to help her with a school term paper. "I'd just like my paper to be the best," she informs him. Alex knows exactly what she is talking about and is immediately interested. "I like your goals of conquest and domination," he tells her. "I'd like to think I inspired that." Unfortunately, Alex gets a little carried away, loading young Jennifer down with complicated reference books, elaborate speeches, and a custom-designed costume to wear as she presents her paper to the class.

Although Jennifer responds and relates to Alex's drive to excel and be the best (remember, she also has an Ambitious Personality), she is a bit uncomfortable with the intensity of his desire to compete and rejects his claim that she is just like him. But he reminds her of an incident that took place when she was a very young child and playing in the sandbox with one of her friends. She and the friend were having a contest to see who could built the biggest sandcastle. As it turned out, the friend's castle made Jennifer's look like a peasant hut.

When I showed that particular segment on videotape to a roomful of Ambitious Personalities, I stopped the tape at that point and asked them what they thought Jennifer would do next. The great majority in the room guessed that Jennifer would find a way to win, to have her castle be the best, no matter what it took. They were tuning in to her Ambitious vibrations.

As it turned out, Jennifer did exactly what the majority had guessed. She diverted her friend's attention by pointing out an ice cream truck down the street, and then demolished his castle when he looked away. While Alex fondly remembers that first clue to his sister's drive to compete and do whatever it took to be the best—her Ambitious Personality—she reminds him that he later bought her poor little friend an ice cream cone to help him forget his demolished castle. "Yes," Alex remembers, acknowledging his turn as Mr. Nice Guy, "but it was just a small cone."

THE RATING GAME: WHO IS THE FASTEST, THE MOST SUCCESSFUL, THE BEST

The essential element that distinguishes you, the Ambitious Personality, from all other Personality Styles is the tremendous emphasis you place on achievement. And to achieve, you must have goals. Reach the goal, or better yet, reach the goal first, and you are the winner. But you can't rate the players in this contest—your competitors or yourself—without a score card. So you tend to score yourself, and others, at everything. I call it the "rating urge," and it comes in many different forms.

"Mirror, mirror on the wall, who's the fairest of them all?" Your first exposure to the rating game might have come from fairy tales. Then it became: Who is the fastest runner on the block, the best dancer on the floor, the greenest thumb on the street, the best backhand on the tennis court, the top salesperson on the staff, the fastest gun in the West? If you're not the best, the quickest, the top, the first, it certainly isn't that you haven't tried: You're *always* trying. But if you're a hair slower or a bit less skilled or a rung below the top, you feel anxious and frustrated. Your ratings are low, or you suspect that others are rating you low. If you're feeling sufficiently good about yourself, you can wait for a better day. If not, you may be tempted to kick the dog. You can watch your Ambitious TV Twins deal with the sometimes tricky game of collecting the best ratings.

On "Moonlighting," Ambitious Maddie is the head of a very

successful private investigation firm. One segment finds her very nervous because her parents are coming for a visit. She hasn't seen them in a long time and is eager to get some good ratings for her hard work and diligence in rising to the top of her profession.

Maddie's father, who apparently shares her Ambitious Personality, is impressed by her office but naturally doesn't want to dillydally or waste valuable time making small talk. So he quickly moves off to more productive endeavors, leaving Maddie alone with Mom. Non-Ambitious Mom is also impressed with the office, but the rating she gives is not so glowing. "This almost makes up for no grandchildren," is her assessment. There is an obvious hint of pain, and disappointment, on Maddie's face. A high rating for a successful career and sumptuous office do not completely counteract the low rating for lack of domesticity and motherhood.

On "Family Ties," Alex is having a bit of trouble with his college geometry class and is threatened by the prospect of a B+ marring his straight A average, so a tutor is assigned. Having to bow to accepting a tutor is bad ratings, but not quite as bad as that B+, so for the moment things are OK. Then comes the Ambitious Personality's nightmare: The tutor is a thirteen-year-old child prodigy who just happens to be attending Alex's college. Bad rating? For Alex, learning geometry from such a precocious upstart is clear off the bottom of the rating scale. But he needs the help, so he does what any other enterprising Ambitious Personality would do in such a dilemma: He arranges a "relationship" between his kid sister Jennifer and the boy genius, just to give the boy a "real" reason to be hanging around the house. Meanwhile, it couldn't hurt to pick up a few geometry tips, since the kid is going to be there anyway.

The rating urge is projected onto all sorts of situations. She likes to be seen with the captain of the football team: That rates a good score. He drives a Corvette: That rates well on a date. She dresses smartly, even a bit seductively: She is inviting a favorable rating. He loses at golf, but buys two rounds of drinks in the clubhouse: He is trying to buy a good rating to offset a low one. Her sales lead for the month and her report is submitted promptly—clean, clear, complete: The sales manager scores her a solid rating on two counts. He brings his wife flowers, guaranteeing himself a favorable rating as the thoughtful husband (even though he had his secretary go out on her lunch hour to buy them while he caught up on some more pressing and important business). As you watch your TV Twins, you realize that you share that same quest, whatever form it takes: to be forever rated first, or best.

For you, that's healthy.

OVERPLAYING THE RATING GAME

Moving through life with a scoreboard on your back, always waiting for the next rating to flash, can be a heavy burden at times. And that is the way the less effective, less confident Ambitious Personality behaves. Sooner or later the rating game can become a losing proposition. If your goal is unreasonable or your plan inflexible, you may run up a series of low scores—even zeros. Then you are in danger of driving yourself into depression.

We can see a perfect example of overplaying the rating game in a segment of "Family Ties." Ambitious Alex's girlfriend Ellen is very interested in the arts—foreign films, poetry readings, and modern dance. Alex, on the other hand, finds such things unproductive, much too passive, and a monumental waste of time. Finally it becomes obvious to Alex that Ellen might be spending a little more time with her arty friends than she is with him, particularly with a male dancer who is going to be her partner in the upcoming dance troupe auditions. Alex decides to improve his rating with Ellen by becoming an aficionado of the arts, a challenge that proves to be beyond his reach. He shows up at the dance auditions, makes a disastrous attempt to perform an impromptu number, and ends up humiliating himself and Ellen. The urge to compete has led Alex into an arena totally foreign to him, and the resulting ratings are very low indeed.

In a potentially threatening situation, such as one in which you feel you are about to come out on the losing end of a relationship, it is better for you, the tense Ambitious Personality, to try to relax and to rate yourself high simply for having made the effort, for having worked hard in trying to achieve your own goals. Examine each opportunity and challenge carefully before acting. That way you can avoid the frustration and anger that are sure to result when you compete indiscriminately or in areas where you have no chance of winning.

At times, the Ambitious Personality might fear that unless he is constantly achieving, he is nothing, no one. Unless he is triumphing constantly, in every arena, he is simply not acceptable to himself. He sees the whole world made in his image and likeness: competitive, aggressive, a bruising, battering battlefield of combat and combatants. Wherever he goes, he keeps an ear open for the fluttering wings of invisible vultures, those covert competitors whom he feels are hovering everywhere: over the business world, the art world, and over his girlfriend.

The healthy Ambitious Personality will have many of those same feelings and urges, as Alex did, in moments of stress. In the end, Alex recovered from his temporary urge to win a high rating in the field of fine arts, a field where he really had no interest or aptitude. He recognized the fact that Ellen loved him and gave him high ratings for what he was, did not want him to be exactly like her, and certainly did not want him to compete in the art of dance.

The lesson learned from that segment, for the anxious, overrating Ambitious Personality, is: step back long enough to evaluate the situation and make decisions based on assessment of the real facts, not strictly on feelings of competitiveness and the indiscriminate urge to rate and be rated.

THE SINGLE-MINDED PURSUIT OF YOUR GOALS: AMBITIOUS TUNNEL VISION

For the Ambitious Personality, the goal you are pursuing stands like an object of desire at the end of a very long tunnel. At times you run at it like a lovesick race horse wearing blinders. There is an unmistakable focus and intensity in your pursuit; you will do whatever it takes to achieve your purpose.

On "Dynasty" we watch Ambitious Alexis marry her ex-husband's arch-rival on his death bed only to take over his oil company after he dies. We watch Alex on "Family Ties" forgo a very important formal dinner to drive seven hours—still wearing his tuxedo—when he decides to win back his girlfriend who has taken the train to another city to marry her former boyfriend.

Tunnel vision—the intense focus that the Ambitious Personality employs in seeking a goal—comes in many different forms. It grows out of a combination of a love of competition, a strong desire to come out on top, and a suspicion that everyone else is moving with equal intensity and desire toward the same goal.

So we can watch "Dynasty" 's Alexis turn an interested ear toward a nearby confidential conversation and understand that she is only enjoying an edge that any other competitor would make use of if he or she were granted the same opportunity.

At times you might find yourself getting a bit carried away in the heat of the contest and with the intensity of your focus. Your Ambitious TV Twins reassure you that you are not alone in your tunnel vision, or in wanting action and results *right now.*

But you may also find that there are times when friends, family, or innocent bystanders pop into your field of tunnel vision, standing between you and the goal, plucking those strings that play "guilt" in your Ambitious heart.

"Sometimes I get so wrapped up in a project at work that it seems as though everything around me, including my family and friends, begins to disappear,'' said one Ambitious Personality to me. ''I find myself working late hours, weekends; everything is subjugated to the goal at hand. My family says they are going to move into my office. I know they are just joking, but I do feel guilty sometimes when the tunnel vision gets too narrow.''

On ''Family Ties,'' Alex finds it very funny when his mother decides to take an auto mechanics course. He's convinced that there could be no contest as to who's the better mechanic: he would be, of course. But Mom disagrees, so they both enroll in the class. Soon after the class starts it becomes obvious that Mom has an amazing aptitude for auto mechanics and Alex doesn't know a camshaft from a gas cap.

Alex is desperate not to be outshone, and his tunnel vision begins to close in. He studies day and night and finally ends up spending an entire night working on the final exam project: rebuilding a starter motor. Mom has already completed hers and gone to bed, but Alex is not doing so well. He ends up dismantling her motor to see how it's done. But he is so intent on making his own project a success that he inadvertently sabotages hers. Mom ends up failing the course and Alex feels guilty. He realizes that his desire to be the better mechanic and have the best project ultimately resulted in a failing mark for mom and a bad rating for him. So, in the end, he apologizes and reluctantly admits to Mom that she might be the better mechanic. But it's still a sure bet that she won't be working on Ambitious Alex's car.

WHEN THE ROAD TO SUCCESS IS BLOCKED, TRY AN ALTERNATE ROUTE

Although our TV Twins' dilemmas are slight exaggerations, we can certainly relate to that urge to focus, strive, and do what it takes to satisfy the goal. But we can also appreciate the price the Ambitious Personality might pay with lost friends, disgruntled family members, and low ratings when the tunnel gets too narrow. That's when it helps to build a few branches off the main tunnel to serve as an alternate route, an Ambitious exercise you and your TV Twins use occasionally.

For example, let's imagine that an Ambitious Personality comes to me, wanting to discuss an affair he has been having for the past six months. Why does he come to me now? What was happening six months ago? He admits to me that about the same time the affair began, his company began a reorganization after a merger with another company; there were duplications at his supervisory level and his position was in jeopardy. Now comes the alternate route: He says he wants to discuss his affair, but the problem that truly concerns him is his endangered career. He is simply building an alternate route. If his career goes sour, he can always blame the affair. This is his insurance policy against having to accept the bitter fact that he didn't compete well in a most important situation: his job and career.

Now switch to Alex Keaton on "Family Ties." He is the star of his college chess team and preparing to play a very important chess match against a skilled opponent from the visiting Soviet team. Alex has the hopes of all the chess players in the country riding on him, but he seems to be more concerned about his opponent's politics and nationality than about the match. He envisions "all those guys sitting over in the Kremlin right now saying 'Keaton is next. We defeat him and nothing can stop us.' " The focus is switched from his chess prowess to the opponent's cold, ruthless character. Another alternate route has been constructed. So, of course, if Alex just happens to lose the match, it will only be because he was forced to play against the "cold and heartless Soviet automaton," not because of any lack of skill or expertise on his part.

The Ambitious Personality finds many good uses for these alternate routes. As any Ambitious salesperson will tell you, "You sell the sizzle, not the steak." The Ambitious careerist benefits greatly when he tapers off a heavy workload after becoming aware of "how much I am missing family life." This is the alternate route, the sizzle. The steak is his coincident awareness that he isn't really going to make it to the top of the corporate structure.

In the same way, the working Ambitious mother can always blame her late arrival at work on having to get the children off to school. The young Ambitious baseball player can blame his poor season on the manager for having switched him from right field to left. And the poor Ambitious student can always claim that he couldn't do his studies because his roommate always had the stereo on.

As Ambitious Personalities, you and your TV Twins sometimes construct these alternate routes as an insurance policy as you go into a goal-oriented situation. You have prudently arranged to avoid the frustration of defeat or a no-win situation. The healthy Ambitious Personality is one who is ready to accept a reasonable alternative, a viable option.

Switch back to Alex Keaton, at the Young Executive Club's formal dinner dance. He knows he isn't the best dancer—but who is going to notice (or give him a poor rating) when he's dancing with the best-looking girl on campus?

YOU'RE ONLY AS GOOD AS YOUR LAST SUCCESS

In many ways, success is the Chinese food of your Ambitious world: two hours later and you're hungry for the next conquest. There is no time to rest on your laurels because everyone else is moving one step ahead while you bask in the limelight. Ratings come and ratings go but the scoreboard is always there. And those fickle fans soon forget. So the one thing you'll always remember is that you are only as good as your last success.

At times you might find yourself getting frustrated: The ratings are down, there are too many road blocks, or success is not coming fast enough. The temptation is there for you to stack the deck, go after the easy wins and the weaker opponents. We watch Alex, on "Family Ties," get into countless predicaments by going for the short-term satisfaction—what looks to be an easy win—only to end up with low ratings as a "flash in the pan." But in reality, Michael J. Fox, the actor who portrays Alex, reveals his Ambitious Personality in an interview with Barbara Walters, as well as a productive and satisfying philosophy. Although he has developed a successful movie career, he has chosen to stick with the TV series "Family Ties." The Ambitious Personalities who watched "Family Ties" and the Barbara Walters interview with me could empathize with Alex's occasional temptation to go for the easy win but found much more appeal in the long-term ambitions of Michael J. Fox. Why?

"I feel much the same as Michael J. Fox," says one Ambitious viewer. "I have a certain amount of loyalty like he does to the rest of the people on the TV show. So it's an integrity thing. Also, I have started to seek a balance between personal achievement and being a team player. I've found that it's often as easy to be the successful coach as it is to be the star player. When a problem comes up, it would be easy for me to let the whole thing drop, or to sweep it under the carpet or shift to an easier or more immediate gain. But the other people on the team get enthused, contribute their ideas, and help me appreciate the long-range purpose, and that gives me far more lasting pleasure."

"I like to distinguish between a short-term aggressive like Alex, and a longer-term 'grinder' like myself," says a second Ambitious viewer. "When I was younger, it was 'action for action's sake.' But now I like to be more pragmatic, not to feel like I'm going real fast, spinning my wheels, but not really getting anywhere."

"I'm interested in the long run, not with being a flash in the pan," says a third Ambitious viewer. "I know that I can work longer and harder, so I naturally look far ahead. And I never look back. As the great baseball player Satchel Paige once said, 'Don't look back; something might be gaining on you.' "

THE AMBITIOUS WORLD OF WORK

When you consider the essential characteristics of the Ambitious Personality, it comes as no surprise that the working world is your natural environment. You can watch J.R. Ewing on "Dallas" and Maddie on "Moonlighting" spend many happy hours at the office, or chuckle at Alex—economics major, member of the Future Executive Club at school, always wearing a coat and tie—and see how the Ambitious Personality would naturally be attracted to a world that allows you to set goals, compete, and proceed purposefully and diligently in a way that can easily be rated. As one Ambitious person noted, "Work is relaxing. There's nothing I'd rather do than work!" Another Ambitious person said, "Work is the best medicine. If you don't work, what do you do? Sit around and rot?"

"Sometimes I exert so much energy at work that there's little left for play," says one Ambitious Personality. "There might be some reserve energy to spend on a round of golf, or an evening of tennis or bowling. But my major goals, usually centered on work or career, provide the real excitement. And not realizing those goals would be devastating."

The Ambitious Personality can be found in almost any field of enterprise—anything that permits you to set goals, to be purposeful, to be rated well, and to keep moving toward the top of your field. You are not likely to be found in a solitary position where there is no opportunity to grow and advance. Even if you were a farmer, you would find a way to compete and compare with another farmer, even at a distance of twenty miles. An Ambitious physician in private practice would be active enough in the local medical society to be able to compare notes, progress in stature among his peers, and gather favorable ratings. But more often, we would find you working within an open-ended organization that offers vigorous competition and opportunity for advancement and promotion.

When the Ambitious Personality focuses on an occupational area, he becomes fully involved. You will work long hours, do your homework, measure the competition, then set goals—always upward, to the top if possible. If you can devise some insurance, some advantage, some special effort, some specialty that gives you an edge over the other person, you will. And you expect that other person to do the same. You're always looking for that ace in the hole. It's part of the game. But you would prefer to bet on a sure thing: That's part of your caution.

The Ambitious supervisor is a surprisingly nice boss. With all the vigorous competition of which the Ambitious Personality is capable, you never compete in a downward direction; that would draw a poor rating. Moreover, you wouldn't consider it competing at all; it would be taking obvious advantage of those who aren't in a favorable position to compete.

In your relationship with those under your supervision, you prefer to be rated as Mr. Nice Guy, a most favorable rating. So you might, at times, let your people stray. But when you realize that things are getting out of hand, that quotas are off, or quality is down, or sales are falling, you can be quick to recover, even if you have to exert strong discipline. You will get the effort going again and revert to being Mr. Nice Guy when the organization is moving along smoothly. And when the signs of success are at hand—recognition awards, bonuses, whatever—you invite all your people to share the winners' circle. You always give credit where it is due. That too is part of being Mr. Nice Guy.

FAMILIES, SIDEKICKS, AND THE BOY (OR GIRL) NEXT DOOR

Not surprisingly, the Ambitious Personality approaches dating and relationships with much the same sense of competition and rating as he does everything else. You are attracted to a person who has an established rating—favorable, of course—who is attractive either physically or intellectually, who is rated in the winning category. It is not at all unusual for an Ambitious Personality to pick out someone who is very popular.

On "Family Ties," Alex peruses the catalogue of incoming freshmen to find a girl to date. Naturally, he chooses the most attractive, and decides, as a matter of fact, that she's going to be the one. But, as luck—and life—would have it, he ends up falling in love with her roommate. The problem is that Alex finds out that the roommate, Ellen, is planning to marry her boyfriend who is a student at another college. At first, it is very hard for Alex to accept the possibility of losing the competition for Ellen, but it's just as hard for him to commit.

There is a productive tendency among healthy Ambitious

Personalities to be very cautious in courtship. They know their competitive impulses going in, and they sometimes break off the relationship, not once but several times, as a way of distinguishing simple contest from true love.

Ellen decides, finally, to take the train to her boyfriend's college to go through with the marriage. Alex drives her to the station and, after some awkward moments, seems to give up the chase. Of course, an hour or so later, he is hopping into his car to drive seven hours, trying to beat the train, to meet Ellen at the other end of the line and tell her he loves her. He just wanted to be sure, and obviously could not bear to lose her to the other boyfriend.

What happens when the Ambitious Personality finally commits, settles down, starts a family, then finds that the high-speed express to action and success has no family accommodations? The name of the game becomes career first, family second, then everything else if and wherever it can squeeze in. It's true that your family might be your sanctuary as well as your biggest source of encouragement and support, but sometimes it is very difficult to gear down from all the vigorous striving, competing, and achieving of the outside world. Sometimes the temptation is to allow work and career to dominate home life.

We can watch this classic Ambitious struggle going on with Alex and his sister Mallory in one "Family Ties" episode. Alex is headed to Princeton for an interview and Mallory rides along to visit her boyfriend, a Princeton student. Acceptance to Princeton would mean a very high rating to Alex and a chance to compete with some of the best and the brightest. But problems strike. As Alex sits in the dean's office waiting to start his interview, Mallory appears outside the door sobbing and distraught. She had walked in on her boyfriend as he was kissing another girl, and now she wants Alex to take her home, immediately. We can almost see Alex being torn in two as his terribly upset sister begs him to take her home while the stuffy dean of students insists on continuing the interview, or else. After a concentrated bout of soul-searching, Alex decides, with obvious reluctance, to leave the interview and take care of his sister.

An Ambitious mother watching that same segment might be

facing the same sorts of options, especially if she has a job outside the home. She can, of course, realize the benefits and responsibilities of home life. But the lure of job and career is not to be ignored. She feels that she is faced with the choice between family and career because she naturally likes to be the best, but she might have some considerable difficulty at being the best at both.

In Alex's case, he did what many Ambitious Personalities will do in an apparent no-win situation: He finds a compromise, one of the "alternate routes" we spoke of earlier. He decides to forgo Princeton and attend a local, less prestigious college. That way he keeps his high rating with the family and puts himself in an academic atmosphere that will give him an even better chance to shine.

For our Ambitious mother, the compromise is not abandoning family or her competitive urge, but learning to leave the job at the office and working off her excess energy with games or projects at home with the family.

Another compromise that the Ambitious Personality sometimes follows is: if you can't bring your work home, just take your home to work. We can watch J.R., on "Dallas," taking his son out to the oil fields, getting him involved with the family business, making the relationship just another part of the work day. Of course, a necessary prerequisite for that compromise is either a very understanding family or Ambitious children.

Support often comes to the Ambitious Personality in the form of a confidante or sidekick, someone you can depend on to listen, reinforce, encourage, and get you through the battle. On "Knots Landing," we watch Ambitious Greg Sumner wallow temporarily in the depression of defeat after he loses the bid for a high-ranking political office. Then his sidekick, Laura, steps in to give him a pep talk. She doesn't berate him, doesn't tell him to give it up or to take life easy. At a time like that, when the Ambitious Personality is suffering the sting of defeat, it's good to hear someone say, "Get out there and do your best" rather than "Why don't you take some time off" or "You have to be number one."

After viewing the "Knots Landing" segment, one Ambitious

Personality remarked, "It's like you can really feel the difference between bare expectation and positive encouragement. If someone just orders you to 'Go out there and knock that wall down' or tells you you're no good if you can't, you probably aren't going to be able to knock it down. But a true sidekick will tell you to just do your best, and you won't have any problem at all knocking down that wall."

The Ambitious Personality might also depend on a sidekick, or team of advisors, to act as shock absorbers, to scout ahead and test the waters or set up an advance deal. If the deal fails, the advisors will insulate their Ambitious leader and take the heat. But if it succeeds, the Ambitious Personality is there to take—and share—the credit.

TAKE JUST A MOMENT TO SAVOR THE SUCCESS AND SMELL THE ROSES

As time marches on, the Ambitious Personality dances along ahead of the parade: up, down, all around, never looking back. But there is the occasional pause when you stop to savor a particular triumph, when you stop to smell the sweet scent of success.

On "Dallas," J.R. Ewing unloads some shipping company stock on unsuspecting buyers because there is a risk that the stock will soon plummet. Unfortunately, he later gets an inside tip that the stock is actually about to skyrocket. He manages to call the buyers to his office and convince them to sell the stock back to him before they get the same information. After the deal is complete, he has his stock back in hand and has ushered the unsuspecting "fair game" out the door, he pauses; a self-satisfied smirk lingers on his face.

"I can identify with the smirk," said one Ambitious Personality after viewing the segment. "I feel very good after I have tackled a goal, pursued it, and guided it through all of the angles, taken advantage of opportunities that others have overlooked or were too timid to pursue, to gain some extra ground. When I come out on top, I feel that tremendous sense of satisfaction and enjoy the short pause to stop and smell the roses. But I like to smirk in private, and don't like to gloat or rub my opponents' noses in my success. You get bad ratings that way and besides, I don't want to divulge any of my strategy to them."

Like a good poker player, the Ambitious Personality never shows the hand he has used to bluff the rest of the field into throwing in their hands. He just takes a moment to sniff those roses—and smirk—as he scoops in that hefty pot.

THE WINNING EDGE AND BEYOND

Work nourishes your Ambitious spirit. But we don't mean mowing the lawn or scrubbing the kitchen floor. That's drudgery. There's no real action in mowing and mopping, unless you intend it as exercise or your goal is to run the most lucrative lawn service or maid service in town. No, the work you love is goal-oriented. And if your goal in reading this chapter was to gain an edge by knowing and understanding yourself better, then that goal has ben satisfied, and the work has been worthwhile.

Let's not forget those TV Twins. Now that you know them, they can be very useful as first advisors, and the advice they give is free for the watching.

We now understand just a little better that ambitions come in many forms. Challenges and competition can be arranged in the family room as well as in the boardroom. They vary according to values, opportunities, training, talent, and temperament. One Ambitious Personality's meat is another's poison. But consciously or unconsciously, openly or subtly, assertively or cautiously, on screen or off, all Ambitious Personalities are hooked on the action, keeping close track of the score and meeting the goals.

So onward, upward, and don't look back.

ALTERNATIVES AND OPTIONS

- Move away from guilt feelings that you sometimes associate with competing and achieving.
- Let your conduct and behavior be self-representing. You don't have to be embarrassed by your excitement over projects and efforts. Enjoy your excitement without fear that you are being overbearing.
- Beware of easy wins and hyped ratings, the kind that come with giving lavish parties, buying drinks for the house, wearing a provocative or seductive dress, seducing an easy conquest.
- Permit yourself to win without trying to explain it away, or without apologizing for having won.
- You don't always have to be Mr. Nice Guy. That's too guilt-oriented; it's a way sometimes of apologizing for your achievements.
- Stop looking for invisible vultures. Not everyone around you is competing with you. Even when you are in a competitive situation, not everyone is hostile or overly aggressive.
- Learn to relate without having to rate, especially to those significant people in your life—spouse, children, friends, or others who are close to you. Realize too that they aren't rating you, except, perhaps, as a lovable person.
- Winning is wonderful, but not at any price. If your goals are prudent and realistic, measured in terms of your real talents and your true opportunities, you can win cleanly and in the open.
- Balance your seldom-received low ratings with your more frequent high ratings. It's the ongoing average that counts.
- Ambition is perfectly acceptable and desirable. Recognize genuine effort and applied talent. Permit yourself the joy that is one of the fruits of victory.

SECRETS

You and your TV Twins function best when you get a good rating. You need to be encouraged to strive, compete, work hard, and practice extra. You need an environment that accepts your intense tunnel vision when you strive so vigorously for success.

The keys to a successful relationship with the Ambitious Personality are:

- Always encourage the pursuit of goals.
- Make every moment productive. No small talk or daydreaming.
- Share the enthusiasm and excitement; get involved.
- Be a good sidekick.
- Keep those good ratings coming.

MATCH AND MISMATCH

Ambitious Personality matchmates:

Accomplishing—You want, above all else, to succeed and to win, and the Accomplishing person's positive nature reassures you and encourages you that you will succeed. Accomplishing Personalities are very quick to lend you a hand or an encouraging word and to assume responsibilities, freeing you to pursue other goals. They try very hard to get your approval, and when you give this you ensure a winning performance.

Influencing—You are drawn to their organized and charming nature. They encourage you to go for as much as you can, being the all-or-nothing type of person. They also enjoy the grand celebrations that follow victories, much as you do.

Persistent—Your life orientation of wanting to succeed is fueled by the creative and clever schemes of Persistent individuals. They want very much to be special to you and consistently feed you ideas. They want, above all else, to make you number one in their life, which ensures personal satisfaction and success on your part.

Determined—You share a goal-oriented lifestyle and you both enjoy working long and hard. Their emphasis on strategy can only aid you in your course of action. Their tendency to remain undeclared while considering their position adds a certain stability to your aggressiveness.

Idealistic—Both of you enjoy challenges in life and strive to make these challenges successful. Idealistic persons allow you the time to pursue these goals. Because of their independent nature they do not get in your way and are content to pursue activities on their own. Their logical approach to life helps you in your pursuit of success.

Patient—You enjoy a sidekick in life who encourages you to get involved with the action, and Patient Personalities perform very well in this role. They value peace and security and will do whatever it takes to keep this, particularly at home which is a haven for you. They encourage you to be a winner, but they don't provide sufficient feedback.

Adaptable—You are initially drawn to the Adaptables' open and sociable ways. Your ability to focus on only one area is counterbalanced by their many interests. However, you enjoy working many hours, whereas they are nine-to-five types. You like to solve a problem quickly and then move on, while they want to obtain many opinions as a way of communicating before deciding which way to go.

Sensitive—Their loyalty and interest in helping you in the pursuit of your goals is a positive factor; however, you want things done yesterday, while Sensitive persons do better when given time to rehearse. You like to receive good ratings, and Sensitive persons are very good at building you up. Their curiosity and questions, however, may get in your way.

Perceptive—This relationship is difficult because of your differing styles. You enjoy a very rapid pace and like to pursue personal interests and goals, while the Perceptive person wants togetherness and may place demands on your time which get in the way of your pursuit of success. Your work is very important to you, while Perceptives feel that *they* should be more important than anything else. Their jealousy often interferes with your work in being victorious.

Conscientious—Your competitiveness and quick pace is slowed considerably by the questioning and doubting you will receive from Conscientious persons. You like to move from one project to another in a perhaps somewhat haphazard fashion, while they have a very set routine. Again, you may be spending your time answering questions rather than moving toward the next opportunity.

Anticipating—This person wants to feel very special and a part of things, which is difficult for you because of your emphasis on action, work, and success. You have a tendency to change things rather spontaneously, which is very difficult for the Anticipating person, who doesn't like change. You have a difficult time with the Anticipating Personality's tendency to worry a great deal, which can be seen as a poor rating for you and can get in your way.

Chapter Four

THE PERCEPTIVE PERSONALITY

PROFILE

- Very compassionate; likes to touch and be touched.
- Down to earth, emotional, and outspoken.
- Champion of the underdog.
- Seeker of fairness.
- Giver and appreciator of gifts.
- Sentimental.
- The original Good Samaritan.

TV TWINS

- Cliff Huxtable—"The Cosby Show"
- Mary Beth Lacey—"Cagney and Lacey"
- Mary—"227"
- Rose—"Golden Girls"
- Archie Bunker—"All in the Family"
- Margaret Houlihan—"M*A*S*H"
- Ann Romano—"One Day at a Time"
- Karen—"Knots Landing"
- Suc Ellen—"Dallas"
- Benson—"Benson"
- Clayton Farlow—"Dallas"

If we had to find one word that would best define the Perceptive Personality, it would be *compassionate*. You are the

Good Samaritan who stops to comfort, to give aid, to console. The Perceptive Personality might notice a lost child crying in a department store and spend the next half hour trying to locate the child's parents. You would likely be the one who stops traffic and carefully lifts an animal that has been struck by a car into your own back seat for a ride to the vet. If you could, you would see to it that every hungry child was fed, that every disease was cured, that the poor had plenty, that every broken heart was mended and every tear wiped away. Every stray cat would be given a home, and every dog would have his day.

The underdog will always receive your special attention. On matters of fairness, you are very outspoken and blunt, shooting verbal bullets from the hip. When your efforts to give aid are thwarted you are frustrated and again you will speak out. Although your outspokenness might sometimes get you into trouble, that usually is of no concern to you. You know that you deserve as much as you give and would expect others to speak out just as loudly for you. If not, their sympathy will do just as well.

Why this compassion? Because as a Perceptive Personality, you are not only quick to perceive suffering in others; you are also able to empathize with another person's pain. The good that you want for yourself, you want for everyone. What you fear for yourself, you fear for others. Thus you react to all forms of deprivation, rejection, abuse, and mistreatment. You have an abiding concern for justice, honesty, and integrity, and do what you can to promote security and well-being in your own environment and beyond.

The Perceptive Personality is a down-to-earth person: responsive and fair, a true friend who wears well over the years. You prize your friends as you cherish family and a good and happy home life.

In matters of love you are an incurable romantic. That first love is your always love and all those sentimental little gifts, remembrances, and memories are carefully tucked away.

At times you wear your heart on your sleeve. And why not? You are a loving and lovable person, touching and warm. You seek affection and expect the same in return. When affection isn't returned, you suffer deeply and for a long time—or at least as long as it takes to find someone else who does respond to your open, affable, and spunky charm.

As a Perceptive Personality, your worst fear is that you might be deprived of your well-being. Friends or family, good health or good fortune might desert you. So you protect what you have, even sometimes to the point of feeling a bit possessive and selfish.

While you see yourself as a giving person, you are prone to think of yourself and your welfare first. And so, as an extra safeguard, especially when your well-being is threatened, you take a self-reliant, do-it-yourself approach to life.

A Perceptive woman I know had never worked during her marriage, but when her husband underwent open-heart surgery her reaction was to enroll in a secretarial course and look around for employment. She wanted to make sure that she would be able to take care of herself if the worst happened.

Survive is a word you hear the Perceptive Personality use often. It ties in with that thrust toward independence. As one young Perceptive woman remarked to me, "Oh, I'm sure I could survive. If you've got enough get-up-and-go, and if you are independent enough, you can always find a way."

Another Perceptive woman admits that whenever her husband shows the first sign of a cold, she mentally inventories the attic and the closets thinking that, if he really got sick, she might raise quick cash through a garage sale. A Perceptive patient once explained to me how, if he lost his job, he could always buy peanuts in bulk, package them in small bags, and sell them on street corners. His father did that during the Depression.

The Perceptive Personality is not only protective of himself; he wants to extend his protection to others. A Perceptive wife may shovel the snow from the driveway rather than permit her overweight and over-forty husband to risk a heart attack. She may continue on to the neighbor's driveway since the woman next door is a widow; she can imagine how it would feel not to have any help around the house. Coming back into the house, half frozen and huffing and puffing, she may feel guilty that she wasn't able to help the teenager down the street push his car out of a snow bank. Before she can get her coat off, she heads back outside to throw breadcrumbs on the snow for the birds.

MEET YOUR TV TWINS

You should have no trouble recognizing your Perceptive TV Twins because, like you, they are compassionate, emotional people.

You and your TV Twins have a strong need to be close to people; you are very protective of those you love. You readily show your affection and concern. You have strong empathy for those who are hurt or suffering. Similarly, you want others to understand and appreciate you. Security, for you, is measured more in terms of home life and close relationships than in terms of finances. A bank account full of warmth and love and a safety deposit box stuffed with cozy affection is all you really need.

Finding your TV Twin can be tremendously rewarding. Your Perceptive TV Twins will be easy to identify because they are:

- Compassionate, tending to be the Good Samaritan.
- Down to earth and outspoken.
- Self-sufficient, demonstrating a do-it-yourself approach.
- Fair; they will protect others and themselves.
- Jealous—very aware of hurt and rejection.

On "The Cosby Show," Perceptive **Cliff Huxtable** is an obstetrician and father of five, living in New York City, married to an attorney. He enjoys a close, loving relationship with his family and becomes actively involved in their lives.

In one episode, Cliff's daughter Denise has a girlfriend who is having some problems. Denise asks Cliff if he will help, and although he doesn't know the friend, he immediately agrees. The Perceptive TV Twin's caring and compassion will always go out to someone in need.

The girl with the problem is afraid to go to her own parents for help. When Perceptive Cliff hears that, he is visibly upset. He states that if one of his family had a problem and didn't immediately come to him, he would just be sick about it. Family togetherness is very important to the Perceptive Personality. And the compassion and caring you give, you expect to receive in equal measure.

Cliff then asks his children if they would come to him first if they were in trouble. Their answer is, they probably wouldn't come to him because they would be afraid he would get mad and overreact. He, of course, immediately denies it, all the while getting angry at the notion that they would accuse him of losing his temper when they needed his help and support.

On "227," Perceptive **Mary** is a mother, homemaker, and resident Good Samaritan in her big-city apartment building.

During one episode, Mary begins to get suspicious when seven raggedy street people, one by one, go up to visit a friend on the third floor of her apartment building and never come back down. She investigates and discovers that they are living there with her friend who has brought them in off the street. When she finds that they are subsisting mostly on beans, she immediately cooks a pot of stew for them. The landlord eventually discovers the situation and threatens to evict all of them, saying that she can't have "bums" living in her building, especially seven in one room. "They're not bums, they're human beings," pleads Mary. Finally, she manages to convince the landlord to find jobs, shelter, and help for the homeless folks upstairs.

On "Golden Girls," perceptive **Rose** divides her time between working as a sympathetic listener at a crisis counseling center and, elsewhere, as a protector of creatures great and small.

Archie Bunker is the Perceptive "lovable grouch": very outspoken about his own interpretation of what's fair and just, but deep down compassionate. He tries to conceal his tender side behind a gruff, "I don't need any help" exterior, but his independence belies his desire for wife Edith's constant pampering and attention.

On "M*A*S*H," **Margaret Houlihan** shows her Perceptive Personality as a nurse at a frontline medical unit during the Korean War. She is tough, independent, and self-reliant; quick to speak out loud and clear when she senses an injustice, or when she has been wronged. But she, too, tries hard to hide her tender side, her occasional tears, and her strong need for love, attention, and affection.

Sue Ellen on "Dallas" has also shown both her tender emotional side and her tough self-reliance as part of a Texas oil family.

On "Cagney and Lacey," Perceptive **Mary Beth Lacey** is a New York police officer, as well as wife and mother. Her Perceptive Personality is evidenced both by her regard for the plight of innocent victims of crime and her concern for her family, which erupts, at times, in outbursts of strong emotion.

Perceptives **Karen MacKenzie** on "Knots Landing" and **Clayton Farlow** on "Dallas" share that same protective urge and react very emotionally when family security is threatened.

Ann Romano is the Perceptive single mother on "One Day at a Time," making it on her own, raising her two teenage daughters with a firm but gentle hand, extending her benevolence to a variety of underdogs and scapegoats.

Benson is an aide and advisor to the governor on "Benson." He is very protective of the governor and his family, candid and direct in his treatment of the devious and dishonest, but sentimental and softhearted under it all.

In one episode, Benson is sitting with some of his friends, playing cards and reminiscing about the past. His own memory is about a girl he met when he was ready to ship off to the Korean War. They're at a club, dancing cheek to cheek to a special song long after the other GIs and their girls have gone home. He tells her he loves her and suggests they get married. The girl is taken aback at first, not sharing Perceptive Benson's surge of emotion and romance. Then she laughs and says, "Oh, I get it, you're just kidding with me like you always do." Benson is crushed but keeps up a steady front and says yes, he was just kidding. But it is a bittersweet moment that he will never forget. Later, after the card game has ended and his friends have gone home, Benson listens to that same special song that had been playing that night, so long ago, and drifts back to that same bittersweet moment.

Mementos, souvenirs, and fond memories hold the key to the Perceptive heart.

For you, tenderness, affection, and romance also provide just the right touch. We can watch Perceptive Cliff on "The Cosby Show" in perfect bliss as he cuddles with wife Clair on the couch, playfully wrestles with son Theo, or gently kisses his daughters goodbye on their way out of the house.

As you follow the video lives of your Perceptive TV Twins, look carefully for examples of:

- Being playfully affectionate.
- Feeling threatened when loved ones aren't paying enough attention.
- Believing in giving and receiving on a measure-for-measure basis; feeling bad when they don't get the affection they feel they deserve.
- Looking back on life in such a way that their past relationships are glorified.
- Wanting to protect so badly that it's difficult for them to let go of children and let them be self-sufficient.

As much as the Perceptive Personality thrives on the closeness and affection of loved ones, your independence and feeling of self-sufficiency are just as important. That might be because you are very aware of slights and rejection and may at times even expect them. With so much pain and suffering in the world, it's a good idea to develop a tough skin and an ability to care for oneself if need be—but it's not easy for you to do.

Your TV Twins will be likeable; they come across as open, caring, and interesting people. In the words of some forgotten philosopher: "If you want to be loved, love and be lovable." You and your Perceptive TV Twins certainly follow that advice.

THE ORIGINAL GOOD SAMARITAN

One of your worst fears is that you may be deprived of your well-being and security: Good health or good fortune may suddenly desert you. Although you are a fair and friendly person, do your part, pull your weight in the boat, and take care of your own, you sometimes feel cheated or come out on the short end. After all, the world is not always a fair and friendly place.

Other people suffer the same unfairness and privation. Since you are quick to perceive suffering, you find it easy to put yourself into that other person's position; empathy is one of your strong suits. That's why you are quick to respond to suffering and privation when they happen to anyone, even to a stranger. After all, it could just as easily be happening to you. So, it is the "protective urge" that best exemplifies the Perceptive Personality. You are truly the Good Samaritan.

You and your Perceptive TV Twins' warm and genuine interest in others frequently prompts others to ask for your advice and counsel. People will pour out their troubles to you, and you can usually be depended on to sympathize and give understanding. You send out vibes that you care, and there are always plenty of takers.

But you do have to be careful not to be too indiscriminate or anxious to shoulder the burdens of the world. There is a difference between understanding and becoming overly involved. Danger or difficulties may arise when your desire to help overcomes the need for caution. When the Perceptive Personality's compassion goes awry, it can cause as many problems as it solves.

On "One Day at a Time," Perceptive Ann is immediately concerned when she learns that a male friend is suffering from temporary sexual impotence. She acts quickly to arrange a dinner at her apartment, inviting the male friend and a female friend who was a former love of his. She also arranges to be called away during dinner on a phony emergency so the two friends can be left alone, hoping that the fortuitous circumstances will reignite the passion and help her male friend overcome his problem. Unfortunately, she doesn't reveal the plan to the female friend until she arrives for dinner, much to the female friend's dismay.

Archie Bunker, on "All in the Family," is quick to step in and offer to arrange the funeral for a relative who has dropped dead in his house. But when Archie discovers the cost and complexity of the arrangements, he regrets jumping to the rescue so soon.

A Perceptive woman came to me with the story of how her willingness to spring to the rescue had backfired. One evening she had answered the door to find a very sad-looking nephew standing there. She asked him in, sat him down, offered him a piece of pie and a glass of milk, and then asked, "Something wrong?" There was. This teenager and his father had had a battle about his staying out late the night before. The young man had left the house in a huff. And now: "Auntie, can I spend the night at your house?" How could she say no? After he was asleep in the guest room, his Perceptive aunt called his parents to let them know their son was at her house: no need to worry. But, when she so informed her still angry brother, he roared, "What the hell are you doing, taking sides?" With no further comment, she slammed down the receiver. "Here I thought I was doing everyone a favor, and what do I get?" Her kindness might have been more productive had she considered the option of calling his parents before she consented to her nephew spending the night, thus avoiding the appearance of having taken sides in a family problem. But in her rush she didn't, and as a result, she suffered. And her family suffered. She felt so put upon and abused that for a week she couldn't put a hot meal on the table. Her family heard so much of her complaining about her brother that even the dog began to shy away from her.

In all three instances, with Ann, Archie, and the Perceptive aunt, we can see how, in the Perceptive Samaritan's eagerness to rescue and assist, he or she can end up worsening the situation or offering aid where aid is not really wanted or needed.

The moral here is not to turn a deaf ear to cries for help, or to refuse to get involved. That would mean ignoring and denying one of your greatest Perceptive strengths. The advice and lesson to learn from your fellow Perceptives, both on screen and off, is to marshal the facts before you offer advice, and then make sure your involvement is truly wanted or needed. Some non-Perceptive Personalities actually pride themselves on their self-reliance and independence, much the way you often claim to—even though you secretly do crave the attention and fuss. There will certainly be no shortage of situations that do call for your compassion, tenderness, and understanding.

We also understand that even the most selfless Good Samaritan has to have his or her priorities in line. You are always open and available, but protection begins at home.

On "The Cosby Show," Perceptive Cliff invites a friend over for a visit. Soon after he arrives, the friend breaks down and admits to Cliff that he is not able to reach one of his children who is having a serious drug problem. Cliff's heart immediately goes out to his friend. He puts his arm around the friend's shoulder and leads him off to another room to talk. Cliff is being the true Good Samaritan, but he's also thinking of his own children.

FRIEND TO CREATURES, GREAT AND SMALL

On "Golden Girls," Perceptive Rose tries to discourage her housemates from calling the exterminator to get rid of a mouse that is living in the kitchen. She then proceeds to tell them how a pet mouse once saved her life when she was a child. It seems that she used to walk her mouse to school every day on a little leash, but one day the mouse stopped dead in his tracks, just as they were ready to cross a bridge. She couldn't get the mouse to budge. Just then a huge wall of water came rushing down and washed the bridge away: the dam upstream had burst.

A little farfetched, perhaps? We'll call it tasteful exaggeration for the sake of TV entertainment. But the segment does serve as an example of how the Perceptive Personality's compassion and understanding extend to all living things.

Feeding birds in the winter would not be an incidental gesture on the part of the Perceptive Personality. You are famous for your love and concern for our furry—and feathered—friends, and would find it very hard to ignore a stray dog or cat, however scraggly. Like Mary on "227," or Rose on "Golden Girls," you will take it in, feed it, and give it a home. One look at you with those sad eyes and you're lost.

Chances are you can appreciate any pet or domestic animal as an affectionate creature that demands little while giving loyal companionship. Since no one is ever lonely with a pet in the house—a loved and well-fed animal will never desert you—you gather them in, great and small.

Horses seem to be particular favorites of the Perceptive Personality. Some people go to the racetrack to bet, but you might spend a day at the track just to watch the grace and the beauty of thoroughbreds in motion. A friend told me that her Perceptive daughter chose to attend a particular college over many others because she would be able to stable her horse not far from the campus.

If by chance the Perceptive Personality is driving down a country road admiring the scenery and happens to see a sickly animal, alone and unattended in the pasture, he might be tempted to drive up to the owner's house to ask what was being done for the poor animal. And the owner had better have a good answer, because when the Perceptive sees mistreatment or abuse, the words will flow hot and heavy.

CHAMPION OF THE UNDERDOG

Because you and your Perceptive TV Twins are so alert to every form of privation and are so concerned about justice and fair play, you are, at times, uncomfortable with privilege because it implies a corresponding *lack* of privilege. You prefer to avoid anything pretentious or pompous and usually find yourself identifying with down-to-earth people. You may find yourself speaking out against bigotry and prejudice, and you will rush to the side of someone who is at a disadvantage or is being victimized by subterfuge or deceit. In other words, you are the champion of the underdog.

Clayton Farlow, of "Dallas," shows his Perceptive concern for the underdog when he confronts J.R. Clayton feels that J.R. has been less than considerate of the fact that Miss Ellie, J.R.'s mother, is bogged down with family problems. J.R. is apparently trying to use his business expertise to force a decision from Miss Ellie concerning the sale of family stock in Ewing

Oil, perhaps taking advantage of her weakened position, so Clayton steps in and warns J.R. to lay off and give her time to clear her mind. Otherwise, says Clayton, J.R. will have to answer to him.

There are many instances, both on screen and off, of the Perceptive Personality going to bat for the disadvantaged, deprived, and the exploited.

A Perceptive father heard his son (not a Perceptive Personality) mimicking another boy who stuttered and made his son apologize on the spot. A Perceptive woman working in a factory put her job on the line by going to management to complain of unsafe working conditions in her department. A Perceptive businessman walked out on a potentially large sales contract when one of the other parties made an unkind comment about his partner's ethnic background. The same Perceptive businessman had quit his country club when he discovered that membership was restricted to white gentiles.

A Perceptive judge I once knew was something of a local celebrity. He grew up in a poor neighborhood, spent years working his way through law school, and gained a solid reputation. Although he was careful with his money—typical of the Perceptive Personality—he helped to finance the college education of several promising young people from the old neighborhood. However, he made secrecy a condition of helping those young people because he knew that not everyone in the old neighborhood could appreciate the limit to his ability to give, and he also knew how hard it would be for him to turn them down.

But the judge wasn't able to protect his secrecy so well when a local paper reported that he had paid the funeral expenses of the town drunk, a man who had been the town mayor before he was convicted of embezzling municipal funds. Few people could understand the judge giving a graveside eulogy that praised the dead man as a good and loyal friend. What they didn't know—or had forgotten—was that the judge and the deceased were once boyhood friends from the same miserable neighborhood and that the convicted embezzler had helped the judge get his start. People shook their heads, but the judge offered no explanation. As a Perceptive Personality, he took it for granted that everyone felt the same compassion and sympathy for an old, less fortunate friend.

AN OCEAN OF EMOTION

As a Perceptive, you are a person of strongly felt emotion. Feelings of love, hurt, fear, joy, rejection, and concern are quick to bubble to the surface. I have heard some Perceptive people describe the early part of their lives as particularly tumultuous. "I was so emotional, I thought I was crazy—at least other people made me feel that way," was how one person expressed it. But, as your TV Twins will confirm, it's certainly not crazy, just Perceptive. And for you, a very natural and healthy way to be.

In one episode of "Cagney and Lacey," Perceptive Mary Beth Lacey comes home to find that her teenage son has been mugged. Her husband tries to reassure her by calmly pointing out that the kid only suffered a black eye, but she is not about to be calm about the situation. When her son informs her that he was putting up a fight for his money until the attackers pulled a knife, Mary Beth really explodes. "You're a stupid, stupid kid, risking your life for money. You are confined to this house for a month." Then we hear her tossing dishes in the sink, banging around the kitchen, and having a loud discussion with her husband while her son retreats to his bedroom.

Sue Ellen's reactions to her troubled marriage and to the problems that come with being part of a Texas oil family are characterized by strong emotions, romantic ideas, the sting of rejection, and the strong pull toward reconciliation after each disappointment.

It is natural for the Perceptive Personality to have a strong show of emotion and, as in Mary Beth Lacey's case, show a strong protective urge when it comes to family and loved ones.

THE SIXTY-SECOND RULE

When the healthy, confident Perceptive Personality comes across an unfair or unjust situation, or when the safety and security of friends or family is threatened, he usually will not hesitate to speak out loudly. Or at least will want to.

Clayton Farlow jumps to Miss Ellie's defense when she is being badgered by J.R. on "Dallas." Cliff, on "The Cosby Show," calls an immediate family meeting with his children when he finds out that they might not be coming to him with their problems. Mary, on "227," immediately goes to her apartment to cook a pot of stew when she discovers a roomful of hungry, homeless people upstairs.

Of course, the message here is not to follow every emotional whim, or to run off immediately to help everyone you perceive in need (remember the overanxious Good Samaritan?), or to always speak your mind with no forethought or consideration of possible ramifications. Once again, I would point out that your TV Twins tastefully exaggerate your Personality Style in action. The point is, you experience a certain immediacy when it comes to your emotions and reactions to perceived wrongs or threats. The longer you hold these emotions and reactions inside without expressing them in some way, the more you suffer.

One husband married to a Perceptive Personality described his wife as "a woman who was always picking up rocks, stuffing them into a bag, and then hitting me over the head with them." What he meant was that she tended to notice every slight or snub, to store them up, and then to unload all of the accumulated hurt at one time. His Perceptive wife hadn't realized her habit of "picking up rocks," but when her husband described the practice she commented, "I guess I do go along getting upset but not saying anything at the time. I don't complain. I don't nag. But then all of a sudden, pow! Some little thing happens and I explode all over the place. Then I feel guilty and wonder, 'What the hell is wrong with me?' "

Well, the Perceptive Personality has been known, at times, to hold on to hurt. It's a combination of being so tuned in to the hurt and unfairness of life, and not expressing your displeasure with what you tune in to.

In one segment of "Cagney and Lacey," we learn that Perceptive Mary Beth still refuses to forgive her father for walking out on the family when she was young. When he finally reappears to ask her about his grandchildren, she says, "I don't know you, and I can't remember loving you." Later, when her son is talking to her about the situation with his grandfather and her refusal to forgive him, her son says he hopes he will never do anything that she would find unforgivable. She tells him that he is her son, so he could never do anything she wouldn't forgive. "Yeah," her son replies, "but he's your dad." It is a scene that shows the Perceptive Personality expressing her feelings many years after the hurt occurred but still, and possibly always, suffering from holding them in for so long.

In most situations, rather than "picking up rocks" and storing them inside, the aggravated Perceptive Personality would be more reasonable, relate better, and feel much more relaxed inside if he would speak up when he feels slighted or put down. Problems begin to appear when you forget or ignore the importance of sharing your feelings. I often hear Perceptive Personalities describe the sensation of holding in feelings as, "I was locked behind my face." And that, of course, can lead to an eventual eruption of emotion. My solution to the problem is the sixty-second rule: you should react to thoughts, feelings, and behavior within sixty seconds instead of storing or suppressing them.

"Oh sure, Dr. Young, that's easy for you to say. But I'm the one who has to pay the price for saying what's on my mind or acting on my feelings without taking time to think." Well, there are going to be times when you offend, or bruise some feelings, or catch people off guard with spontaneous reactions. But that's the purpose of giving yourself sixty seconds. That should be enough time, in most instances, to decide whether your reaction or words could do some serious damage. Otherwise, some toes might get stepped on, some feelings hurt, but you will feel much better for having let it out. It's just part of self-preservation, and part of recognizing yourself as a Perceptive Personality. And that's certainly best for you. Think tact, then react.

I'LL TAKE ROMANCE

What a divine mystery love is. You probably felt the vague sensations of it stirring inside you earlier in life than most other Personality Styles. You are hooked on the warm, secure feeling that touching and affection bring to you. The closeness of family, friends, and later, girl- or boyfriends, was a source of security and an outlet for your powerful emotions. Of course, on the other side of the coin is pain and rejection. But after the fight comes the making up. And, as the Perceptive philosopher might say, the pain only makes the pleasure that much more enjoyable; the two must coexist. So it goes in the world of Perceptive romance.

You thrive on a touching, caring relationship: lots of tenderness and open affection. And of course, you also enjoy a great deal of what comes afterwards: sex. Lots of foreplay and cuddling afterwards is the way to your Perceptive heart. We might even call you a bit of a flirt. Flirting and sex appeal are your hedge against lonely times. The world can turn very cold very suddenly, so you like to test the waters occasionally, just to make sure you've still got "it."

Love comes in many forms. Some people look for it in the right places, some look in all the wrong places. But for you, it comes best as good, old-fashioned romance.

We can watch Perceptive Cliff on "The Cosby Show" respond to the language of love from wife Clair in many ways. In one segment, after an exhausting night of work, Cliff looks for a place to relax and read his paper. He finally finds refuge in his office. Then Clair shows up with a special pizza for an intimate little picnic. Cliff can't resist and quickly locks the door against any possible intruders.

In another segment, Cliff talks about the romantic power of music. He can hear an old song, one that just happened to be playing during an earlier, memorable moment in his life; and when he hears it again, he can almost feel, touch, and taste the moment once more. Then he announces to Clair that he is tired and going to bed and goes upstairs. But Clair has other plans and knows all too well the foolproof method for getting her Perceptive incurable romantic back downstairs: She puts on one of their all-time favorite—not to mention sensuous—tunes on the stereo and sits on the couch to wait. Halfway through the song, Cliff suddenly appears on the stairs with that sultry look in his eye.

Mementos and souvenirs are more to you than just crinkled movie ticket stubs, dried flowers, or old songs played "just one more time." They are precious reminders of love past. They can also be a soothing reminder that times can be much better, when the present is a little too painful to face. Your first love is your always love and the memories will often carry you through.

BREAK UP JUST TO MAKE UP

When I say there have probably been too many times when you led with your heart instead of your head, you might smile and say, "So true." You can meet an attractive person and fall instantly in love, ignoring everything—including the possibility of entering into a poor relationship and getting hurt. When you discover that this person isn't good for you, you tend to think that perhaps with enough love you can change him or her. That's a misconception we're all guilty of at one time or another. But that other person cannot, through the magical power of love, change into another Personality Style. And you are a Perceptive Personality, who suffers from incompatibility more acutely than most people do.

Even in an established relationship you don't always get the love and special attention you need. On "227," Perceptive Mary is doing her exercises one morning when her husband stops on his way out the door to work and kids her about trying too hard. She informs him that she is doing it to look nice for him. He tells her he loves her just the way she is, but she doesn't buy that. "We've been married for twenty-three years," he says.

"You think I've been faking all that time?" But she says she still needs to be reassured. When he comes home that night she is wearing a new dress, but even though she poses all around him, he doesn't notice. They have a fight and she storms off to the bedroom to change clothes. When he asks why, she answers, "Why should I wear new clothes for a man who can't see?"

I asked a group of Perceptive Personalities how they handled a similar situation when the special attention they needed from friends, spouse, or a certain someone was not forthcoming. Most conceded that they probably need a few more compliments and a little more reassurance than other Personality Types might. And most agreed that if they were looking for a compliment or attention and it didn't come, they felt underappreciated. "When I want a compliment and it's not coming, I won't hesitate to come right out and ask for it," said one.

It is true that some of the other Personality Styles are not so forthcoming with affection and compliments. And since friend, spouse, or certain someone might just happen to be one of those Personality Styles, there's nothing wrong with prompting. You Perceptive Personalities are sometimes not content with subtle signs of appreciation.

For every sting of underappreciation, inconsiderate remark, or lack of attention, you often react with a heavy sting of your own. Then the bell rings for round one.

"If I need to hear a compliment from my husband, I'll hear it if I have to drag it out of him," says one Perceptive I know. Another, after watching the "227" episode mentioned above, said, "I have this raggedy old warm-up suit at home that I work in. If I had a new dress on and he didn't notice, I would go back and put that raggedy thing on. Then I know he would say how bad I looked, and I would ask him why it wasn't as easy for him to say how nice I'd looked before."

Of course, it's better for the Perceptive Personality to be up front with feelings and let the other person know how you feel: remember the sixty-second rule. If the other person doesn't understand, it's good to sit down and talk about it, the sooner the better. But, as is more often the case, you might just have to fight it out. Then, after the fight is over and the air is cleared, comes the best part.

Back at "227," Mary is doing the laundry in the basement the day after the fight over the new dress. Her husband surprises her, comes home from work early, flowers in hand, and tells her they are going out for a night on the town. Just to make up.

You know the rest of the story.

MARRIAGE AND FAMILY: THE TIE THAT BINDS

In a relationship or marriage the Perceptive Personality looks for someone who loves as strongly as he or she does, who is as caring and compassionate. Your cozy home and warm bed mean so much to you. They give you your sense of well-being. One of the most gratifying experiences in the world for you can be coming home to the love of spouse and children. So you will do whatever it takes to enrich the warmth, contentment, and security of home life, not just for yourself—although that is important—but also for your family. Because of that you might experience great stress when your spouse or one of your children gets in trouble, or is sick or injured.

On "The Cosby Show," Perceptive Cliff is very concerned for wife Clair when she breaks her toe. She is determined that the toe is not going to slow her down, but Cliff is just as adamant about taking care of her. He insists that she go to the emergency room. He doesn't want her to go to work the next day, but she ignores him and refuses to use the crutches he has gotten for her. As that particular segment ends, Cliff is hurt and complaining because of the way Clair has spurned his concern and efforts to help. But she knows just what to do, giving him some touching and sweet talk. It is a good example of the Perceptive protective urge in action, but also shows the best way to soothe a ruffled, Perceptive mate.

When it comes to family, home, and loved ones, the protective urge sometimes works overtime. You try, sometimes excessively, to shield those you love—spouse, children, *and* yourself—from harm's way.

When the Little League coach chews out your son in front of the team, you rush down from the bleachers to give that coach a double dose of his own medicine. You sit up half the night on prom night to be sure your daughter comes home safely. You get up before dawn to chauffeur your youngest child on his or her paper route. You are so protective of your spouse at a party that you appear to be jealous—and sometimes you are.

In one episode of "Knots Landing," we observe Perceptive Karen keeping watch over her son's hospital bed. He is suffering from some strange illness and is in pain. She refuses to leave the hospital for days. "Look," she says to a nurse who is attending to the boy, "he's in pain. Give him something." The nurse calmly says she'll ask the doctor. But that is not enough for the Perceptive Personality. She informs the nurse that she will ask the doctor herself. Later, after finding that the source of her son's illness is the water he's been swimming in (it has been polluted by chemical waste), Karen gets on the phone and goes into action, going on a rampage against the polluters.

When Perceptive Mary Beth, on "Cagney and Lacey," comes home to find that her son has been mugged but had tried to fight the muggers off, she is very upset with him. At the same time she is hugging him, she is yelling at him: "Stupid, stupid kid, don't you know there are more important things to fight for than money?"

A Perceptive Personality watching that particular segment said she would definitely agree that the security of home and family is much more important than financial security. She could relate to Mary Beth's outpouring of emotion—anger, fear, concern, and love all at the same time—as well as her strong protective urge. "I like money as much as the next person," this Perceptive observed, "but if things aren't going well at home or someone is hurt or in trouble, then money matters just don't seem too important."

THE WORKING WORLD

The Perceptive Personality functions well in any profession or job where his responsiveness to others can be used to advantage, especially in the helping professions and service areas.

On "The Cosby Show," Cliff, an obstetrician, handles a class of expectant mothers with Perceptive style. He listens closely and jokes with them about their concern over losing their figures and gaining weight; but he's firm and protective when he lectures them about the need to take care of themselves, to exercise, and to regain their fitness after the baby is born.

Because you have such a capacity for sensing the problems and needs of others, you would usually be a pleasant and effective supervisor—although a little shy of being called the "boss." You are especially effective in working with trainees, particularly problem trainees.

You usually bring your direct and down-to-earth approach to the job. On "Cagney and Lacey," police officer Mary Beth Lacey arrives at the scene of a murder only to be mobbed by reporters. "Get that thing out of my face," she tells one over-anxious reporter thrusting a microphone at her. But when one of the witnesses laments about there being no justice in the world, Mary Beth reassures him, "That's why we're here."

As a Perceptive employee, you may find yourself experiencing some problems with a boss or supervisor under stressful conditions. A slight, any lack of recognition, or a harsh criticism may send you into a slow burn. You may think—and possibly say—"I'm working my tail off and you want more." Or, in more serious circumstances, you may be tempted to walk off the job, or demand to see the company president to complain about that "scrooge" who runs your department.

Just remember the example of your TV Twins: the sixty-second rule, don't sulk and burn. Pause to let the embers of resentment cool long enough that you might possibly understand your boss's comment and respond constructively to the situation. Constantly lamenting "nobody cares" or struggling to keep it all inside does not leave much energy for discovering that the boss really does care enough to want to discuss the problem.

GIVE A FAVOR TO GET A FAVOR

The greeting card industry would probably collapse without you. The Perceptive Personality seldom misses an opportunity to remember someone he cares about; and not just on holidays or birthdays. You would send a thoughtful gift to Auntie Mae, who is eighty-six and recovering from a broken hip—and she's not even really your aunt. Or you might surprise the kid next door with a generous gift for graduation, or send a sick neighbor down the street flowers and a get-well card.

You are always on the lookout for the good health, good fortune, and well-being of others. But while you are quick to respond compassionately to the other person's plight, inside you are saying to yourself, "Dear God, that could be happening to me!" Thus your second-level response is to look out for yourself. You balance compassion for others with your concern to protect your own well-being. It's almost as if you are putting all that love and concern in the bank, hoping you will get it back sometime when you need it. You give to get.

The Perceptive Personality watches Mary on "227" get very upset when her family does not seem to appreciate her efforts to make a nice home and keep herself looking pretty. One Perceptive comments, "I can really relate to the way Mary feels. In the winter time I go outside in the morning to sweep the snow off my husband's and kid's cars, but I never hear any thank-yous. Sometimes I feel like I'm being taken for granted. I feel like Mary. It wouldn't kill them once in a while just to appreciate what I do for them." You like to give and receive on a measure-for-measure basis. But if it's compliments you want, you might have to come right out and ask for them.

I CAN TAKE CARE OF MYSELF: I WILL SURVIVE

Whenever the Perceptive Personality starts feeling a little blue, or used, or begins to measure what he gives against what he gets and finds himself on the short end of the stick, he might respond by asserting his independence.

As we mentioned earlier in the chapter, *survive* is a word you hear the Perceptive Personality use when he feels threatened by loss of security or disappointment or is not receiving love and care equal to the amount he is giving.

Sue Ellen survives when, threatened by her husband's affair, she creates a successful lingerie company and arranges for her husband's mistress to model the product. Sue Ellen knows perfectly well that J.R. won't approve of his mistress appearing all over the country as a scantily clad model; she also knows that her young rival won't be eager to give up her "one big shot at success." So, the affair is scuttled and Sue Ellen's romance with J.R. is rekindled—again.

On "M*A*S*H," Perceptive Margaret Houlihan is the chief nurse at a military field hospital. She is very firm and distant with the nurses under her charge. In one episode, she is being particularly blunt and bossy, refusing to give one nurse time off to spend with her soldier/husband who is visiting the camp, and reprimanding the other nurses for having a hot plate in their tent, which is supposedly against a rule that is rarely enforced.

On the surface, Margaret is being tough and independent, a survivor in the harsh game of being an officer in a wartime situation, distancing herself from her troops. The other nurses respond by distancing themselves from her. Margaret is hurt and disappointed that her nurses automatically exclude her from any of their social get-togethers, avoiding contact with old "Hardnosed Houlihan" as much as possible. Finally, in tears, Margaret breaks down and confesses her desire to be included every once in a while, at least to be invited for a cup of coffee. The nurses are surprised to see a soft and tender side to Margaret and to see her pull in instead of push away.

Sometimes, if your well-being and security are threatened by a loved one, you may find yourself pushing them away instead of pulling them closer. Like Archie Bunker, the Perceptive lovable grouch, you may try to avoid possible rejection by distancing people with a gruff manner or an "I don't need you" attitude.

I asked a group of Perceptives watching Archie why they might have a tendency to push away or back off from someone at times when they needed that person the most. "I guess a big thing with us is that we're so prone to see rejection and pain. We are afraid of being hurt or rejected so we try to 'head it off at the pass' so to speak," is how one Perceptive put it. "Telling ourselves that we can make it alone is really avoiding what we see as inevitable."

The Perceptive Personality sometimes experiences the same "push and pull" with children who are about to leave home. Cliff, on "The Cosby Show," encourages his children to study hard and is constantly giving them lessons in survival, as does Mary Beth Lacey, on "Cagney and Lacey." But when Cliff's children inform him that he might not be the first one they come to when they're in trouble, he is clearly upset.

One Perceptive, after viewing her Perceptive TV Twins interacting with their children, observed, "I believe very strongly in the importance of family, but I also want my children to be strong and capable of taking care of themselves. They know I am there for them, but it's like with a bar of soap: you hold it too tight and it pops out of your hand. Seeing the way these Perceptive people deal with their kids has shown me that I don't have to push my kids completely out of the nest like other people try to tell me I should. I really can't, and really don't have to."

A PERCEPTIVE SECRET

Question: How do you get a Perceptive Personality to do something you want them to do? What is the best way to motivate them? I asked that question of a group of Perceptives. Then we watched a "Cosby" segment in which Cliff was reminiscing about an experience he and wife Clair had had as teenagers. They were supposed to be going to a Sunday school picnic, but instead went off on their own picnic and spent the day alone, necking in the woods. Clair wanted Cliff to call his mother and confess what had happened that day, but Cliff insisted that Clair should be the first to tell her mother the terrible news. So Clair moved a little closer to Cliff, put her arm around him, nuzzled his neck and disagreed, saying he should be first. That did the trick. Off he went to the phone. Of course, after telling "Mom" all about the secret picnic, he hands the phone to Clair, saying, "Your mother wants to talk to you."

But the real secret is already out: if you want to get on the Perceptive Personality's good side and get them to do something, try some physical contact: a light pat, an arm around the shoulder, or a gentle caress. At that point they are putty in your hands.

Well, almost.

If you want to have a successful relationship with the Perceptive Personality you should know that he or she:

- Likes being praised sincerely and honestly.
- Wants to be listened to.
- Appreciates someone who really cares and is interested in how he or she is doing.
- Wants to feel needed.
- Wants praise, patience, and constructive criticism, in that order.

ALTERNATIVES AND OPTIONS

As we have noted, the healthy Perceptive Personality is very warm, outgoing, and likeable; so decent and fair that he makes friends easily and keeps them.

You are compassionate, attuned to the hardships and ailments, trials and sufferings of others. You will do what you can to remedy their sufferings and sorrows since you can put yourself inside their problems through empathy. You are generous in crises, and hope that everyone else will respond in the same manner. You would be frustrated if you were unable to help.

Above all else, the Perceptive Personality prizes happiness, a good home life, calm and contentment, and security of every sort. You are true to your word, just as you are in your dealings with others, and outspoken in your convictions.

But the less secure Perceptive Personality, especially under stress, is vulnerable to feelings of rejection and deprivation. You tend to see your glass as half empty rather than half full. You are not at all surprised that you get the rock in your beans, the apple with the worm in it. The wishbone never seems to break your way. If you were to find a pearl in your oyster, you would complain to the waiter.

You are the Good Samaritan who rushes to help the little old lady being mugged only to have her yell "Thief!" Your dog has fleas and your cat is pregnant and the kids are growing mushrooms in the back seat of your car. When your mate has heard it all for the ninety-ninth time, he or she goes off to mother's for the evening. You aren't surprised; you expect that too, so you pop open a beer and turn on the TV set to hear comedian Rodney Dangerfield moan his signature line: "I don't get no respect." You laugh and sigh, "So true, so true."

But on good days, you are able to see the silver lining. Give or take your grousing and grumbling when things aren't going well—at least as you perceive them—you are resilient. You are so well tuned to your own common sense that you can respond to changes for the better.

If you are a Perceptive Personality, consider the following:

- Whenever you're feeling lonely get involved. Everything you want is contained in relationships dear to you, so wrap yourself in friendships and family.
- Rejection is usually your own projection. People aren't rejecting you; you are walking away from them, or not giving them a chance.
- Beware of your jealousies. They are signals of your tendency to feel deprived or a fear that you will be deprived—or that someone is getting more than you.
- See the larger good and not the small flaws in things that come your way. Take the long view of life and the small flaws will fall into perspective.
- You draw too many lines, defining just how much you will give or do. You fear that someone will take advantage of you or misuse you or that you might become too obligated. Draw-

ing lines causes friction and challenges the good will of others. Don't set up what you fear most: rejection.

- Relationships can be more frustrating than fulfilling when they aren't reciprocal. When you are giving and getting without taking time out to measure which is which, then the relationship is working. You are sharing. It all begins to flow together. Then who knows who did what and when? And who cares? You did it together and that's the joy of it all.
- Every time you say "Leave me alone," think again. You don't need a corner alone in the bedroom; you need closeness, warmth, and caring people. When you think about it long enough, you may end up saying, "Please don't leave me alone."
- Stop being so sensitive to slights or snubs, real or imagined. And don't always store them up. Rather, speak up. Don't sulk, don't smolder. Say it now. Try always to react within sixty seconds. Think tact, then react.
- People admire you for being open, honest, and candid. Don't spoil the impression by being less than honest and open and candid about your emotions. Again, remember the sixty-second rule.
- Beware of being so involved in compassion and concern for the less fortunate across town that you forget or slight those at home who also need your help and your love.
- Stop viewing your compassion as a curse. People aren't out there ready to drain you of all your concern and care. If you are so busy avoiding and dreading involvement, you are going to miss all the good things—and good people—that may come your way. Let the good times roll.
- Whenever you view the glass as half empty, look again. See if it isn't really half full.

MATCH AND MISMATCH

Perceptive Personality matchmates:

Persistent—This is a very easy match, primarily because of the emphasis the Persistent person puts on the one-to-one relationship. The Persistent lets you know how much he or she cares in both words and actions, which makes you feel very secure. Also, your caring and compassion are given in return, which makes the Persistent person feel very special. This is a relationship in which much attention and affection are shared, a true romantic relationship.

Perceptive—This is the only Personality Style that is truly compatible with itself. You encourage each other to respond quickly when there is a problem. You share the same sense of compassion and caring and you place the same emphasis on fairness. You get along well because you both need the same kinds of things in life, and you do not have a problem telling each other when you need this.

Adaptable—Both of you share an honest and open style of communication. You get a great deal of feedback from the Adaptable person, but he or she is also very willing to listen to your problems. Both of you enjoy leisure time and engaging in pleasurable activities together. Because of the Adaptable's flexible nature, your partner encourages you to participate in a wide variety of activities, something which you enjoy.

Sensitive—The Sensitive person is aware of your needs and wants in life and has a great ability to listen to your problems, which makes it easy for you to respond. The Sensitive's loyalty in a relationship keeps your somewhat jealous nature under control, and your great care and concern encourage your partner to discuss feelings more openly.

Accomplishing—You both share an outgoing nature, which keeps the relationship exciting. The Accomplishing person works very hard to meet your needs and to get approval from you, which makes you feel very good. Your somewhat pessimistic nature is balanced well by the Accomplishing Personality's positive outlook on life. This Personality also encourages you to discuss problems so that they can be corrected, which is very healthy for you.

Idealistic—The Idealistic person is very self-sufficient and independent. This sense of independence is shared by you. You both like to try to solve problems on your own first, before asking others for help. You both are direct and open when communicating to others and to each other. You, however, operate on a somewhat emotional level, while the Idealistic person uses a more objective approach, which may lead to some problems. The Idealistic cool nature may appear to you as uncaring.

Anticipating—You are initially drawn to Anticipating individuals' genuineness and honest nature. They build you up, give compliments, which makes you feel good. Above all else, they want you to be happy. You also encourage them to share their plans and concerns with you because you want to be included. However, your outspokenness can make them feel somewhat unimportant, and their occasional tendency to lash out may be taken too personally by you.

Ambitious—Your independence will be utilized in this relationship, allowing you to be free to pursue your own interests. The Ambitious person is success-oriented, always working on a hot project, which leaves less time for romance than you would like. Your outspokenness is taken as bad ratings by the Ambitious person.

Influencing—While you are initially attracted to the charm of the Influencing person, it is difficult to deal with this individual's need to control situations and to make decisions, especially decisions for you. The Influencing person strives for the grand and glorious experiences in life, and you enjoy sharing in this first-class treatment. You may see an occasional temper outburst as a personal attack on you, and your feelings may be hurt rather easily and often.

Determined—Your outspokenness and honesty are directly opposite to the Determined person, who does not give feedback. This individual feels there is a right and a wrong way to do everything, which often will conflict with your own sense of what is right. Your outspokenness is seen as a lack of respect by the Determined person. The more you press to have things brought out in the open, the more he or she clams up. Again, communication styles are very different.

Patient—Both of you have a great willingness and a need to help others, coming to the aid of someone who is in trouble. The Patient Personality, however, may have some difficulty expressing needs and wants, while you can be very outspoken with yours. This individual often takes a "let the dust settle" approach to problem solving, which is seen as a lack of concern by you.

Conscientious—The Conscientious person's tremendous sense of humor is very attractive to you at first. However, the tendency to doubt decisions—and you—can be hard on you. You see this doubting or constant questioning as personal criticism. The Conscientious person deals in facts and logic, while your world is one of emotion and feeling.

Chapter Five

THE ANTICIPATING PERSONALITY

PROFILE

- A worrier, especially about the future.
- A careful, long-range planner and list maker.
- Likes to be organized.
- Doesn't like surprises or last-minute changes in plans.
- Looks for the genuine, the "real thing," especially in relationships.
- Doesn't like the pretentious or the phony.
- Can be something of a pessimist; firm believer in Murphy's Law.

TV TWINS

- Allie—"Kate & Allie"
- Maggie—"Growing Pains"
- Tom Magnum—"Magnum, P.I."
- Michael—"Newhart"
- Blanche—"Golden Girls"
- Jim Rockford—"The Rockford Files"
- Joan Rivers

THE ANTICIPATING PERSONALITY

Suppose you're wondering whether that fine old chair stored in your grandmother's attic is really an authentic Morris chair. Consult an Anticipating antique dealer. If he says it's the genuine item, you can rest assured. The Anticipating Personality appreciates authenticity and quality in all things, including in himself and his work.

Or let's imagine you're considering setting up a retirement fund, a guaranteed source of comfort and sustenance for your golden years. Look no further than the advice of your favorite Anticipating investment counselor. The Anticipating Personality is fully attuned to the future and would anticipate your needs with great care and planning. This Personality's high regard for genuine quality and careful planning is perfectly illustrated by the Anticipating woman who wrote her husband's obituary while he was in the hospital recovering from open-heart surgery. She wanted it to be correct and complete, not thrown together at the last minute if things suddenly took a turn for the worse.

If you just need a touch of warmth and good feeling, then invite an Anticipating friend over for coffee and conversation; the Anticipating Personality has a knack for generating genuine warmth and good feelings. And don't worry about whether the coffee will be OK or if you're going to take up too much of your friend's valuable time. He or she will worry enough for both of you.

You Anticipating people are the best worriers on earth. You see those potholes coming on the road of life long before you reach them. You feel the bump and see the flat tire long before the blowout happens.

Take, for example, an Anticipating copywriter who is writing an advertising campaign for a new brand of soap. She is aware of her writing talent and realizes how important a good campaign is to the success of a new product. She has read all the laboratory reports on the new soap, so she is confident that this *is* a better bath soap than the others on the market. But she is somewhat hesitant about the scent. If they like it in Louisville, will they like it in Los Angeles? She has studied the market research, and she wonders if the copy she is considering for the East will go over well in the South. How effective are the name, the design of the wrapper, the model's image, the tentative slogan? Will they all mesh into one singular impression of a quality bath soap? She wonders. She worries. If she is that healthy, self-reliant Anticipating Personality who knows she can write well—her copy always reflects her ability to persuade—then she can move ahead, confident that she can put all the pieces together. If the campaign goes well and the new soap is a success, she will be able to assess her own contribution. Even if the campaign doesn't turn out to be an overwhelming success, she will be able to acknowledge her efforts and give herself credit.

On the other hand, if our Anticipating copywriter is less confident going into the campaign—this product and this campaign are somewhat new and the soap smells funny—she may worry too much about Louisville and Los Angeles, too much about the scent and the wrapper and how she will handle the slogan. She may roam around the agency seeking reassurance from colleagues, or she may decide to postpone writing copy until she has a look at proofs of new photographs being shot at the studio. Doomsday looms large, even before she has written the first word.

But worry is not the only result of viewing the future through a telescope. The Anticipating Personality is also a great planner. You know that the best way to avoid problems is to have a carefully thought out plan: step by step.

Planning assures that you do your job well, and whether you are building skyscrapers or planning dinner, doing the job well is very important to you. It reflects your importance as a person. So you don't like to be unnecessarily interrupted, or to have your carefully laid plans subjected to any careless, last-minute change.

When it comes to relationships, you have a tendency to invest your all, your every effort into commitment, and you want a partner or mate who is willing to try as hard and to invest as much.

A good appearance, in your person and in your home, means a lot to you. You want others to think well of you. You like to feel important.

But there are times when you have a hard time accepting praise, especially if you suspect in any way that it isn't genuine.

Sometimes when you are feeling down you will heap compliments on others, feeling that they do so much better than you. You rarely give yourself enough credit for your own good work.

You have a tendency to underrate yourself at times, but it's usually done with humor, and only because you have such high expectations of yourself as well as others. You are wary of compliments and of overselling yourself because you are interested in the genuine. For you, it's the real thing or nothing.

MEET YOUR TV TWINS

"I'll never be able to recognize my TV Twins. And even if I do, what if I don't like them?" That's the Anticipating worrier talking and, as we have found, it's natural for you to fret just a bit.

But I guarantee you that finding your TV Twins will be tremendously rewarding. They'll be easy to identify because they:

- Are genuine and thorough and tell of their interest in a long-term approach.
- Want to feel important and be needed.
- Are somewhat self-deprecatory, especially in their humor.
- Have difficulty accepting compliments.
- Tend to build others up while at the same time not recognizing their own capabilities.
- Need to proceed in a gradual, planned fashion.
- Tend to worry about change.

On "Kate & Allie," Anticipating **Allie** is a divorced mother who shares her New York City apartment with her son and daughter, her friend Kate, and Kate's daughter. Living as a single woman again after years of marriage, in a big city, with a teenage daughter and adolescent son, sharing her home with another single mother, all combine to give Allie plenty to worry about. But Allie's careful planning works well to offset the perils of her lifestyle—at least most of the time.

Have you ever heard of Murphy's Law? "If anything can go wrong, it will." Will Allie's ex-husband and his new wife be the only guests not to cancel out on Allie's Thanksgiving dinner?

Will her ex, who is a doctor, then be called to an emergency at the hospital just after he and his new bride arrive at Allie's? Will Allie, who just happens to be home alone preparing dinner while Kate and the children are at a Thanksgiving parade, have to spend an hour alone with the very woman she has just greeted at the door with, "Welcome to our broken home"? You're the Anticipating Personality; *you* answer those questions.

On "Growing Pains," Anticipating **Maggie** is a wife and working mother with three children, two of them teens. Her husband, a psychiatrist, has his office at home, while Maggie goes out to work. She is a list maker, a planner, and, naturally, a worrier. An Anticipating Personality would know just what Maggie is going to say when she watches her husband open the birthday gift she has bought for him: "I can take it back if you don't like it."

Michael, on "Newhart," is a producer at a small-town TV station. He expresses his Anticipating Personality by worrying that his job is not important enough to impress his snobbish mother, and by putting his girlfriend Stephanie on a pedestal, treating her like a goddess to contrast with his own occasional feelings of inadequacy.

Anticipating **Blanche,** on "Golden Girls," is, on the surface, very confident in her relationships with men. But she is obviously nervous about how her house looks to visiting guests. Everything must be just so, or she is a wreck.

Both Blanche and Michael are great followers of the Anticipating, "look good, feel good" theory: The way you look, and the way your house looks, is a direct reflection of your feeling of self-importance and worth.

On "Magnum, P.I.," **Tom Magnum** is a private detective who approaches his job very carefully, knowing that his chosen field is fraught with danger. Anticipating **Jim Rockford,** on "The Rockford Files," is also a very low-key private detective who disdains the usual flashy, flamboyant approach of the private eye and tends to be rather self-effacing.

We only have to hear Anticipating **Joan Rivers** claim that she was so fat as a child that she was her own best buddy at camp, to understand that the Anticipating Personality has a tendency to underrate self worth. But, as we pointed out earlier, this self-deprecation is usually done with humor, as Joan Rivers so well illustrates, and only because the Anticipating Personality has such high expectations.

You and your TV Twins have a strong need to plan and be prepared. You worry when things aren't going according to plan or when your plan is disrupted. You give it your all in life and want others to think well of you. You can be quite critical, or even blunt, when others aren't as genuine as you and when they interrupt your plan. You recognize that you grow through change, and so you plan for changes.

As you follow your TV Twins' video lives, look carefully for examples of:

- Worry.
- Planning ahead.
- Lashing out or building up others excessively when they feel inferior.
- Panic with last-minute changes or with spontaneous situations.
- Personal growth with praise.

WE'LL CROSS THAT BRIDGE BEFORE WE COME TO IT

I have a friend who has an interesting and complicated problem. He's a writer who has been quite successful, although he has published only two novels in twenty-three years. "I'm a planner," he says, "and a worrier, kind of like Allie on 'Kate & Allie.' So I like to have my work totally laid out in my mind, step by step, before I start. It takes longer, but that's just my way."

If you praise him for his brilliance, he will laugh and deny being anything but a pencil pusher. He is uncomfortable with compliments and puts himself down in a joking way, just as Jim Rockford on "The Rockford Files" and Tom Magnum on "Magnum, P.I." do. But I know how important his work is to him and how much care he takes with it.

The other day he was out jogging (which he does to clear his head and to prevent heart attacks), thinking about whether to move to the West Coast and try writing screenplays. He was nervous about taking a new job, as Maggie on "Growing Pains" would be, worrying, like Allie, about the plane flight he would have to take. What if nobody liked his work after he got there? Maybe the plane will crash. What happens if he has a heart attack when he gets there? Everyone has told him that hospitals back East are much better at treating heart problems.

In the midst of this worry, he failed to notice his dog lying on the sidewalk in front of his house. As he ran up to the front door, he tripped over the dog and fell into the shrubbery. Luckily he suffered only a mild concussion and some minor lacerations.

During the ambulance ride to the hospital the unfortunate events of the day started germinating into a third novel in my friend's mind, just as Joan Rivers's life becomes a monologue on TV shows.

The question of whether to go to the West Coast is now, of course, put off indefinitely, at least until the novel is finished. Then my friend will have to get himself back in shape again. He's a great believer in the "look good, feel good" theory, just as Blanche on "Golden Girls" and Michael on "Newhart" are.

Then there's always that damn flying to think about. But, he says, before he does *anything* he definitely has to get rid of the dog.

On "Kate & Allie," Anticipating Allie is preparing dinner when the phone rings. Kate answers and tells Allie it's Allie's mother calling. "Something's wrong, I know it," are the first words out of Allie's mouth as she rushes for the phone.

You worry when things are going right, you worry when things are going wrong. And you might even project your worries into the future, telescoping a long series of suspected problems. You are thirty-two thousand feet into the air, halfway between home and Honolulu, and you're mentally reviewing your pre-vacation checklist. Suddenly you ask your companion,

"Did I leave the oven on? Do you think the neighbor will remember to feed my cat? Did I leave too many lights on?"

What is this all about?

One of the essential elements of the Anticipating Personality is the importance of careful planning so that things will turn out well, because what you do is a reflection of who you are. You're always afraid, though, that things will turn out wrong, you get caught up in the worrying urge. It can strike anytime, anywhere.

We watch Tom Magnum on "Magnum, P.I." pursuing a bad guy in a high-speed car chase. But Magnum is driving someone else's car, and suddenly, in the middle of the chase, he begins to worry about wrecking the car. After all, it's not his. And at those speeds anything can happen.

If you're feeling good about yourself, you can realistically measure your talents, capability, and confidence against the scope of the task ahead and anticipate the appropriate outcome. If you and the project at hand are reasonably matched, you can be expected to plan and organize efficiently, then move into the project, confident of doing a quality job. But if you're feeling less sure of yourself and your competence to handle whatever is facing you, you might back away. You might begin to worry about every conceivable problem, every possible pitfall, every snag, every danger—even a few that aren't too possible.

On "Kate & Allie," Anticipating Allie is taking a college poetry class. Her handsome young instructor invites her to have tea with him after class, and it quickly becomes obvious that he has more than a passing interest in her. She comes home later and tells roommate Kate about him and Kate immediately encourages her to follow through. "Don't worry," Kate says, "he's a younger man, he's going back to Ohio in two weeks." But Allie is already planning for the worst. "I have to protect myself. I don't want to get involved. I don't want to get hurt. I don't want to be alone with him in an empty apartment."

At times, you are reluctant to let yourself be lifted to the heights of happiness because the inevitable crash is so painful to your tender Anticipating heart. You can never be too sure. As you are receiving your company's annual safety award, you're thinking about that new machine in your department that has too many exposed gears. You're afraid that some worker is going to catch a piece of clothing in the gears before you can get the safety screens in place. The president of the company can't understand that worried look on your face as he hands you the safety award plaque and the audience applauds.

Kate tries to reassure Allie that her relationship with the college instructor will work out, but Allie is reluctant to be carried away by a whirlwind romance. "In six days I'm going to fall apart in little pieces and you'll have to put me back together again," she tells Kate.

Eventually, Allie is able to relax and enjoy the relationship as it happens and for what it's worth.

After viewing that segment, an Anticipating Personality commented, "I have a tendency to blow things out of proportion at times like Allie. But I've also learned not to worry about things that are out of my control. For example, I have to move to a different city soon for my job. It's a big change for me, but it's out of my hands, at least if I want to keep my job. So why should I worry about it and get myself all upset? What I've tried to do is turn it into a positive thing, look at all the positive things I have to look forward to in the new place. I'll still worry, of course, but it can be a positive worry that I use to plan for a smooth transition."

MURPHY'S LAW

Murphy, of Murphy's Law fame, must have been an Anticipating Personality. At least every Anticipating Personality knows old Murph in some way, shape, or fashion.

On "Kate & Allie," Allie is going all-out to prepare a fantastic Thanksgiving dinner. She has her children cleaning the house so it is spotless for the guests. Her daughter comes into the kitchen while Allie is heavily involved in shaking various containers of seasoning over the turkey. Her daughter sets her can of bathroom cleaner on the counter and announces that she is finished. Allie doesn't look up, keeps on working, says "OK, OK." Later, when she pulls the turkey out of the oven to check on it, it is swimming in a sea of bubbles. She panics, "My God, what's wrong with the turkey!" She has Kate taste it. Kate makes a face and asks her what she put on it. "Just the usual," says Allie and proceeds to name the ingredients as she picks up each container, "Parsley, sage, rosemary, poultry seasoning . . . cleanser!"

How do you escape the dreaded Murphy? Well, there's always planning ahead for every possible contingency. Suppose you're getting ready to strip and wax the kitchen floor. What if the phone rings in the middle of the job? Better take the phone off the hook. But what if one of the kids gets sick at school? Better put the phone back on the hook. What if the kids get home before you're finished and want a snack? Better put cookies and milk out on the dining room table. But won't the milk sour sitting out for several hours? Better get out the cooler and ice the milk. What if the floor needs a third coat? Back to the store for another bottle of wax.

Well, OK, so planning for every possibility is not so realistic. How about planing ahead for *most* possible contingencies, and developing a good sense of humor to go along? That might be the best way to foil Murphy's law.

LAUGH IN THE FACE OF TROUBLE

The Anticipating Personality's comedy is often one of despair. Jokes about calamitous situations are the way you bring your worst worries and fears into the open and deal with them without letting them get too close.

Joan Rivers worries aloud about aging, and claims that when she noticed her first liver spots she thought her nipples had moved. When she was young, she says, she was so fat that in her school pictures she was the entire front row.

On "Kate & Allie," Allie is making goose liver pâté for a special dinner. Her son tastes it and says, "Yeck." She tastes it and says, "Yeck." It's obviously a failure. "I think I put in too much cognac," says Allie. "It tastes like the goose died of cirrhosis." Later, after a few more setbacks, she looks heavenward: "Boy," she says to the divine manipulator of fate, "you're good." It is the Anticipating magic of denial through humor.

The Anticipating Personality will see the demon—the fears, mistakes, vulnerabilities, and sorrow—coming in the distance, will hear it creeping down the hall, but will hold it at arm's length, laughing in its face.

IT'S NOT A MATTER OF BEING LUCKY, IT'S A MATTER OF BEING PREPARED

Had you, the Anticipating Personality, been the skipper of the *Titanic*, that good ship might still be afloat. You would have carefully considered the possibility of icebergs in the Atlantic during April and planned your course accordingly. You always have your sights set on the future. You know what you want to do and how you plan to get there. We can watch Maggie on "Growing Pains" carefully plan how the day at home is going to go before she leaves for the office. On another segment, she makes a plan to protect her father's pride. He's about to lose his house because of financial problems but refuses to accept money from Maggie's husband. She discusses the dilemma with her husband. "OK, so what's your plan?" she asks him. "Do you think it's wise to proceed without a plan?" The plan they eventually settle on involves a drinking contest between father and son-in-law with the champion winning—coincidentally, the same amount of money the father owes. Father wins and everyone is happy; maybe too happy.

By planning, you look ahead, set yourself a course past all the possible disappointments and problems. You can move ahead comfortably knowing that the map, personally drawn by you, will bring you safely to your destination.

One Anticipating woman I know told me about her burial plan. Although she had a burial plot where she currently lived, she also had one "back home." She felt that the cemetery back home was much more beautiful and, at first, had planned to be taken back there when the time came. But then she started thinking about how much trouble it might be for her friends to have to travel all that way to visit the grave. So she decided to stick with the burial plot where she lived instead.

In an interview, Joan Rivers tells about writing her husband's obituary—somewhat prematurely as it turned out. He was in the hospital after a serious heart attack. Anticipating Joan was very upset, but still planning. So she decided to write his obituary, just in case. She wanted it to be well written and complete, not thrown together at the last minute if the worst happened. Fortunately, her husband recovered.

Allie, of "Kate & Allie," is usually at home every day making dinner for everyone, but one afternoon her college instructor asks her to have tea with him and they end up spending hours together. Even in the midst of a blossoming romance she plans for dinner, still remembering to bring deli food home for the hungry troops.

In another segment, Allie is looking at pictures of the house her ex-husband has just built for his new wife. Although she obviously is not taking great pleasure in seeing photos of what should have been hers, she spies a freezer in one of the photos, perks up, and exclaims, "Do you realize that if I had a freezer like that I could make a year's worth of meatloaf in one sitting?"

An Anticipating woman I know told me that she first realized her son was also Anticipating when he started asking her, first thing in the morning, what they were going to have for dinner that night.

THE GREAT LEVEL-HEADED LIST MAKER

We have established that the Anticipating Personality is (1) a careful planner and (2) something of a worrier. So, being the resourceful person that you are, you often find that the best way to avoid worry and organize your plans at the same time is to keep careful lists of those things that have to be done. You are the great list maker.

When Maggie, on "Growing Pains," is trying to decide whether or not to give up her full-time job and go back to housekeeping, she makes two lists, one of the pros of staying home, one of the cons, to help her plan her decision. She hands the lists to her husband and he starts reading, "Loaf of bread, dry cleaners," etc. She had used the back of one list to make still another.

Even though some non-Anticipating Personalities may make light of all your lists, you know that when your lists, both on paper and in your mind, and your calendar are synchronized, good things happen. Otherwise, you would be disorganized and fretful.

Speaking of disorganized and fretful, that is exactly the state of mind you can be thrown into when your lists are not carefully followed, when unannounced guests stop in for dinner (or, worse yet, the weekend), or when cruel fate throws a monkey wrench into your well-oiled plans.

We can watch Allie planning her Thanksgiving dinner, spending the whole morning preparing the food, setting the places, laying the blueprint for a smooth day, even though her ex-husband is bringing his new wife, a woman Allie has never met but already despises. Kate tries to reassure her, reminding her that there will be so many other people there that she probably won't have to spend any time alone with the despised woman and probably won't have to talk with her much. As the show goes along, we see Allie's carefully laid plans gradually fall apart. First, the turkey is ruined. Then, one by one, all the guests call to cancel because of illness or some other problem. Finally, the only guests expected are Allie's ex-husband and his second wife. Allie is in the middle of a panic when Kate, who has taken the kids to a parade, calls and says she'll be late getting home for dinner. Allie begs her to come home. It's definitely time for Plan B.

After viewing the segment, one Anticipating woman commented, "I can really see how planning is very important for the Anticipating Personality. Unfortunately, the other Personalities don't always appreciate or consider that. My husband used to invite people over for dinner at the last minute and then tell me about it. It really got to me. Now that he and I both understand my Personality a little better and my need to plan, he doesn't do it as much, although he hasn't stopped completely."

In another "Kate & Allie" episode, Allie is put on the spot when the man she has been seeing suddenly suggests that he move to New York and get an apartment to be near her, and then proposes marriage. She feels cornered, hasn't had any time to plan, and panics.

An Anticipating Personality watching that segment noted, "It can certainly be a terrible experience when someone springs an unexpected situation on you at the last moment or expects you to all of a sudden change your plans. If people only realized that about the Anticipating Personality, they could get along much better with us. Give us time and we'll come out in tremendous shape. But rush us, and it might spell trouble."

Good old predictable Allie managed to overcome her panic and deal with the sudden proposal in true Anticipating fashion: She formulated a practical plan. She joked about her fears, just to relax her companion and herself, then managed to strike a compromise, a happy medium.

You may suspect that that predictability, that distaste for the spontaneous, that fear of the unexpected, and that love for the happy medium make you a dull, uninteresting person. "I used to watch Allie and think to myself, 'God, am I that much of a stick-in-the-mud worrywart?' " said one Anticipating person I know. "Then I began to realize that the predictability and stability were a big part of my strength and my appeal. People were drawn to me because of that. It's just me."

STEP BY STEP

The Anticipating Personality seems to function under the norms of Newton's first law of motion: An Anticipating Personality at rest tends to remain at rest; that is, there are times when the Anticipating Personality doesn't seem sure enough of what lies ahead to get off square one. Sometimes this is interpreted as being laid back. But once the Anticipating Personality is set in motion, he or she tends to remain in motion, that is, the Anticipating Personality continues to function with confidence and efficiency until the job becomes overwhelming, or until a new, unanticipated angle is introduced. Then the Anticipating Personality may back off, returning to the state of rest.

On "Kate & Allie," Allie is taking a college class. The discussion turns to whether the college should continue to own stock in a company that has been accused of illegally dumping toxic wastes. Allie speaks up initially, gets the ball and herself rolling, but when some of her younger classmates try to get her involved in a march on the administration building, she pulls back, moves away from the situation until she has time to think and consider the possibilities involved in that sort of action.

An Anticipating Personality watching that segment remembered voluntarily transferring to a lower position at work from a higher one where he had been expected to attend meetings at the spur of the moment, unprepared. He was pulling away from a situation he was not prepared for.

At times, the Anticipating Personality might even experience a phobia as a means of pulling away from a difficult situation. Any one of us can experience a fear of flying on a turbulent day, but a young Anticipating executive I knew never feared flying until he had to fly to another city to attend a very important corporate management meeting. Suddenly, the thought of flying was terrifying to him. On "Kate & Allie," Allie is asked to appear on a TV talk show. Coincidentally, the usually glib Allie suddenly develops a stutter, a phobia of speaking in public, just as the normally fearless young executive coincidentally developed a phobia of flying. Both were perfect examples of the Anticipating Personality using a phobia to back away from a difficult situation.

But never fear, all of you Anticipating people, temporarily frozen by phobia, there is an answer:

The uneasy Anticipating Personality can be coaxed into action through one form of reassurance or another. Best for you is self-motivation: talking to yourself in a positive, confidence-building way to get moving. On "Magnum, P.I.," we watch Tom Magnum being chased by some rather hungry-looking Dobermans. He gets to his car but freezes and can't get his key in the door to unlock it, so he starts talking to himself in a reassuring tone, saying "Put the key in the lock. Turn it. Open the door." It's the step-by-step method. Magnum knows that once he takes that first step, he can do the job, and avoid ending up as dog food.

I suggest that the Anticipating Personality use a plan called "following the *P*s" in order to function well and effectively in a stressful situation. The *P*s are:

- Pay attention when you first encounter a situation; don't panic.
- Pause and collect your thoughts.
- Plan in a step-by-step manner.
- Proceed; face the situation head-on.
- Pace yourself; life is a cinch by the inch, hard by the yard, and a trial by the mile.

  And, last but not least,
- Praise yourself; let yourself feel proud of the way you have reacted to the situation.

FEEL IMPORTANT, BE IMPORTANT

It's important for the Anticipating Personality to *feel* important, but because your expectations of yourself are so high, you may hesitate to oversell yourself. Like Allie, Maggie, Tom, and the rest of your Anticipating TV Twins, you tend to downplay compliments, responding with, "Oh, anyone could do that."

When the Anticipating Personality is faced with a new or changing situation, he may feel a little scared. As his confidence sags he may come down on himself, looking for and expecting the worst. Kate and Allie sit, waiting for a phone call from a man they think is going to invite one of them to the opera. They are both friends with the man and both apparently have an equal chance of being the one he will ask. But it's Allie who says, "The one he asks goes to the opera; the other kills myself."

The Anticipating Personality may praise and flatter others, putting the object of his flattery on a pedestal to contrast with his own insecure position on the ground. On "Growing Pains," we watch Maggie give her husband extravagant praise for his "invaluable advice" on whether or not she should keep her job. We can also watch Allie diligently preparing dinner for her ex-husband and his new wife and observing, "In three hours a woman who makes me feel totally inadequate is coming over."

The Anticipating Personality might also compensate for feeling down with the exact opposite of flattery, namely, lashing out with criticism or biting humor. Before Allie's ex-husband and his new wife arrive for dinner, Allie rehearses in her mind what she will say: "Oh, Charles, how nice of you to come, and I see you brought that slut you married. Welcome to our broken home." Later, Allie is left alone with Clair, the second wife, after Charles is called away on an emergency. "Well," says Clair, "is this where you let me have it?" "Well, Clair," says Allie, "I have a feeling nobody lets you have it. You just take it."

But ladies, ladies please. There is a better way for the Anticipating Personality to handle both those occasional feelings of inadequacy and praise for a job well done. It's called knowing yourself and being yourself.

On "Newhart," we can watch Anticipating Michael prepare for a visit from his mother. She is a rather pompous woman, and has always expected Michael to be some sort of consummate artist. Instead, he has become a TV producer for a small local station. He is feeling insecure about his position, being self-critical, and minimizing his accomplishments as a producer. He decides to impress his mother, whom he has obviously placed on a pedestal, by trying to impress her as an artist. But his artistic efforts fail. In the end, he finally recognizes that he is what he is, an Anticipating TV producer, and comes to appreciate both the importance of his work and of himself, just as he is. He stands up to Mom in an impressive finale.

After viewing that particular segment, one Anticipating Personality noted, "I really felt good watching Michael stand up to his mother like that. Sometimes, if you hear those negative things long enough, you start believing them. Others are putting you down and you start putting yourself down too. And that's no good."

Another Anticipating Personality commented, "I have had

trouble accepting compliments and my own self-worth just like Allie and Michael. Just the other day I was working on a project at my arts and crafts class but was having some trouble getting started. I was saying to myself, 'You can't do it.' Then this woman walked by and complimented me on my work, told me how really competent I was. I started to say how I really wasn't all that good, but suddenly I caught myself and said, 'Here I am, doing it.' I realized what was going on, so I went ahead and finished and did a really good job."

THE WORKING WORLD

That same law of Newton's that applies in the rest of your world also applies in the world of work: Once in motion you tend to stay in motion. The fear of new challenges, new frontiers, and new encounters may make you hesitant to enter the job market initially. For example, if you are nearing graduation from college you may be tempted to change majors in your senior year or go on to do graduate work as a way of avoiding the new demands of the working world.

We can watch Maggie, on "Growing Pains," anticipating all the pros and cons in her mind as she tries to decide whether or not to take a full-time job. What about her husband? What about her children? Will she be able to make the transition from homemaker to career woman without shattering her sense of self-importance?

But once you cross the threshold, you become an energetic, responsible, resourceful performer. Once in motion you tend to stay in motion, and your planning skills help you to avoid the problems that go along with your particular line of work. Well, almost all.

If you are forced into an unanticipated change, or, God forbid, make some major mistake on the job, you could experience a crippling attack of stress and insecurity, depending on your confidence level. Your progress might temporarily grind to a halt. On that same "Growing Pains" episode we mentioned above, Maggie does decide to take the job and proceeds to make a major mistake at work soon after. She gets very upset and immediately contemplates giving up her job, her feelings of self-importance in tatters. But after some initial agonizing over whether or not to return to the job, Maggie collects herself, follows "the *P*s," consults with her husband, and decides after all to put herself back in motion. She returns to work to remedy the mistake and continue the job.

As we mentioned earlier, the Anticipating Personality always works well from a list and by executing items one at a time in advance of any set deadline. Notes one Anticipating Personality preparing for winter: "All my flowers are out of the ground, bushes are mulched, the trees trimmed. Long before the cold weather hits I had the car tuned, the antifreeze checked, and the snow tires put on. The furnace and the filter are cleaned. The fireplace is checked and the cord wood stacked. That way, I'm ready. If something isn't right, like the furnace, I'm not caught waiting three or four days waiting for the furnace man to come. By planning properly, I can do it all a little at a time and I never have to rush. When I'm rushed, I always seem to bungle the job and have to do it over."

HOME

A good appearance, in your person and in your home environment, is very important to you. A neat and tidy home is just another reflection of the Anticipating Personality's striving for a feeling of self-importance.

On "Golden Girls," we can watch Blanche prepare the house for a visit from her sister. She has always felt as though her sister put her down, so she alternates between giving her sister backhanded compliments—putting her on a pedestal of sorts—and sniping at her to cover some inadequate feelings she has about herself. One way for Blanche to retrieve some self-respect is to have the house absolutely spotless for her sister's arrival. While they're waiting, no one is allowed to even sit on the sofa for fear that the cushions will be wrinkled.

After viewing that segment, one Anticipating woman I know echoed that same sentiment. "If everything in my house is looking good but there are a couple of things out of place in the back bedroom, the whole house doesn't look good to me and I don't deserve any praise. I hate it when people come in and say 'Your home really looks lovely.' I'm sitting there thinking, 'No, you ought to see the back bedroom. It looks like hell.' "

Another aspect of the Anticipating Personality also has a profound impact on home life and is reflected in the "Growing Pains" segment in which Maggie is contemplating quitting her new job after making a major mistake. When trouble comes, one of her immediate reactions is, "What am I doing here at work? I should be at home doing laundry."

This emphasis on adequacy may prompt the Anticipating Personality to divide household chores on a "his" and "her's" basis. Each person functions according to his own competency, and in our changing world the division of labor does not necessarily follow traditional sex roles. As one Anticipating woman noted, "My husband is much better at decorating, so I want to let him use that talent in our home. But the yard is my province."

Whatever you do best—and whatever makes you feel the best about yourself—do. But let's get that back bedroom cleaned up.

THE REAL THING

In love, as in day-to-day life, it is important for the Anticipating Personality to be true, both to himself and to his companion. You do not put much stock in phonies.

You tend to invest your all, your every effort in commitment to a relationship. You hold those close to you in high regard; each is a very important person. But when you find that one person to whom you can be very special, it is usually someone who is calm, easygoing, and fun loving, someone who lets you be yourself.

We can watch Allie go through the whole Anticipating "girl-meets-boy" process on one segment in which she is forming a relationship with her college professor. He approaches her very gradually, asking her to have tea after class, carrying on long discussions about poetry and life. Then they begin to date and everything proceeds according to plan, including one afternoon they spend alone together in Allie's apartment from which she emerges with that certain "luminous glow."

But then things start to progress too rapidly. The professor, who is about to be transferred back to Ohio, announces that he plans to take an apartment in New York near Allie instead and proposes marriage. Not only does that push Allie into unplanned and untested territory, it forces her to make a snap decision on whether his—and her—feelings are genuine. She has been through one failed marriage already. "I don't know if what I feel is love for you, or the need to feel something again," she says as she struggles with the dilemma.

She collects herself for a moment, then decides that the way to the "real thing" passes through Plan B. She tells him she wants him to go back to Ohio and write letters to her, and quote her poetry until she thinks she's the biggest fool on earth for letting him go. "Then I'll come visit you, and we'll have time to sit and think and plan and decide what to do," she says. He agrees.

It *is* the real thing.

THE LITTLE ENGINE THAT COULD

The Anticipating Personality looks to the future and realizes that good, hard, diligent effort will carry him past most obstacles, even the ones he can't plan for. Right? Well, in most instances; I mean, Allie and Maggie and Magnum and Blanche and the rest of your Anticipating TV Twins continue to function, although the worry never stops. The unpredictable future is at the same time an aggravation and the dynamic that keeps you and them going.

The Anticipating Personality might be something like the little engine in that famous children's story that says, "I think I can, I think I can." But you know that the tracks can be very long and rough. "I think I can, I think I can," will never be enough.

ALTERNATIVES AND OPTIONS

All things considered, the Anticipating Personality is usually a contented, self-reliant, generous person who contributes significantly to the human good, even when he isn't aware of how much he contributes. In a culture that often puts more emphasis on image than on substance, the Anticipating Personality is greatly concerned with authenticity and integrity.

Even so, with all of your marvelous traits, you don't always recognize how much you contribute, how much people enjoy your warmth and admire your integrity.

The Anticipating Personality who recognizes himself as less sure of his capabilities can be too pessimistic, too worried to test his confidence. His confidence erodes; he anticipates failure. When these things happen, the Anticipating Personality needs to be aware of a plan that will help the individual move beyond worry and gloom into real productivity and confidence.

If you are an Anticipating Personality, consider the following points:

- Plan ahead. Make a list of things you have to do, then do them one at a time, one step at a time. Remember, life is a cinch by the inch, hard by the yard, and a trial by the mile.
- Put your energy into work, not worry. Worry stops when work begins.
- Be sure to give yourself credit when you do something well, when you make a strong effort, when you try something new.
- Be willing to test your capabilities. Listen for the encouragement of others who urge you to try harder.
- Assume more responsibility for judging your own capabilities and competence. Avoid seeking credit where the situation doesn't really warrant it.
- Always make an effort to function at your true level of capability. If you believe you should be a B student, make every effort to work at that level. If you believe that you are capable of being a supervisor, be willing to assume more responsibility; then make your plans.

- The really important effort is starting. Hear this successful Anticipating Personality: "Once I start, I'm OK. If I don't start, I feel defeated. I used to think too much before starting. Now I plan and just go ahead and do it."
- When things are gloomy, recall some other moments when you were doing well, feeling good. Let your natural optimism rise to the moment.
- Your fears and phobias are messages. Read beneath the surface of fear of flying, fear of crowds, fear of dying, fear of dark places. The underlying message could be fear of *trying*.
- Failure is possible, and when it really happens, it does hurt. But don't let one failure paralyze you for life. The best response to a failure is to look around for other areas of capability. Give yourself credit for having tried. The failure is in *not* trying.
- Expand your interests and involvement. Probe untried areas of interest. If you have always wanted to play the guitar, then rent one. Get started before you have time to think up excuses or reasons why you couldn't possibly play the guitar. If you have always wanted to be a writer, take pencil in hand. Good luck. Begin. Try first, evaluate later.
- Temper your tendency to compliment and flatter others. You may be nibbling away at your own self-esteem. And don't mistrust the compliments of others. Be more prone to appraise yourself and your performance properly. When someone compliments you, say "Thank you." You deserve the credit.
- The next time you feel like saying, "I know I can't do that," say, "I think I can." Then take the first step. Soon you will be saying, "I knew I could."
- Don't hold back. Move ahead. One step at a time. The future is now.

SECRETS

The keys to a successful relationship with the Anticipating Personality are:

- Respect the Anticipating Personality's plans and the need to be organized.
- Don't spring last-minute surprises or changes in plans.
- Allow the Anticipating Personality time to pause and collect thoughts.
- Respect, but don't encourage, worry.
- Encourage feelings of self-importance and the importance of tasks and jobs that the Anticipating Personality is performing.
- Stress the step-by-step approach.
- Give the Anticipating Personality genuine and sincere praise when it's called for.

MATCH AND MISMATCH

Anticipating Personality matchmates:

Sensitive—A very easy match because of the keen awareness of the Sensitive person which safeguards against accidents and problems. Plans flow smoothly and the Sensitive person trusts your judgment. A gentle, modest approach on the part of the Sensitive person ensures good feelings on your part because he or she can readily see how capable you are and will let you know this.

Conscientious—Such Personalities appreciate your tremendous planning and can help with this process because of their own emphasis on details and calculations. Both of you have a strong sense of efficiency and routine. This makes you feel important. There are no false compliments and this is truly a joint effort. You both enjoy fun and good times.

Adaptable—Very good communication skills provide the feedback that you need as an Anticipating person. Both of you place emphasis on a good appearance and both proceed in an organized and planned fashion. These persons are very good at appreciating your capabilities and let others know how skilled you are in your planning abilities. You build them up as well and can share your plans and worries with them because they encourage you to communicate.

Persistent—You are a planner and are "future-oriented" in your approach, which blends well with the Persistents' creative thoughts and imagination. You like to feel important and you will with these individuals, whose emphasis is on the one-to-one relationship. They make you feel very special with their attention.

Patient—This person is quite agreeable to your well-laid plans. Your worry is counterbalanced by the Patient's pleasant, optimistic, easygoing manner. You are such a genuine and thorough person and the Patient's need for security is not threatened. He or she is dependable, which eases your worry.

Influencing—In this situation, both of you are impressed by the thoroughness and organizational abilities that you share. In addition, you both emphasize a good personal appearance. You are initially attracted by the charm and charisma of the Influencing person. However, it is difficult for you to make and carry out your plans because of the Influencing person's controlling tendencies. When he or she takes over a situation, you may feel unimportant.

Perceptive—You look to the future; the Perceptive person often dwells in the past. You are both up-front with your feelings, so the discussions can be heated. The Perceptive person can complain, which does little for your self-esteem. The self-sufficiency of the Perceptive person can also be a problem. You may feel unimportant when, for example, the Perceptive rushes off to aid someone who is hurting.

Accomplishing—You plan very carefully, using a gradual approach, while the Accomplishing person is impulsive. Your pace is gradual and deliberate, while this Personality is fast and furious. Your worry is seen as negative, something that is very difficult for the Accomplishing person to deal with. Your criticism is also seen by the Accomplishing person as disapproval.

Determined—You value feedback, which is very difficult to get in this situation; there is little conversation. When your plans don't work out you hear "I told you so," and your confidence disintegrates. The Determined person has plans also but does not discuss them. In this situation, communication is the biggest problem.

Idealistic—You need to share your plans and worries with others and this is seen as weakness by the Idealistic person whose standards and principles are sure to cause you problems. You need to feel included and important and you get little help from the Idealistic person because he or she can't admit these needs. Because of this, your confidence is threatened.

Ambitious—The Ambitious person wants things done yesterday and you still need time to plan. Praise and credit are hard to come by in this situation because after completing one project the Ambitious person is off in pursuit of the next goal. In this situation, you will probably be spending a great deal of time by yourself, feeling left out and unimportant.

Chapter Six

THE CONSCIENTIOUS PERSONALITY

PROFILE

- Likes detail and tends to give elaborate explanations.
- Likes routine; is very predictable.
- Can be indecisive, and even after making a decision may be plagued by doubt.
- Wry, dry, sly sense of humor.
- Lover of practical jokes, the more detailed the better.
- Lover of gadgets.

TV TWINS

- Dick Loudon—"Newhart"
- George Utley—"Newhart"
- Cliff—"Cheers"
- Christine—"Hotel"
- Dick Cavett
- David Letterman
- Andy Rooney
- Groucho Marx

THE CONSCIENTIOUS PERSONALITY

Quick, tell me what *Pi* is.

If you answered, "A fruit or cream filling baked between two pastry crusts," you are probably a hungry person who can't spell.

But, if you answered, "*Pi* is the ratio of the circumference of a circle to its diameter; a transcendental number having a value to eight decimal places of 3.14159265," chances are you're a Conscientious Personality.

If I happened to be looking for someone who could wade through a mountain of facts, figures, niceties, fine points, and particulars, a veritable connoisseur of detail, I would look no further than the Conscientious Personality. You gather and collect facts and figures the way others collect coins, stamps, or salt and pepper shakers. Your explanations are loaded with them.

Your constant and sometimes meticulous attention to detail is very apparent in your style.

It is the Conscientious student who turns in an immaculate and comprehensive term paper, ample footnotes embroidering the bottom of each page. He or she spends hours and hours perusing reference book after reference book, always looking for still another volume that might add further substance to an already substantial report.

If you're interested in buying a certain piece of property but have doubts about the title being clear, seek out a Conscientious real estate attorney. Whatever doubts you have will be minor compared to the stream of doubts that will run through *his* mind, automatically. He will exhaust all possibilities in trying to locate all past claims to the property, rummage the hall of records, visit the historical archives in the state capital, tour the attics of the last ten owners. He is the kind of person who could turn up the original deed to Manhattan Island.

What is it that compels the Conscientious student to research so exhaustively, the Conscientious real estate lawyer to probe so deeply? It's the Conscientious Personality's great need for certainty.

You tend to identify your own worth with the correctness of a solution to a problem, the completeness of a task, the exhaustion of all options beyond all reasonable doubt. Maybe. There, in even one hint of doubt, however trivial, hangs the Conscientious Personality's sense of worth. So your tendency in most situations is to question, examine, and then reexamine all possible angles, possibilities, and data in the pursuit of certitude.

Doubt, plus indecision, are the bane of your existence. But when the details are all lined up in logical order, certainty is assured, doubt is removed. For the Conscientious Personality, good habits and set routines are the meat and potatoes of daily life. Both eliminate the need to make those annoying decisions that come with a footloose, spontaneous nature, such decisions as what to have for breakfast or which movie to go to.

Routine, the tried and true, is what keeps life uncomplicated for you. The less need for decision, the less chance of making the wrong decision, the less doubt about the decisions you have made. Once you've found an effective and efficient way of doing something, you stick with it. That low-keyed, steady approach to life involves a minimum of risks and a blessed absence of too many alternatives.

If you think all that practical, predictable routine is making you sound dull and boring, I should quickly reveal the next facet of your Personality.

Just because you might be slightly enamored of the minutiae of life, it is a mistake to see you as some sort of humorless computer. In reality, the Conscientious Personality typically has a killer wit, but a subtle wit.

Upon first glance, your mind might appear as a contradiction to some people. Who would ever guess that under that analytical, facts-and-figures front lies an incurable wisecracker. You have a knack for one-liners, the wry remark that breaks the tension in a serious situation and hits the nail directly on the head.

I often refer to the Conscientious wit as an "economy car wit": It goes a long way without much effort expended. You see the full range of possibilities in most situations, including the humorous and the absurd, and can reduce them to one sharp, dry point.

Practical jokes are also far up in the Conscientious Personality's repertoire of humor: the more complex and convoluted, the better.

One famous Conscientious Personality, writer Jerzy Kosinski, tells of a time when he was in the house of a distinguished American government official where he was to meet the foreign minister of a Middle Eastern country. Our Conscientious friend sneaked into the living room and flattened himself full length behind the cushions on the back of the sofa where the foreign minister, his wife, and some other guests were to be seated. After all the others had come into the room and taken their seats on the sofa, our friend began gently kicking and pushing against the pillows. Even though the victims were aware that something very odd was happening, they refused to acknowledge it. Finally, frustrated with the guests' seeming disregard for his kicking and punching, the Conscientious prankster raised his head from behind the pillows and everyone jumped up in shock.

Puzzles, mazes, and games of calculation also hold a special fascination for many Conscientious people. With your painstaking attention to detail, you consider all the facts, facets, and possibilities until all doubt is removed and the puzzle is solved.

My one piece of advice would be: Don't ever make a bet with a Conscientious Personality. As a Conscientious Personality, you only bet on a sure thing. Even so, you usually aren't too inclined to gamble; you don't like to take risks. If the talk were of horse racing, you would be more interested in the horses, their past performance, their best times, how well the posted odds conform to statistical probabilities. And if the electronic scoreboard at the ball park flashes a stumper of a question—who was the last switch hitter to hit consecutive home runs from alternate sides of the plate in an afternoon game?—we would probably catch the hint of a smile on your lips. You know, you always know. You're a walking book of records.

MEET YOUR TV TWINS

Before you begin to study your TV Twins and use their video experiences, trials, and tribulations to help guide you through your own life, you have to solve a puzzle: of all the characters, stars, and celebrities you can watch on TV, which are your Conscientious TV Twins?

Well, that decision should be an easy one to make. There should be little doubt as to which are the Conscientious TV Twins. They'll be easy to identify because they:

- Are humorous in a wry, sly, and dry fashion.
- Are doubting and indecisive.
- Possess many facts and figures.
- Tend to give much detail in their explanations.
- Are predictable in their response to situations.
- Place much emphasis on having fun.

You and your TV Twins have an amazing capacity for storing, sorting, and analyzing a wide range of information. You can handle facts and figures competently and accurately. You have them ready and available when needed. Those who know you feel that when you offer information, you are correct ninety-nine percent of the time. Good habits and set routines are your steady fare. You function well when you can predict what will happen each day. Once you have found an effective and efficient way of doing something, you find it comfortable to continue doing it that way. Thus you have the time you need to pursue personal pleasures and self-fulfillment—and even to take a few risks.

On "Hotel," **Christine** brings efficiency and steady habits to her job as assistant manager of the St. Gregory Hotel, but faces some unpredictability in her dealings with hotel guests and her on-again, off-again relationship with the hotel manager.

On "Newhart," Conscientious **Dick Loudon** is the owner of a Vermont inn and a talk show host on the local TV station. His dry, sly wit is exercised on a variety of guests, oddball locals, and slightly eccentric employees at the inn. In one episode, we watch Dick standing in the lobby of the inn with his wife, Joanna, and Stephanie, the young woman who works for him. In comes Michael, Stephanie's boyfriend. "Hi, all," says Michael, "with an extra kiss kiss to one in particular." Dick quickly responds, "Please, let it be me."

Also on "Newhart" is Conscientious **George Utley,** handyman at the inn. We can watch George as he goes through his paces with an entire collection of tools placed in the bib pocket of his overalls. There is detail: every type, size, and shape of tool. There is doubt: Which tool will be the one I need at any one time? Probably not the one I decide to carry. And there is need for certainty: So I'll just carry all of them. A tool for every job.

George is a meat and potatoes sort of a guy who shows us the Conscientious desire for good habits and set routines and the Conscientious disdain for the need to make spontaneous decisions. In one episode, he tells Joanna that he wants to totally redecorate his room. "Wait," you say, "that doesn't sound like maintaining a routine or establishing steady habits." Well, maybe not until George goes on to explain that redecorating his room is something he does once every ten years, in April, on a Monday, after lunch.

Again we ask, does all that practical, predictable routine make you sound like a tame, monotonous person?

To answer that question, all we need to do is watch Conscientious **David Letterman** on his late-night talk show. Since the show went on the air in February 1982, Dave has shared his off-beat wit with such guests as a man who flew to an altitude of fifteen thousand feet in a lawn chair and was almost killed by a Delta Air Lines jet; a worm farmer; Sidney Miller, Doorman of the Year; and a woman who claimed to have gone shopping on Venus.

When Conscientious **Dick Cavett,** host of yet another TV talk show, was asked in an interview if he had ever been in psychotherapy, he answered, "Yes." When asked, "What kind?" he replied, "The kind between you and another person."

On "Cheers," **Cliff** the Conscientious mailman is a regular at the bar from which the show takes its name. He delivers detailed, factual discourse on a variety of subjects to the other patrons at the bar. In one episode, he is asked by buddy Norm to entertain some people Norm has been trying, but failing miserably, to entertain. Cliff is uninterested at first but is spurred into action when he discovers that one of Norm's friends is in the milk business, one of the many subjects Cliff is apparently conversant in. "Speaking of milk," Cliff says, "here's a little known fact. The cow was domesticated by the Mesopotamians. In fact, it wasn't originally a milk animal. Originally it was used as a guard animal for the Chinese emperors during the Chung King dynasty." On and on goes the highly detailed, if not exactly accurate, explanation.

Andy Rooney, resident philosopher and social commentator on "60 Minutes," is famous for his detailed discourses on such prosaic subjects as soap, exercise gadgets, and holidays. In one segment, he gives a very logical explanation as to why Christmas comes at the wrong time of the year. With Thanksgiving at the end of November and New Year's coming just a week after Christmas, three holidays that close together make no sense, Rooney claims. Also, he continues, a turkey dinner with the whole family at Thanksgiving is fine, but another barely a month later is too much turkey and too much family. He suggests Christmas in mid-February when everyone is sick of winter and needs a break.

You and your TV Twins function best when you approach problems as a puzzle to be solved. Think positively. Be logical. Go with your first decision. The odds are in your favor. Start with one aspect of a problem and let the logic and process flow. Doubt and second-guessing are often the cause of failure, so practice shooting from the hip and going with the flow.

Consider this exchange between Conscientious **Groucho Marx** and one of the contestants on the now classic quiz show, "You Bet Your Life." It's a wonderful example of Conscientious humor, logic, and slightly sardonic wit:

GROUCHO: How did you meet your wife?

COUNTRY BOY: Well, I drive a truck.

GROUCHO: You ran over her?

COUNTRY BOY: No. She was in the barn.

GROUCHO: You drove your truck into the barn?

COUNTRY BOY: No, no! Her family had been missing some chickens.

GROUCHO: They were lonely for chickens.

COUNTRY BOY: No, they had been missing them, so they

turned on a light in the barnyard, and I was driving up to get some turkeys and her father hollers, "The turkeys are in the barn . . ."

GROUCHO: You married a turkey?

COUNTRY BOY: No! As I go to the barn, a big skunk starts for the chicken house and a girl yells, "Get that skunk!" So I jumped on it and she fell on the skunk too—and we both smelled so bad . . .

GROUCHO: That's the most romantic story I've ever heard.

As you follow your TV Twins' video lives, look carefully for examples of:

- Relating by questioning.
- Concern for keeping life simple.
- A tendency to become irritable when doubted.
- Interest in routine.
- Having difficulty when presented with too much data.
- Telling stories and jokes as a way of communicating.

BEYOND A DOUBT

A certain amount of doubting is normal, necessary, and productive in any human enterprise. All of us are bombarded constantly by facts that need to be sorted, utilized, or discarded. Some are useful, some not. Questions are posed to us. Good answers have to be constructed. Many options and angles have to be considered, and different problems demand different approaches, different solutions. The very process of selecting includes challenging and doubting the data at hand. That is the way buildings are constructed, diseases are identified, scientific discoveries are made; it's the process through which most learning is accomplished, friends are chosen, and relationships are formed. Thus doubting shouldn't be thought of only as a negative process; it is one of the necessary phases of inquiry, and in routine day-to-day living it helps us enormously in making decisions.

But even after the Conscientious thinker arrives at a decision, he goes right on seeing all the other possible routes he could have taken. There's always some doubt as to whether he chose the best.

We can watch Dick, on "Newhart", as he tiptoes through the mine fields of doubt. On one segment, he helps his friend Chester campaign for mayor by giving him a "joke" to use in one of his speeches. As Chester is leaving Dick's house after their meeting, Dick tells George Utley the joke, which goes something like this: "Ladies and gentlemen, thanks for your support. Not that I couldn't stand up without it." Surprisingly enough, George does not break out laughing and Dick is immediately stricken with doubt, yelling to Chester to come back: time for another joke.

Conscientious Dick once again deals with the demon doubt when he and wife Joanna are both sick in bed with the measles. Just as Dick is ready to pop a lozenge, Joanna inquires if that is the last one. "Do you want the lozenge?" Dick asks. Joanna hesitates a moment, then assures him that she doesn't. But it's already too late, the seed of doubt has been planted. After some additional discussion Dick hesitantly sits back with his lozenge, still not totally convinced. Then Joanna asks if there are any bananas left in the bag of supplies next to the bed. "Yes," Dick answers, "there is a banana in there. Do you want it?" Again Joanna pauses slightly and assures him that she doesn't. "Sure, you say that now," Dick replies. "But if I eat it, you start making noises like a monkey."

What it is that compels you to doubt? Well, there is only one answer for certain, and that is that certainty eludes us all. Most non-Conscientious people accept that finite limitation with a certain amount of grace. The self-confident Conscientious person is also willing, in most circumstances, to accept reasonable limitations and reasonable risks. And for you, once may be enough—a very careful, thorough, once. Common sense prevails, but doubt is never fully rooted out. The doubting is not simply concerned with a solution to be found or a task to be completed. For the Conscientious Personality, it is wrapped up in the whole feeling of self-worth: If the outcome is questionable, *you* are questionable.

"I can really relate to that tendency to doubt in my Conscientious TV Twins," said a Conscientious Personality after watching Dick on "Newhart." "I remember when my husband and I were building our house, there were so many decisions to make. And it was such a major project. So I kind of wavered at times in the decision-making process. But I knew, and could see by watching my Conscientious Twins on TV, that the doubting was normal for me to a degree. I would listen to the experts, then make a decision about interior colors or landscaping, then be faced with bathroom fixtures and insulation. At times I wanted to just put the whole thing off and go rent an apartment. And I certainly didn't want to end up regretting my decisions once the house was built. My husband was very supportive of my decisions and I finally did decide that I had to live with them."

LOOKING FOR THE SURE THING

On "Newhart," it is time for the town's annual Snow Carnival. The problem is, there is no snow, and Dick doubts that it will snow, even though everyone else seems to be optimistic. Handyman George Utley is convinced that it's going to snow because just that morning he saw rabbits scurrying into the woods and that always means a storm is coming. "You'll have to excuse me, George," Dick says, "but I have this thing about getting my weather information from primates."

Later, three of the town's characters, Larry and his brothers Darryl and Darryl, offer their services to make snow with a slightly bizarre and outrageous plan for which they will charge $1,000; "$2,000 if you want it to stick." The plan includes the use of cannonballs, fabric softener, two pounds of veal, and pimientos. Chester the mayor is desperate at that point and tells Dick he is considering hiring Larry and his brothers. "Chester," doubting Dick says, "what do you want to be known as, the 'no snow mayor' or the 'moron mayor'?"

Finally, even Dick reluctantly gives in to the idea of giving Larry, Darryl, and Darryl a chance, with some grain of doubt still obvious. Larry warns him that there is one little hitch to the snow-making process. "I know," says Dick, "you can't guarantee results." Oh no, Larry assures him, it will snow all right. "It's just that on a rush job like this, we can't promise that two snowflakes won't look alike."

There goes that sure thing.

In a world of infinite possibilities, the careful Conscientious Personality likes the odds in his favor and a predictable outcome. You like to reduce the calculated risk to a certainty.

The more careful the sifting and sorting, the more careful our questioning, the better equipped we are to make good decisions. So far, so good. But the Conscientious Personality tends to want to sift and sort and question just a little longer and more carefully than most Personality Styles, heightening doubt, delaying the decision. This is beneficial just as long as, somewhere in the process, the options narrow, the questioning lessens, and a decision is forthcoming. Sometimes a lingering question and a further consideration of the problem trigger a radical discovery, and in those rarefied moments—as well as in the more routine but necessary moments of doing tax returns, term papers, and title searches—everyone benefits from the contributions of the Conscientious Personality.

On "Newhart," Conscientious George has lent Michael $500 and is having a great deal of trouble getting it back. He doesn't mind being Michael's friend, but doubts that lending money is a good way to continue his friendship. So he goes for the sure thing. He dismantles part of Michael's car and offers to sell the parts back to him for $500. Michael says, "This is the last time I ever borrow money from you." George replies, "I know."

ROUTINE AND HABIT: THE MEAT AND POTATOES OF CONSCIENTIOUS LIFE

Variety may be the spice of life for some Personalities, but not for the Conscientious. You like good habits and set routines. You function at your best when you can predict what's going to happen from one minute to the next: the fewer decisions and choices, the less anxiety. So you find a routine to get you through the day, then shift to auto pilot, sit back, and glide.

George Utley, on "Newhart", shows his Conscientious penchant for routine when he announces that he is planning to redecorate his room. "Every so often I change it around so I don't fall into a rut," George explains. So he redecorates every ten years, in April, on a Monday, after lunch. But this time he seems to be out of ideas, so he asks Joanna to help him. Well, she asks him, what sort of changes have you made in the past? Well, George answers, ten years ago he moved this piece of furniture over there. Ten years before that he had moved that same piece of furniture over here. And ten years before that, the same piece of furniture wasn't in the room. So he went and bought it.

George's employer, Dick Loudon, shows that same love for the familiar. It is 1986 and, at a ceremony for his fifteenth wedding anniversary, Dick is supposed to renew his wedding vows. He repeats the same vows he had prepared fifteen years before, in 1971, at the original wedding. Unfortunately, they contain some slightly dated references to "love-ins," "head trips," "bad vibes," and Cambodia.

"I guess my routines and patterns work well for me just as they do for George and Dick," said one Conscientious woman after reviewing the "Newhart" segments mentioned above. "I am a working wife and the kind of person who can have the children fed and off to school, a full load of wash done, the breakfast dishes back in the cupboard, and myself ready to go to work by 8:30—not just today, but every day. I've been doing it the same way for the past four years without a hitch. I've suffered some teasing and felt a little funny about being so predictable and attached to my routine. But after watching my Conscientious TV Twins with their routines and systems, I realize that it's not only normal, but very valuable to my peace of mind. I take great pleasure in every predictable moment. Structure makes the pleasure possible."

Within the structured existence, the Conscientious Personality thrives. Freed from having to consider all the options, angles, and choices of the small things in life—what to have for breakfast, which is the better route to work, when to take a coffee break, whom to lunch with, when to do the laundry, when to start preparing dinner—you are able to devote your talents and energy quite productively to the task at hand.

TAKE THE CALM, COOL APPROACH

The methodical Conscientious Personality is not in a nervous rush. A mind that is well ordered and devoted to detail does not rush at a problem or situation with wild and crazy emotion. You know the course, you know the destination, so there is no hurry to get there. You approach on a logical path, carefully sidestepping those pitfalls of doubt and rash judgment. You tend at times to be a bit skeptical, even when the subject is ghosts.

On "Newhart," the inn that Dick and Joanna own is being plagued by creaking noises in the night, doors opening and closing by themselves, and books mysteriously falling off shelves. After hearing that a witch had been executed in the house in the seventeenth century, everyone but Dick assumes that it is her ghost. "When it comes to ghosts," says Dick, "I take a lot of convincing."

Even after Dick and Joanna come downstairs one night after hearing noises and find all the books from the bookshelves stacked neatly in the center of the room beside the sofa, which is stood on end, Dick remains skeptical. Joanna is ready to move from the house. But Dick says, "I'm not leaving because somebody rearranged our furniture as a prank. Nothing has happened here that a moderately imaginative moving man couldn't have done."

Finally, Larry, Darryl, and Darryl, the show's resident eccentrics and jacks-of-all-trades, arrive to exorcise the ghost, and Darryl promptly disappears—the blond Darryl—in the basement. Dick still harbors some doubt, although even the staunchest Conscientious will weaken after time. As the show ends, the ghost is revealed. It turns out to be the two former owners who were trying to scare Dick and Joanna into selling the inn back to them, cheap.

The moral of the story is, it pays to follow the deep, cool

waters of skepticism, rather than jumping into the wildly unpredictable rapids of hot emotion. Just ask Dick Loudon. Ask any Conscientious Personality who happens to live in a haunted house.

ONE STEP FORWARD, TWO STEPS BACK—THE CONSCIENTIOUS TANGO

As we have seen from watching you and your Conscientious TV Twins, your approach to life is along the well-ordered path of logic. But, because of your awareness of all possible alternatives and lack of absolute certainty in any of them, your advance will be tentative at times: one step forward, two steps back; one step forward, two back. At those times, in short, you are a procrastinator doing the Conscientious tango.

George Utley, of "Newhart," finds himself doing the Conscientious tango when he takes one step forward and decides to enlist Joanna's help in redecorating his room. "Well," asks Joanna, "what do you use your room for? Reading? Watching TV? To work? "Yes," is George's answer; two steps back.

So Joanna tries again. "Well, what's your favorite color?" is her next question. "I don't know," says George after running over all the possibilities in his mind. "Blue?" suggests Joanna. "Blue, that's my favorite," says George (one step forward) who then adds, "No offense to the others," taking two steps back.

Decisions come slowly and painfully—and sometimes not at all—for the heavily doubting, uncertain Conscientious Personality. After viewing the TV segment described above, one Conscientious Personality remarked, "I have experienced a similar problem with my Conscientious child. We sometimes give her a reward when she has done something good, like letting her choose a treat. She will decide on ice cream. But when she gets into the ice cream store, she is just overwhelmed by all the possible choices and can't make a decision."

Another Conscientious Personality gave his own version of the one step forward, two steps back dilemma. "I could really feel for George having to make up his mind, having to commit to a decision about redecorating his room. I have the same problem when I go out to buy a car. I make the decision to buy, then I go around to all the dealers, listen to all the pitches, gather all the information, and have a very difficult time making up my mind which car to buy."

Well, there is hope for all of you Conscientious tangoers. The secret is to predecide. In other words, before you go out to buy a car, decide the kind of car you want: what color, what options you want, how much you are willing to pay, and so on. That way, you have already considered the countless possibilities and will be less easily confused by persuasive salespeople and better able to make a final decision.

A good example of predecision is practiced by a Conscientious businessperson I know who frequently takes clients to lunch. He has found a very good restaurant which he goes to all of the time. The people there know him, know what he likes to eat. So it's roast beef on Mondays, veal on Wednesdays, and fish on Fridays. He frees his mind from having to decide where to eat and what to eat. He takes one step forward by devoting his time and energy to the important business at hand. He avoids taking two steps back by avoiding a strange menu or an insistent waitress trying to push the five daily specials. After all, it takes two to tango.

TWO HEADS ARE BETTER THAN ONE—SOMETIMES

The time has come in the decision-making process to make the actual decision. It is a big step for the Conscientious Personality. You may look to others to reinforce the decision you have made, to get a second opinion. But that second opinion often comes with a grain of salt.

After George Utley has consulted Joanna on the redecoration of his room, she completes the decorating job and is obviously pleased with the result. But George is still skeptical, although in a very diplomatic way. "It is the most beautiful room I ever saw,'' says George as he carefully avoids stepping on the snow-white rug in the middle of the room or sitting on the 200-year-old antique bedspread. ''You hate it,'' says Joanna. ''No, no, no,'' answers George, ''I love it so much I could never live in it.''

Doubt is still the dynamic in the Conscientious Personality's life, even in the face of expert advice. After all, one can be polite, but never too sure: not of one's self, and certainly not of others. As that famous Conscientious TV Twin Groucho Marx once said: ''I don't wish to belong to the kind of club that accepts people like me as members.''

When it comes to the smaller decisions, you might not ask for a second opinion, but rather turn the entire process over to a second party. After watching the George Utley's room-decorating episode, one Conscientious man noted, ''It's good for me not to get all wrapped up in the smaller decisions that have to be made around the house or the decisions that are best left to someone else. For example, when it comes to deciding what type of furniture or carpet to buy, I leave that totally up to my wife.''

There are times when the Conscientious Personality does not want the decision to be taken away or made by a second party. You follow the process, you make the decision, and the last thing you need is someone undoing the whole thing by doubting your conclusion.

On ''Hotel,'' we can watch Christine struggling with a decision about a relationship with an ardent admirer. The pressure is on but she's handling it—until another acquaintance tries to step in and make the decision for her. Then she blows up. ''Look, I don't need to come to you for permission to have a relationship,'' she says to the interfering acquaintance, who also happens to be her boss. Her boss replies, ''I told you what you do on your time is your business.'' ''Then stop making it yours,'' replies Christine.

''I remember struggling with a decision about a relationship I had been having,'' said one Conscientious Personality after watching Christine. ''I'll admit that it is hard for me to make big decisions at times, and it was particularly aggravating in that case. But now that I'm familiar with my Personality, it's easier for me to recognize those situations that call for my decision, no matter how long it takes, and for me to live with it once it has been made."

On "Newhart," George Utley is also being pursued by an ardent admirer. After he invites her to his room, he decides that she is putting too much pressure on him and begins to doubt her motives. So he makes his decision and asks her to leave. But she wonders why. "I have things to fix," says George searching for an excuse, "like my stove. It's been getting real hot."

The woman doubts George's decision, as well as his knowledge of stoves. "Well, isn't it supposed to?" she asks.

"Who died and left *you* handyman?" George snaps back.

"Sometimes when someone makes a decision for me, or interferes in my decision-making process, I welcome it. That way I don't have to decide for myself and that's nice," said one Conscientious Personality after watching George. "But as for the bigger decisions, I don't want someone else making them for me. On the big things, I like to make up my own mind no matter how long it takes. And I don't need anyone to question it."

DETAILS

In love there is no sure thing, but the Conscientious Personality likes nothing more than a sure thing. So the love of your life is detail. Details lead the way and ensure the results. You hold, caress, and examine each one with rapt attention.

When all the details are noted and lined up, there is order and certainty. On "Newhart," Dick has his details in line when they are needed as an alibi for wife Joanna. The two have planned to repeat their wedding vows in front of a churchful of people on their fifteenth wedding anniversary, but they fight at the last minute. Joanna refuses to go to the church and Dick is left with the task of explaining to the guests why Joanna isn't there. He explains that she spilled mouthwash on her white wedding dress. "I've never known mouthwash to stain," observes one guest. "And grape juice too," Dick quickly adds. "A little cold water and a few drops of glycerin will take care of that," another know-it-all guest pipes up. ". . . and ink, and epoxy resins," Dick says.

You might also find yourself expressing your love for detail with facts and figures. The Conscientious accountant is the sort who will carefully sift and sort through all your records and receipts, scrutinize them thoroughly, and then itemize appropriate entries on your income tax forms. You can be sure that whatever is due from the IRS is carefully reckoned. But you can be sure too that everything legitimately due *to* the IRS is reckoned. If you would like to stretch the legal limits, find another accountant. This one, remember, is Conscientious as well as precise. As one famous Conscientious Personality observed: "God is in the details."

GADGETS, UTENSILS, AND WIDGETS

If details, facts, and figures could become solid, inanimate objects, what would they look like? Well, they would probably resemble gadgets, utensils, and widgets. The Conscientious Personality's love for facts and figures is also naturally shared with tools and gadgets. They are details you can hold in your hand. We have already noticed that Conscientious George Utley carries a variety of tools in his overall bib pocket, but witness Andy Rooney on one of his "60 Minutes" essays—the one on physical fitness.

Andy starts by mentioning that he noticed some flab under his arm as he was driving along one day, so he bought a dumbbell to bring to work every day to exercise his biceps. Then he noticed that he was having problems unscrewing the gas cap from his car; he bought an exercise gadget to strengthen his grip. He then decided that he would strengthen his forearms for tennis, so he picked up another gadget—a spring between two handles. For overall physical fitness, he then bought an exercise bike. But it was frustrating to do all that pedaling and not get anywhere.

Finally, he expressed his doubts about physical conditioning.

How much time do we really want to spend on our bodies? We have some six hundred muscles to deal with. Who has time to exercise all of them? Besides, people who devote all their time to body building look like circus freaks. And after all, the muscles other people see when you wear a bathing suit are the ones you use the least. And so on.

There are, most likely, gadgets for exercising every one of those six hundred muscles. And, if you are doubting your physical well-being or your attractiveness on the beach, you might collect them all. Of course, it's fascinating just to consider those gadgets, there might be some at your local health spa. Then the question becomes: Which health spa do you join?

After viewing the Andy Rooney segment mentioned above, one Conscientious Personality noted, "I have a lifetime membership to two different health clubs, and I don't go to either one of them. I almost bought a third membership because I felt if I had this one I would really use it. But I didn't."

Forget the health clubs. The six hundred gadgets would probably be cheaper.

WIT AS WISDOM—OR THE ECONOMY CAR WIT

We note in considering each Personality Style that humor is usually a sign of good health, and this is particularly evident in the behavior of the Conscientious Personality. Normally reticent in speech, you are at your best when you see the comic or amusing aspects of a situation. And you usually do, since you see the full range of possibilities and options in any situation, even the ludicrous. Your style of humor runs to the pithy, concise comment. Your wit is wry, sly, and dry. But there are no barbs attached. You don't wound. You can tease, but you don't taunt. You love a playful practical joke, but nobody gets hurt. And you can laugh at yourself—the best antidote to your doubting and questioning.

On "Newhart," wit abounds, especially when Conscientious Dick is on the scene. Larry, Darryl, and Darryl decide in one episode to start an escort service and bring in a brochure for Dick to display in the lobby of his inn, advertising their services. A female guest sees the brochure and asks Dick about the escort service, claiming that she is looking for something "innovative" to do with her evening. Dick advises her to forget about the escort service and to rent a duck suit instead. "Rent a duck suit?" wife Joanna asks after the puzzled guest leaves the room. "Well, there's no point in buying one," Dick observes dryly.

Although the Conscientious wit does not particularly like spontaneous situations, if he can get a good sense of how the flow is going, ad-libs might fall from his lips like pennies from heaven. On one "Newhart" show, Dick welcomes a friend he hasn't seen for a number of years. "You haven't changed a bit," Dick says as he greets his friend. "I've lost a hundred twenty pounds," the friend answers with surprise. "Except for that," Dick adds without skipping a beat.

WHAT IS THIS THING CALLED LOVE?

On "Hotel," Christine is trying to decide whether or not to commit herself to a relationship. "Do you love him?" a friend asks. "I don't know," Conscientious Christine answers. "I love being with him. He's very generous and giving. He knows how to make me laugh. But is that love?" For some other Personalities, that *is* love, plus, but for the Conscientious Personality, who has trouble deciding what to have for breakfast, the decision whether or not to plunge into the unknown depths of love can be a difficult one indeed.

The Conscientious Personality will consider the negative fears as well as the positive hopes. If you are confident and self-assured, you will likely put greater stress on the positive side and move toward a decision and a commitment. But if your confidence is down, you might be so ridden with doubt, so concerned that this be the perfect relationship, that you will be unable to decide. While the whole process may be hard work for you, the other person may see it only as procrastination.

On "Newhart," George Utley falls for an actress who is doing a show in town and staying at the inn where he works as handyman. He thinks she might like him too. After all, she asked him to call her Loretta and touched his hand while he was pouring a cup of tea for her. "What do you make of all that?" George asks. "Only a fool could misread those signals," says Stephanie. Still unsure, George asks Dick, a fellow Conscientious, if he thinks Loretta likes him. "Well, I, uh . . . it's starting to look . . . within the realm of possibility, that maybe she might," answers Dick in true Conscientious fashion. "Aw, what would a woman like that see in a guy like me," says George, still doubting. "You ask a pal for a little advice and he blows sunshine up your overalls."

Even though Loretta makes it more obvious throughout the episode that she is, indeed, attracted to George, he remains skeptical. Dick has convinced him that she is just using him, stringing him along so he will help out at the local theater where she is performing. So when she finally comes to his room one night, George decides to send her away, telling her that he has lots of things to do, like wash his feet. "George, what's wrong?" Loretta asks. "Nothing," George answers testily. "Feet get dirty, that's life. If you can't live with it, maybe we shouldn't see each other."

Loretta leaves and goes to cry on Dick's shoulder. Dick confesses that he has given George the wrong impression about her. So she goes back to George's room, helps him make the correct decision, and they all live happily ever after.

Once the Conscientious Personality finally decides to commit, he or she will usually work very hard to make the relationships or marriage a success. Your sense of purpose is very productive, and your ability to consider all the various sides of any situation makes compromise possible. But life, and love, are unfortunately not always that simple; especially for the Conscientious Personality.

"Major decisions have come slowly in my marriage," said one Conscientious woman. "Whether to have children, how many children, buying a home. The biggest one probably came when I was considering taking time out from my career to start a family. Is it a good time? Can we live without my income? Would I be a responsible mother? My mother says being pregnant is awful, I might get varicose veins. Will my husband still love me with varicose veins? Maybe I should wait. But I want a baby now."

The longer she takes to make a decision, the more negative she feels about herself, and she becomes edgy and quiet. She knows, from watching her TV Twins, that a certain amount of doubting is normal for her, but she also sees that if she could break through her doubting long enough to discuss her feelings with her husband fully, he might give her the assistance and support she needs to make a proper decision. That would be a far more productive course.

The thing to remember in matters of love is to be careful not to doubt too long. You may miss the opportunity, then live to regret your indecision. Sometimes not deciding is the greater risk.

THE WORKING WORLD

As a Conscientious Personality, you probably find your approach to work and your organizing skills applicable in most fields, although you might not enjoy a position involving extended travel, living out of hotel rooms, and being away from home.

The Conscientious engineer would come up with six different solutions to a problem while his colleagues struggle with one; he would know every facet of the problem and consider all the options.

She would be the teacher who introduces a dozen techniques in teaching a routine subject, or the executive secretary who so well structures procedures in the office that her presence is considered indispensable.

He would be the internist who, not satisfied with a preliminary diagnosis, would run tests until his identification of the malady was reasonably certain.

She would be the legislator who could always be found doing her homework on a bill or the executive whose attention to detail and careful consideration of both sides of an argument would make her a masterful negotiator in labor relations.

He might be the salesperson who thoroughly knows his product, how it is made, and how it functions; who has the answers to questions that the customers might never ask. Yet he himself would have strong sales resistance; if buying a car, he wouldn't appreciate being introduced to thirteen different models with a choice of twenty-four colors and ninety-two options—that simply would be too much data to process. And few salespersons would enjoy him as a customer; he would have too many questions to ask.

The Conscientious Personality obtains much gratification from his work. By doing what you feel you do well, you grow in confidence; you particularly enjoy any form of enterprise that permits you to finish what you start, pursuing your own methodical, detailed approach.

AFTER WORK, SOME FUN AND THE SIMPLE LIFE

"Aw, give me the simple life. A routine and orderly existence, a real low-key approach to this hectic tumultuous world we live in." That's the Conscientious Personality talking. Trouble is, the rest of the world is not always listening.

On "Newhart", Joanna asks Dick what he plans to do for her on their upcoming fifteenth wedding anniversary. "Oh," says Dick, "dinner and a movie." Joanna is not impressed. "Dick, that doesn't sound very romantic," she says. So he gives her the same answer, only this time with a very exaggerated French accent. She is still not impressed. "Honey, you know how I like for our anniversaries to be special, especially after the unromantic wedding we had." Dick is still not moved. "What was wrong with our wedding?" he asks. "It was short, it was cheap, and it was legal."

OK, so you're not a wild romantic. You like the predictable pace of everyday life, admire the virtues of hard work, and don't like to shoot from the hip. We know that's part of your Personality, just as it is with your TV Twins. But we also know that you like nothing better at the end of a long, tiring day, than to have some fun; lots of fun. A healthy portion of lighthearted tomfoolery is right up your alley.

Conscientious David Letterman even managed to have a bit of fun while he worked. One of his first jobs—and appearances as a TV Twin—was on an Indianapolis TV station where his tasks included weatherman, Saturday morning kiddie show star, news anchor, and late-night movie host. Once, while doing the weather, he reported that the city was being pelted by "hailstones the size of canned hams." On another weather report, he announced that a tropical storm had just been upgraded to a hurricane, then proceeded to congratulate the storm on its promotion.

Even if you don't have the sort of job that allows you much fun during working hours, it is still very important for you to fit some fun in your day somewhere. I have discovered that it works best if you divide your day into three parts: work, transition time, and play time. Many Conscientious Personalities I know who are having problems can trace them to the fact that they are not enjoying enough transition time, or fun time. So take a few moments to decompress at the end of a hard day. Then have some fun.

ALTERNATIVES AND OPTIONS

As we have seen, the Conscientious Personality's approach to life is methodical, painstaking, and purposeful. You enjoy routine and structure and are reliable and dependable. You are quiet, avoid clutter and hassle, and try to inject order and efficiency into whatever you do. You put great emphasis on excellence and performance of a task, certainty, and predictability, so much so that at times you are overly concerned with impeccability. You equate your own worth with the correctness of any decision; so you approach all options and possibilities, all sides of an argument, every solution a problem might have.

You sometimes become so concerned with the possibility of making a mistake that you hesitate to make a decision, tending to doubt yourself; the longer you continue in the doubting, the more you doubt your own worth.

Rather than brood and doubt, rather than remain uncommitted and indecisive, the uncertain Conscientious Personality should consider these options:

- Don't look back. That first doubt can spoil your pleasure in having acted decisively. Your first decision is your best.
- Eliminate the negative by accentuating the positive.
- More and more, it ought to be apparent that only death and taxes are certain.
- Spend more time with children; they resist structure and they invite the playful spirit in you. Besides, it's always safe to do impromptu things with children.
- People love that wry wit of yours. Let it loose—it's a great social asset. It can be the antidote to your negative attitudes, your doubting urge.
- Go out and buy yourself a double-dip ice cream cone. Or a new dress. Or a new tennis racquet. Live a little.
- Accept more responsibility. Reach out and seek it. Test and extend your talents and capabilities. You are always much more successful and enterprising than you give yourself credit for.
- If negative attitudes are habit, then positive attitudes can be habit too.
- Try to break those solemn rituals—getting into bed only one way, muttering little formulas to yourself when facing a decision—or fearing a mistake or doing something wrong. The magic is in positive actions that follow firm decisions.
- Don't make a decision and then invite others to criticize it or tear it apart. They will. Remind yourself that you make good decisions.
- Tell yourself, "Make a decision, then do it. The odds are in my favor."
- Before running through all those options and angles and maybes, tell yourself, "I'm doing great." Keep it simple.
- Let your day be divided into three periods: work time, transition time, play time. Then enjoy that party. You deserve it.

- Use a familiar environment as your framework for flexibility and freedom. There lies the challenge that you can enjoy.
- Plan a lunch date. Your involvement with friends, your need to break out, your need for communication and laughter are very, very important. You're worth a little bulge in the budget.
- You have to let that humor of yours work for you. If you could bottle it, you'd be rich. But you are rich; you just haven't recognized your currency in terms of your friends, your family, and your human worth.
- Ever and always: Accentuate the positive.

SECRETS

The keys to a successful relationship with the Conscientious Personality are:

- Don't plant the seed of doubt. Encourage and support the Conscientious Personality's decisions.
- Be there to advise and counsel when the Conscientious Personality hesitates.
- When it is clear that your counsel and advice are not needed or wanted, stay clear.
- Don't make decisions torturous by offering too many options. Keep it simple.
- Learn to expect a multitude of questions and highly detailed explanations on every subject.
- Look for the humor in unexpected and unlikely places. At times the Conscientious Personality's humor may be a bit understated.
- Make sure there's time for fun.

MATCH AND MISMATCH

Conscientious Personality matchmates:

Anticipating—You appreciate the tremendous planning abilities of the Anticipating person and can aid in the decision-making process because of the emphasis you place on details.

Both of you take your time in making decisions, and most often these will be very good decisions because every contingency is planned for. You both share a sense of thoroughness and completeness.

Sensitive—The emphasis you put on routine makes the Sensitive person very comfortable because of the predictability. Your organized and deliberate approach to life ensures a sense of trust to the Sensitive person. You like to ask many questions, and the Sensitive person's innate curiosity encourages this tendency. Your emphasis on fun and sense of humor are very much admired.

Adaptable—Both of you look at many possibilities when making decisions, and the Adaptable person can go along with your well-thought-out decisions because of their flexible nature. The Adaptable Personality also encourages you to relax and have fun, which is very important for you. Both of you need and enjoy leisure and love time.

Determined—Both of you think things out in a logical manner before making a decision. Neither of you is impulsive and you respect each other's views. You also share similar views on spending: Both of you spend wisely. You both enjoy the practical joke.

Patient—Your comprehensive decision-making style poses no problem with the Patient Personality because of that individual's pleasant, agreeable nature. You utilize a rather deliberate pace in life, which fits in well with the easygoing style of the Patient Personality. The Patient's positive outlook also gives you confidence in your decisions.

Influencing—Schedules and organization are important to both of you. Your routine may be somewhat disrupted because of the Influencing person's tendency to take charge. Both of you compile much information before arriving at decisions, but you don't want someone to doubt your decisions by making them for you.

Accomplishing—Your great sense of humor will be appreciated by these fun-loving persons. They are willing to help and will do so as long as they are receiving your approval. You like to take your time deciding things, while they are spontaneous and might find your routine difficult. They want to please you so much they interfere with your decision making.

Idealistic—Both of you are objective in your thought processes but while you are still gathering information, the Idealistic person has reached a decision. You enjoy a set routine, but this can run counter to the Idealistic individual's strong standards. Your practical jokes won't go over very well with this individual, who prefers logic. Your tendency to doubt and question ideas often conflicts with the Idealist's strong, independent self-image.

Persistent—You enjoy a fixed routine, while the Persistent person drifts from situation to situation. It's hard to maintain an orderly progression when the Persistent person follows where the imagination leads. You like a carefully calculated budget, but that has little appeal to this free spender. This person interprets your questions as frustrating and rejecting.

Ambitious—Your deliberate, methodical approach is directly opposite to that of the Ambitious persons who prefer a "do it now" and "whatever works" method. This pressure leads to more doubt and indecision on your part and frustration on theirs. You need relaxation every day, while their relaxation is more work; this makes for a very difficult interaction.

Perceptive—Your world is one of logic and facts, while the Perceptive individual's world consists of emotions and feelings. You lead with your head, they lead with their heart. Your unhurried manner may be mistaken for a lack of concern and may bring cries of "unfair" from the Perceptive person, whose frequent feelings of jealousy and rejection can make you doubt your love.

Chapter Seven

THE ACCOMPLISHING PERSONALITY

PROFILE

- Very energetic and enthusiastic—at times may seem to be everywhere doing everything.
- Likes to entertain, be the focus of attention; a "ham" at times.
- Upbeat and positive.
- Wants and needs approval.
- Expects much from self and others.
- Can be very bruised by criticism or disapproval.

TV TWINS

- Tony—"Who's the Boss?"
- Samantha—"Who's the Boss?"
- Jason—"Growing Pains"
- Carol—"Growing Pains"
- Mike—"Growing Pains"
- David—"Moonlighting"
- Johnny Carson

If, as Shakespeare said, "All the world's a stage," then the Accomplishing Personality says, "Put me front and center." Onstage is where you like to be, even if acting doesn't happen to be your profession. As an Accomplishing Personality, you're always doing your best to please, impress, and gain the approval of your audience, whether they be family, friends, colleagues, or the guy on the street.

You want nothing more than to perform well—brilliantly, if possible—dazzling others with sheer energy, grand accomplishment, or crazy, irreverent stunts.

If I want to guarantee that an Accomplishing Personality will do what I ask, all I have to do is tell him or her that it's never been done before.

You are the life of the party, a tireless worker, the lovable smart ass who will press the limits, do anything on a dare, and have your finger in every pie—even the cream pie you might be aiming at the back of my head.

Whether at work or at play, among friends, family, or coworkers, the Accomplishing Personality is alive with purpose and exuberance, driving hard and striving to shine. You want nothing more than to earn approval, affection, and applause. So whatever you're doing, you're giving your all. Nothing less will do.

Illness, injury, or exhaustion will not stop you; you will dance on crutches, sing through pneumonia, and keep the show going until you, or your audience, collapses. And if for some reason yours is not quite a stellar performance, it certainly isn't because you haven't tried. If at first you don't succeed, you are willing to try, try again, then try one more time.

The Accomplishing Personality looks on life with a robust passion. You are the sort of high-energy person who might put in an eighty-hour work week, then dash off to the golf course to play eighteen holes before appearing fresh and glowing at the Saturday night party where you can be expected to dazzle until dawn.

The Accomplishing Personality is the homemaker who might leave the dinner dishes in the sink while she sits up half the night writing what she hopes is the Great American Novel. He is the high school trumpeter in the band who blows all the lip-bruising notes until the applause dies or his lip gives out. She is the spunky ten-year-old who jumps off the garage roof with a homemade parachute to impress the other neighborhood youngsters. And if she breaks a leg, that great white cast is sure to dazzle them.

The Accomplishing Personality is always "on." As one non-Accomplishing describing an Accomplishing friend put it, "She's even dazzling in a grocery store, singing and dancing her way through the express line with more than twelve items."

Exaggerated? Not for the Accomplishing Personality. A bit of exaggeration is part of your style. It shows in the way you work, in the way you play, in what you expect to accomplish, in the way you talk, in the way you expect others to respond to the flair and flamboyance of your performance. Your expectations of yourself, like your expectations of others, run high and can only go higher.

Onward and upward. The sky is the limit. Or is it? Consider this version of a dream rather common to Accomplishing Personalities: "I'm flying over the city and people below are waving at me. I had one heck of a time getting off the ground, but I kept flapping and flapping my arms and I finally made it. It took a lot of doing but I kept flapping and flapping, rising and turning, soaring and dipping. Everyone below me on the ground was really amazed."

MEET YOUR TV TWINS

You want to meet some fantastic people? They're exciting, wild, outrageous, lovable, and possibly some of the most dazzling people you've ever met. I've spent hours, days, tracking these Accomplishing TV Twins. It's a major accomplishment just to slow these people down long enough to get them on paper.

You want to reap the rewards that come with discovering your Accomplishing TV Twins? They'll be easy to identify because they:

- Are interested in pleasing.
- Are irreverent; sometimes they find it hard to be serious.
- Are energetic and enthusiastic.
- Want, need, and get approval.
- Are optimistic and positive.
- Expect much of themselves and others.

You and your TV Twins will encourage others to approve of you; you want them to recognize your accomplishments and respond with applause and cheers. You and your TV Twins elaborate and exaggerate until the good sounds better and the better sounds best. You are so naturally optimistic that when things are going well, you expect them to get better. That is why you always perform with so much zip and zest, expending every ounce of your energy. You are always on stage, and when things are going well you don't need a spotlight. The glow of your smile is light enough.

On "Who's the Boss?," Accomplishing **Tony** is the male housekeeper and nanny for a single career woman named Angela. We can watch Tony fly through his video life, taking care of his daughter, **Samantha;** his employer, Angela; her house; her son, Jonathan; her mother, Mona; his bowling team; and half of the attractive young ladies in the state of Connecticut. The only time we catch Tony getting down is when he's on the floor doing pushups.

In one episode, Tony illustrates both the Accomplishing Personality's irreverence and the secret weapon that allows him, and you, to get away with it. Angela, an advertising executive, decides to teach an evening class in copywriting, and Tony enrolls. The first night of class, as Angela is taking attendance, in blows Tony. "Hey, Teach," he greets her. He flashes the killer Accomplishing grin, dashes around the room gathering in the whole scene, puts an apple on Angela's desk, quips, "Hope nobody squeezed the Charmin yet," and takes a seat in the front row, all without pause or hesitation. The room is immediately dazzled.

On the show "Growing Pains," Accomplishing **Jason** is a psychiatrist and father of three children, two of whom, **Mike** and **Carol**, are also Accomplishing. That makes for an interesting and, at times, slightly frenetic household scene. We can watch Jason, with sons Mike and Ben, playing football in the kitchen, tackling each other, knocking over the furniture. Suddenly, in comes Mother with, "You won't be happy until you've broken something." So Accomplishing son Mike says, "OK, punting practice in the living room." Off go Jason, Mike, and

Ben, but Mom blocks the procession into the living room with an arm across the doorway. "Just kidding, Mom." You've got to love those Accomplishing rascals.

On another episode of "Growing Pains," Accomplishing son Mike is trying to dazzle his new girlfriend. He tells her that his mother, a small-town newspaper reporter, is just completing her twenty-seventh novel; that his father, a psychiatrist, is a famous painter; and that his nine-year-old brother is a child genius philosopher. Well, hey, if a little flourish, elaboration, or exaggeration will help the grand accomplishments along, so be it. After all, you have to give the audience what they want.

Accomplishing **David,** on "Moonlighting," is a private investigator who dazzles his female boss and criminals alike with his high-energy style and quick, flashy dialogue. Life in the spotlight often requires him to press the limits, to examine each and every path, to grab opportunity by the butt. In one episode, while simultaneously meeting with reporters, having his hair cut, and solving a crime, David answers the phone, listens, then asks, "A TV show? About me? Sure, why not."

Accomplishing **Johnny Carson** will do absolutely anything on his "Tonight" show that a guest, or his staff, will do or dare. He has let a wide variety of wild and exotic animals sit on his desk, in his lap and, in some instances, on his head. He has done barrel rolls in an aerobatic stunt plane, climbed ropes with commandoes, thrown Indian tomahawks, dived off high platforms onto air bags, and jumped out of an airplane with a parachute. He never fails to rise to the occasion and accept the challenge; people expect it and he loves doing it for them.

Carson has raised his nightly monologue to the level of art: Accomplishing art that captures the audience, even when it's bad. If a joke hits the mark he will smile, smooth his tie, and nod approvingly while the audience laughs. But if a joke falls flat or flies over their heads, the audience will groan and hoot, Carson will look wounded, then drop some self-deprecating remark that gets a bigger laugh than the original joke would have. He turns failure into success.

As you follow your TV Twins' video lives, look carefully for examples of:

- Dazzling, and then asking such questions as "Shall I go on?"
- Reacting to disapproval by trying harder.
- Getting sidetracked from one activity to another.
- Motivating others with contagious energy.
- Feeling bruised when criticized.

You and your TV Twins can be motivated by someone just asking you to do something. No matter what someone asks, if it's within your powers, you'll try. In a new and unfamiliar situation your TV Twins may withdraw and hold back, or they may go to the other extreme and try to impress and dazzle. Your TV Twins benefit from challenges that will encourage them to prove just how good they really are.

THE URGE TO DAZZLE, ASTONISH, AND AMAZE

What is so evident in the style of the Accomplishing Personality is a willingness to work and play hard, to make the maximum effort, and to commit all available energy and desire to the task or purpose at hand.

You do it all with such vibrancy and good cheer, such exuberance and enthusiasm, such verve and vitality, that onlookers are usually impressed. And that is exactly the reaction that you hope for. You want others to recognize and approve of your performance. I call it the "urge to dazzle." The aim is to astonish, amaze, impress. And, more often than not, it happens that way.

When Angela, on "Who's the Boss?," decided to teach an evening class, it was typical of her Accomplishing housekeeper, Tony, to enroll and to make a flamboyant appearance on the first night.

An Accomplishing Personality watching that segment commented, "I remember when I was in school. I always busted my buns to get to the room on the first day so I could sit in the front row, center. Some people thought I was just a showoff, but it was more like I was saying, 'Hey, Teach, here I am.' " Here you are indeed.

Back to Accomplishing Tony in the advertising class. Angela has assigned the students to make their own commercial on videotape for an imaginary laundry soap. The other class members take turns showing their commercials when they are completed. Finally, it's time for the Tony show. "You've seen the rest," he begins, "now see the best." He primes the class for his video and they react, but Angela doesn't seem too enthusiastic. "I'm just warming them up, Teach," Tony reassures her. "Not that you need warming up. This commercial is hot." He then turns back to the class, pointing to a woman in the back. "You look a little short. Would you like to move to the front row?" Naturally, the class loves it. Who needs the video? The real show is just in getting ready to view it.

On "Growing Pains," Accomplishing Jason Seaver and his family have challenged a neighboring family to a bowling tournament. So what could be more natural than bright orange bowling shirts with "The Bowling Seavers" written across the back, just to let those people at the bowling alley, who have somehow misplaced their programs, know just which team is which?

Have you ever done anything like that to dazzle anyone? "Why, yes," you answer, "probably a hundred times a day."

The Accomplishing Personality begins early in life to show that high energy and desire to dazzle. "I remember I was involved in the school newspaper, the yearbook, theater, the band, cheerleading, anything and everything that provided an opportunity to shine," was one Accomplishing woman's recollection.

You know what pleases people. In most cases, you know that the audience loves to be shocked and dazzled and will love the person doing the dazzling. As long as you please the people, you're going to be a hit. And that is the primary goal.

"I used to feel a little self-conscious about being a ham at parties," said one Accomplishing man. "My wife would tell me that I was overdoing it. But the other guests always seemed to enjoy my antics and I always enjoyed making them laugh. Now that I am familiar with my TV Twins and am more aware of my Personality, I know that it's just me, ham and all."

We can watch Accomplishing Tony helping Angela prepare Thanksgiving dinner. "Excuse me, Tony, we need an egg." "Sure, coming right up." But he doesn't just hand an egg over; he tosses an egg in the air, bounces it off the crook of his elbow, flips it behind his back and makes a neat catch, puts the egg in Angela's hands then slaps her hands together to crush that well-traveled egg.

Just keep Tony out of my kitchen. But, on second thought, that was pretty funny. It certainly made a nice break from the labor of preparing Thanksgiving dinner.

GRABBING ATTENTION AND HOLDING IT

The Accomplishing Personality needs to be noticed, to stand out from the herd. You will wake people up, and when they open their eyes they will like what they see. But your alarm clock doesn't go ring-a-ding. It sticks ice cold hands right up the nightgown.

On "Growing Pains," Carol, the Accomplishing teenage daughter, goes out with a friend of the family, Jeff. He is much older than she, but she has a crush on him and wants to be noticed as more than a little-sister type.

As they walk into a restaurant, Jeff eyes an attractive waitress. "She's very pretty," Carol says. "She's OK," Jeff replies. "If she's only OK, I'd like to see your idea of great," Carol says.

Would Carol like to be "great" in Jeff's eyes? Is grass green?

"Oh, looks aren't everything," Jeff observes, "she looks a little dopey to me." Carol is paying close attention. "So your ideal woman should be intelligent?" she asks. Jeff agrees that he likes an intellectual woman. Carol immediately pulls a large pair of glasses out of her purse, puts them on, and strikes a pensive pose. "But romantic too," Jeff adds. Carol quickly pulls a rose out of the vase on the table and puts the stem between her teeth. "But she shouldn't take herself too seriously," he says. Carol puts the flower end of the rose into her mouth. She will do whatever it takes to please Jeff and meet with his approval.

The Accomplishing Personality will reach out and grab you, making sure he or she corrals your attention right away. We watch Tony, on "Who's the Boss?," take daughter Samantha to her first ballet class. The Russian instructor embraces Samantha, kissing her on both cheeks in the continental style. Then he turns to Tony. Tony immediately grabs him and kisses him on both cheeks with great gusto: "When in Moscow . . ."

Accomplishing Samantha wastes no time in reaching out and grabbing the instructor's attention with a dazzling performance. Afterwards, she asks poppa Tony how she did. "You were magnificent, wonderful, beautiful," is his reply. "Just checking," she says. The instructor, apparently impressed with Samantha's initial showing, informs Tony that his daughter has "oodles of talent." "Well," says Tony with obvious Accomplishing delight, "I love oodles."

Sometimes it's downright irreverence that will catch the adoring public offguard. People love the Accomplishing Personality because you bring their secret thoughts out into the open, say what they are afraid to say, do what they are afraid—but dying—to do. And for that they will gladly give their approval.

How many times have you wished you could stand up in the middle of a boring sales meeting and suggest that everyone take off and spend the day at the beach? Or been tempted to liven up a deadly dull party by balancing the host's cheese soufflé on your head? Or come very close to jumping out of your car in the middle of a sweltering midsummer traffic jam and run through someone's lawn sprinkler?

Well, you're not alone in your temptation. And, if you've ever gone so far as to carry out such irreverent stunts, you're in good Accomplishing company.

Accomplishing Tony is doing another assignment in Angela's advertising class; it's a video commercial for an imaginary brand of soap. The other students have come up with the standard commercial material, but Tony uses a different approach: His commercial features female mud wrestlers who use the detergent to spruce up their bikinis after a particularly strenuous match. Angela is not impressed, but a visitor to the class, who just happens to be the vice president in charge of advertising for a major soap company, loves it. "One of you had the audacity to put a couple of half-naked women in mud," he says, "and it is that kind of audacity that sells soap."

Irreverence can also come in the form of sarcastic remarks. Johnny Carson regularly introduces a member of the "Tonight" show band as a man who "brings new meaning to the word *dull.*" Reacting to a slightly ditzy female guest's ramblings, Johnny was moved to remark, "I think she has splinters in the windmills of her mind." The audience will always clap and laugh.

On "Growing Pains," Accomplishing Carol finally realizes that there is too much of an age difference between her and Jeff, on whom she has a crush; she's fourteen, he's twenty-three. Jeff is trying to let her down easily. "If we were both fourteen I'd be one lovesick puppy," he says. "Imagine how much fun it would be if we were both twenty-three," Carol replies with a gleam in her eye. "Well, maybe when I'm twenty-three and you're thirty-two," she adds. "Or when you're thirty-two and I'm forty-one," Jeff says, getting into the spirit of things. "Hey," Carol shoots back, "I'm not gonna be wanting to date any old geezers in the prime of my life." Slightly taken aback, Jeff then recovers and asks, "What if I'm a rich old geezer?" "We'll talk," says Carol, closing on a high note.

She holds her own—maybe a little irreverent, but definitely someone special. And he loves her for it. That's the Accomplishing way.

IF YOU CAN'T DAZZLE THEM WITH BRILLIANCE . . . TRY A LITTLE EXAGGERATION

There are times when the run-of-the-mill truth, the boring facts, the everyday state of affairs are just not getting you the attention and approval you need, so you embellish the story a little, pump it up here and there with a few flourishes. As one Accomplishing Personality puts it: "If you can't dazzle them with brilliance, then baffle them with bullshit."

On "Who's the Boss?," Tony comes home from a bowling tournament with a very large trophy. By the time he finally finishes describing the tournament, it sounds more like a crowning Olympic moment.

On "Growing Pains," teenage Mike is told by his parents that he is not allowed to ride motorcycles. Later, when some of his friends invite him to ride their motorcycle, he is in a dilemma. If he tells them he isn't allowed to ride, he will be called a wimp—very unimpressive. But he doesn't want to disobey his parents. So he decides to try some baffling. "Oh, I rode all last summer and now I'm kind of burned out on it," he says. "Didn't you tell me last week that you've never tried this?" asks one friend, just a little suspicious. "Well, I was just talking about this particular model," says Mike, quickly recovering. "I mean I've ridden other models, the 702, 703, and 704." "But they don't make a 704." Mike picks up the cue. "Yeah," he says, "because when I tested the prototype I told them it was a piece of garbage."

In another episode, Mike is trying to convince his sister to help him learn ballroom dancing. He has been invited to a wedding by a cute girl and has been convinced by his Accomplishing father, Jason, that being a dazzling dancer is a sure way to impress. But sister Carol is more interested in saving her feet than in teaching Mike the way around a dance floor. Mike tries throwing Carol a line: "You know, I often wonder what's more beautiful, the glittering stars on a clear night, or this (meaning Carol's) face." Carol is not convinced. "You are such a jerk."

But Mike is on a roll. He agrees with her, he is a jerk. "No, really, I am," he says, "and that's why I'm so incredibly fortunate to have a sister who is not just a sister, but a saint."

Those are some blatant examples, I'll admit, so write them off to the exuberance of the young Accomplishing Personality and to the exaggeration of television. But they do serve to prove a point: Sometimes the best way to get the audience's attention and approval is to liven things up with a little overstatement.

So you won a blue ribbon for your chocolate cake at the county fair? Later, at home, after displaying the blue ribbon, tell the family that the judges insisted on a copy of the recipe (well, one judge did) and that photographers from all the newspapers took pictures of your prize cake (they photographed the entries displayed together) and that the governor, who just happened to be visiting the fair that day, begged you for the last piece of your prize-winning cake (he hadn't eaten since breakfast).

Truth may be an end in itself, but a good line of bull can turn the stale truth into a never-ending story that can only get better: applause, applause.

THE NONSTOP, ACCOMPLISHING WHIRLWIND

To call the Accomplishing Personality a high-performance person is an understatement. You are a nonstop whirlwind, everywhere at once, covering all the bases, pulling the rest of the world toward you in an exhilarating rush. You'll run them to the edge, jump off, and fly them to the moon.

We can watch Tony, on "Who's the Boss?" as he lights up the household and the bowling alley. On "Moonlighting," David is constantly on the go, solving crimes in his sleep. Mike, the Accomplishing teenage son on "Growing Pains," does his homework while he sings along with rock music on the radio and dances around the room.

"I used to think there was something wrong with me," said one Accomplishing Personality. "Everyone would tell me to slow down, keep something in reserve. But now that I've discovered my Accomplishing TV Twins, I see that it's just me. All that energy is completely normal and natural. Society is always telling us to slow down, pace ourselves, don't exaggerate, don't come on so strong, don't try so hard. That's almost a death sentence for an Accomplishing Personality. I realize that now.''

When something ignites your enthusiasm, the juices flow. Your feet move faster, and your voice rises in pitch as you plunge into the middle of whatever is happening. It's just the natural way for you.

After Accomplishing Tony's daughter, Samantha, has taken ballet lessons for only three weeks, the instructor informs her and Tony that she has real talent. Although that turns out to be the same thing he tells every student, it is enough to ignite both Samantha and Tony. Samantha starts going to lessons five days a week, practicing around the house, dreaming of becoming a prima ballerina. She becomes a ballet whirlwind and develops that ''star quality'' that the Accomplishing Personality is prone to. But she will have to give up her social life and junk food in order to get to the top. ''It's your life and your choice,'' Tony tells her, ''but would you like to be poor and unknown for the rest of your life or would you like to be the toast of Paris?'' That's not even a question for the Accomplishing Personality.

Tony is a matching whirlwind. He is at every ballet class, dancing along. He confides to Angela that he might not be able to afford Samantha's lessons. Angela offers to pay for the lessons and Tony immediately accepts. ''I'll get you free seats when Sam's dancing 'Swan Lake' at the Met, front row center; you'll be so close you'll be swimming in swan sweat,'' Tony gushes.

The Accomplishing Personality's energy will lead him head first into every realm. You can't count the number of ways he can reach you, perform for you, dazzle you. He'll come at you in more directions than a used car salesman.

GETTING OFF THE TRACK—OCCASIONALLY

Self-discipline is not always the Accomplishing Personality's strong suit. You are convinced that you can perform with the best of them, that no job is too big or too tough for you. The world is full of limitless possibilities.

Like Tony, diving headfirst into any number of projects, or Mike, studying for a test with the stereo blasting and suddenly bursting into a dance around the room with his American History book, you have an impulsive streak. You tend to react spontaneously to whatever is going on around you, to get distracted from your main purpose.

Suppose I'm an Accomplishing Personality and my purpose at hand is to write this chapter. But in the middle of my afternoon at the desk, my neighbor phones and tells me he has just bought a new riding mower. Would I like to give it a turn or two around the lawn? Why not? Ten minutes won't hurt. So I take a few laps around the lawn. Fascinating! Another two laps. Terrific! It's hot, so the neighbor brings out a beer. Tastes good. He turns on the ball game and we sit, just to watch for a few minutes. The six-pack disappears and I run out for another one. Our team wins. One more beer to celebrate. Ten minutes has turned into four hours, and now it's dinner time. And after dinner I always take a nap. Oh well, there's always tomorrow.

That, my Accomplishing friends, is called sidetracking and it is ever a temptation. It is a temptation for Mike, on "Growing Pains." He's scheduled to compete with his family in a bowling tournament, but along comes an attractive girl who invites him out; there goes the bowling tournament. It is a temptation for David, on "Moonlighting," who is in his office one minute having his hair cut, shoes shined, and ear bent on the telephone, and is off the next minute to follow the lead on a new case. It is a temptation for Tony, who is helping Angela prepare Thanksgiving dinner when the phone rings: He is invited to Mrs. Rossini's house in Brooklyn for Thanksgiving. Everyone will be there, it will be great, and suddenly Angela and her entire household are packed off to Mrs. Rossini's.

If you are tempted to sidetrack, you're in good company. As

one Accomplishing Personality noted, "I have learned that the shortest distance between two points, whether it be from here to the garbage can, or from here to a job promotion, is a straight line, although those side roads never lose their appeal."

"DOESN'T EVERYONE ELSE TRAVEL AT THE SPEED OF LIGHT TOO?"

They will find each other in the wilderness, two Accomplishing Personalities. And that's probably not as difficult or unlikely as it might sound. After all, how hard can it be to spot someone who is juggling, telling a joke, washing the car, and barbecuing a chicken all at the same time?

Accomplishing Personalities will often be drawn to fellow Accomplishings. Each will complement the other's zany brand of humor and will take obvious pleasure in driving the other to new heights of attention-getting madness.

Even back on earth, in everyday life, Accomplishing Personalities look for partners and friends who can appreciate their humor and need for approval. In one episode of "Who's the Boss?," Tony meets and immediately falls in love with a girl who seems to have everything—well, almost everything. "She's warm, she's beautiful, she's crazy about me," Tony rhapsodizes to Angela. "And she can cook." Angela is convinced. "She sounds like everything you've ever wanted in a woman," Angela says. But Tony, unfortunately, is not convinced. "I need somebody I can talk to, somebody I can fool around with." The two crucial ingredients for any Accomplishing Personality are missing.

You expect the moon and stars from yourself. And sometimes you make the mistake of expecting the same from everyone else around you. You assume that everyone, even non-Accomplishing people, wants to match you stride for stride.

When Tony gets that sudden invitation to Mrs. Rossini's in Brooklyn for Thanksgiving dinner, he gives Angela no chance to protest. Unfortunately, non-Accomplishing Angela ends up having a miserable time, not being ready for the raucous scene at Mrs. Rossini's, even though Tony has automatically assumed that she would love it.

After watching that particular episode, an Accomplishing Personality commented, "I get in trouble sometimes because I want to go and do things all the time and realize later that the friends I'm dragging along don't. It's like that with my wife. She would rather stay around the house, which is OK for her. But I have all this energy and I just don't feel like I'm living if I sit around the house. So sometimes I have to say 'Sorry, honey' and leave her there. I feel guilty at times for leaving and getting on with my activities, but I know if I stay it wouldn't be healthy for me. And in the end, we would both suffer."

There is a danger at times, that an Accomplishing parent will project his or her energy and the need to shine on the rest of the family, the way Tony assumes daughter Samantha will take her interest in ballet straight to the top. He or she may temporarily get carried away with expectations of the Accomplishing child, who already expects so much of himself or herself. Here's how one Accomplishing Personality remembers it: "My mother was a great person. You would have liked her. She laughed a lot and she could do almost anything. She was exciting to be around, and I always wanted her to be proud of me. But I never seemed to be able to please her. She was never satisfied, and she was always saying to me, 'You should be able to do that,' or 'You should do better than that,' especially when I brought home my report card. She would always be able to show me a better way."

The more you become aware of your dazzling energy as one of the great strengths of the Accomplishing Personality, the more you must realize that other Personality Styles don't share that same strength. Each has its own strengths; some people are content to sit and watch. Your increased awareness of the needs of other Styles also helps you to recognize the energy in other Accomplishing Personalities; you are drawn to them and, if your confidence is in place, you can share the spotlight. As long as everyone is enjoying the show, who cares?

THE POWER OF LOVE

Accomplishing energy will carry you along; you can, at times, be swept away with the moment. In the language of love, that's translated as infatuation.

Accomplishing Tony meets a girl he hasn't seen since she was a kid. She has grown up quite nicely and Tony is immediately floored. The next night they are having dinner together, alone, and he is already thinking about marriage.

On "Growing Pains," Carol opens the front door to reveal a family friend who has come to spend a few days in the Seaver home. He is handsome, but much older than she. She is love struck and tries to dazzle him, but he treats her like a little sister. In the end, she feels silly about the whole thing. But her Accomplishing father, Jason, tells her about a crush he had on his teacher in the seventh grade. He remembers kidnapping the class hamsters and holding them for ransom until his teacher/heartthrob promised she wouldn't marry the shop teacher. "Everyone acts a little crazy at times," he tells Carol. "That doesn't mean you're a jerk. It just means you follow your heart." It just means you are Accomplishing.

When two people who are able to have a ball in life get together, they soar. Now that's love, at least in the Accomplishing world. Courtship can be great fun for the Accomplishing Personality, male or female. The newness, the excitement, the approval, all make it a delightful experience.

With all of that newness, excitement, and approval going on, you might be in danger again of assuming that your love interest is moving along the same lines, and at the same dizzying speed, as you are. What you look for and seek may not always conform to the reality of the other person. We all can't be Accomplishing, even in the name of love.

Tony assumes that his new girlfriend will enjoy his Accomplishing brand of outrageous humor. He is helping her in the kitchen and tries the egg trick—the same one he pulled on Angela. Unfortunately, this girl is not amused. Tony has exaggerated and amplified her good qualities while choosing to ignore, at least temporarily, the less attractive ones, especially her total lack of appreciation of his Accomplishing sense of humor. The relationship is doomed.

When you finally find That Certain Someone who can handle an occasional smashed egg, life can be wonderful. Parenthood is most gratifying for the Accomplishing Personality, especially at the birth of a child. He or she is exhilarated, caught up in the moment of awe and wonder, filled with the sense of having shared in the grandest of all performances, the mystery of creation.

It sometimes happens though, in a home with several Accomplishing Personalities—like the Seaver household on "Growing Pains"—that the stage becomes a little crowded with everyone trying to dazzle at once. There can be some jostling and elbowing as one vies with the other for the spotlight. Those who have a hard time doing their number can become frustrated and sometimes resort to sarcasm. But when the Accomplishing family takes turns on the stage, they find that the others serve as a very receptive audience. No one appreciates a sparkling performance more than another dazzler.

DAZZLE WHILE YOU WORK

The working world is always center stage for the healthy Accomplishing Personality. There you can be expected to do your best, perform at a high level, produce great and grand effects.

The young Accomplishing Personality enters the working world with high hopes and great enthusiasms. If your goals are realistic and focused, you will move ahead with vigor and success. Like Tony, Jason, and the rest of your Accomplishing Twins, you don't mind starting at the bottom; you are confident and optimistic enough to believe that you will rise, level by level, to the top. As Tony says to Angela when she is beginning her job as teacher of the evening class, "You're gonna make a terrific teacher." Or doctor, lawyer, or Indian chief, whatever your career choice happens to be.

There are, of course, the usual dangers. There is always the temptation to sidetrack. Writing a sales report is a breeze for you, but your friend Charlie dies a little with each month's report. So you get up from your report to help Charlie. Shirley's having trouble too, so you give her a little coaching. An hour later Charlie and Shirley hand in their reports on time, but the boss is hanging over your shoulder asking where the hell yours is.

On one episode of "Who's the Boss?," Angela confides to Tony that she has just burned the dinner. "That's great," says Tony. "What do you mean?" Angela asks. "You try, you fail, I make the save," Tony answers, ready to take over the preparation of the meal.

Sure, you like the approval that comes from helping out, from being the one everyone can depend on to save the day. But don't let it get away from you.

The Accomplishing woman carries the same emotional equipment into the marketplace, whether on a full-time or part-time basis. If she's a working mother, she'll feel that she has enough energy and productivity to work without shirking her responsibilities at home, and she will find work not only fulfilling but a welcome change of pace. As one working mother commented, "I couldn't sit home and just clean house."

She might tend to overcompensate for time away from home by spending lavishly on the family; the Accomplishing Personality likes to spend money as well as energy. As that same Accomplishing mother noted: "I can't keep money in my pocket. If I had five dollars, I would have to spend it on the kids, my husband, or myself. I'm always broke by payday."

She will always be well dressed and looking good—appearances are important to the Accomplishing Personality—and she will probably be found in the kind of job that provides an outlet for her sociable nature.

And when the weekend comes, she will want to make the most of it. Citing again our working Accomplishing mother, "We have to do something fantastic—a picnic or a day at the lake, dinner out, a movie, something. I want to have some fun." But come Sunday afternoon, you may very well find her asleep on the couch: "Napping is the greatest thing in the world."

Despite her full work week, the Accomplishing woman is able to move through a flurry of housework, with which she expects the children to help, but she never feels caught up: "I'm brushing my teeth and I notice the bathtub needs cleaning. I can't wait to finish my teeth to get at the tub. When company is coming, everything has to look good. All my closets are crammed, but what you see looks terrific." She manages to get most of her housework done while her husband takes the children out for the day. "I can't stand to be alone. I hate it. But when I'm alone, I work really hard." Can she manage the combined jobs of career woman, wife, and mother? "Sure I can," she grins. Her eyes sparkle, and she gets ready to give her next dazzling performance.

What about retirement? It does seem hard to imagine an Accomplishing whirlwind at rest. "Yeah, I had a difficult time retiring," said one Accomplishing friend. "I could handle it for a while, but I ended up going back and getting another job."

For you, sitting still might be the hardest job of all.

RISING TO THE OCCASION

If I want immediate action from an Accomplishing Personality, all I have to say is the four magic words: "It's never been done." You will rise to the occasion like bubbles in champagne.

On "Growing Pains," Mike's friends talk him into riding a dirt bike, even though he has never ridden one before, and his parents have forbidden him to try. The dare, and disapproval if he doesn't, are just too much for him to bear. He'll deal with the disapproval from his parents later.

On "Who's the Boss?," Angela's son, Jonathan, needs a partner for the father-son golf tournament. His father is divorced from Angela, remarried and living in another state, but there is always the housekeeper, Accomplishing Tony. Jonathan knows the four magic words; Tony, who has been a professional baseball player but has never set foot on a golf course, jumps right in. So how hard can golf be? "A ball's a ball," says Tony, "and this one ain't even moving." He and Jonathan appear in the kitchen the next day in outrageous matching golf outfits they've picked up at the pro shop.

DO YOUR BEST AND THE HELL WITH THE REST

While you're soaring through life, that grand and wonderful show with its laughter and sorrow, you never want to quit. Even illness or injury won't slow you down. The Accomplishing Personality would like nothing better than to tape an audience to the ceiling if he is flat out in bed.

When Mike accepts his friends' challenge to ride a dirt bike, he doesn't just ride, he does Evel Knievel—until he falls off the bike and slides across the ground on his bottom. Later, at the hospital, the doctor is examining Mike's injuries. The doctor is a friend of his parents, so Mike doesn't want to tell the truth about what happened. When the doctor asks what caused the injuries, Mike tells him he was at a party and sat on a hot pizza. "How about those abrasions?" the doctor asks. "Those are cheese burns," Mike answers. And the gravel? "Oh, we didn't order that," is Mike's reply.

Later, at home, after Mike has confessed to the family and taken his punishment, they decide to go out to dinner. How is Mike going to sit at the table? Never underestimate the power of the Accomplishing light to shine. He appears, waddling down the steps, with pillows stuffed into the back of his sweat pants.

Illness? Injury? Never mind. But there is one thing that will pull the plug on the Accomplishing Personality. That one thing is criticism or lack of approval. It can devastate you.

We can watch Tony pulling his egg trick in the kitchen with the girl he has just met, trying hard to impress her and make her laugh. But she clearly does not approve of his efforts. "Aw, come on, Gina," he says, "I was just kidding around a little bit." She pulls the plug. "Not in my kitchen. Out!" So much for that romance.

Carol, on "Growing Pains," has a similar experience. You remember her story: she's trying very hard to impress a guy who's nine years older than she. When he introduces Carol to an older woman as "like the little sister I never had," he pulls the plug on that romance. Carol runs off to the ladies' room, obliterated.

Back to Tony again. This time the scene is the adult school advertising class that Angela is teaching. Tony has just shown his laundry soap commercial about mud wrestlers. It was outrageous and the class naturally loved it. Tony is riding high. "Thank you, thank you," he acknowledges the approval of the class. "But I can't take all the credit. My inspiration—Angela Bower." Angela brings him down in a crash landing with her response. "It's the most offensive TV commercial I've ever seen," she says.

There is no substitute for honest, constructive criticism. It's just another way for you to grow. And if you're feeling good about yourself and understand your Accomplishing Personality, you can take a little disapproval now and then in stride. But what happens when you're around people who are constantly tearing you down? Here's how one Accomplishing Personality sees it: "If you're in a relationship where someone is constantly criticizing you, it almost destroys you. Thank goodness you can move away from a relationship like that, or help the person know that this is not the best way to relate to you. But first of all, they have to know that you need recognition and approval and that you'll perform much better if you get those things. Otherwise, there may be trouble."

What happens if you're not getting your positive strokes at work, if your boss or supervisor can't, or won't, recognize your unique Accomplishing strengths and needs? "These people will probably not change and all of a sudden start giving you the approval you need," observes one Accomplishing woman I know. "So a lot of times it's better if you're able to give yourself the approval, to believe that what you're doing is right and deserving of applause, even if the applause doesn't come. It's like a sign I saw on somebody's desk one time that pretty well sums it up: 'Do your best, and the hell with the rest.' "

So criticism occasionally pulls the plug on your dazzling performance. If you know yourself, and are comfortable with what you see, you can generate your own electricity. On "Moonlighting," Miss Dipesto, the secretary at the private investigation firm where Accomplishing David works, tells him that he looks a little down. "Me? Down? No, I'm not down," says David. "A little exhausted, lonely maybe. Cracking cases, collaring criminals, collecting commissions, it's hard. But I'm not down."

NO STOPPING YOU NOW

Quick, tell me the best thing about the Accomplishing Personality.

"I think Accomplishing people are able to draw other people out. They are naturally energetic and feel good most of the time and other people respond to that. I'm an Accomplishing Personality and I know that people at work say that it's really great when I come in and they see me smiling. I know that things are all right, they know that things are all right, and it starts the day out on the right foot."

And how about Tony, on "Who's the Boss?," how does he feel? He is shining a silver tray and stops a minute to admire his reflection. "I would have made a great silver dollar."

RIIIGHT!

ALTERNATIVES AND OPTIONS

As we have seen, the Accomplishing Personality is normally energetic and hardworking, purposeful and productive. You enjoy the reputation of being a person who gets things done with superior skill, a person who performs brilliantly in so many ways. And you relish the approval, affection, and applause that your efforts produce.

Socially you are charming and gracious, hearty and outgoing; your humor is robust and contagious. When you are your healthy best, you know your goals and you move toward them briskly and purposefully—no detours, no charging off in many directions, no sidetracking or wheel spinning. Straight ahead. Onward and upward. First things first. You know your limits and the limits of others and you accept them. "Do your best," you can say, "and then forget the rest."

The less mature Accomplishing Personality is also capable of great success, but the cost can be terribly high and the efficiency low. He can diffuse his energy in too many directions and can try too hard. He can be impetuous, sidetracking, and something of a dilettante. He can't take criticism or a compliment; either can paralyze him or provoke a chain of nonproductive overperformances—or withdrawal.

His social moments can be flash-in-the-pan performances that sizzle, then fizzle. He often fails to be aware of his own limitations and the limitations of others. He is often frustrated, wound up, and wounded. His urge to excel can degenerate into easy dazzles and superficial cleverness.

This unsteady, erratic, and unhappy Accomplishing Personality could be much more productive and much more relaxed in his approach to life if he would reduce his exaggerated expectations, accept his own limits and the limits of others, keep his eye on his goals, and stop occasionally to pat himself on the back. If you are an Accomplishing Personality, here are other alternatives and options:

- Understand your goals and share them with others to test their reasonableness.
- Rather than race off in a dozen different directions, organize your routine. Know where you are going and the straightest route there.
- Be realistic in your expectations. You try to do too much in too little time.
- Accept help. Everyone needs help sometimes. You tend to deny this; you don't have to do it all. We all have limits. We can all use constructive advice, support, opinions, and help.
- Share the stage with others. It's one of the things you do best.
- When you discover you have overcommitted your time, energy, and resources, back off. Reassess your expectations. Be flexible.
- A good performance does not always have to be superdazzling to be creditable and to draw approval.
- Sidetracking is the greatest distance between two points: it is the longest route to the garbage can, the next promotion, the love of your spouse, the achievements you so dearly desire. Learn to move straight ahead.

- Beware of your tendency to exaggerate, especially in terms of expectations for your spouse, children, coworkers, and friends.
- Invite constructive criticism occasionally rather than always insisting on approval.
- Learn to accept compliments graciously. A compliment is not always intended as a stimulus to still greater accomplishments or more dazzling performances. A compliment is only a compliment. Enjoy it, say "Thank you," then take your bow.
- Consider this: You are so much more than what you do. What people love about you, what they so gladly approve of, is simply you; just *you*.
- Do your best, then relax for a minute—you deserve it!

SECRETS

The keys to a successful relationship with the Accomplishing Personality are:

- Keep criticism to a minimum.
- Always give praise and approval where it is warranted. Then give a little extra.
- There might be times when you can help the Accomplishing Personality keep the whirlwind energy focused. But don't discourage the spontaneity or enthusiasm.
- "Slow down, take life easy," is like saying, "Don't be yourself." Avoid saying that. Let the energy flow.
- Learn to appreciate a little embellishment and exaggeration. It keeps things lively.
- Sit back and enjoy the show.

MATCH AND MISMATCH

Accomplishing Personality matchmates:

Adaptable—These persons bolster your confidence; they readily give the approval that you need so much. Their flexibility and ability to communicate make it easy for you to get along with them. They also encourage you to be irreverent, to play, and to have fun.

Ambitious—Both of you like to work hard and play hard. Both are energetic, and try very hard to succeed and enjoy success. The bigger the challenge, the harder both of you work toward a successful outcome. The Ambitious person also appreciates your tremendous efforts which ensure your best performance.

Influencing—You are very drawn to the charming and elegant ways of the Influencing Personality. Both of you are interested in neat and clean surroundings, and the Influencing person's desire for the ultimate experience keeps this relationship exciting and gives you something to strive for.

Sensitive—These persons are adept at listening; they make a very good audience for you. Also, their curious nature provides you with the attention you need. Their loyalty is seen by you as a great strength and as approval.

Patient—You'll enjoy their ability to go along with you on your ideas. The Patient person is also caught up in your enthusiastic and energetic nature. You both like to look good and both like approval, so you do well socially as a couple.

Idealistic—Your fun-loving and adventuresome spirit is counterbalanced by the Idealistic Personality's logical and objective approach to life. Both of you involve yourself in projects with a certain intensity and energy. The Idealist's standards and ideas will show you how to get approval, but you may interpret coolness as disapproval.

Persistent—The Persistent person above all else wants to spend time with you and to be special to you. Both of you have a positive outlook toward life, which helps in this relationship. You may, however, experience some difficulty with your differing life approaches; whereas yours is very energetic and quick, the Persistent person likes to stop and contemplate.

Perceptive—Perceptives will give great amounts of approval as long as they feel they are being appreciated. However, when they feel unfairly treated, their outspokenness may appear to you as disapproval. The Perceptive person's tendency to be rather negative on occasion will also not wear well with your more positive outlook on life.

Anticipating—Anticipating persons like a step-by-step, gradual approach which is difficult for you because of your hurried and spontaneous nature. They need to plan things in advance, while you like to do them at that moment. Your somewhat irreverent and playful nature may bring disapproval from Anticipating persons because of their emphasis on genuineness.

Conscientious—Your emphasis on having fun and your sense of humor are shared with Conscientious persons, but you want approval very much and they doubt you every step of the way. Your orientation to life is very unpredictable and impulsive, while the Conscientious follow a strict routine and do not like to have the routine disrupted.

Determined—It is difficult for you to do anything right because this person, in his or her own mind, determines what is right and wrong. Your theatrical nature is vigorously disapproved of by this Personality. Determineds may see your flamboyance as disrespect. You want to converse and talk at great length with those around you, while the Determined Personality does not share this outgoing nature. You want to keep the party going with your entertaining nature, but with one look from the Determined person you realize that the party is over.

Chapter Eight

THE PERSISTENT PERSONALITY

PROFILE

- Has vivid imagination; is very inventive.
- Can be something of a daydreamer.
- One-to-one relationships are very important.
- Has a great deal of faith and hope.
- Will encourage others with faith and hope.
- Charismatic.
- Perseveres; has a great deal of tenacity.

TV TWINS

- Kate—"Kate & Allie"
- Jonathan—"Highway to Heaven"
- Zach—"The Colbys"
- Spenser—"Spenser: For Hire"
- Pam—"Dallas"

What is your dream? What are you searching for? What makes you happy?

Well, if you are a Persistent Personality, there is some part of the gypsy in your soul. You're not one to sit still for very long, at least in your mind, and your quest is most often expressed in terms of a relationship with another person, or persons. But whatever the object of your search may be—spouse and family; friend or lover; God, government, or the general manager's position; the state lottery, an oil scheme, the home team; peace, plenty, or a day in the sun—you seek it with persistence, deep faith, and high hopes. The search, the dream, the happiness are all tied together.

When the road is smooth and the relationship sure, the Persistent Personality is a genial and gentle person who thrives on the good things in life. You appreciate every moment shared with others and view life openly and zestfully. Even in bad moments, when the road is rough and rocky, you hold out for the happy ending—such is your faith, hope, and love.

You are the believer whose faith just might move mountains. Your dreams are many, sometimes scaled larger than life, but your devotion to them makes them plausible and possible. Whatever your prize, your faith is unwavering; you live that faith, are nourished by it. You could not press on unless you were convinced that the forces were on your side. You trust mightily and you persist.

At times, your faith is so contagious, your belief so rich and vibrant, that some are captured by your charisma. Others may turn away from such an outpouring of devotion. No matter. Your faith endures as the vital core of your life and your actions.

The mortgage may be due and her bank account overdrawn, but she knows that somehow they will manage; they always have. His team is down 11–0 in the ninth inning with two outs, but he is confident that his heroes can turn it around: "You gotta believe." Her child may be sick, terribly sick, but her faith and devotion to that child keep hope alive. The Dow Jones average may be slipping and sliding downward, but he has faith that his stock prices will hold. He isn't selling, he's buying. Nine publishers have rejected her manuscript, but she knows that she has written the Great American Novel, so off goes the manuscript to a tenth publisher. Cynics may say that God is dead, but to the Persistent believer, God is alive and acting in his life. Her date is an hour and a half late, but she still has hope—he must have had car trouble; he'll be here any minute.

In many cases the Persistent Personality's powerful faith will result in a zeal for religion and in a strong sense of the immediacy of God and His will, or faith in themselves and mankind. Or the Persistent may react against the stiffness of institutionalized religion and turn his or her faith to a belief in the unprovable: mysticism, reincarnation, or UFOs, for example.

As a good-natured Persistent, you are a soft and humble soul, often a late bloomer. Due to your amiable nature you will exert a certain magnetic attraction over others, a charisma. Your faith, like your ideas, is so sparkling that it moves others to join you on your journey through life. And you rather enjoy the attention and company.

At times you are so thoughtful, considerate, and attentive to others that you can spoil them. You are lavish with gifts and affection; at times, generous to a fault. Your spirit is nourished by the delight of others. It's no wonder then that relationships mean so much to you. They are your prime source of joy and pleasure and give you that special feeling that comes with a sense of belonging.

The mature Persistent Personality is affectionate, bighearted, and charitable in deed as well as in attitude. He is receptive, open to others, mindful of their needs, responsive. Everyone around him benefits. She is that friend at the office who always bakes a cake on your birthday. He is that good buddy who will lend you $10 until payday and then never ask for it back. She is the good neighbor who, when you mention the loveliness of her roses, snips you a dozen. He is the pensioner who can't pass a charitable coin box without emptying his pockets of change, even when it means that he has to miss lunch. He is the college student who volunteers to do the grocery shopping for the old people who live in his neighborhood. At home, she is forever doing an unexpected kindness for someone; drawing her husband's bath, mending her son's baseball glove, brushing her teenage daughter's hair, singing softly to the baby.

But the Persistent Personality is just as attentive to his or her own needs. One of the Persistent Personality's top concerns in life is to follow his own instincts and motivations, to fulfill his own potential. He listens and pays close attention to his own mind and may at times appear somewhat self-absorbed. He is interested in enriching his own life by taking advantage of and fully appreciating what is around him and up ahead.

In sum, you are a person who sees the needs of others, as well as your own, and tries to meet them. You truly care. You want to share. Your job is the simple pleasure of seeing others enjoy what you do, what you give. The closer the relationship comes, the greater your effort to promote the happiness of others.

MEET YOUR TV TWINS

Imagine what it would be like if you could watch people on TV who shared your Personality Style. What methods would you invent to use their experiences in video life to help you in your own life?

Well, the first step in the process is to identify your TV Twins. They are not the product of your imagination; they are real. Your Persistent TV Twins will be easy to identify because they:

- Are charismatic
- Encourage others to hope and pray.
- Are persistent and not readily giving up.
- Are very attentive and understanding.
- Are interested in a one-to-one relationship.
- Are able to share their dreams and wishes.

You and your TV Twins constantly seek and search. You never rest in your quest for the fresh and the fanciful, the new and the novel, the better idea, and the urge to answer the eternal question "Why not?" But no dream is complete without the imaginative scheme that can bring it to life. This brings you down from the outer space of reverie to the inner space of reflection. There your dreams are purified and molded. Then you test your ideas against reality.

Yours is the faith that can move mountains—and people. You see yourself and the universe as one. You see all things as a child does with innocence, full of beauty and splendor.

Persistent **Kate,** on "Kate & Allie," is a single mother who lives with her daughter, roommate Allie, and Allie's two children in New York City. Kate is something of a free spirit, ready to try new experiences and new relationships, while carefully maintaining those important relationships that have already been formed.

Consider one episode in which Kate tries to convince Allie to demonstrate against the college where Allie is taking classes, because the college is investing in a company that dumps toxic wastes. Kate fondly remembers her younger days when the world was fresh and new and there were plenty of roads to travel—and protest—upon. It wasn't so much the cause as the chance to form a relationship with the group and its members, to explore that feeling of oneness. "You know," says Kate, "you get this incredible feeling when you're part of a movement."

Allie is reluctant to pursue something as extraordinary as a protest, but Kate's persistence is very convincing and appealing. Although she is not a student at the college, Kate wants to join the protest. She has the courage that most Persistent Personalities have, or would like to have, to take a risk and explore the unknown. And she has the imagination to come up with an excellent scheme: a sit-in at the college chancellor's office.

A group of students, including Allie, are taken in by Kate's charisma and proceed to park themselves on the floor of the chancellor's waiting room. Soon the police are called and everyone, except Kate, is ready to give up. She shows her persistence, and faith, in the fact that the protest should continue. "What good does it do to stand up for something when you back down when it really counts?" she asks. Once again, her charisma and staying power draw the group together in a unified whole. Even one of the arresting officers falls for her.

Later, at the city jail, Kate is still holding fast to her dream and trying to keep the group together. Although the university has offered to drop all charges if the students drop their protests, Kate persists. Allie and the other students are, at the same time, doing some serious soul-searching, trying to decide whether or not to give in to the compromise that will kill their protest, but spring them from jail. In the midst of all the soul-searching, Kate is flirting with the arresting officer who has eyes for her, trying to decide whether or not to accept his offer of a date. Allie notices this little digression into the realm of relationships and mumbles, "Here we go again."

That scene shows Persistent Kate's overriding interest in the idea of relationships—particularly one-to-one—but it also shows how the Persistent Personality may appear a little self-absorbed at times, daydreaming or lost in flights of fancy. At times like that, the Persistent voyager is simply examining his own thoughts, meditating on the schemes, ideas, and inventions that he is forming to gratify his search and satisfy and enrich himself.

There is also a higher force at work when Allie and the other students join Kate in letting the police carry them away to jail. It is a force that the Persistent Personality can exert with amazingly little conscious effort. Because you are so amiable, a soft, humble, but very tenacious soul, you are blessed with the power of charisma. And although you may not be using your power to convince people to follow you to jail, it can come in handy to make some feel very special. Just ask that friendly police officer who has his eye on Persistent Kate.

On "Highway to Heaven," we meet Persistent **Jonathan** who is, surprisingly enough, an angel who has come back to earth in human form to help others do good and take care of one another.

In one particular episode, we see Jonathan trying to convince his companion, Mark, to accept a position as counselor at a camp for children who are suffering from cancer. "You've got a chance to get involved with the greatest bunch of kids in the world," says Jonathan. "They're holding their hands out to you and you're running away from them." But Mark is reluctant. "That's 'cause I can't do anything for them," Mark pleads, overcome by the prospect of working at a camp that is filled with tragic cases, and by the cruel mystery of cancer. But Jonathan persists. "You can be there for them, just be there for them. Help them laugh, help them have fun." Finally, Mark gives into the power of Jonathan's charisma and agrees to help.

On "Spenser: For Hire," Persistent **Spenser** is a private detective who uses his imagination and inventive powers to solve crimes. His faith can encourage friends and victims of crime not to give up.

On "Dallas," **Pam** shows the Persistent concern for relationships in her regard and concern for Miss Ellie, matriarch of the Texas Ewings, and for her husband, Bobby.

Zach, a wealthy and cultured businessman, shows his Persistent penchant for close relationships and his Persistent charm and charisma in his dealings with some very lovely and sophisticated ladies on "The Colbys."

As you watch your Persistent TV Twins and share their experiences, recognize the unique power of your ideas and dreams. Pay heed to the thoughts that are constantly churning and let your mind wander in a quiet and reflective way. Look for themes and harmonies. Recognize that your ideas need not always initially be accepted by others. But don't be afraid to share them.

As you follow your TV Twins' video lives, look carefully for examples of:

- An ability to make others feel special.
- Encouraging others to be useful.
- Advising hope and prayer as a way of coping with problems.
- Generosity.
- An ability to share amazement and surprise.
- A need for time to think quietly, daydream, and solve problems.

GOTTA FIND WHAT YOU'RE SEARCHING FOR

You look on life as a journey. Every day you head on down the road, hopes high, pursuing your dreams. What is it that you're looking for? Well, the answer to that question lies in your complex, spontaneous, genuinely caring, and always busy mind.

One Persistent Personality I know remembers wanting to be an astronomer or a physicist when she was a child; she was always looking through her telescope and reading about people who discovered things.

Another Persistent mentioned that, by the age of twenty, she had already grabbed at the sky and touched some stars. "I have always felt that I had a contribution to make and I'm not merely taking up space with my life," she remarked. "And although I'm not sure what the future holds, I'm always open to suggestions."

The Persistent pursuit may lead you through a variety of vocations, studies, philosophies, and disciplines. We can listen to Kate, of "Kate & Allie," describe the different paths her life has taken: student protester, hippie, wife, mother, career woman, then student protester once again. But through it all, one image persists for Kate and you other Persistent Personalities. That is one of a "free spirit."

We watch Kate arrive at her dentist's office, complaining of a toothache. The dentist leaves her in charge of the office while he goes down to the lobby for a pack of cigarettes. While he is gone there is a blackout, and Kate is left sitting alone in the darkness. Another person, from elsewhere in the building, wanders into the dentist's office. He and Kate strike up a conversation. Finally, although she can't even see his face, Kate accepts his invitation to accompany him to a basketball game that evening.

What strange paths that free spirit carries you down! What serendipitous encounters it leads to. It may lead to the realm of factory worker, philosopher, housewife, playwright, or poet. But more often it leads, as it did with Kate, to a relationship.

THE ALL-IMPORTANT RELATIONSHIP

The key to understanding the Persistent Personality is the great emphasis you place on all kinds of relationships.

We can watch Persistent Kate develop and describe her feelings about a number of different relationships. In the episode about the protest and sit-in, we saw her relationship with a unified group, a "movement," and how special she felt about being a part of it.

In another episode, Kate's daughter, Emma, is celebrating a birthday. Kate's ex-husband, Max, has seemingly forgotten about Emma's birthday, and both Emma and Kate are feeling blue about it. But Kate's faith, both in the power of relationships and in Max, comes through and Emma is treated to a special surprise from her father as the show ends. "Listen, let me tell you something about your dad," Kate confides to Emma. "He's not always there like some other fathers. But when he is, it's parades and skyrockets. Cherish every moment. He's like nobody else and he loves you so much."

In still another episode, Kate describes the unusual relationship that she, daughter Emma, and Allie and her two children, have established. A friend has proposed doing a TV show on the new American family and wants to use the Kate and Allie household as an example. "You guys are really something," the friend comments. "You're just like a real family." "We are a real family," says Kate. "But not a typical one," says the friend. Kate disagrees. "Well, you don't have to have a man and a woman and 2.3 children to be a typical family. You just have to live with people who love you and will lend you their support."

Relationships are vital and important to all of us. We are all social beings who need and want to share with others, but no other Personality Style places such consistent emphasis on relationships as does the Persistent Personality. Your basic disposition, your primary orientation is to establish a close bond with another human being. Within the relationship you experience a sense of identity, you find your source of pleasure and joy, your personal enrichment.

In a time when alienation and apathy are too evident in our culture, you and your Persistent TV Twins have much to teach all of us about the value and dynamics of relationships. We talk of "meaningful relationships," but sometimes too glibly, too easily. The very term notes something of a hunger we all have for greater and more gratifying exchanges with those around us. We can be jostled morning and evening in the crowd and deal with customers, coworkers, and clients until we feel numb with all that passing contact with others, yet we experience so much loneliness in our society. Even supposedly significant relationships—marriage, family life, friendships—sometimes hint of shallowness and touch-and-go superficiality. Our human contact is, sadly enough, often characterized more by quantity than by quality. Then along comes the Persistent Personality, on a journey down a long, sometimes unusual, but always steady path to change all that. To you, no relationship is ever static. It grows and flourishes, or it dwindles and dies. But those relationships that, for you, are real, true, and growing have a way of rippling out to touch and enrich the larger community.

On "Kate & Allie," Allie's relationship with Ed, her father, is strained when she suspects him of cheating on her mother and having an affair with his receptionist. Allie refuses to speak to him or to discuss the problem and continues to shut him out until Kate steps in. She has had a close relationship with both Ed and Allie since she and Allie were kids. So she gives Ed her attention and understanding. "Ed, look," she says, "I don't know why you did what you did and I can't say I'm thrilled with it, but that doesn't take away the man you've been all these years. Give yourself a break." Her faith, understanding, and resourcefulness finally bring Allie and her father back together again.

THE PERSISTENT LIKES TO SPOIL AND BE SPOILED

In a special relationship with a Persistent Personality, I might expect a few surprises. After all, you are a person with a very vivid imagination and a desire to make me feel very special.

A close relationship is so central to your life that you may find everything blotted out of your mind when you are with that one special person. You can be oblivious to everything and everyone else. You don't want to share that person; you want him, or her, all to yourself. As Zach, on "The Colbys," tells Sable when she considers parting with him and going back to husband Jason, "Don't you want to be here? Then you must let go of Jason, the past, all of your worries. Think only of here, and now, and us."

You enjoy pampering that special person in your life and you like to be pampered yourself. We can watch Zach bring Sable a lovely breakfast in bed, complete with red rose, after she spends the night at his house. You enjoy making life cozy, comfortable, and pleasurable for your beloved.

Gifts also hold a special place in your heart, both giving and receiving. Kate reveals that when she tells daughter Emma, who is expecting a birthday gift from her father, with obvious enthusiasm, "Whatever it is I know it's going to be fabulous."

The Persistent Personality is a great giver of gifts, but you do it with such grace and make others feel so special that others don't always recognize that you may want a favor in return. You take special delight in wining and dining and entertaining, then hope that as much will be offered to you.

We can watch Zach as he charms Sable, finally has her in his arms. "I've dreamed of this moment," he murmurs. But Sable pulls back, "Zach, I can't." But he persists in his seduction. Sable assures him that she wants him, but asks him to take things slowly. "On one condition," Zach tells her. "That you spend the night here in my bed, alone." She of course asks why. "Because I don't want you going back to his [Jason's] house tonight. Because I've always wanted to have breakfast with you." Oh, Zach, how do you always manage to say the right things?

So attentive, so understanding, so able to make the other person feel so special. But it is a chicken-and-egg situation: which comes first, your desire to spoil, or your desire to be spoiled? When Sable thanks Zach for his thoughtfulness, his reply is, "I don't want your gratitude, I want you."

After watching that particular segment, one Persistent Personality commented, "I really saw myself there. I do a lot of special things for my husband, like special dinners and things, and I'll admit I sometimes have in the back of my mind, 'OK, you owe me one.' "

Indeed, as we watch a little further in "The Colbys" episode, Sable again tells Zach, in appreciation for the wonderful evening he has given her, "I can't thank you enough." "Oh, yes you can," answers Zach, "if you try. But for now, let's just say you owe me."

OK, so you do have some idea in the back of your mind that there might be some return for the special treatment you give. Recognizing that is simply recognizing your Persistent Personality at work. But that certainly does not diminish the pleasure that the other person gets from all that you do and give. Nor does it diminish the pleasure you both derive, in your own fashion, from the relationship itself. Now we know: all you really want, for both of you, is a garden of earthly delights.

SPEAKING OF GARDENS OF EARTHLY DELIGHTS

When the one-to-one relationship is of the intimate variety, the Persistent lover often projects a certain eroticism: a preference for lovemaking that is imaginative, inventive, and fulfilling. The subtle message that you and your TV Twins project is that you want complete, exquisite, and very special gratification for yourself and your partner.

How do those of us who have never had the sublime experience of that sort of relationship with a Persistent Personality know that to be so? Well, we just watch *your* TV Twins and use *our* imagination. We watch Kate, who works as a travel agent, describe a trip to Jamaica that she has just arranged for two of her friends. "Picture the two of you on a deserted stretch of beach, the sun warming your two yearning bodies."

Now flip over to Zach on "The Colbys" as he is leaving the lovely Sable to sleep alone in his bed while *he* sleeps in the guest room. "You sure you can trust me?" he asks as he is going out the bedroom door. "Trust you? I'll show you how much. I won't even lock the door," says the self-assured but very appealing Sable. Zach smiles and starts to leave, then pops back. "On second thought, lock the door," is his parting comment.

Finally flip back to "Kate & Allie." A newfound friend has just taken both Kate and Allie to dinner. They had a wonderful time, both found him very attractive, and both would like to pursue a relationship with him. But how to divide him between them. "I get the half that tells the jokes," says Allie. "Great," says Kate with a satisfied smile.

DAYDREAM BELIEVER

What would you do if you won the big jackpot in the state lottery? Where would all of that money go? Well it just so happens that Kate and Allie are discussing that very topic. So let's listen in. Allie is considering mutual funds, an IRA, a solid stock portfolio, and a corporate trust account; all of those practical nuts-and-bolts sorts of applications. Persistent Kate, on the other hand, is letting fly with one of the greatest Persistent strengths: "A cruise down the Nile . . . an African safari . . . maybe a small yacht to go shopping among the Greek islands . . . all the gowns in Paris . . ." She is showing the rich and vivid imagination that all Persistent Personalities share.

With a mind so rich in imagination, all possibilities are considered and respected. You are not one to scoff at the idea of reincarnation, or ESP, or even UFOs. We can eavesdrop as Kate and Allie tune into a TV talk show. "Our subject tonight," the announcer says, "has been UFOs: Fact or Fiction." Their reaction is immediate, and very telling. "Fact," says Kate. "Fiction," says Allie. "A lot of very smart people believe in UFOs," Kate shoots back. Can't argue with that.

The ticket to the theater in your mind often comes in the form of daydreams. You are prone to let your mind wander, much as Kate, Jonathan, and your other TV Twins do, and may find that daydreaming helps ease the tension between creating ideas and the need to be correct; between discipline and the need to let your mind fly.

TIME TO LET YOUR MIND QUIETLY DRIFT

You are very aware of your own mind and are usually very tuned in to its mechanism. It is the center of your need for gratification as well as the place where the plans to carry it out are formed. For that reason you may be very absorbed in your own thoughts. When you become keenly involved in those inner processes, you don't like to be jarred out of your productive reverie; so the solution is to slip away for some quiet time, meditation, a relaxing float on the sea of tranquility.

In one episode of "Kate & Allie," we watch Kate, just as she is ready to depart on one of those floats. She has been feeling the pressure of living in an apartment with four other people and has not had the opportunity to get away for some time alone—that time for peace and quiet that everyone needs now and then, but that a Persistent Personality has a special need for. She arranges a vacation for some friends and volunteers to feed their cat while they are gone just so she can spend an hour or two alone in their apartment every day, to sit with her feet up, in the theater of her mind.

"I need that creative distance also," commented one Persistent Personality after watching Kate. "All day long I'm working, then I need time to set my mind free, to run the ideas and schemes I come up with through my mind. But there's still a gap between the ideas I have and the opportunity to actualize them."

"I have difficulty sometimes convincing my wife that the time I need alone isn't because I don't need her or because I'm not interested in her ideas or activities," said another Persistent Personality. "I can see now with Kate that it's just a part of my Personality. So I try to trade off things I have to do for the free time. I take my son to his baseball practice and that gives me an hour to sit in the bleachers by myself and let my mind wander."

"I will take care of your cat as long as we agree that as soon as I take care of kitty I can stretch out on the sofa for a little vacation of my own," says Kate to the friends she is sending to Jamaica. The friends agree, so they all make a toast: "To a deserted beach in Jamaica," say the friends. "To a deserted apartment in New York," says Kate. Clink go the glasses.

A LITTLE BIT OF WHIMSY

Daydreams and a vivid imagination are not something you can buy; thank heaven for that. Neither are close, sincere relationships, although a special one-of-a-kind gift can certainly help strengthen the bond at times.

It is Kate's daughter Emma's birthday. When Emma opens her package from mom it contains a slightly damp bandanna. "Gee, thanks Mom, just what I've always wanted, a slightly damp bandanna." "No," Kate corrects her, "it is one of Bruce Springsteen's slightly damp bandannas."

You can, and do, use your nimble imagination to enhance the ordinary, to engage in a bit of whimsy now and then. It keeps life fresh and exciting and keeps those around you happy, if not amazed. "Sometimes, when the check comes at a restaurant, I'll leave as much money for the waiter or waitress as the whole meal costs," said one Persistent Personality I know.

Money is not always such an overriding concern. Faith will provide even if the imagination doesn't. So what's to worry? When you are likely, at any time, to be launched on the wings of whimsy, you may miss a trick here and there, may be seen as a bit absentminded. Friends might say that when they're talking to you, they're not sure you're listening, or even in the same place.

Remember Kate in her dentist's waiting room waiting to have a toothache taken care of? While she's there, lights in the building go off. A man just happens to stumble into the waiting room from out in the hall. A conversation is started. He and Kate hit it off. He invites her to a basketball game and off they go.

Well, the moral of that story is: If you wait for the dentist to come back, you may lose your toothache, but you may also lose the chance for a wonderful relationship.

So go. We understand.

THE INVENTIVE PERSISTENT MIND

With such a creative, inventive mind, you are a likely candidate to build a better mousetrap. A Persistent Personality is usually the one seeking a simpler, faster way of doing things while others pursue the old tried and true way. The more conservative may label your ideas weird until shown that they work wonderfully well. Your inventive ideas and schemes give you more time to think, to imagine still better ways to build a better mousetrap and to come up with even more clever schemes.

Who is a better Persistent schemer than Kate? In one episode, she and Allie have fallen for the same man, Richard. They have gone out with him together but he hasn't shown a special or recognizable interest in either one of them individually, so Kate hatches a scheme to determine which of them he will pursue a relationship with. Richard is an opera buff, so Kate will arrange for her boss's wife, who is on the opera guild committee, to send two impossible-to-get tickets to Richard's house. Since he has just moved to the city and doesn't know anyone but Kate and Allie, he will use one of the tickets for himself, and invite the one he finds most appealing to use the other ticket.

We can also watch how Kate schemes to get Allie and her father together for a talk after they have fought. Allie refuses to stay in the same room, or even in the same house, when her father comes over to apologize. When he comes over one more time, and is upstairs with the grandchildren, Allie comes into the house. "Is he here?" she asks Kate. "No," Kate answers, then proceeds to push Allie into the closet while she is hanging up her coat, and locks the door, making her a captive audience. Then she calls everyone downstairs, offers to take the kids out for ice cream, and leaves Allie, still in the closet, and her father alone to talk.

We watch Zach, on "The Colbys," come up with a scheme to win Sable's affection. Sable would like her sister, who is temporarily living in the US and making Sable miserable, to be transported back to England. "Your sister's husband is with the British Foreign Office?" asks Zach. "I have, as it happens, a modicum of influence in diplomatic circles.'' He will arrange for the bothersome sister to be sent home, if Sable comes around. ''I would be eternally grateful,'' says Sable. ''I don't want your gratitude,'' says Zach again. ''I do want you.''

The Persistent Personality does indeed at times indulge others with the thought of gaining some indulgence in return; you are quite capable of using your imagination and inventive mind to craft any number of creative schemes to get what you want: to make the situation much less obvious and much more appealing.

''Yes,'' admitted one Persistent Personality after watching Kate and Zach, ''I sometimes am aware that I'm manipulating people, and a situation, to get something I want. I'll tell them what they want to hear to win them over. And sometimes when I do special things for people I'll be thinking, like Zach, 'You owe me one.' ''

To some, who don't totally understand you or your Persistent Personality, your schemes to get what you want may show you as being manipulative and slightly self-indulgent.

Allie is busy wrapping gifts at the dining room table. There is no special occasion, she just likes to have an emergency supply of gifts around so that if one is needed in a pinch it's there. Kate spots a watch just as Allie is ready to wrap it. ''That's a nice watch,'' she says. ''I need a watch.'' Allie is obviously not happy about giving in to Kate's hints, but Kate persists. ''Think of all the trouble it will save you. You won't have to wrap it, you won't have to give it to me, and I won't have to act surprised.''

In another episode, Kate bounces in at 1:00 A.M. from a date and wants to talk to Allie about it, immediately. Allie is obviously not too thrilled about having her sleep disturbed and says so. But Kate's response is, ''Remember when you had that stomach virus? Who stayed up with you all night?''

You cherish the other person for his or her human value and you want to contribute to that person's well-being. Great, that's your Personality. You also occasionally have an ulterior motive for your contribution. Great, that's your Personality too. So where's the harm?

Persistent Kate has arranged for those two opera tickets to be delivered to Richard, whom she and Allie both have their eyes on. Remember her scheme? He will use one ticket and give the other to the one he likes best. Allie is sure she will be the loser in this deal, and end up alone talking to herself in the pit of despair. Kate tells Allie she will call the boss's wife in the morning to arrange to have the tickets delivered. "I'll go pack my smocks for the pit," moans Allie. "Don't pack that green silk because that's the one I'm going to wear if he asks me," says the ever-faithful, but slightly self-indulgent Kate.

"If I ever do have something in mind, like Kate or Zach, when I do a favor or something special for someone else," said one Persistent Personality, "it's something good. The real trouble comes when people are always suspecting that what you have in mind is bad."

Another Persistent added her own creative explanation. "If I don't get the things I want, I won't have anything to share. I place a very high value on relationships. So I want to share, and do share. Sometimes I just like to take the first bite."

PERSIST AND PERSEVERE

The Persistent Personality's quest for enrichment, fulfillment, and the fruit of relationships is just that: persistent. You will use your imagination and resources to steadily overcome anything and everything in your path.

On "Spenser: For Hire," Persistent Spenser puts that attitude into words—actually the words of Winston Churchill—when he tried to encourage a friend not to give up hope. "Do you remember Winston Churchill's speech to the graduating class at Harrow?" Spenser asks his friend, then proceeds to recite the speech: " 'Never give in. Never give in. Never, never, never. Never in nothing, great or small, large or petty. Never give in except to convictions, and honor, and good sense.' "

We can watch Kate encourage a group of students to persist in the sit-in demonstration even when the police are on the way to arrest them. And we can watch Jonathan, on "Highway to Heaven," encourage a man, who is terribly ill in the hospital, to want to live. He shows his persistence in asking the man to pray for the strength to live, and conveys a sense of hope.

"I remember when my father was sick and the doctor told him he had to lose weight, or else," said one Persistent man. "I explained to my father that he had to listen to the doctor, to fight the illness and his weight problem, and to go on just like Jonathan did with that man in the show."

Another Persistent commented, "I counsel youths who are thinking about suicide and I try to get them to have faith, to know that the person is greater than what they might happen to be feeling inside at any particular moment."

For the unwearied Persistent, perseverance equals faith. You could not and would not press on in your search unless you were convinced that the forces were on your side. Everything will work out; there's just no question about it. Yours is the faith that can move mountains.

On "Highway to Heaven," Jonathan is trying to convince his friend Mark that he has the courage and strength to work at a camp for young cancer victims. "You've just got to stop being scared," says Jonathan. "None of us knows what's gonna happen tomorrow. What's important is how we live today."

Due to your great faith and your assumption that everything will turn out for the best, you may sometimes find yourself being temporarily crushed by the disappointment of not having your dreams come true. Well, you're not alone. Kate tells daughter Emma about the temporary setbacks her faith suffered when she was still trying to make a go of it with ex-husband Max. "Max's screw-ups were always murder, but his apologies kept me going for years."

Another Persistent Personality saw it this way: "When I lose my schemes, I hurt pretty bad. But I keep the faith."

One serious setback may crush the Persistent Personality, but it's like crushing a bedspring: As soon as the weight is off, you bounce back. You have a facility for resourceful and reflective thinking that produces tactics to match your vision. Whenever things have gone your way you can fully appreciate how well it has all worked out. We can watch Kate, and daughter Emma, persevere through the entire episode when both are afraid that

Max has forgotten Emma's birthday. When at the end the gift is finally there, both are relieved and reinforced. "Oh, I knew he didn't forget," says Emma. Kate smiles, "Me too."

A LIFE FILLED WITH OPPORTUNITY AND JOY

There is a scene at the beginning of "Highway to Heaven" in which we find ourselves drifting and soaring through the clouds. It is quiet, serene, and quite beautiful, almost like heaven. It's an excellent time to meditate on a life filled with opportunities and joys. And if you are a religious person, as Persistent Personalities often are, you may find yourself muttering a pilgrim's prayer of thanksgiving to God for all His goodness.

Of course, not every Persistent Personality finds religion an object for faith and devotion. You may react against organized religion and what you perceive as shallow piety, Sunday-only morality, and rigid attitudes. You may simply look on all of life and all of creation—the dawn, the sun and moon, the snow in winter, fresh buds on the trees—as signs of the presence of a higher force.

You may, as Jonathan on "Highway to Heaven" does, find immediate, everyday channels for your faith, service, and devotion in fraternal, social, or community-action organizations.

Because of your vivid imagination and free spirit, you may have a tendency to pursue the higher plane through astrology, the occult, spiritualism, or the like. After all, as Kate says, a lot of very smart people believe in UFOs.

More often than not, you invest your faith and devotion in close relationships. In these relationships you find many ways to be useful, purposeful, and involved. It's an opportunity to be of help to others and to be the beneficiary of kindness yourself. "You see the happiness you bring to people. They are giving you so much," is how one Persistent Personality describes it. It is also a great way to plug into the greatest relationship of all: the one that binds all life together. "We are all part of God," is how one Persistent Personality sums it up. "We are all part of that force."

You appreciate what you have and what you do: the relationship itself. It represents that larger force that is the sum of all the parts. And chances are, as a Persistent Personality, you find that very gratifying.

CHARISMA: WHERE YOU GO, WE'LL FOLLOW

As a Persistent Personality you enjoy attention as much as the next person, maybe more. Attention shows that you're being appreciated, and that's something you crave. But you have your own unique method of drawing that attention, a method that doesn't involve a lot of flash or horn tooting. Most often it's your humble nature and the great power of your faith that combine to draw others in. It's a personal magic: the magic of charisma.

Charisma is not easily defined, although a couple of Persistent Personalities I know have tried. "It's genuinely loving other people, looking at and appreciating what they have to offer," says one. "You mirror that for them, as well as what they can do, and they are naturally attracted by the image." Another Persistent Personality sees it as "my faith and hope as the impetus for others to keep going."

Who knows? Maybe it's the way you communicate pleasure and joy. Maybe it's that you're just a lovable sort of person. Maybe it's your ability to inspire confidence and hope. Maybe it's because, secretly, you are dying for attention. Or maybe, just maybe, you are a person "through whom the light of God shines," as one famous Persistent observed.

ONE-TO-ONE: THE BEST KIND OF RELATIONSHIP

The more actively and intimately you participate in a relationship, the better. What could be more intimate, or satisfying, than a one-to-one relationship?

We might ask that question of Persistent Zach on "The Colbys" as he charms and seduces the lovely Sable. Zach comes up with an imaginative scheme to catch Sable's attention by offering advice on how to display her priceless art collection. Later, he entertains her in his luxurious home and gently kisses her shoulder as he helps her remove her diamond necklace, asking her to "think only of here, and now, and us."

I think it is safe to say that the answer to the question: "What could be more gratifying to the Persistent Personality than a one-to-one relationship?" is "Nothing." It might be a relationship with husband, wife, child, friend, or lover. It might last for a week, or a year, or forever. But for you, it's the top of the mountain.

Marriage is a great opportunity for the Persistent Personality to utilize his faith and devotion, his caring and sharing capacity. He can be a considerate and affectionate spouse and parent, his normally mirthful and optimistic attitude prevailing. The Persistent Personality may give up her own educational or career opportunities for the sake of her spouse's career, placing greater value on the relationship. This devotion will show in countless little gifts of self: "I'm a devoted wife. When my husband wakes up in the morning, I have his juice and toast beside the bed and his bath water running. While he is getting dressed, I'm out there warming up the car." And he is no different: "If she sees something she likes, I'll put in overtime if I have to to get it for her." But in return, the Persistent spouse may expect some show of appreciation—if nothing else, the abiding presence of the other person, which can be burdensome at times for that person. "When she's not home, I get irritable," says the Persistent spouse. "I hate to be alone."

Sometimes though, the Persistent Personality can do too much for either spouse or children. He can be too giving in a way that burdens others. One Persistent wife told me of always being so considerate and thoughtful that her husband found her threatening and just "too good." The more he resisted her giving ways and her desire for constant togetherness, the more she tried to do. The marriage ended in divorce, a crushing experience for the Persistent Personality.

In her next marriage, this Persistent switched directions in her search for a happy relationship, going toward the loose and easy side, trying to find a chic lifestyle, a free and casual relationship. That marriage also ended in divorce; the woman was fighting her own values and inherent characteristics—she simply wasn't moving in a direction that was good or natural for her. Moreover, she really didn't make a commitment after her disappointment in the first marriage. Still, she persisted in the second marriage, hoping, feeling wretched. When the marriage finally broke up, she was terribly depressed. Even today, though more wary, she is still searching for a relationship and marriage, one that will permit the security and opportunity for sharing and mutual happiness.

"Some of my friends think I'm foolish, looking for another partner," she says. "But knowing my Personality and knowing my TV Twins has made me aware of how essential relationships really are to me."

Our Persistent friend will need to accent the word *mutual* lest she run the risk of overpowering still another partner. She will need to learn that others too have a need to do and give.

THE WORKING WORLD

Work and career are meaningful to the Persistent Personality according to the value assigned to relationships. Appreciation and feeling special are important, but the Persistent worker can be too finely tuned to a supervisor's reactions and comments, or lack of them. He can easily feel slighted. If the working environment promotes a spirit of closeness and offers supportive feedback, however, the working Persistent feels at one with his work. Once he commits himself to the task, he will pursue it with his customary devotion, searching for ways to do it better, seeking to contribute at the same time to the human environment of his job. When he believes in his employer and the product, when he feels that he is valued as a productive person, he is a devoted employee.

The Persistent worker often welcomes retirement, sometimes even when she is involved and committed to her work. Like Kate, Jonathan, Zach, and her other TV Twins, there are so many facets of life she yearns to explore—travel, a wealth of good books, good music, fellowship, sports, good moments alone with the beauty of nature, or just quiet moments for reflection and meditation. The search goes on.

Like most things in his life, the Persistent Personality's disposition toward money can take opposite directions. He can be prudent, handling it carefully, putting away regular savings for security. The unhealthy version of this drift is miserliness. On the other hand, the Persistent Personality can be the easy come, easy go spender; if this tendency goes awry, he can be prodigal. It all depends on how he appreciates the fruits of his labor; does he want to enjoy it now or later?

As we have seen, she can be very generous either in helping others or in giving gifts. She can also be self-indulgent, enjoying the immediate benefits of her earnings—spending on expensive clothing, household luxuries, hobbies, and recreation: "What the heck. I'm working. So what's wrong with a few luxuries? I've earned them."

When she has the money available, she is just as likely to rush to the financial rescue of a friend in need. Savings are gratifying. The luxuries are gratifying. Helping a friend is gratifying. The bottom line is the same: appreciation.

IT'S GETTING LATE

Well, it's getting late in the chapter, almost time to move on to the next group of TV Twins. "But wait," you say, "we're just now really starting to get to the good stuff." Just think of this as a good time to stop. Go to a quiet place somewhere and meditate on everything you've learned or recognized about yourself in this chapter. And understand that this chapter, like the Persistent Personality, Kate, Jonathan, Zach, and all the other Persistent TV Twins, is very often a late bloomer.

"And why," you may ask, "is the Persistent Personality a late bloomer?" Well, it does take a long time to find the fruit of such a continuous and exhaustive search as the one you're on. Then there are the relationships you stop to form and enjoy along the way. But you are gratified by every minute of the journey. Remember that from the bloom comes the fruit; from the fruit, the seeds of a new plant, then blossoms bear more fruit; then more seeds; then . . .

ALTERNATIVES AND OPTIONS

The Persistent Personality sees life not only as a continuous search, but as an opportunity: to give, receive, to share, to sacrifice, to be gratified by the many occasions to bring pleasure and joy to others.

The Persistent is greatly appreciated, even when she doesn't notice how much people appreciate her. It may be that she is just too busy scheming and inventing more ways of developing her rich talent and of being useful to others. The search goes on and on.

The less mature Persistent Personality is also searching, but in all the wrong directions and in all the wrong ways. He is less prone to contribute to others, being more likely to draw on the environment, even to the point of draining every possible source of gratification. His appetite, emotionally and physically, can be enormous, voracious.

Although the happenings in the Persistent Personality's mind may be of utmost importance, the rest of the world has a tendency to continue operating all around him. Unless the introspective Persistent keeps his self-absorption under control, he may miss a trick here and there.

Even the healthy Persistent Personality can be stronger in certain characteristic areas while being perhaps a bit more vulnerable in others. Any Persistent individual may find the following recommended alternatives and options helpful:

- When you reach a dead end in your thoughts, try switching to some other area, then move on.
- On the journey through life, take regular pauses to appreciate all that you are, all that you have, all that you do. Appreciation is the key to enjoying all relationships and the continuous search for greater opportunity to utilize your talents and your faith, devotion, and love.

- Don't wait for others to appreciate you. Appreciate yourself. Make it a habit.
- Ask yourself why you give so many gifts. Recognize that you make yourself special by giving gifts and your special treatment. Don't be unhappy if others don't give to you in return.
- Beware of how easily you find all the shortcuts—pretty sly, but pretty creative.
- Relationships work best when the give and take flows easily in both directions. Let others give and do also.
- Today is a good day for taking inventory of all your assets: your talents, your efficiency, your competency on the job, your generosity toward others, your regard for others, your appreciation of friendships.
- The best way to get attention is to do things well.
- Start from the present, from where you are, as opposed to where you want to be, and then move forward.
- It's nice to dream dreams, but life is usually a series of the little things done well. Keep on dreaming, but then put the dreams into action.
- The greatest discovery of life comes when you discover your own resourcefulness, your own great capacity for loving and doing and sharing.
- The best way to overcome confusion, wondering, and questioning is to *do* something and then appreciate what you have done.
- Faith is more than a virtue; it is your great strength. Invest it wisely. Persisting in faith, whatever its object, is the best way to overcome faults and frailties.
- Be frugal but not miserly. Be generous but not lavish. Moderation is the key.
- There is an old and wise saying: "Pray as if everything depended on God; work as if everything depended on you."

SECRETS

The keys to a successful relationship with the Persistent Personality are:

- Appreciate the one-to-one relationship.
- Encourage the Persistent Personality's inventiveness and utilize the invention.
- Don't discourage daydreams; they are often the source of great ideas.
- Give the Persistent his or her time to examine thoughts, to meditate.
- Recognize what you consider "stubbornness" as persistence.
- Enjoy the gifts and the attention.
- Keep the faith.

MATCH AND MISMATCH

Persistent Personality matchmates:

Perceptive—You are both people who prize a close, loving relationship. This person makes you feel special and will share your compassion and caring.

Anticipating—These individuals put your interest and happiness above everything else; when you spoil them, they hold you in higher and higher esteem. Anticipatings are interested in your visions and dreams, and their planning encourages your ideas and wishes to flow.

Adaptable—You eagerly share ideas. This partner listens and explores your interests; this is someone who loves to communicate and listen. Your quiet time to think blends in with the Adaptable's need for an occasional night out for other interests.

Ambitious—You and this partner form a team that is a balanced blend of conniving and striving. The Ambitious values your keen dreams and clever schemes; you two are never bored.

Sensitive—Your partner is very loyal and affectionate in a quiet, thoughtful way. At times, he or she knows you better than you know yourself. You need quiet time, and your partner needs private time, so you go together. This partner's curiosity piques your ideas and interests.

Influencing—Your partner will lavish you with all the good things in life; will show you special attention; will encourage you to hold onto your convictions and approaches but will want you to follow his lead, to listen and do things his way.

Accomplishing—This person wants very much to please and win your approval but goes off in so many directions and interferes with your need for special attention. The Accomplishing will encourage your visions and dreams but has so much energy that you do not get your needed quiet time. He or she needs so much approval that it stifles your imagination.

Patient—Your Patient partner often misreads your offers of friendliness as demands; when things go wrong, look for an "I told you so" attitude. This individual gives little feedback and does little to acknowledge your wish to be special. He or she takes a factual and practical approach, whereas you can be a bit fanciful.

Conscientious—The Conscientious are constantly doubting your wishes and ideas; at times their sense of humor can be sarcastic. Your brain burns with novel ideas and innovative notions, whereas they want to deal only with facts and details. You can be very spontaneous, while they follow a regular routine. It is hard to share your visions and dreams in this relationship.

Idealistic—You deal with imagination and intuition, while these individuals deal with shoulds and oughts. You're emotional, while they prefer to relate in an intellectual fashion. When you make Idealistics special, they feel threatened. You want to work together; they are aloof and uninvolved. In this relationship your ideas aren't encouraged to flow and your thoughts aren't encouraged to wander.

Determined—You want to carry on a conversation and this person lets deeds speak for themselves. You share your ideas and intuitions, and the Determined reacts with a scowl and "the look." You are rarely appreciated for the special things you do; your creative ideas are ignored or even ridiculed. This person views your need for quiet time or daydreaming as wasted time.

Chapter Nine

THE INFLUENCING PERSONALITY

PROFILE

- Wants to be in charge, very willing to take responsibility.
- Demands order and organization.
- Wants everything spotless, on time, and in its place.
- Looks for the best, the ultimate.
- First class or nothing.
- Can be very direct and to the point.

TV TWINS

- Blake Carrington—"Dynasty"
- Dr. Mark Craig—"St. Elsewhere"
- Stephanie—"Newhart"
- Dorothy—"Golden Girls"
- Winchester—"M*A*S*H"
- Lance—"Falcon Crest"
- Fonzie—"Happy Days"
- Jennifer—"WKRP in Cincinnati"
- Higgins—"Magnum, P.I."
- Jason—"The Colbys"
- David Hartman—"Good Morning America"
- Bryant Gumble—"Today"

Let's get right to the point. In the world of the Influencing Personality, there is no hair out of place, no crooked pictures, no cluttered desk or grimy tennis sneakers, no handprints on the refrigerator. Everything is spic and span and in tip-top condition. "Just don't give me anything messy or disorganized," you say. "There's a place for everything and by God that's where it belongs."

The Influencing Personality is a supremely organized person who approaches every task in life in the same way: thoroughly and systematically. He expects the maximum effort from himself and from everyone else—nothing less will do. Whatever he starts, he finishes, come hell or high water. He is keenly observant of what is going on around him and can spot the smallest flaw in technique and product.

She is the neighbor you see leaving the house every Saturday morning exactly at 9:30 for the hairdresser, her house in pristine order. He is your auto mechanic whose garage floor is spotless. When he says you can pick up your car at 5:00, he has it ready at 5:00 with the invoice tabulated and itemized. The cost may be high, but the engine is humming like new, or even better than new—and there is never a grease smudge on the steering wheel. If the job is not the best, up goes the hood and the work starts all over again.

Whether at work, at home, or at play, the Influencing Personality is possessed by an undying urge for the ultimate—the ultimate sales record, the ultimate garden, the ultimate tennis game. Whatever he does must be done superbly, flawlessly. To attain the ultimate, he must be unerringly on target—the perfect salesperson, the perfect gardener, the perfect tennis player. Moreover, the ultimate results demand complete and total control over the process.

In order to have first class you have to be first class, and the only way to be first class all the time is to take, and keep, control of yourself and your environment. You want things in order and on time. Not three-minute eggs cooked for two minutes and forty-seven seconds. Not a hem with one dangling thread. Not your car back from the shop with even a tiny black smudge on the whitewalls. Not a partner with the wrong color eye shadow or the least little bit of dirt under the fingernails.

In the Influencing world, only the finest will do: the best

brands, the finest labels, the top of the line. Your world is a first-class place. It has to be or you won't live there.

Taking charge and leading the way comes naturally for you. You have that certain flair, that sense of elegance and style that command attention. But as a leader you make following virtually painless. You'll charm the socks off your audience with endless absorbing stories. At the parties you throw, no glass goes unfilled and you preside over the festivities like the Mardi Gras monarch. For you there is no more tedious and trying curse than mediocrity.

You do have a tendency at times to elevate minor calamities into major crises. It's likely to happen when things are getting out of control or you're being cut off or interrupted, or you are being discouraged from taking the reins and putting the situation in order. At times like those, your temper can resemble a sudden summer thunderstorm: dark clouds gather from nowhere, you explode in a fury, set things straight, then just as quickly it's blue skies again.

Your conversational style follows the pattern of your other activities. The Influencing Personality isn't much for small talk and tends to limit his conversation to those areas in which he feels competent. Even in seemingly casual conversation he is in control. Whether speaking of building bridges or fishing for trout, he is a talking technical manual, covering the full scope of the enterprise and the most minute specifications.

But buried in the talk is a hidden agenda: you are taking over; you are influencing the direction and disposition of the situation. However subtle or indirect, however charming and gracious, you are delivering the message: "Let's do it my way." And if I miss the point or choose to challenge it, you will repeat the message less subtly, even bluntly. You are not bashful and you do not give up easily. If my attention lapses, you may very well clear your throat or tap my shoulder and then repeat everything you have said from the beginning. So the message to us non-Influencing Personalities is, "Relax and listen." We will find, more often than not, that the Influencing Personality is knowledgeable and informative, whether the topic is raising money, pouring concrete, or grilling the perfect hamburger.

When the Influencing Personality tells you that he knows a better way, believe him. If you want the name of a good restaurant or the brand of a fine champagne, ask the Influencing Personality; he knows only the best. But if you inquire about the price, he may look at you unbelievingly: "You only get what you pay for."

MEET YOUR TV TWINS

When your Influencing TV Twins come on the screen, heads turn. They bring a certain commanding presence into a room—a presence you can see, hear, and feel.

Finding your TV Twins can be tremendously rewarding. Your Influencing TV Twins will be easy to identify because they:

- Are charming, stylish, and persuasive.
- Are great storytellers and always ready to give an opinion.
- Take charge of and are responsible for situations.
- Are threatened by criticism.
- React vigorously at the time of a crisis.
- Are interested in the highest quality.

You and your TV Twins have a certain flair that commands attention. Your very presence exudes excellence and elegance. You abhor anything messy or disorganized. There's a place for everything, and that's where it belongs. You are the king or queen of clean. You tend to think in terms of all or nothing. You make the maximum effort to obtain the best results. This is the way you approach everything.

On "Dynasty," the air is blue with tension when Influencing **Blake Carrington** strides into the boardroom at Denver Carrington, the multinational corporation he commands. His chair is strategically placed, so that the rest of the room rotates around him like lesser planets around the sun. The board members all wait for a sign: when Blake sits down, they can start breathing again. But he toys with them, adjusts the hand-tailored shirt cuff, straightens the Italian silk tie, checks the time on the gold

Rolex watch. There are still two minutes before the meeting starts and he will start it precisely on time. He is the boss.

Influencing **Jason** fills a similar position on "The Colbys."

Dr. Mark Craig presides over the operating room on "St. Elsewhere." He shows the Influencing penchant for first class while planning the ultimate Christmas party in his home. He has genuine bayberry candles from Cape Cod, the best Vermont cedar garlands, and just the right balsam wreath from Maine to hang on the front door. "We should invite more people to the party," he says to his wife. "Well, there are twenty people coming already," she says. But to Dr. Craig that's small potatoes. That's not a party, that's a minor disturbance. "This year I want a houseful of people," says the doctor, "packed to the rafters, with everyone having a good time."

At the 4077th M*A*S*H, an Army field hospital operating during the Korean War, **Major Charles Emerson Winchester** still insists on the finest and the occasional grand celebration, even if it is taking place in a tent. In one episode, he is welcoming a visiting Swedish surgeon with a bottle of vintage wine. "I brought you a bottle of Chateau Lafite '37, a modest little welcome of inestimable value," he announces as the dreary tent is lit by the charm and elegance of the fine wine.

Meanwhile, back in the US, Influencing **Jennifer,** the alluring, cultured secretary at "WKRP in Cincinnati," a fictional radio station for which the show is named, is throwing a bash in her opulent apartment. She is the true Influencing hostess: the guests have been selected so that they complement each other, the bar is stocked, and the meal is prepared to perfection. Everything is just right. The guests are all enjoying themselves when the doorbell rings announcing more guests. But Influencing Jennifer's doorbell doesn't just go ding-dong. It plays "Fly Me to the Moon."

Influencing **Stephanie** works as a chambermaid at a country inn on "Newhart" but manages to maintain her expensive tastes, her designer wardrobe, and the exclusive adoration of boyfriend Michael. Of course, having millionaire parents is a big help.

On "Golden Girls," Influencing **Dorothy** is one of three single, middle-aged women sharing a house and the trials and tribulations of life in Miami. Her Influencing Personality is exhibited most often by her blunt comments and her tendency to step in and take over in any situation where she sees help might be needed.

Influencing **Higgins** is the guiding force behind his private investigator friend Magnum of "Magnum, P.I."

Bryant Gumble, of the "Today" show, and **David Hartman,** of "Good Morning America," are ready at the controls at 7:00 A.M., directing a sleepy America into another day.

Influencing **Lance,** on "Falcon Crest," and Influencing **Fonzie,** on the classic, "Happy Days," typify similar aspects of the Influencing Personality. On "Happy Days," Fonzie is a small-town tough guy who has stayed around to dispense his wisdom and keep the local high school cutups, who worship him, under his thumb. On "Falcon Crest," a show about the rich and powerful in California's wine country, Lance is a wealthy, contemporary young man who shares Fonzie's desire to be in charge and to unleash his killer charm on the young ladies.

You and your TV Twins function best in an organized, structured environment. You are most effective when you have your priorities established. When you are stressed, you benefit from an understanding, solicitous approach that will encourage you to relax and get a new perspective. You don't profit from being given illustrations, or being ordered around yourself.

As you follow your TV Twins' video lives, look carefully for examples of:

- Talking with their hands when communicating in order to emphasize the message.
- Dislike of being interrupted.
- Moving on from one intense interest to another.
- A reluctance to back down from a confrontation.
- Frequently being referred to as "perfectionists."

DON'T GIVE ME GOOD OR BETTER, GIVE ME THE BEST

Nothing about the Influencing Personality is casual. Your quest is always for the best.

That's right. No mundane cross-country flights or everyday trips around the world. Make it a flight to the moon. And make that first class, please. First-class fare was invented for you. You are the connoisseur, the Personality who understands the details, technique, and principles of the ultimate. You are possessed by an undying urge for the ultimate, the best, the finest: the best sales record, the finest antiques, the ultimate tennis game, the first commercial flight into outer space.

Even in dress, the quest is for the best. She shops the best stores and the best labels. She wants style and fashion, but today's style and an elegant label aren't enough. She must also examine the fabric, inspect seams and stitching, and study every detail meticulously. He will call for the head tailor to fit him. The price tag may warrant a glance, but it isn't that important. What is important is the supreme, the superlative, even in appearance, and the Influencing Personality, male or female, is willing to pay the price.

"I am a great subscriber to the saying: 'If it's worth doing, it's worth doing well,' " said one Influencing Personality. "And when I say let's do it right, I mean let's do it the best way. That's my way. People used to make me feel like I was being picky or like I was always going to extremes because of my attitude. But the way I see it, whether I'm fixing a light switch or launching a space vehicle, I can't be satisfied until I'm sure that the very best tools were used, the finest materials selected, and all the correct procedures followed. That way, there's no question that when I flick the switch, the light goes on, or the rocket lifts from the pad, on time and on course. After watching my Influencing TV Twins, I know that they feel the same way."

No matter what he is doing, the Influencing Personality is presiding and calling the shots. In a restaurant he expects to be seated immediately and to be served well. If he orders a two-inch New York steak for dinner, measure it before you bring it from the kitchen. And if he requests it medium rare, well seared on both sides, only that will do. Anything else will be sent back with a sizzling comment. If he is really displeased, he may walk out, but only after he has fully registered his grievance. When the fare is excellent and the service attentive, he may say nothing, but he will tip generously. And he will come back. He tends to return to familiar places where he can expect high quality and good service, whatever the price.

Ultimate results demand ultimate command over the process. Thus you insist on being expertly knowledgeable about all phases of the enterprise you are undertaking. For you, there's nothing worse than being a struggling beginner, or even worse, a mediocre journeyman. It's just not in your blood.

Ultimate results also demand the best ingredients. Charles Emerson Winchester of the M*A*S*H 4077th knows perfectly well that you don't throw a first-class welcome with cheap wine or GI gin. Dr. Craig, of "St. Elsewhere," was born with the knowledge that one does not give a proper Christmas party with a cheap dimestore garland or paper cups. And at the crown of his Christmas tree you'll never find a plastic angel; at the top of his tree is the same silver star that has graced the family trees for the past 120 years, complemented by an ornament forged in Philadelphia by Samuel Craig at the time of the Continental Congress. When it comes time for the toast to be made, Dr. Craig does it in the traditional Middle English dialect. Now that's real class.

NOT A BETTER, BUT THE BEST MOUSETRAP

You're not interested in building a better mousetrap; you want to build the perfect mousetrap—the paramount, definitive mousetrap. This passion for the ultimate shows in everything you attempt—or you wouldn't attempt it. If you don't have the opportunity for perfection and the control it takes to achieve it, chances are you'll avoid getting involved in the first place. As we observed earlier, there's nothing worse for the Influencing Personality than to make an obvious effort and be mediocre.

An Influencing woman came to me, telling me of the problems she and her non-Influencing husband were having decorating their home. She wanted the ultimate; he was willing to settle for adequate. 'I would leave the window bare rather than buy inexpensive drapes,'' she said. ''And I wouldn't really mind going into debt to have them custom made and professionally hung. It's just the way I like things. But before we watched Dr. Craig, Charles Winchester, and Jennifer, he didn't understand. Now he does and is willing to concede.''

Well, Charles Emerson Winchester would not turn out to greet the visiting Swedish surgeon at all if he could not at least present her with a bottle of vintage wine. Dr. Craig would not even bother with a Christmas party if he couldn't treat his guests to the finest. And you are not going to take up tennis unless you can buy the best racquet, take lessons from a pro, and dress in appropriate clothing. So whether it's home decoration, wine, Christmas parties, or tennis, if the opportunity for the best is not there, then you will probably avoid involvement altogether. It just has to be that way.

And what about the cost? As Blake Carrington says, ''I don't care how much money it costs. I don't care how much time it takes.'' You only get what you pay for.

AT THE CONTROLS

How does one arrive at the finer things in life? Well, put someone at the controls who appreciates and desires the finer things, of course. And so it is with the Influencing Personality. You know better than any that there is no faster way to the sloppy, the shoddy, and the mediocre than to leave things up to chance. So who better to put in charge than yourself?

On ''Dynasty,'' we can watch Blake Carrington stride into the boardroom where the board of directors is mulling over a decision as to how to rescue Denver Carrington stock from a downward plunge. Blake immediately takes command of the situation without a blink. The solution, of course, is to take over the rival company, Colbyco, that is the source of Denver

Carrington's problems. "Now, once and for all, let's get them," says Blake.

I guarantee you have never seen Fonzie, on "Happy Days," hesitate to take over a room, or even an entire restaurant. In one segment, there's trouble at Arnold's, a local teen hangout. In walks the Fonz to calm the situation. "There is a rule," he announces. "There's not a word spoken in this room unless it's warm and loving." It begins to warm up immediately.

On "Newhart," there is trouble also. The town's annual Snow Carnival is about to be canceled due to lack of snow. But Influencing Stephanie has been chosen Ice Maiden for the festival, and it's an honor she's not about to give up. So she stands up at the town meeting where the cancellation of the carnival is being discussed and takes charge. "I'm Stephanie VanderKellen and I've heard just about enough. Not only do I insist that the carnival continue, I demand that it snow, immediately."

An exaggerated example? Of course. But it serves to show the Influencing Personality's need, and knack, for being at the helm. "Yes, I can see the need to control things in myself," said one Influencing Personality after watching Blake, Stephanie, and the Fonz. "It used to drive me crazy when my wife and I would go to a party, or shopping, and only take one car. She would want to stay for hours and I couldn't stand not being able to leave when I felt it was time. We had a lot of arguments over that. But after we recognized the problem, the solution was clear. We would just drive separate cars. That gave me an escape hatch, the control over the situation, so I had a way out in case I got bored or just wanted to leave before her."

As we concluded earlier, ultimate results demand ultimate control over the process. In a "WKRP" segment, we see Herb, a guest, begin acting up and causing a disturbance at Influencing Jennifer's party. But she has the situation totally in hand. "Herb," she says softly, "Andy would like to see you in the kitchen." The hint is taken, Herb removes himself from the scene, Jennifer maintains her control, Herb maintains his dignity, and the party rolls right along.

On "Magnum, P.I.," Influencing Higgins exerts his control in a less subtle manner. He needs to speak with his associate, Tom Magnum. It is very early in the morning but Higgins knocks on Magnum's door anyway. "I must speak to you," he says through the door. "I'm sleeping," mumbles Magnum. But in walks Higgins anyway. There is no time to sit and dawdle while others sleep the day away. There is important, pressing business.

Some who do not understand the Influencing mind might interpret Higgins's action as downright rude. But for the Influencing Personality to be his best, he has to do, and be able to do, his best. And the best cannot always wait until others decide that the time is right. The best cannot be subject to whim.

We watch Stephanie, on "Newhart," try to carry on an important conversation with her boyfriend. His mind is elsewhere; she takes charge and judo-flips him onto the sofa. His attention is immediately captured.

There are, of course, more subtle ways to exercise and maintain command over your life and surroundings. One Influencing Personality recounted this example after watching her TV Twins: "A group of my friends were kicking around the idea of a ski vacation. But out of the twelve people in the room, there were twelve different ideas of where to go and when. The debate could have gone on until the snow melted. I knew I would have to step in and bring the trip together, but I didn't want them to feel like I was just taking over. I've seen, from my Influencing Twins on TV, the good and bad points of assuming that everyone wants you to be in charge. So I took the position of pointing out the merits and disadvantages of each suggestion, sharpening the focus, organizing the information, and moderating the discussion until I finally had all twelve agreeing on time and place. Naturally, they put me in charge of coordinating the trip itself. They knew that I would arrange a ski trip to end all ski trips. Everyone ended up happy. They got what they wanted." Proof again that the Influencing Personality is born to lead.

THE THREE-OPTION SOLUTION

You are a take-charge person, wanting and willing to take responsibility for whatever is going on around you. "I'm never at a loss as to how to cope with a situation," is how one Influencing Personality explains it. "I have to have a way of reacting, whether it be the right thing or not. That's just how I am." For you, it's just a matter of seeing the need for your fine touch in every situation.

There are times when the need to react, take charge, and exert your influence calls out to you with too many voices. It seems that everyone in your family is having a problem; everyone needs some sort of assistance, a commanding presence. Your ability to keep things under control and moving along smoothly is stretched to the limit. Then you begin to lose control.

"When people need assistance I jump in first," says one Influencing woman who is familiar with the problem. "I watch Dorothy on "Golden Girls" and can see how she steps in to take over other people's problems. In one episode, Dorothy's housemate Blanche's niece came to stay but was having some real problems handling herself around men. Blanche was at a loss as to what to do, but Dorothy immediately stepped in. In another episode, housemate Rose's sister, who was blind, came to stay and was experiencing some difficulties in accepting and coping with her blindness. Dorothy automatically stepped in there also. But sometimes in my life I bite off more than I can chew. I get angry and don't know what else to do. Sometimes I can't control all the things that go on around me, but I have great difficulty letting someone else take over."

Another Influencing empathizer agrees. "I get very frustrated when I can't figure out what to do about my children's problems. But I don't like it when someone points out to me that I'm not in control of my own children."

An Influencing man came to me with the same sort of problem. His brother had gotten a divorce and for financial reasons had to move back in with his father. Our Influencing friend's brother and father had been arguing, fighting, and struggling.

When he went over to talk to his brother about the situation, the brother would get angry, resent the interference, start an argument, and the entire scene would quickly deteriorate. What to do? How to remedy a situation that was out of control? How not to feel like a failure when the situation seems beyond you?

Well, let's sit down for a moment and watch Blake Carrington on "Dynasty." It seems that Blake has finally come to terms with a family situation that had looked hopeless. He had been struggling for quite some time to accept the fact that his son Steven was a homosexual and the situation had reached a standstill; Blake lost control and was alienating his son in the process. Then he discovered the perfect way to resolve the dilemma: he followed the "three-option solution." Instead of locking himself into a power struggle, he decided finally that he could shut his son out of his life, continue to struggle, or accept the fact that he could not make the choice of sexual preference for his son. In the end, he accepted the fact that he could not be responsible for Steven's sexual preference, but would continue to love him as a son and feel good about himself, even though he wasn't in total command.

After viewing that segment, my Influencing friend was able to apply the three-option solution to his own personal dilemma. "I finally realized that my brother and father didn't want me to take over, but they did want my support. So I guess I gave myself three choices: I could either continue to try to take over, be a good listener, or just walk away from it. I finally settled on option number two and things have worked out well. They both feel better for having someone to talk with and I don't have to take on the responsibility of the situation." For him, the pressure was off.

Another Influencing Personality was also having a problem that called for the three-option solution. She had retired from her job in order to care for an invalid aunt, but she was torn between the need to take care of her aunt, and the very strong need to take command of her life and enjoy a much needed vacation.

We watched Influencing Stephanie, on "Newhart," as she wrestled with a similar problem. The inn where Stephanie works is in the midst of a measles outbreak. The owner, his wife, the handyman, and even some of the guests are bedridden, and Stephanie is left in charge. The work is getting to be too much, she is losing control, and she is afraid of how bad she will look with the red spots all over her own beautiful face. She gives herself three choices: she can call the doctor to stop by and help; she can abandon the situation and go home to mother; or she can continue to handle the whole thing by herself. In the end, she decides to stick it out and handles the situation quite well.

"After watching Stephanie, I was able to relate her situation to mine and give myself options concerning the care of my aunt," said my Influencing friend. "I told myself I could either take off and let someone else take over, give up the idea of a vacation, or have someone come in and take over part time. I finally decided to have some part-time help. Before, I probably would have felt like I was being wishy-washy by giving myself three options and letting someone else take over part of the responsibility. But now I can see how giving myself options takes the pressure off and enables me to make the best decision."

THE GRAND CONVERSATIONALIST

"You can always tell when an Influencing Personality is riding the bus," an Influencing man said to me one day. "He or she will get on and start telling a story to the person in the next seat. When the bus comes to the Influencing person's stop, if the story is still going on, half the people who were within earshot will get off too, whether it's their stop or not, just to hear the end of the story."

The Influencing Personality's conversational style follows the same basic pattern as his other activities: an appreciation for, and striving after, the ultimate. You can capture any crowd by weaving a spellbinding tale, controlling their attention by a scene that is alive, right down to the smallest detail.

On "Golden Girls," Influencing Dorothy's sister is visiting and she reminisces about the mesmerizing bedtime stories Dorothy used to tell when they were both young girls. "Oh yes," Dorothy recalls, "stories like the bogeyman and the little girl, the zombie in the hamper, and cannibal parents. I think between the ages of five and seven you might have gotten two hours' sleep."

Meanwhile, at the 4077th M*A*S*H, we once again watch Charles greeting a visiting surgeon with a bottle of vintage wine and immediately launching into a story: "Ah, the grape, whose mist of skin is a pale membrane between the workaday and the holiday." When he discovers that the surgeon is Swedish, the story continues: "Ah, Sweden, the jewel in the crown of Scandinavia," he begins, then proceeds to tell of a Swedish scullery maid his parents had when he was young.

And what better time to gather the group around for a wonderful story than at the grand and glorious Christmas party Dr. Craig is having for his fellow doctors from St. Elsewhere. He tells the story of how his Christmas tree became an archive of the family history: the same star has been placed on the top for the past 120 years, the ornaments have been made by his family members since the eighteenth century. And while he has the room's undivided attention, he continues the spell by proposing a toast—in Middle English dialect.

But Dr. Craig has had a bit too much to drink and accidentally drops his cup of punch to the floor in the middle of the toast. One uncomprehending guest, thinking that was part of the ceremony, drops his cup also. Dr. Craig is interrupted and the spell is temporarily broken. "Now I have to start all over again," says the disgruntled doctor.

An Influencing woman, who had just watched that segment, was able to relate to Dr. Craig's annoyance. "I don't like to repeat myself when I'm telling a story or making a point," she said, "but, like Dr. Craig, I insist on not being interrupted."

When an Influencing Personality speaks, even E.F. Hutton listens. You tell a story so well that you are rarely interrupted. But God help the thoughtless person who cuts in before you've finished. That sorry soul might get a silencing stare that could pierce a two-inch steel plate. Just catch the expression on Dr. Craig's face when his toast is interrupted. Or listen to Charles, on "M*A*S*H," when his story to the visiting Swedish surgeon is rudely interrupted by his associate Hawkeye, an interruption that humiliates Charles in the process. Afterwards, he comments to Hawkeye, "If I have ever led you to believe, in any way, that you are above contempt, I am profoundly sorry."

A bit less pompous, and certainly more cool in his approach to verbal control, is the Fonz on "Happy Days," as he deals with a conversation intrusion by announcing, "Don't interrupt me. I'm having a moment here."

"Well, I certainly don't feel uncomfortable now about reacting to interruptions the way I do," said my Influencing friend after she had watched Dr. Craig, Charles, and the Fonz. "I tap the offender on the shoulder, lock eyes, and we all get to hear the story again from the beginning. But it is, after all, always one hell of a story."

When you weave a web of words that is short and smooth, the audience is engrossed. But you are never simply entertaining. You are, in fact, attempting to impose verbal mastery over the occasion. "I tend, at times, to monopolize the conversation," observed one Influencing Personality after watching Charles, Dorothy, and Dr. Craig. "And when someone else is speaking, I might lose interest and let my mind wander away." It's true that you might be less interested in what others have to say than in what you have to say. But, like your Influencing TV Twins, you do it so well and with so much charm and grace that others usually want to listen. Not that they always have a choice, of course.

"I'm not much for small talk," admits one Influencing woman I know. "I tend to limit my conversation to areas where I feel competent. But even in casual conversations I like to be in control." Well, as we have seen, the desire to capture and hold your listeners with your conversation is certainly healthy for you. But just try to get those poor folks off the bus at their own stop from now on. Tell them you'll finish the story tomorrow, just for them.

FLASH! THE EXPLODING TEMPER

"When I lose my temper," observes one Influencing Personality, "I go to war."

Well, if that is so, it is simply a war against annoying interruptions, irritating criticism, and presumptuous efforts by others to take responsibility out of your hands. Those are the three major forces that can make your blood boil. Some might accuse you of making mountains out of molehills and major crises out of minor disturbances, but that is just the way a person with very high expectations of himself and the rest of the world operates.

We can watch Charles, on "M*A*S*H," blow up when Hawkeye criticizes him in front of a fellow surgeon. Or watch the storm clouds gather when Blake Carrington is being interviewed by a particularly annoying magazine reporter. The reporter is trying to corner Blake and momentarily gain the upper hand with his probing questions. When the otherwise calm and poised Influencing is crossed, the thunder and lightning strike quick and sure. "You print one word of this conversation and I'll have your head," is Blake's final word on the subject.

A short but explosive show of temper is the Influencing Personality's perfect method for bringing an unrestrained situation under control and is a perfectly normal reaction to some meddler who might mean well but is obviously out of line. On "Newhart," we watch Stephanie blow her top at her boyfriend Michael because he is letting his mother's unreasonable criticism and badgering get him down. "You are not letting that woman push you around any more, and that's an order," she tells him. Just then Michael's mother walks in. "Michael," Stephanie decrees, "carve her up."

"Some of my friends used to accuse me of making every situation into a crisis, including those who made me blow up," said one Influencing man who had come to me. "But I recognize now, after watching my Influencing TV Twins, that a grand and glorious display of temper is the quickest way to get everyone's attention, clear the air, and get things put back into line. I explode, and then it's over."

GETTING RIGHT TO THE POINT

The Influencing Personality knows that one way to keep critics, friends, family, and everyone else under tight wraps is to be brutally honest and blunt. It saves time and, while the recipient of your blunt remarks sits with his or her jaw hanging, it gives you the upper hand. As one Influencing Personality sees it, "My friends know that I can be the most charming, amiable, and gracious person on earth. But there are times when it does no good to dance around the obvious. They know I'm going to get right to the point."

We can watch Dorothy, on "Golden Girls," get right to the point. She has met a handsome doctor and is pursuing a relationship with him, but housemate Blanche informs Dorothy that the doctor has been making passes at her also. Blanche has developed a reputation over time as having a rather large appetite for the attention and affection of men. Dorothy does not want to face the fact that the doctor is not totally devoted to her, so she accuses Blanche of lying. "You're jealous," Blanche says. "You know something?" Dorothy answers. "You could never be a real friend to another woman. And you know why? Because you're a slut."

On "St. Elsewhere," Dr. Craig's wife is getting ready for a party and asks him how she looks. "Tone down the rouge and lipstick," is the doctor's assessment. "You're starting to look like Raggedy Ann."

"When something is on my mind, I let others know it," said one Influencing woman whose bluntness was causing some trouble in her life. "Like one time my husband had a friend over. They were sitting in the other room talking and I was trying to watch TV. They kept getting louder so I kept turning the volume up. Finally, I just walked into the other room and said to my husband's friend that I was sorry but he had ten minutes to leave. He did and he never comes over anymore."

We sat then and watched Dr. Craig on "St. Elsewhere" as he put it very bluntly to his mailman. It was Christmas; the mailman had just delivered a package to Dr. Craig, and was lingering in the doorway. "Don't you have some junk mail to deliver?"

asked the doctor. "It's customary for folks to give their mailman some kind of bonus at this time of year," answered the postman. "Oh yes," says the doctor, "and the amount is reflected by the quality of the service rendered. You get the Christmas goose egg. Now get out of here." Slam goes the door.

"I can't see myself reacting like him," was my Influencing friend's reaction. "But I can identify with him. It's super to be able to hear other Influencing people and how they feel and react. I learned it's OK to be myself, but I will try to control my tendency to bully. It's a technique for controlling situations, but it could destroy a good friendship or relationship."

THE KING AND QUEEN OF CLEAN

"Some of my friends call me a perfectionist," complains one Influencing Personality. "I suppose in a way it is true, but I don't really like to hear it. It's just that I like to have things just so."

Well, we've seen the top of your desk: bright and shiny, no nicks, a cup of the best brand of number two pencils, each one sharpened to a fine point; one well-ordered file open, its contents neat and tidy. And we've seen your kitchen: meticulous, never a dirty dish in the sink, floor shiny and truly clean enough to eat from, although it would be much nicer to use the Royal Doulton.

We only have to watch Dorothy create an absolute crisis over finding a mouse in the kitchen to discover that "cleanomania" is a universal Influencing trait. "Oh my God, I can't believe it," says Dorothy. "A rat." Non-Influencing housemate Rose is calm. "It wasn't a rat, it was a cute little mouse." But Dorothy is unmoved. "Rose, it doesn't wear little white gloves and work at Disneyland. We're talking about a rodent here."

"My home is a showplace," said an Influencing woman after watching Dorothy, "and I guess you could call me an immaculate housekeeper. I like the towels and linens folded just so, and the cap put back on the toothpaste tube. And I guess I do get a little carried away sometimes like Dorothy. I remember asking my husband over and over again to quit leaving his coat and sweater draped over his chair in the living room, but he kept ignoring me. Finally, I took them both out to the garbage can.''

Your lawn is cut and trimmed twice a week, whether it needs it or not, and looks like the cover of *Better Homes and Gardens.* Even your garage is as clean, spotless, and well organized as a hospital operating room. Don't let those cries of ''perfectionist'' from the untidy and unruly get to you. Take heart from your TV Twin, David Hartman of ''Good Morning America,'' who once revealed in an interview that the best therapy for him after a hard day is to go home and clean out his refrigerator.

GOOD LOOKS, GOOD HEALTH, AND THE UNIFORM OF THE DAY

Just watch Fonzie, of ''Happy Days'' fame, check out his pompadour in the mirror. He walks by, takes a look, raises his arm to comb, then decides that the picture is perfect. Now watch Stephanie, on ''Newhart,'' as she frets over having to care for a houseful of measles sufferers. ''Doc Wiley,'' she groans to the visiting doctor, ''I'm sick too.'' The doc gives a quick once over. ''Well, you look perfect to me.'' ''Of course,'' is her reply.

The Influencing Personality takes just as much meticulous care with his appearance, personal habits, and health as he does with his surroundings. Sharp creases, well-groomed hair, shined shoes, and a dazzling smile can only make you feel comfortable and in command.

For you, looking good applies to all situations. Even the casual is calculated, and the Influencing Personality will always dress for the occasion: the ''uniform of the day.''

When you show up for a cookout, it's jeans and tennis sneakers, that's true. But the jeans are the best designer style, freshly pressed, and the sneakers are spotless, snow white. The old sweatshirt you wear for the coed touch football game says Harvard. Friends of ''Today'' show's Bryant Gumble claim that Influencing Bryant will try on five or six shirts in the locker room before a golf game to achieve just the right look.

"I don't think there's any excuse for looking sloppy or being inappropriately dressed," is one Influencing Personality's assessment of the "uniform of the day" theory. "An executive should dress like an executive, not a college student or a tourist in Miami. Wherever you are and whatever you're doing, you should look sharp and be sharp. That's the best way to command attention and respect."

For the well-dressed and -coiffed Influencing Personality, it's not enough to look good on the outside. Mastery of good health and fitness is also of utmost importance. Illness, a potbelly, or a sagging behind are all signs that you're out of touch and out of control.

Firm, sleek Blake Carrington radiates good health and power. And Stephanie, of "Newhart," expresses what might be a universal Influencing view of an unhealthy state. When she is stuck taking care of the measles sufferers, she complains to her mother on the phone: "Oh, I'm terrible. I'm surrounded by sick people here. And you know, I don't even like to be on the same planet with mucus."

"It's true," commented one Influencing woman on her TV Twins's view of health and fitness. "If I miss a day of work because of the flu, it's torture. I don't like to be sick and don't like others to know that I can't keep myself well and healthy."

Another Influencing Personality had been wrestling with a weight problem, but had finally gotten the upper hand. "If you can't manage yourself, how can you expect to command any attention or respect from others?" she asked. Incidentally, when she finally did reach the size she wanted to be, she treated herself to a new wardrobe. For her, the uniform of the day became the look of thinness and power.

THE INFLUENCING PERSONALITY AT WORK

The adult Influencing Personality is usually a very productive person in whatever occupation he or she chooses. But you especially like those areas that permit you to function at a high level of structure, organization, quality, and control. You will function well in any group enterprise where there is a clear line of responsibility, especially when you have the opportunity to exert leadership. You are quite comfortable doing detail work, systematic analysis, and planning—anything that permits you a logical, structured approach: logic permits consistency and control.

The Influencing woman will enter the marketplace with the same energy and purpose as her male counterpart. She will pursue her goals with the same quest for excellence and control. If she encounters sexual discrimination in the working world, she won't hesitate to fight for her rights; remember, the Influencing Personality would rather fight than flee.

Male or female, the Influencing Personality is not driven so much by ambition and competition—as the Ambitious Personality would be—as by the need to be productive and efficient, and to maintain control of his or her enterprise. Again, winning is simply a by-product of playing one's own game—by one's own rules.

"I don't necessarily have to be corporate president, or a Blake Carrington," says one Influencing executive, "but I do want to rise as high as I can commensurate with my ability to maintain quality of product and control of my own working environment. It's the 'big fish in the little pond' theory." In other words, if more power can be wielded from the trenches than from the throne room, then stay in the trenches and redecorate.

Another Influencing Personality noted, "I've watched Dr. Craig on 'St. Elsewhere' and Blake Carrington, and I've noticed how they're always taking charge of the situation. I have done that too. But I also know how draining it can be if you try to handle too much or take on too much responsibility. It's hard to walk away from it, although I know now that I have to. But I can see the pressure it puts on them when things get out of hand. I know I just can't let my eyes be bigger than my reach."

The Influencing Personality often extends his reach by gathering and grooming a loyal group of followers. You may also find, in the ranks of the faithful, one who is especially suited to continue the search for excellence: a protégé. After watching Blake Carrington groom his son Adam and send him off to carry on the family enterprises, one successful Influencing businessman was moved to comment, "In order to reach those who are hesitant to follow your path, surround yourself with a cadre who isn't." And that, my friends, is the Influencing business commandment of the day.

The Influencing woman who chooses home and family is no less interested in maintaining control over her environment and performing efficiently and well. She too will be driven by the urge for the ultimate, and she tends to be an immaculate housekeeper. (Note: no matter where the housekeeping responsibilities may fall, many Influencing Personalities have found, after a tough day, genuine therapeutic value in "cleaning out the refrigerator.")

COURTSHIP AND MARRIAGE

The Influencing Personality is drawn to the person who is physically attractive, neat in appearance and dress, and attentive. Dirt under the fingernails is a kiss of death for any potential suitor. The Influencing Personality's courtship rite is deliberate; he or she wants to make a strong showing and a very good impression—extensions, again, of a desire to be top-drawer and to maintain control. He or she will take a date places that reflect a tendency to extravagance and quality: always the best.

"I tend to maneuver my date into following my direction, especially if he seems indecisive or suggests something I don't really feel I'm going to enjoy," says one Influencing woman. "I have watched Influencing Stephanie, on 'Newhart,' and how she almost bullies her boyfriend into doing what she wants. Of course, it's exaggerated, but it does serve to prove the point. I'm not a bit hesitant about suggesting dinner at a good restaurant or good seats at the theater. I'll coax my date into trying skiing, which I like, even if he's not particularly interested. If a boyfriend pleads poverty, I'll invite him up to my apartment for some gourmet cooking. I tend to guide the relationship, or at least I try. It used to seem pushy. But now, after becoming acquainted with and watching my Influencing TV Twins, it seems natural."

The Influencing Personality may choose a partner in marriage whom he can dominate—or at least one who will permit him enough scope to pursue his quest for control and the ultimate in all essential matters. The Influencing woman may choose a man "who needs me" so that she dominates. The male, similarly, may choose a submissive woman. But this need to structure and control a relationship sometimes creates tension and conflict. Not surprising would be a marriage where the partners maintained independent careers and separate interests, a style of peaceful coexistence that would keep the marriage afloat.

The Influencing woman might be content early in the marriage to be a homemaker and mother. Given the opportunity, she might blend a career outside the home with her role as homemaker, but only if it did not jeopardize her image as the quintessential wife and mother.

The Influencing partner likes to maintain tight schedules, long-range blueprints of family life, and control of the budget. He is tempted to instruct everyone on how to do the various housekeeping tasks. The Influencing husband would not hesitate to show his wife how to make a bed with hospital corners or how to iron his shirts or even how to vacuum the carpet.

The Influencing parent and spouse may have a difficult time avoiding seeing things only from his own perspective and interest. He is prone to go his own way, and expects others to accept his determination of how things ought to be. One example is an Influencing wife and mother who viewed her husband's company Christmas party as a chore and a bore. It was outside her sphere of interests—and her control. But something happened one Christmas party to change all that: "I didn't want to go. It was all so boring until suddenly I began to see it from my little girl's point of view: Just relax, have fun, spend one evening going with the flow. Then I had a ball." This remarkable insight was productive for both Influencing mother and non-Influencing child.

TO THE EDGE AND BEYOND

There is something very addictive about taking charge and taking things to the top, or at least to the very edge. When you triumph over yourself and the elements, show that you are the master of any possible adversity or opponent, there comes a sublime satisfaction that only you, the Influencing Personality, can experience.

"I like to be on the edge sometimes," is how one Influencing Personality explains it. "Once you've done something well, reached the heights, established a certain command over it, it becomes boring to keep doing it over and over again. You look for new worlds to conquer."

Doing something well, and with the precise control it requires, will keep you on top of the world. Watch Influencing Lance, on "Falcon Crest," as he pushes his motorcycle to the limits; he is dressed in the best leathers, riding the best, superbly tuned high-tech bike, leaning into turns, floating over the road with the finest of balance. But his non-Influencing passenger is urging him to slow down. She doesn't understand. And when he swerves and barely slips between two trucks, she insists that he stop. "Promise that you'll drive like a sane person or I won't go on," she orders. Yeah, sure, he promises. But he is perfectly sane and healthy. He is an Influencing Personality. Zoom, the motorcycle is immediately back up to dizzying speed and he is leaning perfectly into the next bend.

Case closed.

ALTERNATIVES AND OPTIONS

The Influencing Personality's great productivity, his pursuit of excellence, his great efficiency, his leadership ability, his diligence and tenacity, offer much to his personal life and to the life of his community. But his singular point of view and his drive for control and constant demand for the ultimate can be limiting and debilitating when carried to excess. He can avoid such a narrow and rigid approach by conquering the fear of failure and imperfection and by learning to recognize life in all its richness and diversity. Those persons close to him, whether family, friends, or working associates, can also benefit by being aware and by contributing to his own awareness of his style of behavior.

The key to understanding the Influencing Personality is recognizing his identification of worth with his urge for the ultimate, his passion for perfection, and his need to control his environment. The best way to prevent his tendency to excess is to help him to relat openly to others in a free-flowing way—and without always attempting to exert control over the relationship.

The Influencing Personality needs to understand that making mistakes is an acceptable part of learning and proving. Failure doesn't necessarily lessen self-worth.

The Influencing Personality needs to know that in the journey through life he doesn't always have to be the driver to enjoy the ride.

If you are an Influencing Personality, consider the following:

- Establish what your life priorities are. Frequently remind yourself of them.
- Consider the high price you pay sometimes for your struggle for control—being overly responsible can take its toll on you.
- Give yourself three options before beginning any project or undertaking.
- Realize that you are capable of many feelings other than anger. Don't deny, minimize, or suppress feelings of tenderness, closeness; they are very productive and healthy emotions.
- Beware of your bullying tendency. It is another way to control a situation but it destroys good relationships with your children, spouse, coworkers, and friends.
- Stop trying to change people. Try working with them and enjoying what they have to offer.
- Don't let your attempts at organization become manipulative. When genuine interaction and open communication are smothered by your efforts, order becomes a dictatorship.
- Look for the small pleasures in life. Don't expect life to provide an endless series of grand and glorious experiences. En-

joy the company of friends for the sake of friendship, and the simple things.

- Don't let your concern for neatness and appearance become a fetish for perfection. People judge your worth by your total person and not by the clothes you wear.
- Let the spontaneous into your life. Good things, and good feelings, have a way of popping up unexpectedly.
- When it's your highest priority, don't be afraid to go for the ultimate.
- Let yourself laugh. It is very human and a perfect antidote for anger.
- When you find yourself losing control of your temper, try counting to ten. But count our special way—one, two, three, five, seven, nine, ten. It will give you pause enough to collect yourself.
- The quality of life is measured more by feelings than by purchasing power. Love, human contact, giving, *and* receiving bring out the best in all of us. And you do, after all, want the best.

SECRETS

The keys to a successful relationship with the Influencing Personality are:

- As much as possible, allow the Influencing Personality to be in control, at least of his or her own movements and activities. Give three options.
- No black smudges on the whitewalls, no handprints on the refrigerator, no loose ends or dangling threads.
- The Influencing Personality is not interested in second-class substitutes. It's all or nothing. The best or forget it.
- Don't interrupt that terrific story.
- Those sudden flashes of temper will soon cool, those blunt remarks are not always to be taken to heart.
- Enjoy the ultimate treatment. You're in good . . . the best . . . hands.

MATCH AND MISMATCH

Influencing Personality matchmates:

Accomplishing—Both of you share a strong sense of enthusiasm, energy, and social ability. The Accomplishing person tries hard to please, and all you have to do is give your approval. Both enjoy neat and clean surroundings, and there is never a dull moment.

Ambitious—Both of you are powerful Personalities, hard workers who enjoy challenges and opportunities to succeed; then come the grand celebrations. Both have somewhat extravagant tastes. Only the best will do for you.

Idealistic—The Idealistic shares your desire for top quality. Communication between the two of you is straightforward and plentiful. You both tend to be rather intense in your actions and life style. The Idealistic Personality encourages you to explore options and live on the edge.

Persistent—Persistent persons are very attentive to all that you do and make you feel special. They encourage you to relax, to take life easy occasionally, and share your love for the grand and glorious. However, you tend to be more down to earth, while they have their head in the clouds. Neatness is not so important to them, which can be very aggravating to you.

Sensitive—Sensitive persons may admire your take-charge abilities and verbal nature. They make it easy for you to have time for your top priorities. They're always aware of your moods and inclinations, but your temper can be overwhelming to them. They need time to prepare and rehearse, while you want things done right now.

Adaptable—Adaptables will listen to your ideas and opinions, share your enjoyment of the trendy, the current, the finer things in life. They also share your desire for socializing and entertaining. Their interest in your opinion should not be mistaken for wanting you to take the responsibility for a problem. They seek many opinions, not just yours. You like control in all areas, but the Adaptable person has many and varied interests and friends. This is a source of conflict.

Anticipating—They praise you for your capabilities and are impressed by your desire for quality. You emphasize time and schedules, but this interferes with Anticipating individuals' plans. You move quickly, while they use a gradual approach. Your temper can harm their self-importance. You can be extravagant; they are practical.

Conscientious—The Conscientious shares your desire for facts and figures and your need for an orderly approach. But you like to charge ahead, to be in control, while the Conscientious person wants all the facts first. You arrive at a decision quickly and implement it, while the Conscientious is still gathering data. The Conscientious person's humor may ease the tension, but only for a while.

Determined—Both of you are responsible and desire organization and structure, but so much for the similarities. While you fight openly, the Determined person fights in a very covert fashion. You're rather verbal, while this person is not. Push too hard and the Determined person goes on strike, clams up, becomes quietly defiant. You are a person of the moment, while the Determined Personality likes to sit on dead center and wait for the right moment.

Perceptive—Tempers can flare rather quickly here. You are both affectionate and feeling-oriented, but demands made by you will meet with strong, overt resistance. The Perceptive complains quite readily and feels mistreated. Your willingness to take charge is seen as unfair.

Patient—You are attracted initially to what you perceive as a great tolerance and willingness to listen. Your giving instructions and making decisions will meet with apparent acceptance but little or no follow-through. You're up front, while the Patient person deals with things in an indirect fashion and may hide problems from you. You play the heavy and he or she comes out smelling like a rose.

Chapter Ten

THE PATIENT PERSONALITY

PROFILE

- Wants security for self and others.
- Does not like to rock the boat.
- Appears very generous and giving.
- Will be reluctant to make own needs and wants known.
- Promotes peace and calm, often acts as "referee."

TV TWINS

- Krystle—"Dynasty"
- Maggie—"Falcon Crest"
- Alex—"Taxi"
- Jeff—"The Colbys"
- Miss Ellie—"Dallas"
- Jenna Wade—"Dallas"
- Lester—"227"
- Ben—"Knots Landing"
- Dr. Westfall—"St. Elsewhere"
- Edith Bunker—"All in the Family"

Imagine that I told you, a Patient Personality, that I was going to explain your Personality to you. Then we were interrupted, there were some other delays, and a great deal of time passed.

If you are truly a Patient Personality, you would probably sit quietly and calmly waiting for me to finally get around to it.

After a while, you would probably start dropping some subtle hints, giving an undetectable nudge here and there. You'd give a little sigh, make an offhanded comment about how well all of those other Personalities have been described, hoping that I would finally pick up on the fact that you were ready to read about yourself.

But you would be very hesitant to come right out and ask me to get to it. That might cause a confrontation, or worse the answer might be a "no." And neither response would be a pleasant experience for you.

Don't get me wrong. You do have wants and needs, and you do manage to get your message across and get what you want sometimes. But yours is a very subtle way, and because of that your patience serves you well.

What the Apostle Paul wrote of love in his first letter to the Corinthians comes remarkably close to describing the strengths of the Patient Personality:

> Love is patient; love is kind. Love is not jealous, it does not put on airs, it is not snobbish. Love is never rude, it is not self-seeking; it is not prone to anger; neither does it brood over injuries. Love does not rejoice in what is wrong but rejoices with the truth. There is no limit to love's forbearance, to its trust, its hope, its power to endure. (1 Corinthians 13:4–7)

The Patient Personality is indeed patient and kind, even humble. His forbearance, tolerance, and endurance are remarkable. He is known to be a bit jealous and to brood (no one is perfect), but he softens this with silence.

What is so noticeable about the Patient Personality is his great generosity. He is always doing something for others in a quiet, unpretentious way. The Patient father will willingly rake the baseball diamond after his son's Little League game. The unmarried Patient aunt might help finance a niece's college education. The Patient neighbor would be willing to babysit your children while you keep a doctor's appointment.

But before we get carried away here and hand out the Nobel Prize for generosity, an important point should be made. The

Patient Personality really isn't that prone to volunteer. Rather, others sense that you are usually available and apparently willing to give assistance when asked. You, sometimes to your regret, are just as aware of your availability. But you find it hard to say no. And, as with all good things, many will take advantage of this unceasing service. You will seldom ask for anything in return. It's not that you don't want or need; it's just that you find it very hard to ask.

You need to be wanted and liked and you have a tendency to dote on those you especially care about and love. That explains your reluctance to say no. You go along with what's asked or needed because you don't want to risk hurting feelings or alienating those whose affection and attention you thrive on. It also explains your hesitation in coming right out and asking for anything you want or need. You might put an undue burden on someone with your request, or they might refuse. For you, it's safer and easier just to keep on giving.

But even you have your limits. There always seems to be someone who abuses your good nature and stretches your limits. You still won't come right out and refuse, even if the demands are coming hot and heavy; you just have your own special way of saying no. You will just go about your business at your own pace, in your own sweet time. Or you will just quietly do nothing. Then heaven help the poor devil who still doesn't get the message. He or she is about to witness the rarely seen eruption of the Patient temper.

The Patient Personality is the peacemaker. Confrontation, fights, and arguments are things you steer very clear of. If you are forced to face them, you usually are the referee who will step in between, urging both sides to step back and cool off.

You have a tremendous ability to find the good in everyone and everything. You know that if you wait out a situation long enough, chances are you will come out of it looking good. You believe that if you just let the dust settle, problems will work themselves out.

Some might accuse you of seeing the world through rose-colored glasses; and it may be true that you are, at times, just a little too tolerant and a little too ready to hide your disappointment. But you'll still take peace at almost any price. Speaking of price, the Patient Personality knows the price of real security and stability. You avoid the risk of having to depend too much on others by carefully tucking away a little nest egg as a hedge against having to ask for anything.

Total financial independence would be nice, but you don't want to separate yourself from the warmth of human contact. Home is where the heart is. So the next best possible alternative is to look for a lover or a mate who is sensitive to your wants and needs.

MEET YOUR TV TWINS

The Patient Personality is always on the lookout for the person who has that peaceful presence, someone who exudes security and comfort, is keenly alert to needs and meets them.

Who better meets those qualifications than your Patient TV Twins? They'll be easy to identify because they are:

- Optimistic and positive.
- Reluctant to express their own needs and wishes.
- Unselfish.
- Interested in their security and the security of those close to them.
- Willing to help others.
- Reluctant to react under pressure and will move at their own sweet pace, or not at all.

You and your TV Twins maintain a pleasant, peaceful exterior. The look on your face ranges from serene composure to a smile—a rosy, radiant smile that reflects your attitude of tolerance. You believe that if you let the dust settle, problems will work themselves out—nudged along gently by your good common sense. You like to look good and you like everyone else to look good. When too many demands are made of you too often, you can erupt and let others know in no uncertain terms, "You're asking too much of me."

On "Dallas," Patient **Miss Ellie** is the glue that holds a large

Texas oil family, the Ewings, together. She is mother, confessor, peacemaker. When the situation calls for it, she guides the course of family affairs with her gentle, subtle, but powerful Patient persuasion.

We can watch Patient **Krystle,** on "Dynasty," as she exercises her patience and forbearance with powerful and demanding husband Blake. It is Krystle who offers to help and advise others when they are upset about their relationship with Alexis. Krystle will even go so far as to offer her advice and help to Alexis herself, despite the fact that Alexis obviously despises her.

Maggie, on "Falcon Crest," exhibits similar patience with her husband and friends, all the while working, like Krystle, to develop her own feelings of security and seeking to have her own needs met in an unobtrusive way. She carries on the Patient "silent struggle" against her husband, who is pressuring her to come home after she has gone off for a while by herself to try and collect her thoughts. She is very sweet, but firm, when she informs him, "You can't push me on this."

On "The Colbys," Patient **Jeff Colby** listens carefully as a young woman describes to him how she was forced to pawn some of her jewelry soon after she arrived in town in order to meet her living expenses. A bit later in the episode, Jeff presents the jewelry, which he has redeemed, back to her. The woman immediately offers to reimburse Jeff. "That's not necessary," he says, "just consider them a gift from a new friend."

It takes a great deal of patience to be a big-city cab driver and **Alex,** a cab driver on "Taxi," exercises his forbearance in dealing with fares and friends. In one episode, he keeps the peace and endures the homemade wine that his friend Latka has brought for dinner. "I make it with honey," says the proud Latka of the gooey brew. "Oh, it goes equally well with fish, meat, or waffles," observes Alex as he chokes it down.

Patient **Jenna Wade,** on "Dallas," also does her best to keep the peace in the rough-and-tumble world of oil-rich Dallas.

On "227," Patient **Lester** is father and hardworking family man who appreciates the security of home, wife, and child. In one episode, he is recalling the night his daughter was born.

Wife Mary had had a very difficult time with the birth, and she couldn't recall whether or not Lester had stayed around through all of the screaming and moaning. "I couldn't leave you there like that," says Lester. "I mean, they'd have had to drag me out of that hospital." If Patient **Dr. Westfall,** of "St. Elsewhere," had been on duty that night, he surely would have understood.

The Patient Personality's feelings toward life and the security of family and home are probably best summed up by **Ben,** on "Knots Landing," when he observes in one episode, "I'm an old-fashioned kind of guy. I love my wife and I love those babies. My family is very important to me."

Who gets the award for the longest-suffering, most forbearing, even-tempered, unflagging Patient TV Twin of them all? That has to be **Edith Bunker,** Archie's better half on "All in the Family." Always supper on the table, certainly loving through better or worse, but a strong-minded Patient Personality after all, who knows just when to draw the line between martyr and loving family life preserver. She is forever keeping the peace between husband Archie and son-in-law Mike, between Archie and the neighbors, and in her own life.

As you follow your TV Twins' video lives, look carefully for examples of:

- Reluctance to ask for help.
- Hinting—persuading in a gentle, indirect manner.
- Attraction to generous, giving persons.
- Promoting peace and disliking violence.
- Ability to see the good in others.
- A calm and unruffled life approach.

You and your TV Twins are practical and factual persons. You're flexible and concerned with the reactions of others. You lead gently by your own silent demonstration of strength. When you are given a task, you like to carry it out at your own pace. You learn best by being given instructions and then being allowed to follow them in your own style. You become creative when you make a project your own, get at its basic and practical points, then carry on from there.

HELP AND HELP SOME MORE

One of the first things we would recognize in the Patient Personality is your generosity. You are almost always giving or doing for others in a quiet, unpretentious way.

When a young couple he knows are having financial problems, Alex, on "Taxi," steps forward to offer a personal loan.

Nobody gives so much soothing advice and reassurance around Dallas and the Ewing ranch as Miss Ellie. She will do and give far beyond the call of duty to keep the impossible Ewing clan together.

The Patient Personality fears for his security and the security of friends and loved ones, so he responds to anyone in his environment who seeks or needs his assistance. "I'm in a position to help people," says one Patient Personality, "and I would be wrong not to help them."

The last doctor in town to make house calls very well might be a Patient Personality. No doubt there is a disproportionate number of Patient Personalities among the ranks of scout leaders, Sunday school teachers, Big Brothers, and candy stripers. Wherever and whenever help is needed, you are likely to find the Patient Personalities on the scene. They just find it so hard to say no.

"I usually find myself going along with what's asked or needed, like Alex and Miss Ellie," commented one Patient Personality, "even though I can tell that a lot of times they feel like I do, that it would be easier to say no. You find yourself going along because you don't want to chance hurting feelings or alienating those you love. There are times though when you just have to refuse."

One Patient father I know told me how he had finally learned to say no. "I could always be depended on to provide transportation for my daughter's gymnastics team. I never said no. Finally, one sunny Saturday afternoon, I noticed the other parents waving from their doorways and shaded lawn chairs and thought to myself, 'There they sit on their duffs while I haul their kids everywhere.' After I watched Alex and Krystle and Miss Ellie, I could see that it was my Personality to want to help, but that I could also say no occasionally and make myself a lot happier." In his own gentle and patient style, he arranged with the other parents to form a carpool. "The other parents really didn't mind. They were only surprised that I hadn't asked earlier."

There might be times when you carry your generosity and service to extremes, becoming a martyr to the urge. We can watch Dr. Westfall, on "St. Elsewhere," as he celebrates Christmas with his family. Outside it is cold and snowy and the dog is barking at the door. "Let the dog in, it's too cold outside," says the doctor. "Dad, what about your allergies?" his daughter asks. "Oh, they won't bother me as much as that," he replies. So the dog is let in. The Patient doctor has made both the dog and his daughter happy. Meanwhile he sneezes and suffers in silence.

"I used to feel that helping others and doing for them was the only thing that I knew how to do," said one Patient woman. "I lived through other people, sacrificed myself like Dr. Westfall and got lost in the shuffle. It wasn't until recently that I realized I'm an individual, and I need some things out of life as well."

Another Patient Personality found some counterbalance for her lopsided giving by watching her TV Twins find their strengths. "My husband used to call me from work all the time and say 'I'm tired, I don't feel good,' and I'd always say 'Well, why don't you come home?,' even though it would interfere with my time and work. I had been watching Maggie, Jenna Wade, and Krystle and how they had all started getting a little more assertive with the men in their lives. Even though they were all like me in wanting to help, they showed me that you don't always have to go along with the wishes of others to keep their affection and respect. You can let others know how you feel, and they'll get used to it although they might be a little surprised at first. Now when my husband calls I say, 'I know you don't feel good, but it's very important for you to stay at work. And I have my work to do here. You'll be all right.' I'm still helping him to do what's best, but now I'm helping myself too."

I HATE TO ASK YOU THIS, BUT . . .

It would be perfect for you if you were surrounded by mind readers. That way you would never have to bother making requests, asking for favors, or letting your wants, needs, or desires be known. But mind readers are few and far between. If, after waiting patiently, nothing happens, you shrug and say to yourself, "I really didn't need it after all," or you simply go and do it yourself.

"I hesitate to come right out and ask for things that I want or need because I don't want to put any undue burden on anyone," says one Patient Personality. "Or worse yet, I might just get a flat-out refusal. So for me, I guess it's just safer and easier just to keep on giving and doing."

"My husband used to get upset with me," another Patient Personality confided, "because I would never ask him to take me out to dinner, even though I really wanted to go. And then when he finally did get the hint, he would ask me where I wanted to go and I would tell him it didn't matter, wherever he wanted. It drove him nuts. But after we watched Miss Ellie, Dr. Westfall, and the other Patient TV Twins, he could see how they were, how they would go along and do what needed to be done without always asking for their own needs to be met. Now he knows to be more patient with me. And I am trying to make my own needs and desires known."

So there aren't enough mind readers to go around, and you don't feel comfortable imposing yourself on your family and friends, at least not with any direct requests or demands. Does that mean that you are doomed to a life of missing all the movies you really want to see, reading restaurant menus you never want to see again, and giving up that piece of pie that your overweight lunch date should have never set eyes on at all? Not necessarily. Just read on, you sneaky devil.

PLANTING THE SEEDS OF THOUGHT

The Patient Personality does have a way, at times, of getting what he wants in a painless, although covert and almost undetectable, way. It may be those subtle hints and clues you drop. You leave the newspaper open to the page where a review of the newest restaurant in town just happens to be. Or you describe to your wife, with great enthusiasm, how much difference those clubs that the pros use make in their golf game. Your birthday just happens to be coming up and your golf game is on the skids? What a coincidence.

Some may call it underhanded, some may call it conniving. We call it Patient sleight of hand: now you don't have it, now you do.

Let's watch Patient Miss Ellie, on "Dallas," in action. She is desperate to keep daughter-in-law Pam from selling grandson Christopher's shares in Ewing Oil to Weststar, a rival oil company. She and Pam are sitting by the pool, watching Christopher and his cousin John Ross play. "I did what I felt was best for my son," says Pam of her decision to sell the stock. "I know you did," says Miss Ellie, "and I always did what I thought was best for mine. But what I thought was right and what was right weren't always the same things." That starts Pam thinking.

Miss Ellie then goes on to explain to Pam how she herself had considered selling out to Weststar at one point because she felt that doing so would end the struggle and pain within the Ewing family. But she soon realized that if she sold, her son J.R. would leave Southfork and take his son John Ross with him. "I'd always pictured Christopher and John Ross growing up side by side, and then they'd start running the business," she tells Pam. But now she knows they won't get that chance. "Now, besides Ewing Oil coming to an end, the Ewing family is as well," Miss Ellie closes with tears welling in her eyes. Pam is obviously thinking very seriously, but still not convinced.

Later, at the annual Oil Barons Ball, Miss Ellie is asked to accept the Oilman of the Year Award for her late son—and Pam's late husband—Bobby Ewing. "This award means a lot to me and a lot to my family," says Miss Ellie. "It would have meant a lot to Bobby . . . it would be a shame if all that Bobby lived for died with him, if he couldn't pass it on to his son as Jock [Bobby's father] did to him, those things that were important to him." So to protect that legacy and perhaps to someday encourage grandson Christopher to follow in his father's footsteps, Miss Ellie asks that she be able to pass the award on to Christopher. She asks Pam to come up and accept the award on his behalf. At that point it comes as no real surprise when Pam announces that she has changed her mind and will never sell Christopher's stock to Weststar. For Miss Ellie, it's mission accomplished, albeit by a very indirect route.

"That's how I do it," observed one Patient woman after watching the Miss Ellie segment. "When I want something or want someone to do something for me, I use an indirect way like that. I plant the seed of thought in their mind and then help it grow with a little gentle persuasion."

Another Patient planter described her method of sowing the seed of thought this way: "I always felt that no matter what I did for my husband, he demanded more. He didn't really seem interested in my needs, only his own. But I finally learned that instead of backing off all the time and waiting, I could get the message across to him that there were some things I wanted too. So I started telling myself what I wanted. Then I would drop a few hints to him and, at the same time, I began to say no to more of those things that I felt he could do for himself. He finally got the message. Now, even though I still do most things myself, I feel like I have a better relationship with my husband—and, come to think of it, with everyone."

"I use the same sort of connivance that Miss Ellie used on myself when I go shopping," said one Patient Personality. "I just take someone else shopping with me who I know will buy a lot for herself. That way I don't feel so bad buying a few things I want. It's really a form of giving yourself some sort of indirect permission to have your own needs met. You get to do nice things for yourself and feel less guilty."

As a Patient Personality, you may not always be exactly as you seem, but it is perfectly normal and healthy for you to be exactly who you are. Now, about all those new car advertisements you accidentally left on my desk . . .

KEEPING THE PEACE

The Patient peace lover wants nothing more than to avoid violence or confrontation of any kind. You will go out of your way to keep everyone happy, will bring all sides together and smooth everything out.

When the neighborhood kids are fighting, you are the one who steps in to referee. You'll gulp down the meatloaf that your friend took so long to make even though others at the table are describing it as "something that assumes a life of its own after nightfall."

On "Taxi," Alex's friends, a newlywed couple, are having serious problems because they don't have enough money for both of them to continue their educations. They are beginning to fight and argue about who will stay in school and who will drop out. So Alex goes way out on a limb to offer them a personal loan and preserve the peace.

Edith Bunker makes the mistake, in one episode of "All in the Family," of telling husband Archie that a house guest has given her a special food order, including some very expensive items to add to her shopping list. When Archie explodes and demands to see the list, Patient Edith manages to keep the peace and avoid a conflict by conveniently "forgetting" where she put the list.

Meanwhile, on the show "227," Patient Lester is on a peacekeeping mission of his own. His wife Mary is wearing a new dress when Lester comes home from work. Unfortunately, Mary's feelings are hurt and the peace is disrupted when Lester fails to notice, or compliment, the dress. So Lester shows up after work the next day with a bouquet of flowers and an invitation for a night on the town, just to smooth things over.

"I'm like Lester in that I aim to please and keep the peace," observed one Patient man after viewing the segment. "But I'm also like him in that I don't always notice things right away, and my wife gets mad like Mary when I don't. When she brings up something like my never giving her flowers or something like that, I don't run right out and buy some because if I did she would say it was just because she reminded me to." As any Patient Personality will tell you, keeping the peace is not always a simple proposition.

There are times when the Patient Personality might find himself putting up with too much for too long just for the sake of peace. We can watch Jenna Wade, on "Dallas," go along with the advances of a male friend rather than taking a chance of upsetting him by telling him that she still has another man, Bobby Ewing, on her mind. And we can listen to Alex, on "Taxi," as he explains to the young couple to whom he is considering making a personal loan how he has endured bad results from such loans in the past. "I'm not really sure that lending you the money is such a good idea," says Alex, "because I've lent money to friends a few times in my life. And it's not only getting the money back, although that's a very important factor. It's just a question of how it affects the relationship."

"I know just what he's saying," was one Patient Personality's reaction to the segment. "I lend money to people and they don't pay it back. But I don't want to cause a lot of trouble or embarrass them by asking. I used to go out at night with some friends who never brought enough money along and so would always end up borrowing from me, but they never offered to pay me back. Rather than confronting them with it, I just don't go out with them anymore."

You put up with the neighbor's barking dog or a friend cheating on the golf course because you don't want to challenge anyone or upset the apple cart. You lean back on your high degree of tolerance to make the best of a bad situation, saying, "My shoulders are broad, I can take it." Well, just remember that British Prime Minister Neville Chamberlain's "peace at any price" approach helped to launch World War II.

PEACE AT ALMOST ANY PRICE

People tend to see you as calm, relaxed, and easygoing, and most of the time you are. Even when things are going badly—as long as they remain within your tolerance level, which is enormous—you, Miss Ellie, Edith, Krystle, and the rest of your Patient TV Twins will remain the picture of poise and serenity. Again, you're looking good, and you're trying to maintain peace at any price. Just as long as you're not pushed too far, it works.

Put the Patient Personality's back to the wall once too often, load on just that extra ounce of pressure, or threaten the security and well-being of friends and family, and you will witness the rare, but impressive, display of the Patient temper. The "read my mind" approach quickly expands into "read my lips" and feel the heat.

We can watch Miss Ellie as she lets Dusty, a friend of daughter-in-law Sue Ellen's, know in no uncertain terms that he should stop interfering with Sue Ellen's recovery from alcoholism. "I only want what's best for Sue Ellen," says Dusty. "Even if it means staying away from her?" asks Miss Ellie. "I don't think it does," is Dusty's answer. "I do," says Miss Ellie, "and I'm asking you to respect my wishes." Dusty is still not satisfied. He pushes Miss Ellie just that one step further. "Miss Ellie, it's not that simple," he pleads. "Let me make it simple for you," is Miss Ellie's final word. "She knows this is her last chance. Don't take it away from her."

We can also watch as Patient Edith endures one too many "stifle yourselves" from husband Archie, and finally shoots back, "No, you stifle." Archie is shocked but definitely gets the message.

Then there are those times when the need for security and well-being for yourself and your loved ones simply takes precedence over your abhorrence of violence. You dislike violence in any form, physical or emotional. But you dislike bullies, tyrants, and tormentors even more intensely.

Patient Jeff Colby, on "The Colbys," shows his temper when his mother suddenly appears out of nowhere after having abandoned him as a small child. Jeff makes it quite clear to his mother that he has no intention of embracing her or showing any tolerance for her unexplained absence from his life. "I've followed your life, your career. You've become quite a man," she says to him. "I was quite the boy too. You should have known me then," he shoots back. "Life gets complicated," mother pleads. "Complicated? That's why you ran out on me when I was three years old?" is Jeff's angry reply.

"People are shocked when I erupt after tolerating a bad situation for a long time," one Patient Personality commented after watching Jeff Colby. "One of my neighbor's dogs had dug a hole under the fence in my backyard and had gotten into my flower beds. I wouldn't say anything, just put him back in his own yard and fill in the hole. But it kept going on all summer long. Finally, I had reached my limit. I almost strangled the poor dog dragging him over to the neighbor's back door. I ranted and raved and threatened to call the police if they didn't keep Rover out of my yard. I thought their eyeballs would drop out."

Another Patient Personality observed, "When I reach that 'I've had it' point, at first I almost scare myself. But after it's over I feel relieved. It's frightening at first because I don't like to feel anger or hate. But when the anger comes out, it comes in a flash and then it's over."

The message here is: never underestimate the Patient Personality, or his temper.

GENTLE IN MANNER, STRONG IN DEED

At first glance, the Patient Personality's gentleness is probably more obvious than his strength. The irony there is that your gentleness is, in fact, to a large degree your strength. Your strength comes in a quiet, nonaggressive way. It has more to do with your ability to endure or resist the impulsive actions and demands of others, your ability to grind down the opposition with steadfastness and calm.

We can watch Jeff Colby as he pits his Patient strength against the aggressive, take-charge power of Uncle Jason Colby. Jason is trying to buy out Jeff's share of Colbyco, the family business, and has called Jeff to his office to talk. But Jason applies just a little too much pressure, pushing Patient Jeff just a little too far. And now it's Jeff's turn to take action. "When I came in here you might have persuaded me to sell out," says Jeff, letting Jason have both barrels. "But as I see it now, it's not that simple . . . no, instead of buying me out, you just bought yourself a partner."

"If he had asked Jeff for the shares instead of saying 'I'm going to take them,' Jeff might have given the shares to him or sold them to him," said one Patient Personality after watching the segment. "But Jason came on too strong. So Jeff said, 'I'll show you,' and will just grind Jason down."

"When I'm in a situation like that I just make my decision and leave," another Patient Personality commented. "Many times in the past I've stayed around too long, trying to make sure everything was all right, to make myself look good. But I've figured out that it's better if I just leave; put the ball in the other person's court, so to speak."

Finally, we have the "take a drink of water" approach to outlasting an aggressor. "When I'm in a situation like Jeff where someone is trying to pressure me or wants a decision 'right now,' I just get a drink of water and sit and wait to see what happens," is how one Patient Personality describes it. And take it from me, the Patient Personality can drink a whole lot of water, if you know what I mean.

THE SILENT STRUGGLE

For the Patient Personality, the usual give-and-take process of life is often lopsided. Unless you are surrounded by extremely sensitive, insightful people, you may find yourself constantly meeting demands and maintaining silence about your own. As we have seen, however, there are limits, even for you. So you have developed your own special coping mechanism for surviving the deluge of demands, your own sweet way of saying no.

"When I feel pressured to do something," says one Patient Personality, "I don't say no—but I don't do anything. When my husband is heading off for his Saturday round of golf and he calls back to me, 'Honey, pick up my shirts at the laundry, will you?' I say to myself, 'The laundry is only one block out of his way. He knows how busy I am.' Come Wednesday morning, he's muttering in the closet, looking for a clean shirt. I just give him a sweet smile. Next time he'll pick the shirts up himself."

Another Patient Personality remarks, "I'm like Miss Ellie and Alex. I'll usually do whatever you ask of me, but I'll do it when I'm ready. You pressure me for something on a bad day and I won't say no, but it might be next Tuesday before you get it. Nag me some more and it might be Thursday. Actually, it's no without saying no."

Actually, the silent struggle is your way of protecting yourself without risking total abandonment or rejection. "When you decide you want to meet me on my terms, you call me. OK?" OK.

LOOKING GOOD WHEN THE DUST SETTLES

On "227," Patient Lester comes home from a hard day's work, kisses wife Mary, then settles back to read the paper before dinner. A neighbor from upstairs stops in to talk to Mary for a minute and as she leaves, she says, "And Mary, I do love that new dress." Lester has not noticed the new outfit. Mary is not happy. Lester has not been paying enough attention to her. He hasn't been showing her he loves her. "You could be a little more attentive, you know," Mary pouts. Lester will hang in there and weather the storm. "OK, what do you want me to do?" he asks. Well, Lester, you should probably do what any other Patient Personality would do in a similar situation: keep calm, wait until the dust settles, then come out in the end looking good. So Lester does just that. He doesn't argue with Mary. He comes home the next day from work with flowers and an invitation to dinner.

After watching that segment, one Patient Personality was moved to comment, "There was this girl at work. She was really loud and a flirt and acted like a phony. Nobody liked her and I didn't care for her too much myself. But I'm her supervisor so

I had to be nice. One night she asked me to go to the movies. Well, I found that the loud, obnoxious front was not really her at all. Once you get to know her, she's sensible and a true friend. Now one of my favorite things is to ride in the car with her and talk for hours. I guess the others have developed a better attitude about her too, and they kind of admire me for hanging in there. I kept my opinion to myself, gave her the benefit of the doubt, waited until the dust settled."

So the neighbor's kids are running through your yard and tearing it up. Do you suggest that the neighbors keep them in the house or build a holding cell in the basement? No. You bowl with those people every Monday night, and kids will be kids. You build your own fence. You're out the time and money, but you're still at peace with the folks next door, and they would vote you neighbor of the year. In the end, you're looking good, just the way you like it.

ROSE-COLORED GLASSES

On "Dynasty," Krystle is wearing them when she stands up for Blake's wayward son Adam. Even after Blake describes how Adam has betrayed his trust and taken advantage of him while he was ill, Krystle asks Blake to look at the bright side. "No matter what he's done, he's still your son."

Miss Ellie wears them on "Dallas" while she's explaining to grandson John Ross how and why his mother and father have decided to live apart. "Sometimes people have times with one another when it's very difficult to live together. If you can get through the bad times, the good times will always come."

Edith Bunker is wearing them the morning after a house guest has kept everyone awake all night flushing the toilet. Husband Archie is very angry and ready to tear into the guest as soon as he comes downstairs. "It could be insomnia," Edith offers, looking to the positive side, "Some people listen to water to help them sleep."

And on "Knots Landing," Ben wears them while he is watching one of the twins born to his wife, not totally sure whether they are his children or not. He looks at the child with obvious tenderness and says, "Well, whoever you are and whosever you are I love you kid, I always will."

Those famous rose-colored glasses always let some ray of light break through, even in the darkest moments. Wearing them is just your way of maintaining, holding out for better times, not rocking the boat, not giving up the security of family members or friends, not blowing your stack until all possibilities of the good and positive have been exhausted. "I guess I just like to give the other guy the benefit of the doubt," is how one Patient Personality sees it. "You can always make the best of a bad situation if you're willing to try hard enough. You look at the other person and say, 'He's only hurting himself, not me.' "

There are times, though, when keeping the rose-colored lenses on and keeping the closed sign on your emotions can cause some problems. Sometimes the boat will spring a leak or two, no matter how careful you are not to rock it. Then the feelings and emotions come rushing out all at once.

"Sometimes when my efforts are ignored, I feel abandoned," says one Patient Personality. "Then I find myself keeping quiet instead of saying I'm hurt."

We can watch Maggie on "Falcon Crest" enjoy her solitude, the time alone to think and sort things out when her relationship with her husband is not going well. In fact, the Patient Personality does enjoy moments alone, prizes solitude and time away from demands and pressures. But it can become a problem when it goes on for too long.

On "Dallas," Jenna Wade has been hiding her feelings about the late Bobby Ewing from Jack, her new boyfriend. Jack senses that something is wrong when Jenna turns away, but he's not sure what it is. "Jenna, we're both grownups, grownups talk to each other. Talk to me." After Jenna finally does open up a little she apologizes. "I'm sorry," she says. "No, I'm sorry," he says, "I read you all wrong." "I guess you did," says Jenna. Had she been more open with her feelings, things might have worked out better, and she would have come out looking better.

On "St. Elsewhere," Dr. Westfall has kept his feelings about his wife's death and their handicapped child inside for far too long. It is Christmas, a holiday he has not really allowed himself to enjoy since the two tragedies struck his life. A friend invites him to a Christmas party, but once again Dr. Westfall declines. "Every year I invite you and every year you're a no show," the friend says. "The holidays are something I endure, not enjoy," is Dr. Westfall's reply. Finally, as the episode ends, Dr. Westfall brings himself to join the family at midnight services on Christmas Eve. He has decided to face the situation and come to terms with it. The catharsis finally comes as he steps inside the church and his son spots him and runs down the aisle to give him a hug. The feelings are finally let out and accepted.

THE SIXTY-MINUTE RULE

Sure, you have a right to moments of solitude, but don't let those moments stretch into isolation. And you do have the right to remain silent, unless your silence is making you, and others, unhappy. My suggestion to the Patient Personality is to try the sixty-minute rule: allow yourself to react to a situation within sixty minutes after it occurs or you become aware of it. Let your feelings out within that time and let people know how you feel. Chances are, after sixty minutes of contemplation, any damage your reaction might cause will be less than if you hold it inside indefinitely.

One Patient Personality who came to me had been feeling the pressures of a threatened layoff at work and the unpaid bills that were piling up. He had hesitated to say anything to his wife or friends. "If I ask people to help me I'll be vulnerable," was his feeling. So he sat, saying nothing, giving the impression that he was uninvolved or that nothing was bothering him or that he was just plain stubborn.

We discussed the sixty-minute rule and then watched Jenna Wade and Dr. Westfall; how they had kept their feelings and needs bottled up, how finally letting them out was a tremendous relief.

"I've been trying to follow the sixty-minute rule," my Patient friend said to me some time later. "I found out that my wife and friends were beginning to feel as if I thought they weren't good enough to help and that I didn't like them as much anymore. It's funny, my keeping quiet was having just the opposite effect I thought it would. I thought it would prevent trouble and hurt feelings, but it ended up causing them."

So, my Patient friends, here's the message: wear your rose-colored glasses (after all, that's part of your Personality), but after sixty minutes, try taking them off. The harsh light of day may be a little uncomfortable at first, but not as uncomfortable as the dark currents crashing around inside you.

PATIENCE AT WORK

The Patient worker thrives on a job in which supervision is casual. When supervision is rigid and demanding and the schedule hurried, you may be tempted to resort to the silent struggle as a way of expressing your discontent. Otherwise, you are typically a well-disciplined, responsible worker.

If you hold a supervisory position, your patience and tolerance of the faults of others may be viewed from above as weakness. "I like to give people the benefit of the doubt," says one Patient supervisor. "And I suppose, like my Patient TV Twins, I like to hold my fire and come out in the end looking good. So sometimes, if I find that my people aren't doing the job that's expected, I try to help them by doing the job myself. Sometimes I'm so busy making other people look good that I end up looking bad myself. It's something I'm working on."

Another Patient Personality ran into some problems when he accepted a promotion. "I was given more interesting and challenging projects, and the best people were assigned to my group. Whatever we needed to complete a project was made available. But late one night I started to realize how much of the time I was spending away from my home and my family. It was a struggle: demands of work, the security of my home. Watching my Patient TV Twins confirmed my final decision. I located a new position that paid less, has less prestige, but left me with evenings and weekends to spend with my family. That's where I feel most alive and secure." As Miss Ellie, Lester, and the rest might say, "Home is where the heart is."

In a working world that values aggression, ambition, and

competitive drive, the great worth in low-key contributions of the Patient Personality is often undervalued. This is a Personality who has a great capacity for reducing issues to their essence. He insists on dealing with facts in a straightforward, thorough, and deliberate manner, resisting impulsive actions and pressure tactics. She keeps the goal always in mind. Her unassuming style invites others to share in the enterprise. He is able to promote conciliation and consensus through Patient persuasion. And he is able to reduce risk by proceeding cautiously and patiently, always advocating "letting the dust settle."

All in all, the Patient Personality is a highly productive person. You know how to achieve and enjoy success and are willing to share it.

LOVE AND MARRIAGE

Since the Patient Personality is warm and friendly and responsive, you usually enjoy a good social life. Dating tends to follow one of two patterns: (1) you may date those persons whose needs you can meet; or (2) you may be attracted to the kind of person who spends freely, who is attentive, who anticipates your needs, who is outgoing—the kind of person who goes places and does the things that you would like but never request.

Thus you are often attracted to the dazzling style of the Accomplishing Personality, the take-charge ways of the Influencing Personality, and the winning manner of the Ambitious Personality. These outgoing Personalities are the Patient Personality's entree into the social scene without having to assert himself or to reveal his needs.

You enjoy the glitter and glow and the good times, and have no trouble taking it all in. You just love it—so long as you don't have to ask.

"Strange," the lovely young Fallon says to Jeff Colby on "The Colbys," "we've barely met, but you know something? I really do trust you." Well, that doesn't seem so surprising when we realize that what the Patient provider wants, more than anything, is security, both for himself and for those he feels responsible for. In your work that means doing a good job and keeping everyone harmonious and productive. For your family that means a stable, happy home.

For you, home and family are a haven, a place where you can find your center and stay there. You work hard to keep it peaceful and productive.

Patient Dr. Westfall describes his thoughts on home and family during one "St. Elsewhere" episode: "When we're young, we tend to take our families for granted. We figure they'll always be there. Then we get a little older and we realize how fragile families really are."

"I'm sure my whole life has been wrapped around my husband and my family," says one Patient woman. "I usually give in and let them have their way, and it's difficult to change. But lately I've been watching Krystle Carrington on "Dynasty" and I can really relate to how she handles her relationship with her husband, who is very aggressive and demanding. She goes along with him to a certain degree but makes sure that she gets the things that she really wants and that her true needs are always met in the end. Then I saw an interview with Linda Evans, the actress who plays Krystle, in which she talked about getting 'wiser' as she got older. I couldn't believe she used that word, because it's the same word I use to describe my acceptance of my Personality. She talks about her lack of ambition and drive, that she wouldn't have any trouble giving up her acting career for love and a family. It's the inner beauty that's more important than the outer beauty. It's the beauty of learning to care for yourself and at the same time for your family and loved ones."

Another Patient woman found that she could really relate to Miss Ellie, on "Dallas," as she summed up her feelings about home and family. In one episode, Miss Ellie is talking with her grandson about her late husband. "Your granddad, in his own way, was a very difficult man to live with. The oil business was always first with him for a very long time," she remembers wistfully. But she continues, "In the end, being together and raising our family together has made my whole life worthwhile."

The Patient husband may be willing to take his aging mother-in-law into his home. The Patient wife will care for the children of a sick neighbor or take in a foster child. Others tell you that you would serve yourself and your family better if you would insist that your family do a bit more for themselves. But when you finally sag into a quiet corner of your home with a glass of wine after everyone else is asleep, that small moment is the one you cherish. All is well under your roof and you're refreshed.

At times, the Patient Personality is prone to be a self-contained or self-sufficient person, even in marriage. It may sound strange and incongruous, but one Patient Personality once told me, "My belief is that I'm the only one who can make me happy. I have always worked very hard to be self-contained and to not need anyone too much. My security is in myself. You've got to be able to meet life on your own."

This, again, is the product of your essential need for security. The security that comes through marriage and love of another person reinforces and enhances this quality of self-sufficiency—it produces that serenity which is so much a part of the charm of the Patient Personality. But it also produces that sense of reserve, that hint of the loner about the Patient Personality.

In fact, you do like moments alone and prize intervals of solitude. Spouse and family will grant you that, recognizing that the busy, giving Patient Personality needs a break from so much doing and going along with others.

Problems can arise, however, when the Patient Personality is also reluctant to share his needs, when he is practicing his grand silence. The danger is that others can misread your solitude and silence. It would be beneficial for the Patient Personality to remember that the root meaning of the word *mystery* is "a secret shared."

LET ME TAKE YOU AWAY FROM ALL OF THIS

If you're careful with your finances, don't live with a lot of flash, and use your good common sense, you won't put yourself in a position where you might have to depend on somebody else. And you won't make anybody mad if you're not the

"Jones' " they have to keep up with. That is some down-to-earth Patient philosophy.

There is an obvious practicality to the Patient Personality. On "227," Patient Lester is talking with wife Mary. They're reminiscing about the hotel where they spent their honeymoon. Mary remembers it as a glorious place; Lester remembers it otherwise. "The complimentary bottle of champagne was nice," says Mary. "Yeah, but they made up for it in the bill," says Lester. "The place was a rip-off. And the room was freezing. Did they really think we were going to bring our pajamas on our honeymoon?"

For all of your seeming practicality and common sense, you may see yourself at times as a bit of a bore. Although there is something to be said for a secure position where nobody's feathers are ruffled, that's not to say that you would not jump at the chance for some glitter and excitement.

"I dream of traveling to exotic and faraway places like Kenya, Peking, and Tibet," confesses one Patient Personality. Another describes how, on her fortieth birthday, the most romantic man she knew planned a flight to Paris for both of them for dinner. And a Patient man confided to me that he loves more than anything when he comes home after a hard day and his wife surprises him with some champagne and cozy pillows arranged next to the fire.

As the Patient poem says:

> So take me away, read my mind if you can,
> Love's not always a thankless task.
> A cruise to the islands, a fine dinner out—
> Love means I don't have to ask.

ALTERNATIVES AND OPTIONS

Friends and family and working associates all note that the Patient Personality is modest and moderate in all things. He can be something of a loner, tending to be a bit reserved and self-contained, and he also tends to define the ground rules of his relationships. He is noticeably soft-spoken and indirect, never threatening, and given to ending statements with comments such as, "Don't you agree?" or, "Isn't that right?"

Whether at work or in social circumstances, the Patient Personality is a gifted listener, always attentive, responsive, and understanding. He can also be an artful talker, although he tends to guide the conversation away from his privacy and any declaration of his needs, wishes, or desires. Sometimes he is evasive, but always in a kind and gentle way. He is also prone to protect the status quo as another tactic for defending his privacy and security. This sometimes gives the impression that he is shy or conservative; while he maintains a wide circle of friends, only a few know him intimately.

Given his tendency to do for others too readily, the less mature Patient Personality can find demands excessive, and then he has the urge to withdraw or to engage in a will-struggle that is silent yet tenacious. At other times, he can be the selfish giver who paralyzes the recipients of his largesse, often making them feel inadequate. He can stifle the need of others to meet his needs or to make him happy, frustrating them by evasive responses such as, "Whatever you say," or, "Whatever you want to do."

When troubled, his greatest fear is that others will desert or abandon him. Giving in is his way of paying dues for membership in the human family—he fears that if he fails to pay his dues in the currency of service and giving, he will be expelled from the company of other people. So he pays and then overpays. He tries very hard to hide his own needs and wishes, fearing that he will burden others who might then hurt him by abandoning him. He finds it hard ever to admit his needs or to say no to the demands of others.

There are options and alternatives for the overburdened Patient Personality to consider, insights to ponder, choices to be made so that what may seem like vulnerable moments may, in fact, be great opportunities for happiness.

If you are a Patient Personality, consider these points:

- No one can read your mind. Share your needs and desires. Plant the seeds and nurture them until they bloom.

- Don't hesitate. Communicate. Let others be as giving to you as you are to them. Reality is sharing—giving *and* receiving.
- Your quest for security is potentially a great building block; used wisely, it can be a solid part of the structure of your happiness. Otherwise it can become a stumbling block or a road block.
- Keep an open-door policy. Let people and ideas flow in and out and all around you without supposing that you will have to give more in return.
- "Peace at any price" comes at a terrible price: no peace at all, only an illusion. Reality has to be faced, decisions have to be made, risks have to be taken. Happiness has a price: dealing realistically with problems on a day-to-day basis.
- Beware of paralyzing others with excessive giving. People feel helpless and inadequate when they are never permitted to do things for themselves. Or they may begin to overexpect, not realizing that you too are human.
- You have a right to moments of solitude, but don't let those moments stretch into isolation.
- Beware of the will-struggle, that stubborn streak in you that runs silently and deeply through your threatened moments. You fear that everyone is demanding too much of you, but the real pressure is only from you. Stop struggling. Better yet, open up. Let someone do something for you. Ask, and don't fear a no. Those close to you are just waiting for a chance to give to you.
- You operate well from the stance of "letting the dust settle," but too often you're still waiting long after the dust *has* settled. After the dust settles, settle your problems. Settle them within sixty minutes. Then comes genuine peace and security.
- Practice saying no. Learn to distinguish the appropriate from the inappropriate request.
- Don't play the martyr. Martyrs are venerable, but they can also be very inaccessible.
- Ever notice that you are a different person when you're out for an evening, away from the demands of home and family? If you haven't, your spouse and friends have. You are delightful and radiant, not that serious and burdened workhorse al-

ways doing and giving. So go out more often; you deserve it. And having you relaxed and having fun is something others deserve also.

- To those whom you need, say, "I need you." They would very much like to hear it. To those whom you love, say, "I love you." Love thrives on communication. And to those who give to you, say, "Thank you." You both deserve it.

SECRETS

The keys to a successful relationship with the Patient Personality are:

- Be on the lookout for subtle hints. The Patient Personality is not always so direct in communicating wants, needs, or feelings.
- Try to let the Patient Personality avoid having to ask.
- Don't always go along with those polite refusals. The Patient Personality really does want to go out to dinner, or to have his or her back rubbed.
- Don't underestimate the mild and mellow. There is power, and a surprising temper, hidden under the surface.
- Avoid arguments and confrontations.
- Provide a loving, secure atmosphere and enjoy the results.

MATCH AND MISMATCH

Patient Personality matchmates:

Anticipating—Security and stability are guaranteed with the Anticipating Personality. Your opinion will often be sought and prized. You get a good feeling of being needed and being significant. This person will try hard to prevent any discord in your relationship.

Accomplishing—The Accomplishing Personality would do almost anything to please you. You are both optimistic and love to be with people. There is always something exciting going on. Everybody likes this person, so there is little discord or confrontation involved.

Determined—The Determined Personality seldom makes rash moves, so there is no threat to your security. You both have a lot of common sense. The Determined avoids hassles and confrontations and has a strong sense of responsiblity. It's peace without any price with the Determined Personality.

Sensitive—You don't have to tell a Sensitive Personality what's on your mind; he or she can read it. Curiosity is the name of the game for both of you. Sensitives also enjoy experiencing many different things and won't infringe on your need for private time.

Adaptable—The Adaptable is comfortable with almost anyone, so this is someone with whom you can easily converse. This individual gives you the space to do what you want to do and on your time. The Adaptable's need to get out, alone, and socialize occasionally might begin to wear on you.

Conscientious—Conscientious persons are fun to be with because of their sense of humor. They have a carefully thought out approach to decision making, which makes you feel secure. Like you, they want to know what makes things tick, but their dry remarks might catch you off guard. And their doubting might magnify your reluctance to ask or make your needs known.

Ambitious—Such an individual always has an exciting project in the works. He or she shares the action with you and wants you to work with them. This makes you feel needed. But the long hours the Ambitious spends on projects might keep him or her away from home; there might be a disturbing lack of togetherness. Your own outside interests could be seen as counterproductive by the Ambitious Personality.

Persistent—Makes you feel special and can openly display their interest and concern for you. They may give you many gifts, but these can get to be too much. You're a practical person and these individuals are dreamers, which threatens your security. Also, their self-absorption, combined with your reluctance to speak up, can leave you in the cold.

Idealistic—Their independence is admired by you, but you like a little more togetherness. Idealistics have high standards for you and not all of them are to your liking. They do not share their problems with you and you feel left out. Your needs are often out the door.

Perceptive—This is a down-to-earth, caring person whose outspokenness can put a damper on the way you get along. You like peace and this person's emotional outbursts disrupt tranquility. You often feel that many demands are being made upon you by the Perceptive's volunteering of your time and energy.

Influencing—Charming, clean, and neat but they seem to take control of you. There's no give and take and you do all the giving, on their terms. Silent war is often declared.

Chapter Eleven

THE IDEALISTIC PERSONALITY

PROFILE

- Takes a cool and logical approach.
- Lives by standards and ideals, "shoulds" and "oughts."
- Does not like to reveal weaknesses or innermost feelings; may back away from emotional intimacy.
- Rebels against conformity or mediocrity.
- Likes to verbalize thoughts, debate, intellectualize.
- Independent and self-reliant.

TV TWINS

- Clair Huxtable—"The Cosby Show"
- Sam Malone—"Cheers"
- Hawkeye—"M*A*S*H"
- Joyce Davenport—"Hill Street Blues"
- Denise Huxtable—"The Cosby Show"
- Grace Van Owen—"L.A. Law"

Of all the Personality Styles, yours is the most fiercely independent, the most proud of the unique image you forge as an individual. Because of this trait, you may not feel comfortable with the idea of being lumped in with any particular group or classification. But the image you share, as an Idealistic Personality, is just as important as your individual view. The aspects of your Personality that you hold in common with your Idealistic TV Twins can help you recognize and polish that image. So bear with me. Let's get to know you just a little better.

The Idealistic Personality looks on life in two ways: the way it really is and the way it ought to be. You compare the real to your ideal and spend your lifetime trying to make one match the other.

You conduct yourself according to your own high standards that never give way to mediocrity or expediency. Others may shrug and say, "But everybody's doing it." Everyone may, perhaps, but not the Idealistic Personality. You make a concerted effort to be uniquely yourself.

As an Idealistic Personality, you look on yourself as you look on life. There is your flesh-and-blood self, complete with a full array of fears, flaws, and feelings, and there is your image, the self you would like to be to match your ideals.

Whatever you are and whatever you do, you are attempting to elevate blood and bones to the lofty level of your demanding image. Image and ideals impose a set of standards and a code of conduct that the Idealistic Personality resolutely adheres to.

"When I was a child," one Idealistic Personality remembers, "I was taught certain standards: 'Always be a gentleman; always open the door for a lady.' I feel bad when I'm not allowed to act that way. I really enjoy being the gentleman, lighting her cigarette, opening the door—I even enjoy putting on a tuxedo for a formal event."

Pretense? Male chauvinism? Never. Another Idealistic Personality might be the liberated woman who wants to light her own cigarette and open her own doors—or the man who finds blue jeans and bare feet a more suitable image.

The essence of the Idealistic Personality is the individual's complete identification with his or her own standards. Your ideals, thoughts, and actions merge into an integrated image of yourself as an individual.

Your image reflects the kind of person you feel you should be and try to be. "A good car dealer ought to sell only quality cars, keep a clean shop, and tend to customers promptly." "A good mother ought to supervise her children's homework, regulate their TV watching, and discipline them when they misbehave." "A dancer should eat properly, get plenty of sleep, exercise two hours daily, and practice four."

You pursue life and your goals with an exacting sense of what is good and true and proper in the life you lead, whether you are a police officer or a politician, a florist or a fashion designer, an undertaker or a used car dealer. Thus there is an appropriate way to make an arrest or to design a dress or to arrange a floral display. No ifs, buts, or shortcuts.

If I happen to be shopping for a used car from an Idealistic dealer, I won't be afraid to accept his word on the vehicle's condition—I don't even bother to kick the tires. His image means more to him than profit. His standards are high and his word is his bond. More often than not when dealing with any Idealistic Personality, these traits are guarantee enough. "You can depend on me," he will tell you. And you can.

Whatever the Idealistic Personality is doing, he goes by the book. And well he should; he wrote it.

As the dedicated Idealistic Personality, you will follow your own drummer and pride yourself on the fact that you conform to no other. Because of that, others may see you and your Idealistic Twins as rebels or nonconformists; your red socks, vintage car, or overgrown lawn may well invite those labels. But, like your Idealistic Twins, you will debate and defend your way of life, no matter what. That's the way it should be and everyone ought to realize that.

All Idealistic Personalities share the desire to be individuals, to hold fast to cherished ideals, to adhere to high and sometimes fixed standards that each has set for himself and the world around. The Idealistic Personality pursues these standards with a sense of purpose that is rarely compromised. His thoughts on any topic or activity are filled with definite standards and regulations: do's and don'ts, shoulds and shouldn'ts, prescriptions and prohibitions.

The Idealistic Personality lives in a world of codes and convictions chiseled in stone. He embraces them tenaciously, and he expects others to abide by them, or at least to abide by standards of equal integrity. His is a rather exacting world of black and white. There is little middle ground, few areas of gray, and little that is relative. When his standards and ideals are challenged, he would rather fight than switch, at least on first impulse. If healthy, he will listen to the other person's point of view, but in a stressful moment even the healthiest Idealistic Personality feels his backbone stiffen. His ideals and standards are so dear to him, so deeply felt, that he bristles when they are challenged. The more mature he is, the greater his openness to others' ideas. The less mature, the greater his rigidity.

Although every Idealistic Personality takes himself and his convictions seriously, a certain style and grace, wit and charm, soften the flinty edges of his standards. His courtesy, confidence, and commitment impress others. His spirit of high purpose is contagious, and his dedication and dignity attract others to his ideals. He is a persuasive spokesman for his beliefs, articulate and forceful in communicating his ideas. His vision, integrity, and courage of conviction often prompt others to rally to him as a leader.

Still, there are times when the Idealistic Personality finds himself standing alone. Given his dedication, his adherence to ideals and standards, his tenacity, and his individuality, it is not surprising that the Idealistic Personality cuts against the grain of conventional wisdom and the status quo.

He is a rebel with a cause, and there are always causes for the Idealistic Personality's choosing. One may advocate food for the world's hungry masses, while another may campaign for the legalization of marijuana. One may advocate abortion, while another opposes it. Whatever his ideal—profit sharing or profit taking, open marriage or closed shop, communism or the corporation—the Idealistic Personality believes his ideal is correct and that everyone really *ought* to see it as clearly as he does. They *ought* to be as dedicated and committed as he is. They *should* be willing to embrace standards, no matter how demanding. They *should* . . . they *ought* . . . the imperatives never end. There is always another standard to be pronounced because there is always another situation ahead that demands one.

You scorn those people who drift through life without cause or concern, people who blend into the latest fashion or the grayness of ambiguity and those who are quick to compromise, sell out, or simply stand for nothing. You can't help but admire someone who sticks to principles, even if they are opposed to yours.

You look for a kindred spirit who has values and principles, a person who respects your need for personal space and freedom and thinks on a lofty plane. You're not interested in someone who is gushy or clinging, who tries to force closeness and togetherness on you or makes too many emotional demands. A partner who can argue with the best, stand on his or her own two feet, and not slide from one viewpoint to another holds a special appeal for you.

Would-be friends and lovers would be hard-pressed to find a chink in your design for life. You are a cool customer and keep all those who would ransack your emotional baggage at a safe distance, either physically or with knife-edged comments. A true friend does not probe for weaknesses in your hard-earned image.

Although you would never admit it, beneath that tough, independent exterior beats a tender heart. You would probably prefer that no one knew about that warm and gentle person within. You may tend to equate tenderness with weakness. Although I don't totally agree with that analysis, I won't debate the issue with you; not yet.

MEET YOUR TV TWINS

You and your TV Twins live by your image. It is very important to you. It isn't a false facade. What you and your TV Twins believe is the crux of your being, it's the very thing that propels you through life: the ideals and principles that set you apart, that express your individuality.

Finding your TV Twins can be tremendously rewarding. Your Idealistic TV Twins will be easy to identify because they are:

- Very interested in their image.
- Reluctant to reveal needs and tenderness.

- Likely to set standards for their own behavior and that of others.
- Objective and dispassionate.
- Verbal and very definite in their statements.
- Independent and individualistic.

You and your Idealistic TV Twins openly rebel against mediocrity, against compromising principles and ethics, against whatever seems to lessen the quality of life and human dignity. You are incorruptible—but sometimes you and your TV Twins may be thought of as incorrigible.

On "The Cosby Show," Idealistic **Clair** is a fiercely independent and self-reliant attorney who also manages to fill the role of loving wife to husband Cliff and caring mother of five active children. She faces an assortment of family crises coolly and, at times, with a slightly detached air, but imparts her valuable sense of self-reliance to her children with obvious love and affection and manages quite successfully to split her image to fit the ideals of both career woman and parent.

Her image as "smooth" is tested in one episode when she and Cliff decide to go out to dinner to celebrate the anniversary of his proposal of marriage to her. There is a debate as to who will win the "smooth contest"; they will have to see who looks the best for the night on the town. Cliff claims that he will be looking so good that the headwaiter will put him at a special table in the center of the room and have the spotlight shine directly on him. But he is no match for Clair's cool calculation; there's no topping an Idealistic Personality with an image to protect. She acknowledges Cliff's feeble attempt at usurping the title of Smoothest but proceeds to put him in his place. "Yes," says Clair, "but when people look they're going to say, 'Who is that smooth, gorgeous woman sitting next to that pitiful man in the spotlight?' "

Clair's daughter **Denise** is an Idealistic young woman who always dresses in a unique and individual style and often expresses her independent attitude to her parents.

On "Hill Street Blues," **Joyce Davenport** is an attorney working for a big-city public defender's office. She is very efficient and no-nonsense, devoting herself to the cause of protecting the legal rights of the indigent. She also shows the Idealistic coolness and detachment at times in her personal relationships.

On "L.A. Law," we find still another Idealistic female attorney, **Grace Van Owen.** Grace works as a deputy D.A., bringing her Idealistic skills and standards to the prosecutional side of the law, while Joyce Davenport hones her legal image on the defense side. But Grace and Joyce both exhibit the Idealistic Personality's coolness and occasional aloofness, especially in the area of emotional intimacy and relationships.

Hawkeye Pierce is devoted to his image as chief surgeon at the 4077th M*A*S*H, an Army mobile field hospital unit during the Korean War. He is also adept at fulfilling the image of camp cutup and "love 'em and leave 'em" lady-killer. The former is a very good method of masking his true and tender emotions with jokes and witty repartee. The latter is a very convenient way of romancing all the nurses in the camp without letting any one of them get too close.

Idealistic **Sam Malone** is an ex-professional baseball player who carries his macho-jock image into business as the owner of "Cheers," a bar from which the show draws its name.

In one episode, barmaid Diane tries to convince Sam to help Carla, a waitress at the bar, by being her partner in a dance contest. "Sam, are you going to help Carla?" asks Diane. "No I'm not," answers Sam. "I am a jock and I've got an image to protect. I don't want people to think I'm too graceful, if you know what I mean." Finally, Sam is convinced to help Carla. They go to the dance contest, but Carla ends up dancing with her ex-husband and winning. Sam and Carla come back to Cheers, trophy in hand, and Diane exclaims, "Oh, you two did it." Sam corrects her, telling her it was Carla and her ex who actually did it. "I guess I just wasn't graceful enough," says Sam, secretly happy that his image as a slightly ungraceful jock was not tarnished. "Come on, Sammy," says Carla, "you were plenty graceful." But Sam quickly corrects her well-meant compliment. "No, I wasn't," he replies.

As you follow your TV Twins' video lives, look carefully for examples of:

- Occasional conflict with their image.
- Tenderness concerning the needs of others.
- Identification with their personal standards.
- A tendency to distance others when there is too much closeness.
- Being critical of others who don't adhere to their standards.
- Use of the words *should* and *ought*.

You and your TV Twins function best when you think before you act. It's important for you to talk about any apprehension, conflict, or problem. Let yourself be objective, think about the issues, and approach them in your uniquely intense fashion. Think out your moves, practice them. Imagine where you want to go and how you will get there. Let yourself gradually, logically, and objectively turn your image into reality.

THE ALL-IMPORTANT IMAGE

While we were all in school studying the three *R*s, you were carrying on an extra study of your own. As an Idealistic Personality, you had already begun your mastery of the four *I*s: independence, individuality, integrity, and ideals. And those four *I*s were always centered on a very special fifth *I*: image.

You were born with the disposition toward image, ideals, and standards, but you've been molding the shape of your image throughout your life. Sometimes it is absorbed from parents, relatives, teachers, clergy, and other obvious sources. Or it could have been formed in direct opposition to the ideals and standards of that same group of authority figures. It could have come from history books, biographies, or the sports page. Whatever its source, you have modified, altered, and adjusted it until it became fully the measure of the individual: you.

Picture yourself as you want to be. Now, devote your life to developing that picture, matching that picture, merging with that picture so it finally becomes you and you become it. The whole world around you will see that picture so clearly that they will give it a name: an image is born.

For Idealistic Sam, on "Cheers," it's the image of macho-jock. For Hawkeye Pierce, it's the image of chief surgeon, the man with flawless fingers and the delicate touch that can just as easily be applied to the camp's entire female population as it can to an injured soldier. For Clair Huxtable, the image is attorney, mother, and supersmooth woman of the hour.

Whatever your image, you develop, define, and refine the standard with care, just as your Idealistic TV Twins do. That much you do have in common.

WHICH IMAGE IS THE FAIREST OF THEM ALL?

Let me complicate things just a bit; then I will come back again later and straighten it all out. (Just think of my image as "Dr. Fix It" for the time being.)

Although the idea of image is very important to you, you don't always have just one single image of yourself. Modern existence can be very complicated, and each stage in your life may demand a separate set of standards that reflect on the circumstances: there is an image of the ideal single person, the ideal spouse, the ideal working parent, the ideal employee, the ideal employer, the ideal student, the ideal teacher, the ideal liberal, the ideal conservative.

On "M*A*S*H," the fun-loving jokester Hawkeye is put in charge of the 4077th when commanding officer Colonel Potter is called to Seoul. Suddenly Hawkeye, the devoted cutup, becomes Captain Pierce, company commander, calling for efficiency and protocol. The rest of the camp is very confused and antagonistic toward "Captain Pierce." But Hawkeye is simply temporarily shifting, albeit not so smoothly, his image.

On "Cheers," Sam is contemplating the temporary transformation of his image as former baseball great and present tavern owner. "This is it," he muses, "the end of an era. Well, maybe I can finally put my career in perspective and enjoy it for what it was . . . I guess I'm no longer Sam Malone, ex-baseball player. I'm Sam Malone, ex-ex-baseball player. Just an average guy doing an average job. That's something I can be proud of, right?"

"I find myself trying too hard to fulfill the image," says one Idealistic Personality. "I put a lot of pressure on myself and I sometimes get overbearing to the point of giving other people a hard time. I find more and more that it is important not to force this image or to let it be the only factor in my life. Now I can be more flexible than before."

For the self-assured Idealistic Personality, tailoring your image to meet the exigencies of modern life is not so much of a problem. Clair Huxtable can be a fiercely independent and self-reliant attorney but still be a caring wife and mother. Sam Malone can be the macho ex-jock but still lend enough of his "grace" to become a dance partner for a friend in need. And Hawkeye can become—although reluctantly—camp commander Pierce, for a few days anyway, even though he commands wearing a red chenille bathrobe.

The need to mix and match several layers of situations and standards can create its own problems. Idealistic Jeff is a young motorcycle mechanic, husband, and father and for each situation in life he has an image. He demands of himself a very high standard as a competent mechanic, and he knows he is that. But he also feels that there is a way that a mechanic working with the motorcycle crowd ought to dress and behave. So Jeff wears the regulation jeans, heavy boots, beard, and bandanna tied around his head, and he is rugged enough and unflinching enough to conform to the code of his motorcycle friends and customers. He has experimented with drugs but gave that up when he became a father. As a "good parent" he limits himself to a beer or two when he is with his friends.

At home, Jeff is a much gentler person. He is affectionate with his child and he enjoys caring for her while his wife works in the evening. He doesn't mind doing the dishes; he believes that a good husband should help in the house. But one evening two of his motorcycle buddies happened to walk in while he was finishing up in the kitchen and he was terribly embarrassed. He felt that his masculine image, so dear to him, was irreparably damaged. He was glad the baby didn't wake up crying; to have to put on a bottle and feed his daughter would have been the absolute last straw.

Until he learned to be more flexible with his exacting standards, Jeff experienced problems at work, also. He didn't feel that the owner ran the shop as it ought to have been run. The shop was messy, parts were never maintained at a working inventory level, the bookkeeping was totally out of whack, and the customers were treated with indifference. On top of that, the owner was away from the shop more often than Jeff thought he should be. "When a man owns a business, he ought to be around to supervise," was Jeff's assessment. He was often chilly with the owner and sometimes downright hostile, but the owner tolerated the chill and the chiding from his mechanic because Jeff was so good at doing all the things he didn't care to do.

Jeff came to me and we immediately set to work, integrating the different images he was contending with into a manageable form. "I have learned from watching Hawkeye, Clair, and the others how important it is to the Idealistic Personality to stick to his standards and maintain his image," said Jeff. "But I have also begun to realize how rough it can be, always expecting others, and myself, to be the same person in every single situation. The world just doesn't work that way."

In time, Jeff has been able to ease up on his rigid standards without losing himself. He is getting more relaxed in each role he plays, although he is just as devoted to each as the situation demands. Even the customers noticed the difference. And now he has one more image to fill—that of part owner of the shop.

TAKING THE NOVEL APPROACH TO STYLE

If I were trying to convince you to read this book, to discover your TV Twins and how they can make a difference in your life, it might be hard to come up with just the right appeal. If I tried taking the approach that most advertisers and promoters take, I would probably be a dismal failure. "Everybody's doing it," I would be saying. "Everyone maybe," you would be answering, "but not me."

As we have seen, image is very important to you. But we're not talking about some false front that can be switched on and off to impress people or curry favor. Your style does not come from Madison Avenue or change with every new TV season (Idealistic TV Twins notwithstanding). As a dedicated Idealistic Personality you enjoy being original and taking the novel approach to the standards of style you set. It is unmistakably marked as yours.

On "Cosby," when Clair is preparing to go to dinner with husband Cliff and outdo him in looking "smooth," she unfortunately has to contend with a broken toe. She refuses to wear the protective boot the hospital has given her, and she can't slip her throbbing toe into the shoes she bought for the evening. She really doesn't want to wear the shoes Cliff bought her—comfortable for a broken toe, but decidedly ugly—so she maintains her smooth image by dressing the ugly shoe that Cliff has bought (and her ailing foot) in a unique collection of decoration and jewels, including rings on her toes.

Later, at dinner, Clair creates her own individual style of dancing with a broken toe; she and Cliff sway, cheek to cheek, while sitting side by side. "Cliff, did you notice the way everybody was staring at us while we were dancing?" Clair asks. "That's because they have never seen people sit at a table and dance before," Cliff answers.

An Idealistic architect summed up his original approach this way: "Why would a client come to me to see the same buildings he could see everywhere else? And what the hell good would I be if I designed them? I have always made a sincere effort to be different."

"WHATEVER IT IS, I'M AGAINST IT"

—line from a Marx Brothers movie

You would probably not go so far as the Marx Brothers in your rebellion against the status quo, but you might be described as a rebel. When the pressures and conflicting standards of society come up against your own, you won't hesitate to revolt and take style to the streets. In fact, your Idealistic brothers and sisters have carried their distinctive banners in some of the most successful cultural rebellions we've seen.

Take Hawkeye Pierce. His personal rebellion on "M*A*S*H" is against Army regulations and protocol. He is not about to subject his standards to those of Uncle Sam. So when Colonel Blake calls him to a conference, he appears in a bathrobe with a distinct five o'clock shadow on his face and proceeds to chew out the Colonel for disturbing a wonderful dream he had been experiencing. "So typical," says by-the-book Margaret Houlihan, the camp's head nurse, "Colonel Blake calls you into his office and you chew him out." Margaret then attacks Hawkeye's choice of uniform. "The idea of reporting to your commanding officer wearing nothing but a robe." But Hawkeye is unfazed: "Would you like me to take it off?"

REBEL WITH A CAUSE

In your youth, your Idealistic rebellion was probably against the imposition of too many standards by parents, teachers, and other authority figures. As you grew older, rebellion may have taken the form of establishing and declaring a standard as to how your adult life was going to be led. Then, as your image of how your life (and the rest of the world) "should" be emerged, your mission became changing the world to fit that image: you took up "the cause."

On "M*A*S*H," Hawkeye Pierce wages a constant battle against the tragedy of war. His cause is pointing out the absurdity of his position as chief surgeon in the midst of war. Joyce Davenport, on "Hill Street Blues," advances her cause of bringing justice to the downtrodden by laboring as a public defender.

On "The Cosby Show," Clair decides to pursue "the cause" as she is reading the newspaper in bed. After she reads an article concerning the city's plan to install water meters in city buildings to monitor water usage, she immediately wakes her sleeping husband Cliff. "The problem is that the city is letting these developers put up these high rises all over the place like the one that's going up on the corner," she tells a sleepy and indifferent Cliff. "Do you know that the high rise will bring a thousand more people into this neighborhood and they'll be using our water?" But Cliff is not yet taken with the cause; his eyelids droop. "Water meters will cost $350 apiece, and you know who's going to pay for that?" says the now incensed Clair as she pulls Cliff's eyelids up with her fingers. "We don't have to pay for the water meters. We're going to write the city a letter." Never mind the fact that it's very late and way past non-Idealistic bedtime. The cause has been launched.

"My latest cause was getting people in my office to start being prompt in returning phone calls," said one Idealistic after watching the episode with Clair. "I'm very punctual about returning phone calls, but the other people in the office aren't. It reflects on my business. And the worst abuser is my partner. So the other day I finally picked up his phone, handed it to him with a stack of phone messages, and said, 'Here, get busy.' "

The "causes" come in any number of forms. They can range from working for world peace to cleaning up the litter along Main Street, or even cleaning up the dirty socks along the upstairs hallway. But whatever the shape, size, and scope, the common fact is that the Idealistic Personality will work very hard to match the world of "ought" to the world of "is." That's just the way it should be.

YOUR DECLARATION OF INDEPENDENCE

You don't need the Fourth of July to remind yourself of the value of independence. The Idealistic Personality celebrates freedom and independence every day. And you certainly don't want to be tied to another person's view of what you are or what you should be. You will decide that for yourself.

Clair celebrates her independence when she discovers that a long lost family painting is coming up for auction at an art gallery and she decides to bid on it. Husband Cliff offers to go to the auction with her and help out. But Clair can handle it alone. "No, Cliff, I want to buy it by myself," she informs him. "See, it's been out of the family now for thirty years and I want to be the one who gets it back." She does indeed manage to outlast all the other bidders and bring the painting home. But after it's over, Clair's daughter's boyfriend, a young man who obviously does not comprehend the Idealistic mind, asks her if her husband Cliff has given her approval to buy the painting. Clair proceeds to straighten out the young man. "You see, in your mind it's OK if Dr. Huxtable buys the painting because he works and he's a man, right?" asked Clair. The young man agrees. "Well," Clair continues, "I work, and it's OK if I buy this painting too. But not because he says so. But because it *is* so." OK, the young man can probably—no, *will*—live with that.

"It's true, I do like to go where I want to go, do what I want to do, and say what I want to say," was one Idealistic Personality's comment after viewing the segment with Clair and the young man. "I guess you could say I'm very much my own person."

On another "Cosby" episode, Denise, Clair's Idealistic daughter, wants to spend her savings to buy a car. Clair does not approve: the clash comes when these two independent Idealistic spirits go up against each other. "It's my money, my bank account, in my name," Denise protests. "It's my money and I can do what I want with it." Clair undoubtedly empathizes with Denise's demand for autonomy, but she also knows that independence has its price. "At this point in your life, you can pretty much do what you please because you know, in the back of your mind, that we are always there to bail you out; we're your safety net," says Clair. "Well, your father and I accept that responsibility because we're your parents and you better remember that young lady. Because if you ever take this attitude with us again, you can take whatever's in that bank account of yours and go discover America."

"I could never be that abrupt with my child," said one Idealistic woman after viewing the segment. "But I do see the emphasis on independence that is so important to me. When my daughter got pregnant by her boyfriend, I tried to be calm and logical and tried to tell her what to expect if she had the baby and what her life would be like. Then it was up to her to make the decision and to live with it."

Another Idealistic Personality related the segment to an incident with his son at school. "One of his teachers had called me in to talk about my son's grades. The teacher suggested I give my son some help and I told her that he was quite capable of getting the grades by himself. He would either sink or swim, but it was his choice."

IN SICKNESS AND IN HEALTH

The stouthearted Idealistic treats injury and illness with the same disregard and toughness as he does any other challenge to his independence and image of self-reliance. You might be down temporarily, but you're never out.

On "Cosby," Clair is discussing husbands—obviously non-Idealistic husbands—with her sister, who is about to get married. "You see," explains Clair, "a woman can have a cold, pneumonia, influenza, and malaria at the same time and still keep going. A man gets the sniffles and he has to stay in bed for a week."

In another episode, Clair breaks her toe. When Cliff brings her home from the hospital, he immediately tries to start babying her. But she will have no part of it. He wants her to use a cane. "I'm fine, I don't need that cane, thank you," she tells him. Son Theo comes into the room and says, "Mom, don't worry, we'll all pitch in and help out." "Thank you, but I don't need your help," is Clair's reply once again. And when she announces that she is going to work the next day, Cliff tries in vain to draw the line. "Cliff, I don't want to hear another word about it. I'm going to work tomorrow," she informs him, and proceeds to put down the cane and hop all the way upstairs on her one healthy foot.

An Idealistic friend told me that when she noticed a bump on her finger that turned out to be arthritis, she said to herself, "Well, it's finally happened. I'm a middle-aged broad."

After watching the segment with Clair and her broken toe, another Idealistic Personality, who has had a great many medical problems, summed up his attitude this way: "I'm not ready for the Olympics, but so what. I'm not afraid of dying and I never have been. It's not that I want to die, it's just that I don't give a damn."

TAKE THIS PITY AND SHOVE IT

The Idealistic Personality would certainly agree with the saying that when the going gets tough, the tough get going. You may be fearful when a principle, or an ideal, or any part of your code of conduct is at stake, but you rarely seek help or break down. The white flag almost never goes up your flagpole. If you have to, you'll go it alone. (At least that way you know you're in good company.)

Down at Cheers, Idealistic Sam is having a rough time of it. He has donated the baseball jersey he wore as a pro to the local public TV station for their celebrity auction and, to put it mildly, the bids are not exactly rolling in. Finally, someone does make a bid and buys the jersey. Sam is relieved until he finds out that it was his friend and barmaid Diane who made the bid. "I want you to take that back," he tells her. "It'll sell, I know it will." Unfortunately, it doesn't and his image as a former baseball great is fading fast. Diane tries to console him. "You have more great days ahead," she tells him, "you have a real job now and friends and you've got your health."

"God, that's low," says Sam. "What is?" asks Diane. "That health crack," Sam answers. "I know what you meant. That's pity talking. You don't tell someone that they will have their health unless you mean that's all they've got." Diane tells him to forget she even said it. But for Sam, it's not that easy. "No, I'm not gonna forget it. You told me I have good health. I'm not gonna take that," Sam raves. "Sam, you're sick," says exasperated Diane. "It's too late to make up," says Sam. "You were pitying me and if there's one thing I can't stand from you, it's pity."

What was the official Idealistic reaction to that segment? "If there's one thing I can't stand, it's pity," said one Idealistic viewer. "I'd rather be hated than pitied." Another empathetic Idealistic agreed. "I feel the same way. It's like, if you see me fighting a bear, help the bear, don't help me."

The helping hand sends out different signals to the Idealistic Personality. "I get confused when people are nice to me. I don't want to accept help because I don't want to owe them anything," says one. Another Idealistic puts it this way. "If a person is in a hole, let him pull himself out. When you try to offer help, you're putting him down and implying that he can't, or won't, do it himself."

At times, though, even the most self-reliant among us needs a little boost. The rest of the world is just not ready to cooperate in just the way you would have it. The stiffest upper lip can sag occasionally. "So, OK," you say, "there are times when I could use a hand. But it's the way that hand is offered that can make the difference." OK, so let's take a look at just what the difference is.

On "M*A*S*H," Hawkeye has just performed some brilliant surgery on a casualty, but the patient is not recovering the way he should and Hawkeye is perplexed. How could he have made a mistake? What could the mistake have been? He becomes totally absorbed and preoccupied with trying to find some logical explanation for the patient's condition. No poker, no movies, no dates; and finally he moves out of his tent and goes into seclusion. A nurse comes in and tries to romance him out of his funk. No luck. Fellow surgeon Trapper comes in with a drink. Sorry, no. Then Colonel Henry Blake comes in and tries the direct approach. "You're losing your perspective. You've got your guts in a knot because one patient has gone sour. That's bad," says the Colonel. Hawkeye tells him he doesn't buy that. "You don't buy that because you're dedicated," says the Colonel. "Well, shouldn't I be?" asks Hawkeye.

"That depends on whether you're dedicated to your patient or your ego," is the colonel's reply.

Finally, Margaret offers her helping hand in a way that also offers Idealistic Hawkeye an acceptable solution. She simply asks if it is possible that he missed something during the surgery. She appeals to his logic and starts the wheels rolling.

"When I'm in a crisis like that I need to talk things out," says one Idealistic Personality after watching the segment. "But I really hate to put myself in other people's hands. If someone comes at me with a 'you've got to deal with it' angle instead of offering pity or affection, it works a lot better. Then I don't mind discussing a possible approach to the problem."

"Both Henry and Margaret were a little too abrasive," said another Idealistic, "but their approach was generally OK. You can motivate me with some facts or a rational approach, but sympathy or an attempt to distract my mind from the problem will turn me right off."

My own logical advice is to step back and think about the problem objectively. Take some time to separate the immediate emotion and let it cool. Then use whatever help you need to come up with your own solution. That advice, and a little motivation from your Idealistic TV Twins, can go a long way in helping you solve your problem, your way.

THE WAR OF WORDS

It's time for a little fun. So what do you want to do for enjoyment? How about a movie? No? Well, OK, how does a round of golf sound? You say you think golf is silly? Well, it is good exercise. OK, so it doesn't do much for your cardiovascular system. Don't knock it until you've tried it . . .

This is starting to sound like a debate on the merits of golf. What was that magic word: debate? Now you're having fun. A lively discussion will keep the Idealistic mind honed to a fine edge. It's a war of the words: you say torpedo, I say torpado.

On "The Cosby Show," Clair's discussing the state of matrimony with her sister, who is about to tie the knot. It seems her sister has been reading up on the subject of how to have a successful marriage, and one book says that when you're having an argument with your spouse you should both sit down, calmly write down your grievances on a piece of paper, then exchange the papers. "When do you get to yell?" asked Clair. "You don't," answers little sister. "Well, darling," says Clair, "if I've got to sit down and write out why I'm mad at someone, I might as well throw the book at them."

"To me, a good discussion or debate is like a fencing match," said one Idealistic verbalist. "You feint, parry, and thrust with words, and may the best win. The moment anyone starts a discussion, I see the challenge. And the more confident and eloquent the other party is, the better."

So what can I say: en garde!

THE IDEALISTIC PERSONALITY AT WORK

Let's imagine for a minute that I'm interviewing the Idealistic Personality for a job. What exactly can I expect?

Every Idealistic Personality runs on IST—Idealistic Standard Time. If you tell me you will be at my office for a sales call at 8:00 A.M., I'll bet you'll be there sitting, waiting in my outer office no later than 8:00 A.M. And if I tell you that I'll be there for an 8:00 A.M. appointment, I know I'd better be there. "Time is extremely important to me," says one Idealistic Personality. "I'm always on time—usually well before time—and I don't like others to be late. It really bothers me. I have to control myself or I'll say something snide."

The person with the best record for the fewest sick days might be an Idealistic Personality. Like Clair, Sam, and your other Idealistic TV Twins, you hate to admit to sickness or injury. It shows a weakness that violates your standards: "A good worker doesn't get sick." So, like Clair with her broken toe, you will hobble through somehow, ignoring both the offers for help and the pain.

I know of a case in which an Idealistic worker missed only one day in thirty-five years, the day he had a small ulcer removed from one eye. He was back to work, eye patch and all, the very next day. And then there's the story of the Idealistic man who had an operation on his throat. His doctor told him not to talk for a week afterwards. But he showed up at the shoe store where he worked the day after the operation, and he had a card that he handed to every customer: "I'm not supposed to talk."

The Idealistic Personality's self-assured manner might, at times, annoy coworkers who might consider him a bit too aloof or even arrogant. Then too, he might feel—and show—contempt for a fellow worker who doesn't behave or look like a fully committed or competent member of the organization. We only have to watch Hawkeye Pierce and his constant annoyance with the bumbling surgical technique of some of his associates to see the point. Although he is the casual soldier outside the operating theater, Hawkeye expects and enforces the image of crack surgeon when the cutting starts. "My attitude is like that," says one Idealistic craftsman. "A shoddy job reflects poorly on everyone; not only on the person performing it, but also on me if I'm working with him."

Another thing that bothers the Idealistic worker is the fixed nine-to-five routine. He finds rigid work schedules oppressive, restrictions that limit his freedom. More, he finds fixed procedures boring: "It's like living in hell." The Idealistic Personality believes that he is more productive and efficient when he can work as long and as hard as he wishes. And it's true—he is very responsible, very trustworthy.

High standards and an exacting sense of time might pose other hazards for the Idealistic careerist. One engineer confides that his career must progress according to his standards or he leaves. "If I don't make the kind of money or develop the kind of products that I feel I must, then I'll be leaving in five years." He means it; he's on his third five-year plan, and he is still bothered by living up to his image as a successful engineer.

Another hazard that he might share with other Idealistic Personalities is his hesitance to make a genuine commitment. As in personal relationships, an Idealistic worker can go along in a position for six months or so without really being involved, or without being fully aware of the standards expected or the devotion required. Suddenly, he realizes just how much of himself must be committed and he quits. He might tell others that the working conditions were poor, the company standards were shoddy, and so on, but his real problem is facing up to the full standards required for commitment.

Another ploy sometimes heard from an Idealistic careerist is this statement, often repeated as the demands for commitment intensify: "Always hold back a little of yourself." That means about eighty percent is available but never the full commitment. The trouble is, holding back twenty percent means he is cheating himself that much. There might be additional risk in full commitment, but only twenty percent more risk, and it's usually worth it.

Retirement is not a problem normally for the Idealistic Personality. "I'm looking forward to it," says a rather young Idealistic worker. "I've always thought that it was kind of ridiculous to work all your life. Early retirement makes a lot more sense."

LOVE MEANS NEVER GETTING TOO CLOSE

"I love getting close to people—up to a certain point," says one Idealistic Personality. "But when they get too close, I feel engulfed. I want room to maneuver."

Another Idealistic Personality feels this way: "I don't make friends easily. I have one or two close friends, but I don't feel I need anyone else. If someone else tries to impose their standards, I pull away."

"Some people say I'm hard to get to know," says another Idealistic. "Others claim I'm cold and snobbish. But I just like to keep my distance and for them to keep theirs. We can still be friends."

On "L.A. Law," Grace is attempting to deal with the advances of a determined suitor, who also happens to be an attorney and colleague. He is moving in too fast and too close, inviting her to an intimate dinner spot. So she throws up some verbal interference to fend him off and maintain her distance. She informs him that she has three rules for dating. She does not date attorneys, and she does not date men she works with. He asks what the third is, but she wonders why because he is already disqualified by the first two. He won't give up and finally, as they are getting on a crowded elevator, she tentatively agrees to meet him for dinner. But make no mistake, the distance will still be kept. "So, are you gonna tell me number three?" he asks. "I never sleep with a man on the first date," she announces in a rather loud voice. The elevator is immediately hushed and Romeo is kept in line.

On "M*A*S*H," Hawkeye's alone in his tent with a visiting Swedish surgeon. He has been trying to seduce her, as usual, but she has turned the tables and is moving in herself—a bit too fast for his taste. She kisses him, then pushes him down on the cot and kisses him again. It's time to make a little distance. "Can I ask you something," says Hawkeye. "When you go dancing, who leads?"

You might say that you prize your independence and freedom, and because of that you like to be able to stand back a bit and evaluate what is going on. Well, I know that's true up to a point. But what you're not saying is that you like to maintain the subjective, emotional distance because if I got too close I might catch a glimpse of some weakness, some need, or a crack in the armor of your standards; an unsightly smudge on the shiny surface of your image.

If an Idealistic Personality was not the first to formulate the axiom, "Familiarity breeds contempt," he certainly fears its truth. For you, letting someone get close enough to see you fall short of your ideal would be contemptible, so you keep them at arm's length—physically, emotionally, or verbally.

"I'm like Hawkeye," says one Idealistic woman. "I'll fire off a few snide remarks to keep people from getting too close. At work they gave me a surprise birthday party with a cake. There was a roomful of people and they all started clapping. I just froze. Sometimes in a situation like that I do like they do in the Westerns. I come out shooting, with words, and I don't care whose feelings get hurt. I just want to get out alive."

On "Cheers," Frazier, one of Sam's acquaintances, is trying to console Sam because he thinks Sam is depressed over a love affair with Diane. Frazier walks up behind Sam, who is sitting on a chair, leans over, and puts a hand on either side of Sam's head. "Go ahead, tell her," says Frazier in a soothing voice. But Sam bolts. "Frazier, I don't like guys touching my head," Sam says, protecting his macho image and keeping Frazier's sympathy at a distance.

One Idealistic Personality told me of an incident at work. He had been injured, and as the emergency crew wheeled him from the building, his coworkers lined the path and clapped for him. "I know they were just recognizing me for doing my job and trying to make me feel good," he said. "But in a way, it made me feel uncomfortable; it was an honor and a debt at the same time."

For the Idealistic Personality, closeness can be a double-edged sword.

MARRIAGE AND OTHER RELATIONSHIPS

In matters of romantic love, the double-edged sword of closeness and intimacy can strike the hardest. For you, the lure of love sometimes lies more in what you don't have to disclose and share than in what you do.

On "Hill Street Blues," Frank Furillo sees the blossom of love beginning to open with Idealistic Joyce Davenport. But Joyce is already feeling suffocated. "It's too complicated," she tells him. "I'm making my own way now and I want to keep it that way. Anything else is too complicated." Frank asks if she is still going out with another friend, Evan, and she admits to him that she is. "Why him and not me?" asks Frank. "He is safe," says Joyce. "With you, I'm not so sure."

Now consider the case of Idealistic Sarah. Sarah is twenty-seven, single, but living with a young man she has known for four years. She attended three different universities but was never graduated. She is actively involved in interests ranging from scuba diving to macramé, from water skiing to gourmet cooking. Sarah isn't a competitive person; in fact, she leans the other way: "I want to be different. I don't feel I can compete with the frilly-frilly types with all that mascara and eye shadow and long hair. I guess I don't want what everybody else wants." Sarah would rather pack up her water skis and head for the dock with her boyfriend MacArthur.

Sarah and MacArthur had what she called a beautiful relationship for over two years. They had interests they shared and interests they each pursued independently. She might have lunch with male friends, and he might lunch with other girls he knew and worked with. Fine. Life was interesting and very good for both Sarah and MacArthur—until recently when they purchased a house. Suddenly, Sarah began taking another look at the girls MacArthur was taking to lunch. She also began to feel a little less sure of herself.

What happened to Sarah often happens to Idealistic Personalties. Her relationship with MacArthur involved a good deal of outward affection, but Sarah maintained a certain inward detachment—a safe emotional distance. However, when she and MacArthur bought the house together, she suddenly felt the emotional distance shrinking and she wanted to push away. She began to fear that she might not be the strong, clever girl she saw herself as; her weakness might show.

This sudden awareness of getting close can surface at seemingly strange times. An Idealistic husband has been married five years and the marriage is going along smoothly. Then one Christmas he gives his wife an expensive and thoughtful gift. Suddenly, he has to take a business trip for a week. What happened was this: that special gift after five years of marriage signified that the Idealistic husband had really begun to feel close to his wife for the first time, so he had to back off.

"Sometimes I get in trouble because I never tell my wife how I feel," said one Idealistic man who came to me about matters of the Idealistic heart. "I have a bad day at work and can't discuss it with her. I don't know if I could handle all the affection and support she'd offer. I'm emotional inside and sometimes outside. I do have soft, tender feelings, but sometimes they come out as harsh and critical."

Hawkeye is having similar problems on "M*A*S*H." It seems that he and Margaret, who are stranded overnight in a hut in enemy territory, have closed the distance between them temporarily and enjoyed a romantic interlude. But then it's the next morning. Margaret is starry-eyed, kissing Hawkeye's finger and putting it to her lips. Hawkeye is terrified. When the rest of the camp finds out about their tryst, there goes his image as playboy; here comes Margaret's smothering love. True, he does have some warm and intimate feeling for Margaret. But he starts pushing her away almost immediately with snide comments and sarcasm. She starts firing back, and their wonderful moment is soon forgotten. But eventually a compromise is reached. As far as the rest of the camp knows, the two still share a cool, professional aloofness, but Hawkeye will continue to know and share the knowledge that an impossible love did shine for a few hours.

"I can see that there's nothing wrong with keeping a safe distance," was one Idealistic Personality's conclusion. "As long as it doesn't get so wide that all the warmth and tenderness falls through the cracks. And if you do have to lean on someone once in a while, it's your loved ones who can be trusted to keep the secret."

ONE COOL CUSTOMER

Poise is a nice word to describe your stance. You like to keep your wits about you, whatever the circumstance. No hasty actions, no emotional outbreaks, no offhand remarks that might trip you up later. As a matter of fact, we could probably sum up the Idealistic Personality by admitting that you are one cool customer, under wraps.

When two attractive young men approach Clair Huxtable and her sister in a restaurant, Clair handles the situation without a flinch. "Let me guess, you two are models," asks one young man. "Right," says Clair. "When I first looked at you from over there I knew you were special," is the young man's next line. "And that's what you do" asks Clair, "you go around buying drinks for special women?" Our young friend really thinks he's rolling now. "Yes, but there aren't that many special women out there," he says, delivering what he feels is the coup de grâce. "Well, thank you," says Clair, delivering her final blow. "You know what? My husband thinks I'm special too, and so do my five children." "That's all I have to hear," says our young Romeo, his fantasy suddenly doused with cool, cool water.

OK, you're one cool customer; I'll grant you that. But just for the sake of argument, let's say there's a warm, tender layer under that smooth, self-reliant surface. Let's say that when Sam Malone finally agrees to show a little grace and be Carla's dance partner; when Hawkeye does give in to an intimate, tender moment with Margaret; when Clair Huxtable does succumb to husband Cliff's neck nuzzles, that it does show an openhearted, compassionate side you would rather not reveal to just anyone.

Although your powerful ideals, uncompromising standards, and courageous independence are the obvious strengths of your Personality, your less obvious feelings of warmth and tenderness are also among your strengths.

ALTERNATIVES AND OPTIONS

The healthy Idealistic Personality is an independent, intellectual, and forceful person who prizes his own standards and ideals while respecting those of the other person. He holds to convictions with great fidelity, always adhering to values and standards, even when others choose expediency and lesser values. He can be a glimpse of grandeur in a ho-hum world of apathy and indifference.

His independent style often elicits the admiration of others, while his conduct and confidence prompt him to follow their lead. He insists on maintaining an impeccable image, one that communicates trust and loyalty.

Whether healthy, or a little less than comfortable with himself and his exalted standards, the Idealistic Personality is something of a natural resource in his community, an asset in his profession, and a source of pride and admiration to his family. He might further enhance his image and be a little more accessible if he would learn to relax a bit more, to share a bit more, to be more flexible, to relate to others without setting standards for the relationship. Then he might have his life of high purpose while enjoying warmth and closeness. With fewer mountains to climb he might enjoy the view from the heights already obtained with much greater satisfaction, simply because others can then share his moments of glory.

If you are an Idealistic Personality, consider these points:

- Warmth and closeness are not weaknesses but great inner strengths. They don't need the rigid armor of ideals for protection.

- Love and being loved enrich a person's image. Far from rendering a person helpless, love shared is an endless source of energy.
- When you learn to accept the help of others, you are better able to offer them your help and the benefit of your wisdom and ideals.
- Practice saying "I need" rather than "I should," "I want" rather than "I ought," and "We are" rather than "I am."
- You have a delightful sense of humor, but sometimes you use it to nudge others back a bit.
- You love a compliment; that means you are meeting standards well enough for others to notice and comment. But you can also give more compliments if you are not so rigid in your standards that others can't possibly live up to them.
- Others could admire you more if they could come a little closer, instead of looking at you from a distance.
- With all the integrity, confidence, self-reliance, and strength that you project, others may find it truly unbelievable that you could ever feel helpless or weak. Don't be afraid to reveal your vulnerability.
- Whenever you get the feeling that you want to run from a relationship, *stop*. Making a commitment may be less risky, and more satisfying, than walking away. Don't flee from your feelings.
- Be logical when there's a problem, get the facts, do whatever research is necessary. Your way is to think out your moves and solve the problem.
- Let others know that they should be clear and objective with you.
- A relaxed smile is much more comfortable than a stiff upper lip—not only for you but for everyone around you.
- You cherish your freedom of choice. Fine. But do you sometimes limit the choices of others by forcing your standards on them? When you deny them their freedom of choice, you forfeit your own.
- *Compromise* doesn't have to be a dirty word. Compromise is the art of the possible in a world of conflicting standards. When you hold your convictions so rigidly and so inflexibly

that they become unattainable, you are the one who has compromised them.
- At times it may be the feelings that are real and the images that are dishonest. You prize honesty, so don't let the images fool you.

SECRETS

The keys to a successful relationship with the Idealistic Personality are:

- Don't expect elaborate displays of emotion; it's not the Idealistic Personality's style.
- If you sense the Idealistic Personality backing away when you feel you should be the closest, don't take it personally. It's just his or her natural reaction to intimacy.
- Accept the fact that the Idealistic Personality has some very resolute standards, but compromise is possible with rational, intellectual debate.
- Stick to your own views, even if they are not in agreement with the Idealistic Personality's. He or she will admire your steadfastness.
- Appreciate the subtle signs of love and affection.
- Respect the Idealistic Personality's love of personal freedom and independence. Give them space.

MATCH AND MISMATCH

Idealistic Personality matchmates:

Influencing—Responsibility is very important to both of you. Your idealism and the Influencing Personality's perfection form a very strong team. Your image will remain intact with this person, and the Influencing person admires your independence. You share a desire for logical, objective thinking.

Ambitious—The Ambitious person allows you complete freedom, seldom stifles your independent ways because they are so busy pursuing challenges and goals. Both of you put emphasis on winning and success.

Determined—Both of you have high moral principles and neither compromises these principles easily. Both of you are responsible and pursue causes with tireless determination. You like debate and controversy and the Determined person avoids this, but the Determined also encourages you to strategize and plot your moves.

Accomplishing—Both of you are energetic and willing to work. The Accomplishing person will go to great lengths to get your approval. Your intensity is counterbalanced by his or her playfulness, but the Accomplishing also profits from your structure and standards.

Sensitive—You have many standards and Sensitives have only one, the Golden Rule. You are rather verbal, while they are rather reserved, but not unaware. You value independence, they value private time. The Sensitive's loyalty is very important to you.

Persistent—You can really appreciate and profit from the Persistent Personality's creative thinking. They like your ideals. But here the battle is between independence and togetherness, between standards and imagination. You can survive with bare necessities and they want to spoil you with extravagant items.

Conscientious—They encourage you to be logical and objective. They contribute a lot of facts and information. You present your standards and ideals in a clear, concise fashion and are met with a barrage of questions and maybes. Your shoulds and oughts lead to indecision and doubt on the part of the Conscientious person.

Patient—You make your standards known, but this is not the Patient person's style, who wants you to read minds. You enjoy confrontation and debate, but the Patient person avoids confrontation at all costs. The more you push, the more silence you get.

Perceptive—Here it is a "head versus heart" argument or "logic versus emotion." They want affection and attention and you want independence, which leads to cries of unfairness by the Perceptive person.

Anticipating—You need independence; they want to plan your life. They want to receive credit and you aren't one to make a fuss. You want your freedom and they want to feel important. You have a difficult time understanding all of the worry; it isn't logical to you.

Adaptable—Your standards are rather rigid and the Adaptable person is the essence of flexibility. They listen well but not only to you; to everyone else as well. Your image and your exploits become public record. They like a close, communicative relationship, which may seem threatening to you.

Chapter Twelve

THE SENSITIVE PERSONALITY

PROFILE

- Very alert and tuned in to their environment and surroundings.
- Brief and cautious in speech and actions.
- Curious.
- Very expressive eyes, but tends to avert or keep them shielded with sunglasses.
- Loyal to friends and family.
- Values privacy.

TV TWINS

- Peter McDermott—"Hotel"
- Mick Belker—"Hill Street Blues"
- Ray—"Dallas"
- Norm Buntz—"Hill Street Blues"
- Stingray—"Stingray"
- Claudia—"Dynasty"

"It's the eyes that you notice first; eyes that tell a story. It's almost as though they have a life of their own." That's how one person described the Sensitive Personality to me. "Just watch the eyes, how they express the exact feeling of what the Sensitive Personality is saying. Even when he's not talking, the eyes still communicate. When he looks down, it's just a pause in the conversation."

Another person compares the Sensitive Personality to a certain creature that lives in the sea. "It's a shy creature that will usually find some out-of-the-way spot and plant itself there. Then it extends these long, supersensitive tendrils that are constantly probing and examining, responding to the most subtle, unseen currents."

In public, we can often find the Sensitive Personality behind sunglasses, even at night or on a cloudy day. Why? Because if the eyes are truly the "windows of the soul," the Sensitive would prefer the shades drawn. Although the Sensitive has a tendency to be rather shy, he is intensely curious. The glasses are one way to allow him to see without being seen.

A Sensitive can easily disappear in a crowd, which serves the same purpose as sunglasses. It allows him to do what he likes best: to watch, observe, and feed his curiosity from an anonymous vantage point.

The Sensitive Personality is so keenly aware of himself and others, so tuned in to the environment around him that it seems, at times, that he has some sort of secret antenna in operation. At times, these antennae may be so finely tuned that he hears what others miss and feels their movements and motions before they do. (It is no surprise that a large number of athletes, artists, musicians, and actors have Sensitive Personalities.)

But these "antennae" are, in reality, just a part of this reflective, introspective Personality: highly sensitive to his own moods, feelings, and thoughts as well as to the moods, feelings, and thoughts of others. Curious about and highly observant of everything in the world, he is just naturally alive to all the signals, good and bad.

When his feelings about himself harmonize with the feelings of others and the events going on around him, the Sensitive Personality is a very content and serene person, happy to be alive. He feels one with the world, one with his fellow human beings, and he is quite willing to work diligently to effect and preserve that harmony without, and that tranquility within. And what he wants for himself, he wants for everyone. Otherwise, there is no true harmony, no real peace—there is only discord and chaos; and the Sensitive Personality cannot abide chaos.

If the world were his, the Sensitive Personality would see to it that all the trains ran on time, that all energy sources were managed prudently, that all the foodstuffs were distributed equitably, that all wounds were healed, and that every worker received a good day's pay for a good day's work. There would be a chicken in every pot and a car in every garage—not coq au vin perhaps, and no super-deluxe gas guzzler; just a nice plump bird and an economical, sturdy means of transportation.

The Sensitive Personality is always looking for the efficient, dependable, purposeful solution to a problem, avoiding the pretentious and the extravagant. Even worse, to him, is the kind of fuzzy thinking that produces pretense and extravagance—those kinds of solutions, he knows, throw the system out of balance to produce waste and want. He is frustrated when the equilibrium is disrupted and outraged at the sight of waste and want—he can't see them without wanting to do something about them. He wants to make all things whole and harmonious.

Not only is the Sensitive Personality intensely observant and sensitive to other people, he is also adept at organizing, ordering, and integrating the various elements and opportunities within his confidence and environment. He produces results. His goals are usually high and he is creative in pursuit of those goals. Whether studying better ways to care for the aged or devising better traffic signs for the corners in his neighborhood, the Sensitive Personality brings to any task his unique resources of keen observation, organization, and a sense of justice, care, concern, and curiosity.

The healthy and mature Sensitive Personality is as aware of the characteristics of his style as are his friends and colleagues, although he is too shy and modest to acknowledge them to others or to want them praised. Here is how two Sensitive Personalities, a man and a woman, described their strengths to me:

"I think loyalty is one. I've seen other women I would have liked to date but I wouldn't. I'm very loyal to my girlfriend."

"Friendship is another strength."

"I think we're open-minded. You always try to think of the other guy; you try to see his side."

"A way of backing off, finding a quiet place, and thinking over a problem."

"A sense of humor. That helps a lot. It gets you through."

The more healthy the Sensitive Personality, the more he can use these qualities for his own benefit and for the benefit of others. Those around him note that the Sensitive Personality is also honest, kind, and considerate, but he is so prone to maintaining a low profile that it is possible to miss some of his many productive attributes. He finds deserved praise uncomfortable, and, being sensitive and shy, he hears a compliment as if it were amplified ten times over and winces. He reacts no differently to criticism—it too is amplified by his sensitive feelings, and he suffers. Yet he is so well organized and purposeful that he can integrate constructive criticism, even when it hurts. He is capable of maintaining a placid exterior while his feelings are shouting angrily inside.

The Sensitive Personality is a lover and maker of tranquility. So the Golden Rule, "Do unto others as you would have them do unto you," makes a shining path for you to follow in your pursuit of peace. As one Sensitive put it, "I'll scratch your back, and I expect you to scratch mine."

Honesty and loyalty are the traits that form the fabric of the Sensitive Personality's relationships. Your friends describe you as "loyal and true to the end." Friendship is not a casual thing, and a relationship is usually a long time coming. But once the bond is established, you'll stick by it through thick and thin.

MEET YOUR TV TWINS

Little escapes your watchful eye, so it should not be much trouble for you to distinguish those TV Twins who share your Sensitive Personality. No doubt, your unquenchable curiosity will be cause enough to make you seek out and examine the ways in which they can help you to know and be yourself.

Your Sensitive TV Twins will be easy to identify because they are:

- Very expressive with their eyes.
- Shy and sensitive.

- Brief in their speech.
- Loyal to friends and family.
- Curious.
- Alert and reactive to their environment.

You and your TV Twins are thoughtful people who want this to be a decent world where everyone and everything coexists in harmony. You greatly value loyalty and, above all, trust. You accept your responsibility to be accountable for your actions, to follow the Golden Rule. You are rather shy and at the same time intensely curious.

Peter McDermott is the manager of the St. Gregory Hotel on "Hotel." He exhibits his Sensitive Personality in a number of ways: through his expressive eyes, his studied, rehearsed actions and reactions, his loyalty and agonizing over relationships.

On "Hill Street Blues," Sensitive **Mick Belker** is an undercover cop who uses his powers of observation and ability to assume disguises and mimic various characters as a cover. He also shows his sensitivity and loyalty during the phone calls his mother is always making to him at the station house. He takes the time to talk and always tells her he loves her.

Norm Buntz, another Sensitive cop on "Hill Street Blues," also exhibits his loyalty to friends, particularly in one episode when he stands up for a fellow officer who is in trouble. Although the fellow officer has not developed the greatest reputation as an honest, upstanding type, he comes to Norm for help. And Norm finds it very hard to turn him down.

Ray, on "Dallas," is part of a Texas oil family, the Ewings. He frequently shows his loyalty to Miss Ellie Ewing, the family matriarch and his stepmother. In one episode, Ray is discussing with his friend Jack an attractive offer that Jack has received (and Ray is about to receive) from one of the Ewing family's competitors to buy his Ewing Oil stock. The rival company is apparently planning a takeover. Ray knows that Miss Ellie is very concerned about keeping the Ewing family and Ewing Oil together. Since she has been a valuable friend to Ray, he is not about to let her down. Jack has asked Ray if he was aware of the offer. "Yeah, I heard of it," says Ray. "Pretty hard to pass up." "And?" asks Jack. "I'm gonna stand by Miss Ellie," is Ray's answer. "Whichever way she decides to go, that's the way I'm going."

Claudia, on "Dynasty," also shows her Sensitive Personality by her loyalty, awareness, and special feeling for children.

The eyes are what you notice about **Stingray,** a mysterious figure who travels the country in his vintage Corvette Stingray, gathering and returning favors, helping those in need. He assumes many disguises and personae in his work. But the eyes always tell his true story. In one episode, Stingray is posing as a surgeon to help a friend find out why there have been so many unexplained fatalities in the hospital where the friend works. While there, Stingray also befriends a rather attractive female surgeon who seems to be as observant as he. "You're no surgeon," she tells him soon after they meet. "Surgeons are cold, distant. There's too much going on behind those eyes."

As you follow your TV Twins' video lives, look carefully for examples of:

- Their need for private time.
- The importance they place on being rehearsed and prepared in life.
- Being accountable and expecting others to be accountable.
- The way they utilize a "Golden Rule" approach in making judgments.
- Not hesitating to praise others.
- The value they place on trust.

You and your TV Twins can be motivated by a positive, constructive environment. You benefit greatly from observing a situation and then responding in your personal, intuitive way. Your curiosity is among your greatest strengths and your antennae are always out. It's your curiosity that allows you to go beyond the superficial and to explore that which is underlying, then follow your intuition.

THE SIX SENSES OF THE SENSITIVE PERSONALITY

Here's how a Sensitive friend explained how it feels to be so highly aware and sensitive in her everyday life: "You're sensitive in every way—your whole body is sensitive. But mostly your feelings are so acute. I think you feel everything just a little more sharply. When you enjoy something, you enjoy it more perhaps than the average person does. If you hear beautiful music, you hear the different notes and how they weave to make the whole. If you rub your hand over a piece of wooden furniture, you feel everything—the smoothness of the surface, any tiny nick or blemish, even the grain of the wood. If you smell your favorite dish cooking in the kitchen, the aroma fills your entire head. You're excited by the sound of a bird singing or the beauty of a sunset with all of its subtle color changes. And when you grieve, it's terrible—the loss is heavy, and it lasts a long time. But when you love somebody, somebody you can know and trust, you love that person completely. They fill all of your senses."

Let's sit back and observe Ray as he tunes into life on the Ewing ranch, Mick Belker as he observes very closely the unsavory activities of his latest "Hill Street Blues" undercover assignment, and Peter McDermott as he reflects on the intrigue unfolding all around him at the St. Gregory Hotel. Then we'll ask you what prompts the Sensitive Personality to be so observant, so keenly aware, so sensitive.

"I like to keep the peace in my own self and in the environment around me," was one Sensitive response. "So I guess by being observant and aware of what's going on it's easier to keep things in order. It's easier to see how things fit together, and catch it right away if they start to fall apart."

Another Sensitive put it very simply: "We like to have everything going smoothly with no ripples." (And we know how those ripples that are barely detectible to non-Sensitive awareness can shout "surf's up" to your delicate receptors.)

"When my feelings about myself harmonize with the feelings

of others and the events going on around me, I am a very content and serene person," said one Sensitive observer. "I feel one with the world and my fellow human beings."

Your acute awareness and sensitivity can sometimes form a radar screen in your mind, a tracking system that lets you see things before they appear, feel things before they strike, and hear the delightful sound of that song that will be coming up on your favorite radio station, right after the next commercial message.

We can watch Ray, on "Dallas," scan the coming attractions in his mind when he takes the words right out of his friend Jack's mouth as they are discussing Jack's business dealings with J.R. Ewing, the sometimes ruthless head of Ewing Oil. "I'll bet old J.R. suggested you get more involved in the oil business. Maybe even said you can have an office down at Ewing Oil, huh?" says Ray as his friend acknowledges the fact that those very words had come from J.R.'s mouth. There is, of course, no mystical secret to Ray's ability to predict. He has simply paid very close attention to his own—and others'—dealings with J.R. and has correctly carried his conclusions one step further by assuming a similar experience for Jack.

There are times, though, when the Sensitive mind is so attuned to the environment and surroundings that you even detect the direction in which the subtle combination of events we call the future is heading. That is an ability that gives your TV Twin Stingray an almost mystical quality as he moves through the shadows, just ahead of the revealing spotlight. That ability is sometimes called ESP, the sixth sense.

"I can remember when I felt pains in my back at work at the very same time that my wife was in labor," recalls one Sensitive man of his experience with the sixth sense. "It was somewhat of a strange feeling, but I was right."

Another Sensitive Personality remembers one of her experiences: "I recall a time when I was driving on the highway and something told me to slow down and pull off the road. Well, I did slow down, but kept driving, and sure enough two or three miles further on down the road there was a truck that had dropped a whole load of lumber in the middle of my lane."

"I know a lot of times what someone is thinking and when that happens I'll tell them about it," said another Sensitive. "I can answer their questions before they ask them. That irritates a lot of people but I know now, after studying my Sensitive TV Twins, that it's not that unusual for me to be able to do it."

Actually, experiences with the sixth sense are not limited strictly to the Sensitive Personality. We all probably manage to tune in and out of it occasionally. But the Sensitive does seem to be much more aware of his ability to experience it. And, true to form, it is a Sensitive Personality whose curiosity had led him to observe and reflect upon just how this amazing ability might work. "I think it's just a matter of my mind working slower than my eyes and ears. Things have actually happened, and I have seen and heard, but my mind just takes a little longer to catch up, digest the information, and become consciously aware."

Sounds plausible to me. I certainly don't have any better explanation. Of course, you probably knew that a couple of paragraphs ago.

THE EYES HAVE IT

What exactly is going on behind those eyes? The answer to that question is something that the Sensitive Personality likes to keep to himself a great deal of the time. You are very aware of what can be seen in the eyes—particularly Sensitive eyes—as well as through them. Not only vibrant color and a variety of textures and hues, but also naked emotion and identity pass through those tiny windows, coming and going on the path from your Sensitive soul. And you don't want just anyone traipsing up and down that path.

Sunglasses are the way many Sensitive Personalities continue to observe the world around them without having it observe them too closely in return. Those sunglasses provide the perfect vantage point.

On the other hand, the Sensitive Personality can also carry on a great deal of nonverbal communication with the eyes. One Sensitive woman described Peter McDermott's unspoken conversation on "Hotel." "His eyebrows arch when he is pleading or puzzled, the eyes glare when he is angry or being pushed or pressured, and he will look down when he wants a minute to think or when the situation is getting uncomfortable. Lieutenant Norm Buntz is the same way. I can almost tell what he is going to say, or would have said next, just by watching his eyes."

For the Sensitive Personality, one look can say a thousand words, or it can say nothing at all.

ALONE IN A CROWD

Just as sunglasses or a downward glance can conceal and protect your Sensitive inner self, an unassuming, modest approach to social situations can keep you in the background where the observing is good and the profile is low. Those who do notice you will probably say that you are just being shy.

"I don't mind being in a big crowd of people as long as I'm not standing out in any way. That way I can be anonymous and people-watch to my heart's content," observed one Sensitive Personality. "But if I walk into a roomful of people and feel like all eyes are on me, I'll turn around and walk out."

A friend of mine with a Sensitive Personality recently took up the guitar, and while she loves it dearly, she finds the lessons and the awkwardness of the beginner to be something of a challenge to her sensitivity. Still at the "plunk, plunk, plunk" stage, her husband enjoys teasing her and she reports, "I get a little upset by his sly remarks." Her shyness really surfaces in the group instruction she is taking. When the teacher has each student play a piece individually, my friend feels the strain. "But I have been watching my Sensitive TV Twins," she says, "and have begun to realize that the shyness really comes from my extraordinary sensitivity, not only to possible criticism from the teacher, but also to all eyes in the room. I feel like I've got a better handle on it now. I'm still trembling away inside, but outside I'm doing my darndest."

Socially, the Sensitive Personality tends to move in a tight circle of friends whom he has come to know gradually. The shyness will normally disappear when you are with that small, comfortable group. While you think of yourself as an open and friendly person, which you typically are, you still place a high value on privacy. There are times when even that small group is too much.

On "Hotel," we hear Sensitive Peter McDermott's assistant, Christine, verbalize it so well when she says, "Peter, sometimes I feel so close to you and sometimes I feel so shut out."

"It's true what she's saying," said one Sensitive Personality after watching Peter and Christine. "There are times when you have to regulate the constant flow of stimuli from people and your surroundings. What some people see as shyness or even as my being 'stuck up' is just my way of avoiding overwhelming public contact."

We can watch Sensitive Claudia, on "Dynasty," as she informs her ex-husband why she has decided suddenly to leave town. "It's partly business. It's partly just to get away and think," says Claudia. "There is so much to think about."

After watching Peter McDermott and Claudia, one Sensitive commented, "I guess it's because you're so finely tuned to everything going on around you, absorbing so much of the environment, that you need moments away to be able to sift and sort, then to give it all meaning."

"I can certainly relate the need for privacy to myself," said another Sensitive. "When I'm home I like to lie on the couch with my stereo headphones on and listen to music. Or I go down to my workshop in the basement alone, tinker a bit, smoke my pipe, and turn the stereo on down there. But what I'm really doing is kind of thinking things over, taking a look at how life's going. If the pace has been really hectic, then I try to take a weekend off to go up to the farm."

When the much needed privacy cannot be maintained, the crowds trample the fence and overrun your solitude, or the isolation is broken, your reaction can come in many different forms. On "Hill Street Blues," Mick Belker turns back those who would invade his space by growling like a dog. Most Sensitive Personalities have found a more subtle method.

"I haven't tried growling like a dog yet," said one Sensitive woman who had come to me, "but I was getting pretty upset with my husband and his constant invasion of my space. He had been working second shift, so when I got home from the office he was gone. Some nights I did wish that he could be there—too much time alone isn't good—but other nights I'd be content. Then he changed to first shift and I couldn't get a minute to myself. Then we started watching and learning from the Sensitive TV Twins. It was easier for me to explain to him that he shouldn't take it personally when I escape upstairs and lock the bedroom door. And if he forgets, I'll just growl at him from the other side. He'll get the message.''

INTENSE CURIOSITY SOMETIMES BECOMES SUSPICION

Curious about what? Well, in the case of the Sensitive Personality, curious about anything and everything. After all, it only makes sense that someone who is so aware and tuned in to what is going on all around would be very interested in the how and why of it. ''I like to examine things firsthand,'' is how one Sensitive described it. ''I want to feel them all around me.''

You are so curious that, at times, you may assume that everyone else is just as curious. (Of course, with other Sensitive Personalities you are probably correct.) That assumption can become a problem if it begins to get out of hand. You become guarded or secretive, especially when you aren't feeling good abut yourself. When you don't fully trust yourself, you project that mistrust onto others. Curiosity becomes suspicion.

On ''Dallas,'' Ray explains to his wife why he is just a little suspicious of Jack. ''Jack was out there helping me mend some fence I had to get done. That guy's quite a character,'' says Ray. ''What makes you say that?'' asks his wife. ''Well, I don't know,'' answers Ray, ''he just comes into town out of nowhere. Don't take him very long, he's got ten percent of Ewing Oil. I don't know. I think the more time I spend with the guy, the less I think I know him.''

Earlier in that same episode Ray had been relating his suspicions about J.R. Ewing to Jack. ''Don't trust J.R. He doesn't trust you," he tells Jack. "And watch out if you've got something to hide, because you're just liable to be reading about it in the morning paper."

On "Hill Street Blues," Lieutenant Norm Buntz is just a little suspicious of the intentions of a female cop who has just asked him to have dinner with her. She doesn't understand his hesitation. "If I'm not mistaken, the last time you and me conversed I had the impression that you thought I was a scum bucket," Norm tells her. But she persists and Norm finally gives in to the invitation, although he is still curious as to her apparent change of heart. Later, at dinner, he asks, "So how come the sudden change of temperature?"

"I find myself really caught up in this 'life is a jungle' idea sometimes," said one Sensitive Personality after watching Ray and Lieutenant Buntz. "And sometimes it's really true. But I really do try to avoid being oversensitive to every slight or criticism. It can really make you paranoid. You just have to learn to separate the legitimate suspicions from the silly ones."

"There were times when I would walk into a room and feel as if everyone was looking at my hair, or my hips," said a Sensitive woman. "I know now that it's our nature to be suspicious. But it's one thing to be suspicious of the motives of others, like Ray or Buntz, and another thing to just project your own insecurities on everyone else. I guess you just have to find that balance between your curiosity and the need to reflect on your own mind; between being sensitive to other people's feelings and being sensitive to your own. I guess you just need to learn to trust."

TRUST AND THE GOLDEN RULE

Trust is the very hub of the Sensitive Personality's existence. It ties together all the pieces of your life to form the whole. The more you can trust in everyone and everything, the greater the sense of harmony and tranquility. And the surest, most dependable method of developing that trust is to be equally trustworthy. You are helpful and loyal to others, so you want them to be loyal and helpful too. You know how you want to be treated, so you treat others the same way. I trust you, you trust me, and the equilibrium is preserved.

Well, that certainly does make sense. As a matter of fact, on "Stingray" we can watch Sensitive Stingray conduct his whole life according to the "I do you a favor, you do me a favor," philosophy. He travels all over the country, handing out and collecting favors. And it all seems to work. So we seem to have an axiom here, a rule that goes: "Do unto others as you would have them do unto you." But what should we call it? The Sensitive Rule? Nah, a little too presumptuous. The Stingray Rule? Maybe not. How about the Golden Rule?

The Golden Rule, in whatever form and by whatever name, is a very important dynamic in the Sensitive Personality's life. It is really as if you had invented it. One Sensitive Personality once told me, with a show of excitement, "I remember when we were kids and the teacher passed out wooden rulers that had the Golden Rule printed on them. I read it and said to myself, 'That's what I want to do. I'm going to remember the Golden Rule.' I remember the good feeling I had. I always remembered the Golden Rule and I still think about it."

LOYALTY AND FRIENDSHIP

For the Sensitive Personality there is no safer port from the chaos of the world than a true and trusted friend. But true and trusted friends seem to be a rare commodity. Once you've found and made a friend you can trust, you've made a friend for life. And from trust flows loyalty.

On "Hill Street Blues," Mick Belker shows his loyalty to an old friend, a street person who has disappeared for a while but has turned up again, a victim of AIDS. Mick is obviously a bit uncomfortable at first, but stands by his friend, sitting with him in his shabby apartment, going out to buy him the ice cream that he wants, sticking with him until the end.

"I used to look at the loyalty and sensitivity in myself and not like it," said one Sensitive Personality. "I wanted to be more like friends of mine who are aggressive and assertive. But once I started watching characters like Ray and Mick Belker, I became aware that it was OK, because I was just being myself. If it's the right thing for me, then I shouldn't be concerned with what someone else thinks."

"I guess I'm like Mick Belker in that episode in which his friend had AIDS," said another Sensitive Personality. "Even though it was very difficult for him, like when the police came after his friend died and asked him if he had had intimate relations with the friend. They assumed Mick was a homosexual also. But Mick didn't back away. It's like Peter McDermott said to a lady friend who had come to him in one episode for help: 'I'd never turn a lady—or a friend—in trouble out of my house.' I feel the same way."

Loyalty does meet its tests at times, and there are situations that really do defy you to stand by your friends. "I'm not depressed very often but I live with someone, my wife, who gets depressed quite a bit," says one Sensitive Personality who came to me for help. "So out of loyalty, I think I sometimes take on her depression. The problem is, she can function when she's depressed but I can't." We watched an episode of "Dallas" in which Ray is visiting his wife in the hospital just after she has suffered a miscarriage. She is very depressed and refuses to respond to any of his efforts to help, but Ray refuses to give up on her or on himself. "I know how badly this hurts you," Ray tells her. "But you can't go on bottling it up inside you like this. Sooner or later you and me are gonna have to talk about it, and I am not gonna let you shut me out like this. Whatever happens, we're gonna see it through together."

My Sensitive friend with the depression-prone wife commented after seeing the episode and thinking about his own situation, "Ray's wife was obviously very upset and depressed. He could have just given up too, but he didn't. He just told her he would be there when she decided to talk. I guess in my own situation it would be better not to show my loyalty by sharing the depression, but by making sure my wife knows I'll be there for her when she gets down. I guess loyalty makes more sense that way."

Another Sensitive Personality was having problems remaining loyal to both parents who were going through a divorce. "I work for my father so I can't really be loyal to both of them. So I stick with my father, but I feel like I am betraying my mother." We watched Claudia, on "Dynasty," who decided that she needed to move away from the city, and from her estranged husband—her second husband—to have some time to think. In this segment, she has stopped by to see her first husband, Steven, with whom she has remained friends, before she leaves. It was a case of deciding to be loyal to herself by leaving husband number two, but still maintaining her loyalty to an old friendship with husband number one. "I'm so sorry that our marriage didn't work out," she tells Steven, "but I'm glad that we've stayed friends."

"I guess there are times when your cup of loyalty just runs over," said my Sensitive friend after viewing the segment. "The loyalty is still there, but it just takes different forms to fit the situation. I guess you just have to let people know, one way or another, that no matter how it looks, you're still with them."

"I was so impressed by watching the episode in which Ray was concerned about his wife in the hospital," said one Sensitive Personality in summing up the loyalty urge. "He was so kind and gentle. A real inner strength showed through that I'm sure will help me when I'm in a situation like that."

Because trust and loyalty run so deep with the Sensitive Personality, and you exhibit both so intensely, you can be stung with equal intensity by betrayal. "I'm always totally knocked out by disloyalty," says one Sensitive woman.

Once someone has betrayed or destroyed the trust in your relationship, the bond is shattered and the relationship is severely impaired, if not totally destroyed. Another Sensitive woman gives what sounds like the final Sensitive word on the subject: "I'll always help someone once, but if they turn on me, that's the last time."

A LITTLE SAYS A LOT

You are very aware of the impact that words can have, so you don't waste them. Like Peter McDermott, Stingray, and the rest of your Sensitive Twins, you are probably not a person who enjoys a lot of small talk, although at times it can get you through an awkward situation. Your eyes, and a few words, will usually express all that you have to say.

A Sensitive Personality came to me saying that she had been very envious of others who were able to talk freely, especially in social situations. She found herself avoiding social situations whenever she could and said that when she was forced to mingle, she had a tendency to be a bit laconic; the conversation was short and sweet. "But I've been watching Peter McDermott and Stingray, how they are able to get their point across with a lot of nonverbal communication," she said. "I'm beginning to recognize that my response to small talk is quite appropriate and normal for me. I'm beginning to put less pressure on myself to have to carry on those long, drawn-out conversations."

The Sensitive Personality may have occasional problems expressing himself. You are so aware and tuned in to possible criticism or ridicule. It can be difficult to reduce all that you feel and experience into the sometimes limiting world of words. But you are not alone. "You know how I am about expressing myself, my feelings," says Peter McDermott to Christine. "It's difficult for me, always has been."

"Sometimes I try to compensate for my inability to make small talk and express myself spontaneously by trying to make jokes or by saying something outrageous," says one Sensitive Personality. "Sometimes it works, but sometimes I end up later regretting what I said."

IMPROVE COMMUNICATION WITH REHEARSAL

My advice to the Sensitive Personality who is feeling unsure about what to say, and when to say it, is simply to rehearse. Ray, on "Dallas," does it. When he and wife Donna are talking about how they will fill their big house, Donna tells him not to worry, that she is a lady who knows how to shop. But Sensitive Ray has had something else in mind. He tells Donna that he has been thinking about adopting a child. "How long have you been thinking about that?" asks Donna. "Been kickin' it around for a couple of weeks," Ray answers.

The more you rehearse, the less you leave to chance. That can mean a lot to a Sensitive Personality whose finely tuned radar ears receive compliments amplified ten times over and criticism amplified twenty. "I really do like to have time to run over my response a few times in my head before I come out with it," said one Sensitive. "Even in the middle of a conversation, I'll play for time: stall, come at answers slowly, light a cigarette. It's really a Sensitive art form to be able to stall without losing the flow."

"I've been getting ready for parties or public gatherings I have to attend by rehearsing," said another Sensitive after watching her TV Twins go through their dry runs. "I try to find out who's going to be there and what they are interested in or likely to talk about. That helps me to be relaxed and prepared for what might go on."

Let's walk through this one more time: you want to protect your delicate inner self from the slings and arrows that might come with an off-the-cuff performance; you like to say exactly what it is you want to say. But you have some problems at times expressing yourself in a way that everyone will understand and catch on to. That's it in a nutshell.

So rehearse. It's good for you and it's advice well taken, not only by your Sensitive Twins but by others who see it work. On "Hotel," Peter McDermott's assistant tells him that a friend has quite suddenly asked her to marry him. Sensitive Peter asks her what her response to the unexpected proposal was. "I told him I needed more time," she answers. "That's something I learned from you, Peter."

SENSITIVITY AT WORK

A Sensitive machinist told me that his hands were so sensitive that he rarely needed a micrometer to gauge the level of tolerance on certain jobs he was familiar with. When quality control ran spot checks, they always found his tolerance was well within the range that he said they were.

It comes as no surprise that you will probably work best at a job or professional situation that allows you full exercise of your strength: the observational powers of Mick; the loyalty and dependability of Ray; the inner strength and character of Peter and Stingray.

A Sensitive Personality as an inspecting officer in the military could be a terror. You would immediately be able to note any small detail out of order, yet you would probably be so aware of a frightened recruit's feelings that you might choose to overlook offenses that you felt were trivial.

TV set on the blink? I would suggest a Sensitive TV repairman; might be quicker to spot the trouble in your set. Playing in the symphony orchestra tonight? Watch for the Sensitive music critic in the audience. He or she will be the one to hear a rushed beat or an instrument out of tune, as well as the exceptionally fine tone of a solo instrumentalist. Big game today? I would tread softly around a Sensitive official. He or she will probably spot a foul or penalty long before anyone else.

One Sensitive Personality described to me how he had used his curiosity and sensitivity at work to detect a rather large percentage of error in his division. "I came up with some ways that the people I work with and I could improve on the job. Some of them thought I was crazy because I didn't run to management right away and claim credit for the ideas. But I just told them to watch Stingray. It's the Golden Rule at work. They'll know what I mean when I come around to collect the favors. But in the meantime, things are running a lot smoother in my division."

After a good day's work for a good day's pay, how about a little time to reflect? A leisurely horseback ride under the wide, blue Texas sky with Ray on a tour of the Ewing ranch. Then a dash down the highway with Stingray, the wind in our faces. A night of comfort and luxury with a sumptuous meal and fine wine at Peter McDermott's hotel. Finally, a walk on the beach. "There's nothing more appealing than a vacation at the beach," says one of my Sensitive friends. "Wiggling your toes in the warm sand, feeling the salt air in your face, and hearing the rhythm of the crashing waves. After working so hard, that's the most relaxing thing in the world."

MARRIAGE AND RELATIONSHIPS

The Sensitive Personality, so careful in relationships, tends to date fewer people than other Personality Styles. He tends to be attracted to a warm, outgoing, and friendly person, and is most comfortable with someone who is carefree and pleasant yet sufficiently serious about life. A smile is a beacon to the aware Sensitive Personality, a sign of openness and friendliness. "That smile; it could light up the night." "He was very gentle and kind and he liked to talk to me. He seemed to always make me feel good. He lifted my spirits." "He is always happy, and he likes other people to be happy. If you have a problem or are upset about something, he'll help in any way he can."

A relationship, with all of its angles, facets, and sometimes bewildering complexity of emotion, is not something to be approached casually. At least not for the Sensitive Personality. You will normally take your time, noting all the positives and negatives about the other person: an annoying twitch here, an obvious overdose of after-shave or perfume there, an unsuccessful kick at your cat while he or she thought you weren't watching, and this potential heartache is history.

"I refuse to accept romance as a function of spare time," is how one Sensitive Personality put it. "It's almost painful to watch Peter agonize over his relationships on 'Hotel.' But I know exactly what's going through his mind. Once I decide to commit to a relationship, I invest heavily. That's why I take my time and consider everything there is to consider."

On "Hill Street Blues," Lieutenant Norm Buntz is still very suspicious of a lady cop who had burned him in a previous encounter and is now back, asking him to take her to dinner. The eyes say there is a definite attraction, the old Sensitive radar is picking up some mixed signals. "You've been on my mind since I quit," she tells him after having quit the police force and then suddenly returning. "I just kept imagining being back at work, having my job back, and I was always talking to you," she says. But Norm is leery. "You weren't hollering at me?" he asks. She answers no. "You stepped on my onions pretty good last time we talked," says Norm, still not convinced he wants to subject himself, or his Sensitive feelings, to her again.

A Sensitive woman who was going through a similar experience with an old boyfriend told me she could readily relate to Norm's dilemma. "This old boyfriend came up to me at a party two weeks ago. We talked for a while and he grabbed my hand. I told him I had to go. It all stirred up a lot of old feelings but I also felt that it wasn't the same as it used to be. I had gotten burned, like Norm, and the situation scared me and made me suspicious, just as it did him. I tend to want to block out feelings because they overwhelm me. Sometimes I get intensely angry. I don't know if I'll ever marry. I suppose it really hinges on meeting the right person."

When that "right person" does come along, and the wedding bells ring, the investment in home and family is once again heavy for the Sensitive Personality: mutual sharing, tenderness, and an intense loyalty. "I felt my lip quiver when I watched Ray talking to his wife while she was in the hospital after having her miscarriage," said one Sensitive Personality. "He stood by her through it all. Then afterwards he was the one to suggest adopting a child to start a family. It made me feel good."

"My husband is the person I'm closest to," said another Sensitive Personality. "He showers me with warm, loving feelings. He also has an attractive body and I like to watch him when he doesn't know it, like when he's mowing the lawn with his shirt off."

The healthy Sensitive Personality arranges a relationship in which he and his spouse share and enjoy mutual interests that contribute to the growth of their marriage. He doesn't compete with his partner; rather, he supports the outgoing and spontaneous style of his spouse. In turn, his partner appreciates his gentle ways, his kindness, his sensitivity toward the other person's needs and feelings.

The partner of the Sensitive Personality may very well be the sort of person who recognizes, appreciates, and encourages the strong prearranging and organizing talents of that Style, both at home and in his career. If sufficiently attuned to the Sensitive

Personality's need for solitary time and reflection, the partner will not only tolerate this need but encourage it.

The less secure Sensitive Personality may be tormented in marriage by jealousy, his own lack of confidence prompting him to be suspicious, accusing his spouse of infidelity. His spouse benefits by knowing that this climate of suspicion is really the Sensitive partner's excessive awareness and preoccupation with everything going on outside himself—to the detriment of his own positive feelings. The problem is, again, one of sharing and understanding. Rather than responding with indignation and retaliation, however tempting, the spouse might reverse the situation by offering calm reassurance while inviting the Sensitive mate to consider his feelings as projected self-criticism.

The problem is also lessened by mutual giving, especially if the Sensitive partner is able to go beyond the moment of jealousy by reflecting on the much larger moments of mutual sharing and tenderness that he values so much.

The Sensitive parent tends to be loving and doting, gladly sharing his or her insights, observations, experiences, and interests with the children. And the Sensitive child, no matter how old, tends to give back to his or her parents as he or she has received; the Golden Rule once again.

FROM THE MOUTHS OF BABES

There are probably no better conduits for beauty, honesty, and unguarded love than the minds and senses of children. They are curious and open to all of the experiences of life, looking on each for exactly what it offers. It is not surprising then, that the Sensitive Personality has such an appreciation for the world of children, or that slipping into that world is usually an easy passage.

On "Dynasty," Sensitive Claudia is not on the best of terms with Sammy Jo. In fact, "enemies" would probably best describe their relationship. When Claudia stops by Sammy Jo's house to take care of some business, though, she notices Sammy

Jo's son at the piano. So she sits down to join him. She can't resist the appeal of putting aside the feud, or the appeal of a little boy at play. When Sammy Jo appears and demands to know what Claudia is doing, she answers, "I was just in the neighborhood and I thought I'd stop by and see a little boy that I love very much."

We can watch Peter McDermott in one episode of "Hotel" sit and have a very warm and fruitful discussion with a young girl about problems she is having with her mother. "I guess I'm able to see the world on the same level as children," said one Sensitive Personality after viewing the segment. "They are close to the ground and their communication is simple. They haven't learned to complicate all of their conversation or cover their tracks with too many words."

On "Dallas," Ray is discussing children with friend Jack. "You like kids?" Ray asks. "Yeah, I guess I like kids, as long as they're somebody else's," answers Jack. "You just say that now," says Ray. "You wait till you find the right lady. You'll probably have a house full of rug rats." "Why," Jack asks Ray, "is that what you want?" "Yeah, more than anything I can think of," is Sensitive Ray's reply.

"I just like to take kids into the woods on a spring day, or to a circus or the movies," says a Sensitive friend of mine to explain the attraction between the Sensitive Personality and the little folks. "They can really appreciate the green buds and blossoms and smells in the woods, and at the movies we share the candy and popcorn. And when something's really good, they won't hesitate to cheer or to boo if it's bad."

"Children see a part of you that the grownup world can't, or won't," is another Sensitive Personality's explanation. "Kids know better than anyone else if someone is good or bad, and kids love me."

And who could argue with that?

ALTERNATIVES AND OPTIONS

We have seen that the Sensitive Personality is a gentle and kind person who, despite a tendency to be shy, is keenly aware of everything and everybody around him, who desires to respond in a healthy way to the needs of others. He pursues the Golden Rule as a basic disposition toward others and as a guard against disruption and chaos in all parts of the environment. Above all else in life the Sensitive Personality desires happy and harmonious relationships, especially in marriage.

He likes to work in a position that utilizes his skills in observing and organizing while permitting him to be productive and to contribute in a personally satisfying way. He makes friends slowly and he tends to restrict his friendships to a few; but, as a friend, he is loyal and trusting. Always he is a person who wants and works for a peaceful life in which he and his family and friends can enjoy serenity and safety.

These very worthy goals are quite possible and available to the healthy Sensitive Personality. The more he knows his strengths and weaknesses, the more available they are. For the less healthy Sensitive Personality, the same goals are possible, but the struggle to achieve them is much greater. He can try too hard to be helpful and nice, so much so that he doesn't lead his own life. He can be so loyal and sacrificing in his love that he is willing to give up his good feelings about himself to be the person he believes others apparently want him to be. He can be so influenced by the environment that he feels responsible for every mishap, and he can assume the blame for every fault and failing; he can be his own worst enemy. He tends to be so aware of the possibilities of hurt and harm that he fears he might cause them to happen; then he is prone to retreat into solitude as a defense rather than as an opportunity for objective evaluation. He hides. He has emptied himself of all trust and confidence in himself. The solution, then, is to work back into the environment, into human company, into communication and trust. He needs to restore equilibrium within himself and with the world outside.

If you are a Sensitive Personality, consider the following:

- First, don't keep it all inside. Turn it outside by opening up to a close friend and family, people you trust.
- Begin by rehearsing, taking small steps—one step at a time. Get to know people. Let friendships grow, however gradual the growth rate. The more you are involved, the more you will learn to trust yourself.
- Getting involved means, for you, the ability to relate to others without being so guarded.
- Stop blaming yourself for every tragedy, major and minor—you really aren't that negative an influence; you just think you are. It's only that you magnify and amplify perceptions, and convert flaws and failings in the environment into personal flaws and failings.
- Loyalty is a great virtue, but try being loyal to yourself more often.
- Let others know that you need your private time and silent moments.
- Use an occasional moment of reflection to tally the good jobs you have done, the kind deeds, the thoughtful gestures. Each night before you go to sleep, you might make it a practice to review the day with its many good moments.
- Don't let shyness rob you of opportunities for communication and interaction. Try the new restaurant you've been wanting to try; go to that party that interests you. The more you try new experiences, the more you mingle with others, the easier it will become.
- Trust your own wishes, your own feelings, your own hopes.
- Trust that other people really care about you and your needs. Trust is the first step in growth. Acting on that trust is the second step. Acknowledging your effort is the third step. Feeling good about it is the fourth. Once you've gone that far, each step gets easier.
- People find your shyness and reserve refreshing in this aggressive society. Did you know that?
- Build and depend on your intuitions.
- Don't let your easily embarrassed feelings make a quitter of you. If you would like to cut your hair or grow a beard, do

it. Sure, people might tease—that is a strange, tribal sign of recognition in our society. It also means people like you. So try that new dress, take guitar lessons, wear that new swimsuit. Enjoy.

- You have an engaging, subtle sense of humor. People enjoy it, so use it, but don't push it; and don't back off if you do use it. Just be yourself: a gentle person of gentle humor.
- Stop thinking that everyone is watching you. This is your projection of your own tendency to be so aware. Besides, since you have become so accustomed to looking at the ground, how can you know if others are watching you? Look up. Look around. Smile.
- You can see what you want to see in a mirror. If you feel your image is poor, you'll see a poor image in the mirror. If you want to see a fat man, you'll see a fat man. If you want to see a drab woman, you'll see a drab woman. The true mirror of your whole self is your ability to trust yourself and others.
- Always accept the opportunity to be with children. Relax, play the clown, laugh, enjoy. The more you experience the company of children, the more you will gain in confidence and the better you will interact generally. Remember: an adult is a child who has kept his sense of wonder intact while growing in wisdom and age.
- Acknowledge that timing for giving good or bad news is important. There's never a good time for giving bad news, but there's a best time.
- Keep your open mind, your great curiosity. Really try to understand as much as you can about everything you do, then hunt for the themes and patterns in life.
- Don't conceal, close yourself away, or be trapped by your shyness. Instead, try to step back, regroup, rehearse, then act. Consider your response and the response of others.
- Don't hold back the laughter. Laughter is a healthy sign that you are becoming more realistic, more relaxed about yourself. You are learning to trust enough to be happy. So laugh, love, and be happy. You deserve it.

SECRETS

The keys to a successful relationship with the Sensitive Personality are:

- Always be aware of the Sensitive Personality's heightened sense of awareness: no loud noises or glaring lights.
- Respect the Sensitive's need for quiet, private time.
- Don't probe too deeply into thoughts and feelings. The Sensitive Personality will discuss what's on his or her mind eventually.
- A little gentle persuasion will help to overcome shyness.
- Loyalty is of utmost importance.
- Pay attention to and learn from the Sensitive Personality's keen powers of observation.
- Learn to expect extraordinary curiosity.
- Make a peaceful, gently stimulating environment and watch the Sensitive Personality glow.

MATCH AND MISMATCH

Sensitive Personality matchmates:

Conscientious—Both of you enjoy a steady, deliberate pace in life. Nothing is hurried, which gives you adequate time to prepare. The Conscientious person treats those around with honesty, warmth, and a good sense of humor, which makes it easy for you to get along with this person. He or she likes to ask many questions, which piques your natural curiosity. An emphasis on routine makes for a pleasant environment, which is essential for you.

Anticipating—You won't go unprepared with this planner. The Anticipating person is able to give positive input, which builds up your confidence and the confidence you have in your decisions. He or she is also very genuine and authentic, which makes it very easy to have a trusting relationship. Your partner's planning and your rehearsing go hand in hand.

Persistent—You thrive in a positive environment and here is someone who gives plenty of attention and positive strokes.

The Persistent makes you feel very special with the emphasis on a one-to-one relationship; this translates into a loyal and trusting interaction. You need time to be alone, your private time, and the Persistent person does well when given time to daydream and be creative.

Influencing—With this person your natural curiosity is utilized because with the Influencing, life is constantly interesting and exciting. You are drawn to this partner's charming manner. You listen very well, and the Influencing is rather verbal, which provides for good communication. You both take pride in orderly and pleasant surroundings.

Ambitious—The Ambitious person enjoys the role of a first advisor, which can be very beneficial to you. You have a great need for private time, and the Ambitious will allow you plenty of time for this. The Ambitious person is always striving toward new goals and your curious mind can help generate new ideas. The successes are also shared, a real team effort. However, your partner is willing to compromise on an issue, and changing directions catches you off guard.

Patient—You both enjoy peaceful and pleasant surroundings and you like to share your ideas and experiences with each other. Because of your intense awareness, you are able to understand most of what the Patient person feels and wants. This partner does have some difficulty with the direct communication of needs and feelings, which may arouse some suspicion in you. The Patient person wants to come out looking good in the end, which could leave you looking bad.

Idealistic—You are attracted to Idealistic persons' independence. They have such definite opinions and you are not opposed to discussing these issues. You enjoy your private time while they need independence, which may work out as long as the timing is right. They do have a tendency to set standards which can be difficult for you. Your tendency to be somewhat self-critical can be seen as a weakness. They can also keep you at a distance emotionally, which may lead to some self-blame.

Adaptable—You two possess vastly different communication styles. They enjoy talking quite a bit, while you can be reserved, especially when around strangers. Your need for privacy is not shared by these outgoing types. They can be very flexible, while you need time to prepare and rehearse for new situations. Your personal matters may also become public information because of their "open-book" philosophy in life. Their multiple interests, while attractive at first, can later become somewhat threatening.

Accomplishing—Private moments are tough to come by with Accomplishing persons. You enjoy a calm quiet, unhurried pace, while they are always on the go, impulsive and energetic. They love attention and approval from others, while you can do without the attention. They love the limelight and you shy away from it.

Determined—It is important for you to have a positive environment and you do not get many positive strokes from this person. You may assume blame when things do not work out between the two of you, which can be reinforced by a cold stare from the Determined person. This partner has a tendency to sit on the fence and not make a decision, which is difficult for you to understand, particularly because of the minimal amount of feedback given. The Determined person is always strategizing but again does not discuss this to any great extent, which may raise your level of mistrust.

Perceptive—Your need for private time is very important, while the Perceptive person wants much of your attention and affection. Outspokenness and complaints can easily overwhelm you. The communication between you is difficult at best. Also, your failure to give constant attention and affection can produce cries of "unfair" from the Perceptive person. There is also a right and wrong time to approach you with problems, but the Perceptive person usually reacts very quickly and does not wait for the right time.

Chapter Thirteen

THE DETERMINED PERSONALITY

PROFILE

- Wants to be right and do the correct thing in all circumstances.
- Goes by the book.
- Very responsible.
- Strives for respect.
- Says a lot with just a few words, or one look.
- Does not tolerate a lot of nonsense.
- Likes to proceed according to a strategy and refuses to be pushed or hurried.

TV TWINS

- A.J. Simon—"Simon and Simon"
- Chris Cagney—"Cagney and Lacey"
- Frank Furillo—"Hill Street Blues"
- Chase Gioberti—"Falcon Crest"
- Cole Gioberti—"Falcon Crest"
- Michael Kuzak—"L.A. Law"

For the Determined Personality, the watchword is *right*, because the essence of your Personality is your prevailing concern for being right and doing the right thing. By doing the proper thing you become a responsible person and show your concern for what is right. And by being such a responsible person you gain the utmost respect of family, friends, and associates. With that formula, "right, responsible, and respect," the Determined Personality can never go wrong.

As a Determined Personality, you are a persuasive person, going about the business of doing what you believe is right in a quiet, yet tenacious—even stubborn—way. To you, part of doing something the right way is doing it all the way, but your tenacity is usually softened by your composure. You avoid overt confrontation or haggling, choosing instead to solicit the support of others in the pursuit of goals, making efforts to be aware of the other person's feelings and needs. You want to be agreeable and, more often than not, you *are* agreeable; abrasive attack and indifference are not your style. You can be competitive but never a back stabber.

Your striving for the right and responsible is done in an unassuming, low-keyed fashion; properly understated to the point of being disarming. Your plans are not always clear to everyone around you. In fact, "reserved" is often the description given the Determined Personality. We know something is happening inside your head—but just *what* is happening may not always be apparent.

The Determined Personality is not given to overt emotional or physical displays. There is no backslapping, gushing tears, or wild laughter here. The exchange may be friendly and warm, but at the same time is usually businesslike and to the point. The action in the Determined mind may be so subtle, so abstruse, that we may miss it or its significance. Few clues are given and no action is taken until the Determined person has sorted through all the angles and decided on the right strategy. Don't bother to ask the Determined Personality what's happening before it becomes obvious; he might find it difficult to explain, or he might prefer not to tell you. Still, rest assured, something is happening.

Consider the following example:

Negotiations between the local police association and the city council were deadlocked at contract time. The police were prohibited by law from striking, and the council, well aware of the law, was sitting tight, rejecting the association's demands. So what were the police to do? Capitulate—simply give in—or go out on an illegal strike, an alternative that was unacceptable to most of the police officers?

The police did neither. Instead, they chose a rather simple tactic: they enforced the local traffic ordinances rigorously. They ticketed every misparked vehicle, cited even the slightest moving violation, and wrote up every jaywalker, noisy muffler, and broken taillight. All week long, city hall's switchboard glittered and buzzed like a pinball machine; traffic court overflowed, frustrated citizens wrote irate letters to an irate editor who tried vainly to reach the mayor, who was trying vainly to appease his twice-ticketed wife. At the next council meeting, a packed gallery of concerned citizens watched as the council voted to grant the police association its new contract with the major portion of its demands intact.

Not surprisingly, a Determined Personality suggested this non-strike, no-capitulation tactic; rather typically, he found the oblique approach, the roundabout strategy, that broke the deadlock to produce victory without wounds.

The healthy Determined Personality has the knack of putting together a strategy that can make a difficult situation productive. The Determined's approach seems to be governed by a clear vision of goals and values pursued, sometimes openly, sometimes surreptitiously, whether in search of a working contract, uniforms for the girls' hockey team, lights in the park, or a better budget for running the household. He always tries to take a calm approach, to consider both sides of an issue, to work things out in a fair and equitable way. He is willing to consider compromise, if the situation so indicates.

Thus the Determined Personality is often cast in the role of mediator or negotiator. As we saw in the case of the police association's negotiations, he functions well as a catalyst who can make things happen. He also has a respect for authority, even when he disagrees or disputes the actions or position of those in authority. He works to keep opportunity alive, to keep his options open, and, if at all possible, he will try to avoid head-on confrontation and hard-nosed stalemates. His preferred tactic is persuasion, low-keyed and constant; he tries to avoid bloody wounds that leave scars and bitter resentment. However right he believes his views and his position, he is concerned that justice be done. That is his understanding of what it means to be responsible.

If, in the pursuit of the right and honorable way, the Determined Personality does run into obstacles that seem insurmountable, he may apply a tactic that certain well-known Determined kinsmen have made famous—the notion of passive resistance. There is no violent demonstration; that would not be constructive or responsible. There is no direct confrontation; that would show a lack of respect. There is only a gentle and constant persuasion, an absolute refusal to act or react, a calculated use of nonaction that gradually wears down the opposition.

MEET YOUR TV TWINS

Your Determined TV Twins are usually not the kind of characters who stand out at first glance as obvious examples of their Personality. But that is simply due to their quiet strength and subtle ways.

A closer look will make your Determined TV Twins easy to identify because they:

- Are interested in doing what they feel is right.
- Strive for respect.
- Try to avoid embarrassment.
- Stay on the fence to avoid being wrong.
- Give "the look" or "a look that could kill" when displeased.
- Go by the book.

You and your TV Twins place much emphasis on being right. You want to be sure—not just right, but *really* right. So you eliminate wrong by avoiding rash judgments and by mulling things over in your mind before you're ready to discuss them openly. You think first, speak later. You would rather your deeds speak for you. You do your duty without complaining. You handle your obligations no matter what. Often silence is your way of making a point, but when you do speak your mind, you pull no punches. A few crisp words convey the message.

On "Hill Street Blues," Determined **Frank Furillo** is a captain of a big-city police department, trying to maintain justice and ethical behavior both on the streets and among his officers.

Furillo finds himself in a Determined dilemma when he considers a campaign for the office of mayor. One of Furillo's men, Lieutenant Buntz, has just been involved in an incident in which another police officer has been shot, and Furillo's campaign manager, Grant, warns him that the Buntz affair might discredit him. "But don't worry," says Grant, "there's something in the works that'll take care of that." Furillo is immediately concerned about the ethics of Grant's plan, and questions him about it. "Frank, in politics being uninformed is sometimes simply expedient," is Grant's answer.

In reality, Grant wants Furillo to publicly announce his disdain for Officer Buntz's actions and state that Buntz is being transferred. And that puts Furillo in a dilemma: he is being asked to do the expedient thing in terms of his political campaign, but it might not be the right thing in terms of his responsibility to his man Buntz. Finally, despite Grant's plea to the contrary, Furillo decides that his position in the eyes of the voters is much less important than his duty to his officers. "I've told you before, Grant, I'll not use my job here to serve the needs of any political campaign," says Determined Frank, sacrificing his bid for mayor to the cause of right and responsibility.

A.J. Simon is half of a two-brother private investigation firm on "Simon and Simon." He is a low-key, no-nonsense kind of guy who, like Frank Furillo, shows his Determined Personality in one segment in which he is considering a campaign for public office. He is a promising candidate, and like Furillo, is being groomed by a capable advisor.

But when evidence is uncovered that one of A.J.'s opponents might be involved in the illegal dumping of toxic waste, and someone is murdered as a result, the situation gets complicated. A.J.'s firm is hired to solve the murder case and A.J. figures that the best, and right, way to bring things out in the open is to question his opponent directly on a televised political debate about the alleged wrongdoing he is involved with. A.J.'s political advisor thinks that move could be potentially distastrous to A.J.'s campaign unless he has irrefutable proof that the opponent is guilty. But A.J. has made up his mind as to the right move. "You want to solve this case or do you want to win this election?" the exasperated advisor asks. The correct question, of course, would be "Do you want to be right or to be city councilman?" And the answer, for Determined A.J., is not a question at all.

On "Falcon Crest," **Chase Gioberti** and his son **Cole** share both a Determined Personality and the responsibility of operating a winery in the California vineyard country. Although either would not hesitate to jump on a good opportunity if it came by, they would never resort to the cutthroat competition that sometimes surfaces, at least in the television portrayal of the wine business. They go by the book, or not at all.

Determined **Chris Cagney** is half of a two-woman police team on "Cagney and Lacey." Her police work is also strictly by the book. She shows the Determined penchant for wanting to be, and to appear, right in one episode in which she is offering wisdom to a niece who is contemplating leaving home. "I like my life, and I like the choices that I've made," Chris tells her. "But you've got the wrong idea if you think everything was perfect. I made mistakes, and they were big ones. If you quote me on that, I'll say you lied."

On "L.A. Law," Determined **Michael Kuzak** is a partner in a prestigious law firm. He carries his ideas of right and responsibility into the courtroom in a low-keyed, but very tenacious manner. One episode shows him defending the rights of a convicted murderer, who has received the death penalty, by arguing the man's appeal. All of his associates in the law firm feel that the condemned man is getting what he deserves, but Michael feels that the death penalty is very wrong and is determined to oppose it, no matter what the reaction of his colleagues. Executing people is just not something that is done by an enlightened society, is Michael's rule of law.

As you follow your TV Twins' video lives, look carefully for examples of:

- Communicating love and concern by deeds rather than words.
- A tendency to state their idea of right and wrong.
- An "I'd rather be right than president" approach to life.
- A tendency to declare their purpose and want others to do so.
- A reluctance to compromise on moral or ethical issues.
- Being the strong, silent type.

You and your TV Twins function best in an atmosphere of mutual respect. Your strategy is directed toward long-term goals. You need an environment that is consistent. You do not need to be confronted with hostility. Those who relate to you best do so by approaching you many times when an issue is important to them. They should not expect an immediate "yes" or "no" from you. You are a master of strategy. You are the catalyst who works by persuasion and calm discussion.

At times you need a diversion, a movement away from whatever is the issue, of doing something differently, and then returning to the issue. You are a person who places much emphasis on right, respect, and responsibility.

"I'D RATHER BE RIGHT THAN BE PRESIDENT"

—Henry Clay

Lucky for you, the choice is not always as extreme as be right, or be president. But the choice is one that, in the Determined mind, is being made constantly.

You may ask yourself, "What exactly is the right way of doing something?" Everyone has his or her own opinion. Everyone sees the world through different eyes. The key to the Determined Personality is not only seeing, but seeing in the correct focus, from the proper perspective. Out of many, many ways to see, there is only one right way for you, and that is the way you seek.

For Chris Cagney, on "Cagney and Lacey," the right way for the police department to proceed on a complaint against her by a disgruntled citizen is to believe her side of the story. "I don't want this on my record," she argues. "Fifteen years on the job and they take his word over mine."

For the Determined woman who had come to me with a problem, the right thing was a very difficult decision, but one that was reinforced by her Determined TV Twins. "My fiancé had impregnated another woman, a friend of ours. He admitted his mistake and said he was sorry. He insisted that ours was the marriage he wanted. And I wanted to believe him. He even offered to financially support the woman and her child after we were married. But I decided finally that he owed more of an obligation to her and the child. The marriage was off. I know after watching Michael Kuzak, Chris Cagney, and the other Determined Personalities that doing the right thing is not always such an easy choice. And to some people, it might seem that the choice you make is crazy. But the right choice is the only way. It's the only one you can live with."

"I guess I can be kind of a demanding person at times," says one Determined woman. "My husband complains that I am always lecturing him about thinking the right way. But I had him watch Frank Furillo, A.J. Simon, and Chris Cagney, and now he can see that being and doing right, is not just some excuse I use to make him take his feet off the coffee table. I guess if you were willing to give up the office of mayor or president because of a decision you've made, it's not something you take lightly, or that you want anyone else to take lightly."

In one episode of "L.A. Law," Michael is upset, although he has won a case. His client had refused to settle and had insisted on a jury trial. He went ahead and tried the case and won. Afterwards he discovered that the only reason his client had refused to settle was because she'd been promised a $450,000 advance from a publisher only if she went through a jury trial. Even a victory does not make Michael happy. In his view, the client's reasons for refusing to settle were wrong, as was her failure to inform him of her plan. And so his success was overshadowed.

"I sometimes have problems with other people who misinterpret my urge to be right," says another Determined Personality. "They can make your strong feeling of wanting to justify existence into something crazy."

So we watch A.J. Simon as he struggles through an episode, trying to make the right decision about testimony he is giving concerning a shooting he witnessed. Sure, he saw the suspect after the shooting had occurred, standing with the gun in his hand. But he didn't actually see the suspect do the shooting. As A.J. is being questioned on the witness stand during the suspect's trial, he tries to recreate the scene in his mind. "Is this the man who did the shooting?" A.J. is asked. The suspect's freedom is on the line. A.J. has run the scene over and over again in his mind. He has even begun to dream about it. People are beginning to question his sanity. Why can't he just answer the question? Finally, he remembers, he saw another man walking calmly away from the murder scene in the midst of the resulting and surrounding chaos. As it turned out, that man had pushed the gun into the suspect's hand after the shooting had occurred. The suspect was innocent. And A.J.'s struggle to make the right decision has come to an end.

"He just wanted to be right," says my misunderstood Determined friend after watching the segment. "It's not only a moral and ethical issue, it's what makes life make sense. Doing right and being right is a big responsibility. I guess you could say that for A.J., and the other Determined Personalities, *not* making the effort to live your life the right way would be acting crazy."

BY THE BOOK

It is no coincidence that, for the Determined Personality, the "right way" is often synonymous with the "by the book" way. Just open to the correct page, follow your finger down to the applicable line, and there it is, in black and white.

So what is this "book" that you are going by? Is it in the library, or on the bestseller list? I'm not so sure myself, but

Determined Chase Gioberti, on "Falcon Crest," seems to have found it. In one episode, an observant friend comments to Chase, "I've followed your career since you came to this valley. You're a lot like your daddy, everything by the book."

Determined Chris Cagney seems to be acquainted with it also. When she is temporarily suspended from her job because of allegations of misconduct, she tries to join with partner Mary Beth Lacey to clear her name and get back to work on the police force. But Mary Beth warns Chris that she will have to stay in the background and let Mary Beth handle the official investigation. Chris assures her that she will "go by the book," and stay out of the way.

And A.J. Simon is seen, on one episode of "Simon and Simon," actually reading from "the book." He is being hassled by a police friend about the problems he is causing in a case in which he has been solicited by the police as a witness. The problems arise because A.J. wants to be absolutely sure that the testimony he gives is correct. His friend is more concerned with expediting the case. "You got us into this to begin with," says A.J., "remember, 'raise your right hand . . . ' Besides," A.J. continues, "let me refer you to Sunday's lecture by one of the leading criminal psychologists still at large." A.J. then proceeds to open the book and recite to his friend.

So OK, how do we get our hands on this book? Well, you and I know that "the book" is nothing more than the tried and true method that avoids embarrassment, offends the least number of people, and assures that life, as well as modern existence, will indeed continue to make sense. "The book" represents the unerring, sane, sober, time-tested method. "Rules and regulations of society are there for a purpose," says one Determined Personality. "They represent the collected wisdom of a lot of years. So when the sign says that the speed limit is fifty-five miles per hour, I drive fifty-five miles per hour."

"I go by the book with my income taxes," said another Determined Personality. "I know you can bend the rules and get away with it. And my friends think I'm foolish to ignore all the loopholes. But it's like the "Hill Street Blues" episode where Frank Furillo is being pressured to hold a suspect. The popular decision would be to hold the guy because that's the general emotion among the other officers and the public. But Frank goes by the book and the book says that there isn't enough credible evidence to hold the guy. I'm sure if we could see an episode where Frank Furillo or Chase Gioberti were doing their income taxes, it would be the same with them as it is with me."

But wait a minute; before we are accused of painting a picture of you as some sort of self-righteous, closed-minded saint, we should point out that being right does not necessarily jibe with what the rest of society dictates. And the book that you are going by would not always qualify as a Reader's Digest selection. "My choices are not always the most popular," says one Determined Personality. "As a matter of fact, they might raise a few eyebrows now and again. But I'm only human. And at the time I made them, they were right for me. It's like Chris Cagney trying to explain to her niece that just because she, Chris, dropped out of school when she was young, ran off to Paris, and fell in love, that it wasn't right for her niece to leave school in California and move to New York without telling her parents. I guess sometimes right is relative."

"The world is, after all, a very complex and complicated place," explains another Determined Personality, "but in the end you stand by your decisions. They were right when you made them and right for you."

A VIEW FROM THE FENCE

"If you want a quick decision, the answer is no." That message has probably graced more than one Determined Personality's desk or back bumper. You like time to study all sides of an issue, its long-term effects, and how any possible decision is going to be received. And you certainly don't want to make a hasty choice that will come back to haunt you, one that you might later regret.

So you hover over the decision, give it the bird's eye—or in this case, the Determined's eye—view. As the old saying goes, you can't rush a good thing.

A Determined Personality, who also happens to be a very fine photographer, came to me complaining about the pressure he was getting from his wife to decide whether or not he was going to open his own studio. "I've been saving my money, and scouting out some rental space. But I want to wait until the time is right," he said. "But she claims I'm just avoiding the issue."

We watched the episode of "Simon and Simon" in which Determined A.J. is trying to come to a decision on whether or not to run for city council. His brother, Rick, who is also his partner, tries to convince him: "The reason you like being a private investigator is you get to help people. You'd have a hell of an opportunity to help people if you had a say in how the city is run." But A.J. is concerned about how the business will be run in his absence. Is it right to leave his brother alone to handle it? When A.J. is pushed by his campaign manager, he is curious to know exactly what the campaign manager is going to get out of it. Is it ethical for his campaign manager to profit from his election? Finally, A.J. holds a little conversation with himself: "I've always thought government was there to help people so they wouldn't have to face overwhelming problems alone . . . if I do this, I want to make a difference. I was lucky enough to grow up in a wonderful city like San Diego, and I want to be sure that city is just as wonderful for my kids and their kids . . . I think I just talked myself into it."

After watching the segment and giving it some careful consideration, my Determined photographer friend commented, "There are a lot of reasons for me to open a studio and go into business for myself. But even though those might be enough for my wife, that doesn't necessarily mean that they're enough for me. I guess, like A.J., I have to be convinced and convince myself that they're the right reasons."

So you might appear at times as though you are straddling the fence between two plans of action. Both might be right, depending on the perspective, but you aren't going to commit yourself until you can make a proper and responsible decision. Otherwise, the answer is still "no."

WHAT EXACTLY ARE YOU UP TO?

Some people might say: "There she is, sitting on the fence again," and you'll say: "I'm just not going to take any action until it feels right. I always want to think things out before I do or act on them."

Other people might say: "I know she's up to something, even though she's not making any moves. I can almost see those wheels turning. But what exactly is she up to?"

You aren't saying anything. When the time is right, your strategy will be revealed. If those other people just paid enough attention, they could probably figure it out. Besides, you're certainly not going to make a big production out of it.

The Determined strategist is skilled at taking the calm, deliberate approach to a difficult situation by considering all viewpoints and bringing all sides to a respectable and equitable solution. If a compromise is called for, so be it.

On "Simon and Simon," A.J. and his brother have been hired by a rich client to gather evidence against his wife as grounds for divorce. The fee is very attractive, $20,000, and they are successful. But afterwards, A.J. discovers that he has been set up by the client. The evidence in the situation that implicated the ex-wife was contrived. It's too late to recant his testimony to the divorce court, and the unscrupulous client's ex-wife has been unjustly left with nothing. So for A.J., the strategy becomes: give the $20,000 fee that he had received to the ex-wife to repay the mistake and help her get a new start, then go after the ex-client to try and uncover some damaging evidence against him, and write the whole thing off to experience.

On "L.A. Law," Michael has two cases going at the same time; a dog bite case, and a very important discrimination case. He doesn't want to deal with the dog bite case so he forms a strategy: he convinces one of his associates to take his place in the dog bite trial and request a continuance. But he knows that the judge will not grant the continuance and that his associate will have to end up arguing the case. That will free Michael to concentrate on the more important case: sneaky, opportunistic, maybe, but a good strategy nonetheless.

On "Hill Street Blues," Frank Furillo is just as skilled at bringing a clever Determined strategy into play. But his technique is not always easy to spot. "What's Furillo up to?" asks one officer. "Whatever it is, he doesn't want us to know about it," is another confused cop's answer.

To give you a real-life example of the sometimes puzzling, clandestine strategy, consider a Determined friend of mine's experience. The local school board was considering various ways of trimming its budget for the coming year. One item that board members thought might be reduced significantly was the cost of maintaining the high school marching band once the football season was over, so its budgeted allowance was to be cut in half. But my Determined friend, a band mother, knew that the reduction would eliminate two trips very important to the band's pride: one to compete with other high school bands in the state capital, and one to play at opening day ceremonies for the major league baseball team in a nearby city. More significant, she felt, were a number of small shows that band members put on each year for residents of the local home for the elderly, the school for retarded children, and the children's hospital. These events were simply not allowed for in the new budget figures.

So my Determined friend came up with a strategy and went to work. She arranged for a band show to be scheduled for the children's hospital a week before the next monthly meeting of the school board. Meanwhile, she recruited a task force of other band mothers to (1) invite the school board president to present the band at the hospital; (2) contact the local newspaper editor, supplying him with background information, and ask if he might send a feature writer and photographer to cover the event; and (3) solicit the support of the hospital public relations director to have the children write and illustrate their own thank-you notes to send to the school board.

Later that week, a full-page photo feature ran in the newspaper. Prominent in one of the photos was the school board president being hugged by two children in hospital gowns. On the evening of the board meeting, some forty delightful handmade cards from hospitalized children were displayed in the school board building. Outside, fifty uniformed band members serenaded board members as they arrived for the monthly meeting. Needless to say, the hospital and school board were delighted with the favorable publicity they received; the newspaper editor was glad to have the opportunity to run a good human interest story; and the board members praised the band for bringing credit to the school. And, by the way, the band's budget was not cut.

But wait a minute, who was behind all of this? Well, one tired but very happy Determined Personality. "I know that I can bring things together and make them happen when the need arises," she told me later after relating her experience. "It's a skill I've found I share with my Determined TV Twins. I've even picked up a few strategic pointers by watching A.J. Simon, Michael Kuzak, and Frank Furillo."

And what are some of these points of strategy, you might ask? Trust us. You'll find out when the time is right.

RIGHT IS RESPONSIBLE

It is no small job to keep your constant sense of purpose, to continue sorting through all the possibilities that life offers until you can come up with that one that will serve both you and those around you, in just the right way. But you will settle for nothing less, and gladly accept the responsibility.

A Determined young women who came to me had, despite her own limited means, taken her sister, brother-in-law, and their three children into her apartment when the brother-in-law was out of work. She found her brother-in-law disagreeable and rude, and had never been extremely fond of him, but she took them in anyway. "I was tempted to say no, but I just couldn't do it," she said. "I had to let them come in." Such is her sense of responsibility. "But the rest of the family thinks I'm crazy," she told me.

So we settled back and watched Chris Cagney take her niece, who had left college and her family's California home to run away to New York, into her apartment and under her wing. It was the only responsible thing to do, even through Chris's life immediately became more complicated and uncomfortable.

Then we watched Cole Gioberti confront his ex-wife on how she is caring for their son. Cole does not approve of the expensive gifts that his ex-wife's male friends have been giving to the child. "I will not have my son turned into a spoiled brat while your lovers use him to make points with you," Cole tells her. "Don't start moralizing to me," she tells Cole, "my private life is none of your concern." But Cole sees his responsibility, and it is to his son. "I may have signed a joint custody agreement," he tells her, "but I'll be watching you. Start acting like a tramp and I'll move heaven and earth to take him away from you."

After viewing the two segments, my Determined friend was reassured that her sense of responsibility to her sister and brother-in-law was in no way crazy. On the other hand, she assured me that she fully expected her brother-in-law to be equally responsible. She told me that to make sure he kept looking for work she was clipping the want ads from the newspaper every morning and leaving them beside his breakfast.

WHEN OPPORTUNITY KNOCKS

When wayward relatives or family members come knocking at your door, the responsible thing to do is to take them in, at least until they are back on their feet.

When opportunity comes knocking, the responsible thing to do is to let it in; provided, of course, that it knocks at the right door.

The Determined Personality is certainly not one to shy away from opportunity or, for that matter, from the competition that creates it. But the competition cannot be of the cutthroat variety. That would involve too much unethical and improper behavior. And the opportunity cannot be at another's unjust expense.

On "Cagney and Lacey," Chris is trying to sell her car. On the outside it is a beautiful, canary-yellow Corvette convertible. On the inside, it is a broken-down, lemon-yellow wreck. "How is this car on repairs?'' a prospective young buyer named Kevin asks her. "I'd be putting my last dime into this baby,'' he tells her. "If the taillight went out, I'd probably have to take out a loan.'' "Oh,'' Chris tells him diplomatically, "any car you buy is going to have repair costs.'' Then he asks her how the car starts on cold mornings. "Oh, it's consistent,'' she tells him euphemistically. He tells her he hopes it starts easily because he has to drive his grandma to early mass every morning. "Kevin,'' Christine says, "can we talk?'' Needless to say, Chris ends up dissuading Kevin from buying the car. It would be an easy, but tainted opportunity to sell and she cannot take advantage of Kevin's naïveté.

Later in the episode, Chris goes to a garage that has been recommended to her to see about making the necessary repairs on her Corvette. Again, easy opportunity knocks. The mechanic tells her he couldn't take her money for working on the car; it's a hopeless case. But he does have a solution. "I have a brother-in-law who, for a modest fee, will see to it that your auto is professionally appropriated.'' (He doesn't realize Christine is a cop.) "You mean stolen?'' Chris asks. "I assume you are covered for theft,'' the helpful mechanic adds. "Oh, yes,'' says Chris, realizing again that opportunity has knocked, but at the wrong door. "The police endowment association gives me terrific coverage.'' Her friendly mechanic quickly recognizes the error of his ways. "I was only kidding. You look like a woman who could take a joke,'' he quips. "Oh yeah,'' says Christine, "what makes you think that?''

"You would be naive if you didn't realize that this is a cutthroat world,'' was one Determined Personality's comment on easy opportunity and Chris Cagney's car-selling problems. "And you too have to be willing to stretch and bend once in a while to get along; as long as you're not hurting the little guy. The thing is, the opportunities that you do jump on have to be the ones that you can live with. That's the bottom line.''

THE DETERMINED PERSONALITY GOES ON STRIKE

Although I'm sure many Determined workers have taken part in labor disputes—particularly if the dispute was totally justified—the strike we are talking about here is just a way to describe the Determined Personality's reaction to a distressing, irritating, or pressure-bound situation.

We watch Chris Cagney as she is playing poker with her male officer friends down at the precinct house. She is still rather new at the game and is trying to decide what to do with the hand she has and the pot that's in the middle of the table. Should she stay or shouldn't she? "Just put in the dollar," says one of the impatient players. That is, unfortunately, exactly the wrong thing to say to a Determined, fence-sitting poker player. Chris goes on strike, sitting, humming a tune, stalling just that much longer.

"I'm like Chris Cagney when I get pressured or irritated," says one Determined striker after viewing the poker game. "I guess it's just an indirect way of making a point. I won't argue or fight with you, I'll just refuse to talk, or move at all."

In pursuit of the right and honorable way, the Determined Personality may run into obstacles. It may be others who are convinced that their way is right. Maybe so. It may be laws or social conditions that are unjust. Or it may just be a breakdown in communications that needs repair.

If you can't negotiate or compromise the obstacle away, you apply gentle and constant persuasion; that is your way. There is no violent demonstration. There is no head-on confrontation or hard-nosed stalemate. There is only the strike—passive resistance.

On "Hill Street Blues," Frank Furillo is practicing passive resistance to demands that he release a suspect named Russ. The pressure is on from all sides, but he refuses to knuckle under or budge. There are no confrontations, just Furillo's statement, short and sweet: "Russ doesn't walk. That doesn't happen."

"My wife calls me a delayer," says one Determined Personality. "Maybe I am. I'm like Frank Furillo or Chris Cagney. If someone tries to pressure me into making a decision or acting before I'm ready, I just sit down and clam up or remove myself totally from the situation. Now, if my wife persists in asking me what I'm doing or what I'm up to, pressuring me before I'm ready to talk, I'll just go out and ride my motorcycle until I calm down. I think we're both beginning to understand the situation a little better from watching the Determined people on TV. I'm beginning to share my feelings a little more. But there are still times when I'll just clam up and go on strike."

JUST PLAIN STUBBORN

Some call it "going on strike" some use the term "passive resistance." Others don't bother to call it anything; they just fold their arms, set their heels, and unplug the sound system.

On "Cagney and Lacey," Chris Cagney's niece has refused to call her father in California, will not make a move to return to college, is steadfast in her plan to stay in New York, and blames it all on the fact that she's just like Determined Aunt Chris. "You're right," says Aunt Chris, finally conceding (well, sort of). "We're exactly alike. You're just as pigheaded as I was."

On "Simon and Simon," a friend is describing the Simon brothers—Determined A.J. in particular. "You don't know these guys like I do. They get something in their heads and they won't let it go."

Well, of course the Determined Personality may be just a little hesitant at times to simply throw in the towel and let it go. You may even appear to some people as downright stubborn or unbending.

"At least my husband knows now that I'm not the only person in the world who is a little headstrong at times," says one Determined Personality. "We watched Chris Cagney, A.J. Simon, and the Giobertis and he can see that it is just a part of my Personality."

"My wife doesn't even care about shopping right," says another Determined Personality, "and I can't stand her buying things that aren't on sale. I'm usually calm about it, but after

I've said nothing about the prices, she pays twice what she should. She tells me that I should just go shopping with her, but that's not my job. Saving money is an issue that is very important to me, and I'm not going to budge on it, although sometimes I end up getting very angry about it and blowing up."

Does our Determined friend feel guilty about his bursts of anger? "Why should I?" is his reply. "By God, I'm right." Time to tune in our Determined TV Twins here for a little understanding and compromise. We might be approaching "pigheaded." But seriously, the simple fact is that for you, part of doing something right is doing it all the way. Once the determination has been made, you act on it. And that, I suppose, is that.

THE DETERMINED PERSONALITY AT WORK

What do you give the decent, responsible person who is determined always, and in everything he does, to do what is right and responsible? No slaps on the back or loud, boisterous parties are necessary. No parades. No gold watches. Just give him a little respect, some mutual regard. That's all he really wants.

The striving for mutual respect (the third Determined *R*) is nowhere more obvious than in the world of work. Chris Cagney's father calls her "Sergeant Officer Daughter." "If you don't mind me saying so," says her partner Mary Beth Lacey, "I think that's one of your problems, Officer Daughter. You're thinking cop all the time." "That's what I am," says Chris. "No, that's what you *do*," replies Mary Beth. "I'm proud to be a cop, Mary Beth," says Chris. "I've never been this great at anything in my life. I want to hold on to that."

For you, "that" is the respect that comes with doing a good job, the best job you are capable of, and doing it with honor, decency, and regard for your coworkers as well as your competition.

The Determined Personality will approach his work or career with the expected deliberate style of considering, choosing, and forming a strategy. He may have a fairly clear idea of what he wants to do with his life, but he may be hesitant to announce his plan. When asked, he might reply, "I don't know." He wants to make sure that his goal is clear and his blueprint is right, and he wouldn't want to discuss it lest he be embarrassed by failing to reach his goal.

He looks for a job that will result in a completed product, something concrete or tangible, or at least some conclusive step that says the process is complete. For that reason, he might not be as attracted to an academic career as he would to a job in the practical world. He is the activist who isn't too interested in the speculative and abstract.

The Determined worker enjoys working with others, but he likes a job that permits him, and others, a defined area of responsibility. "On the job, my attitude is like Frank Furillo's or Chase Gioberti's," says one Determined Personality. "I want the working situation to be well structured and well defined. Sloppy supervision irritates me as much as low quality and poor safety standards. It's like that one guy said about Chase Gioberti on a segment of "Falcon Crest," 'Everything by the book.' "

The Determined Personality doesn't particularly like anyone standing over him watching him work. He feels that he is a responsible person and doesn't need to be watched: "Just by the way I work, people can, or should be able to tell that I'm doing my best," is how one Determined Personality puts it. On the other hand, the Determined Personality likes to watch the work someone else is doing for him: the mechanic tuning up his car, the furnace repairman installing a new motor. He's not comfortable when he can't see whether or not they're doing it right.

No matter what his work assignment, the Determined worker often derives great satisfaction from assuming job-minded responsibilities such as being actively involved in union affairs, accepting a position on a safety or incentives committee, serving as chairman of the annual charity fund drive, or such. He enjoys the feeling of responsibility, and the respect he earns is a very large bonus.

A Determined Personality was moved to comment on her working situation after watching Chris Cagney being suspended from the force in one episode because of a citizen's complaint that she had not acted properly in handling a case. "I could really relate to Chris Cagney's disbelief that the police department would take some irate citizen's word over hers, a fifteen-year veteran of the force. For me, my word is my bond. It's the equivalent of a written contract. I always weigh all the elements, take my time in coming to a decision, and invest my own sense of responsibility in any project I'm working on. My integrity is on the line. So when I offer my word, there is no escape clause, no iffy fine print."

I guess we can shake on that.

DETERMINED LOVE AND MARRIAGE: THE STRONG, SILENT TYPE

Let's imagine for a moment that I am a Hollywood casting director. I'm casting a love story and I want a Personality who can convey the feeling of love, caring, and concern without a whole lot of overt expression or emotion.

Just watch Frank Furillo on "Hill Street Blues" when he was in the early days of his relationship with Joyce Davenport, an attorney with the public defender's office. It was all very cool and calm. No flowers, candy, or outlandish efforts to get her attention. No love letters or skywriters. Just some business conversation, a few knowing words, and a few knowing looks. After their first date, Frank closes her car door for her, leans his face in her open window, and sends her off, not with a kiss but with, "See you in court."

There won't be any overcharged, public displays of affection, no heartrending emotional scenes, no crying, screaming, or sex on the beach. Chris Cagney knows the part. We can watch her as she reacts to the efforts of a man she has just met to put his arm around her as they are walking. His casual expression of public affection is like an annoying fly, and she is determined to shrug it off.

In another scene, a man with whom Chris is much better acquainted and has just spent the night, is taking a shower in her bathroom and invites her to join him. She accepts the invitation and steps in but is still wearing her robe.

What I am really looking for is a Personality who is willing to share a sense of mutual trust and respect, a Personality who conveys love on every level: woman to man, wife to husband, parent to child, by actions and deeds rather than by overt expression.

On "Falcon Crest," we can watch Chase Gioberti express a great deal of love and respect for his son Cole, just simply by being there in tough times and giving him some encouragement. Cole is going over the joint custody agreement that he and his wife have formed after their divorce, and is feeling depressed. "Why don't you and I have a bachelor's night on the town?" Chase says, trying to offer some consolation. "Cry in our beer, huh?" says Cole. "Sure, why not," says Chase. But Cole begs off, explaining that he's just not up to it. "Son," says Chase, "I know this is all scary, lonely, embarrassing, frustrating, a million other things for you and for Melissa too. It probably feels like it is the end of the world. But it isn't." There is no embrace, no emotional lament over the divorce, no badgering or blame. Just a respect for the need for quiet dignity and the offer to be there.

I guess when you get right down to it, you could describe the Personality I'm looking for as the strong, silent type. Kind of like the Determined Personality.

"I feel the need to do something substantial to gain respect," says one Determined woman. "Even though I know I am physically attractive, I sometimes feel it's a curse. When someone tells me I'm beautiful, it's like they're saying 'but you don't have a brain in your head.' I guess I'm a lot like Chris Cagney. Part of my beauty is my strength and dignity."

"The kind of person who is attractive to me is someone friendly and considerate," says another Determined Personality. "Someone who will give me my own counsel, some quiet moments. And someone who is strong and independent enough that they are not going to burden me unnecessarily with worries and problems. Just bring me the big issues, not the little bitty ones."

Just as you don't enjoy being burdened unnecessarily with the worries and problems of a weak-willed mate, you will take pains not to do the same yourself: that's where the silent part comes in.

"It used to be, when I came home from work my husband would always try to open me up, ask me how my day went," says one Determined woman. "At times it was very irritating to me and I'd let him know it in no uncertain terms. I would just want to sit in my chair in silence. He would ask me what I was thinking and I felt he ought to know without me having to tell him. Things weren't going well."

My suggestion was to watch Chris Cagney as she deals with her non-determined partner on Cagney and Lacey. When the time is right, Chris will confide in her partner, open up, and accept her advice. But there are other times when Chris will come into work, give her partner one look, and say "Don't ask." Watch Cole Gioberti: there are times when he welcomes the questions and counsel of his father, and there are times when he simply says, "It's my house, let me worry about running it, OK?"

Things are going a little better now, reports my not-as-silent Determined friend after watching, with her husband, her Determined TV Twins. "I'm opening up a little more now, sharing some of my hopes, plans, and day at work. And he is being a little more understanding of those times when a look should be enough."

The Determined spouse might not want to have children until he or she feels life is sufficiently established. It's a matter of being responsible, making sure that everything is right for having and raising children properly. What the Determined Personality wants is a clear reckoning of goals, within and without marriage, and the strategy for obtaining them. Once children come, Determineds can settle into parenthood with the same purpose they bring to whatever they do.

A LOOK, AND THE ONE-LINER

How can I describe "the look," that unique method of communication that Frank Furillo uses to express the utter contempt he feels when his ex-wife humiliates him publicly with a harangue about problems with his support checks. It is a look that could peel the bark from a tree.

Or how about the glare that Chris Cagney gives to a smart-mouthed, cocky cop who is giving her a hard time. It is a scowl that would silence the Mardi Gras.

Actually, "the look" is not used solely as the social equivalent of the neutron bomb. It is simply a part of the efficient, and very effective repertoire of Determined communications, designed to get the point across with a minimum of fuss and bother.

But when Chris Cagney's wide-eyed look of utter astonishment as a reply to a mechanic's suggestion that she junk her beloved Corvette, her icy glower at the pushy poker player, or her confounded sigh in response to her niece's familiar hard-headedness fail to communicate, there is still the one-liner.

Frank Furillo has been having some financial problems and has just been reminded, in a public display of emotion by his ex-wife, that his latest support check has bounced (remember "the look"). Unfortunately, his current romantic interest has also witnessed the scene. So Frank recovers nicely with a one-liner: "You know," he says to her, "I'd really like to ask you out, but I just can't afford it right now."

Chris Cagney shoots a good one at a certain doctor who has been uncooperative and rude with her. "Thanks a lot," she tells the doc, "next time you need a cop, take two aspirin and call me in the morning."

The Simon brothers have just collected a very nice fee from a client and are discussing what to do with the money. Rick, the non-Determined brother, is thinking in terms of the slightly frivolous. "Boy, I can see it now. Me and Bambi Risolli drifting aimlessly off the coast of Cabo San Lucas," says Rick. "Boy, I can see it now," counters the much more practical A.J., "my own backyard."

"I guess I use silence sometimes as a way of making a point," said one Determined Personality after watching Frank, Christine, and A.J. deliver their lines. "But when I do speak, I speak my mind. I don't pull any punches. Just a few clean, crisp, well-chosen words convey the message."

And finally, there was the famous Determined senator's somewhat affectionate one-liner to his wife during a fund-raising dinner for his presidential campaign. As the senator sat, preparing his after-dinner speech, an aide arrived unexpectedly from Washington, D.C. "Well," the senator's wife asked of no one in particular, "who's minding the store?" The senator looked up over his reading glasses and said, "This is the store, honeybunch."

For the Determined Personality, 'nuff said.

ALTERNATIVES AND OPTIONS

We have seen how the fully alive and fully mature Determined Personality is always moving toward realizing his goal for life as a purposeful, harmonious whole. He keeps his eyes on the goal and goes about organizing his strategy calmly and deliberately.

What can appear at times as stubbornness may only be his fidelity to the purpose, his determination to pursue his goal in a resolute way, so unhurried that it may annoy more aggressive colleagues and friends. But he is moving ahead, arranging his strategy. He is so dedicated that he is willing to make sacrifices to attain his goal. Those around him, sensitive to his style of communicating through actions, realize that this sometimes enigmatic person is simply involved, fully immersed in his process, acting to make the dream a reality.

Yet in his quest for his goal, the Determined Personality is concerned for others. He very much wants to maintain respect for and from others, to remain open to change even while keeping a steady pace in pursuit of his agenda. And while he doesn't mind competing, he never does so at the expense of others. He wants to win his share of victories, even if only symbolic ones, but he can accept compromise if that seems the proper course.

When he does win, the Determined Personality knows that he has obtained the prize honorably and responsibly—then he can share the sweetness of victory. He knows when to celebrate with family, friends, competitors, colleagues, and the community.

The less healthy Determined Personality is less likely to share the victory and celebrate. Achievements are fewer. His tendency to restrict verbal communication can generate into a battle of silence and an uneasy game of stealth.

His seeming calm can be a concealing of frustration and anger, and he can become so fixated on the strategy that he loses sight of the goal. He can so fear embarrassment that he never moves off center. He says little and does less, and is so rigid about being right that he runs the risk of being wrong. He risks little else, fearing that miscalculation might wreck the plan; so he tends to mince, point by point, until all purpose is lost. Nothing ventured, nothing gained—but frustration. Dreams become nightmares of struggle and anguish. The intended doer of deeds temporizes, postpones, and becomes immobile. He can't communicate. After a while, he can't move. All that splendid dedication and sacrifice are buried in a heap of unexecuted plans and tired strategies.

Transition from immaturity to maturity is largely a process of the Determined Personality identifying his tendencies to restrict communication and sharing his goals and strategies with those he lives with and works with, those who are most able to give him support in pursuit of his goals. Since he has the natural grace of setting goals and negotiating and forming strategies, these talents will serve him well in effecting the transition to maturity. Then all things are possible.

If you are a Determined Personality, consider these points:

- Don't conceal. Reveal. Sharing is the ferment that makes things happen.
- Speak up. Express yourself in more than one or two terse sentences. Say what you really mean.
- Don't take your many good works for granted, and don't take the good works of others for granted. Compliment others on

their achievements and permit others to compliment you on yours.

- You are like an iceberg; so little of you is visible and so much of you is hidden. Share your strategies, values, and feelings. Make a deliberate effort to say what you are thinking to those persons who would benefit most by knowing; that way the plan moves forward.
- Let people know the principles from which you are operating. Saying, "That's just the way it is," explains nothing, and it's frustrating and irritating to those who are interested and involved in your activities.
- Don't be so critical of others. That suggests that only you have the right way of doing things, which can appear very pretentious.
- Humility is real when it displays the total you—the strong, capable person as well as a person with some weaknesses and fears. Being humble doesn't mean self-effacement; it means recognizing—and announcing—your strengths and your weaknesses.
- Try making fewer judgments and more observations; that way you will be more open to other people's observations.
- "By God, I'm right," has been the motto of many tyrants and dictators. Is that the company you want to keep?
- Planning the right strategy is the beginning of an action, not the end. When the opportunity presents itself, be ready, then move on it. But recognize that overall, yours is the long-term approach.
- Review those grand moments when you fully pursued your strategy and reached your goal. If you've been successful in the past, why not again?
- Stop hiding and holding back. Assert yourself—without exploiting. Take a chance. Strive for the respect you dearly desire.
- By keeping your communications open, you also keep your options, and the feedback is so helpful in keeping the plan alive and working.
- Don't sulk. Don't pout. Don't blow up. Any of these negative reactions is an indication that what you really need to do is to assert yourself. So find a constructive approach, a positive expression, a declaration of your strivings.

- Ponder this statement attributed to Abraham Lincoln: "I am a slow walker, but I never walk backwards."

SECRETS

The keys to a successful relationship with the Determined Personality are:

- The Determined Personality is a no-nonsense type, so respect his or her conservative tastes and reserve.
- Don't pry. The Determined Personality will reveal his or her thoughts or strategy if and when the time is right.
- Learn to recognize "the look" as a definite sign of disapproval.
- Avoid gab, gossip, and small talk, or any behavior that could be potentially embarrassing to the Determined Personality.
- Don't engage in any public ridicule or criticism of the Determined Personality. Being right is very important, and being respectful and respected is of utmost importance to the Determined person.
- Be responsible, on time, and forthright.

MATCH AND MISMATCH

Determined Personality matchmates:

Ambitious—A very good match because both of you are goal-oriented. The Determined person's thoughtful approach makes for many successful outcomes and potential profits which the Ambitious person also strives for. The respect you have for each other also helps this relationship.

Conscientious—Both use a thoughtful approach to decisions; no stone is left unturned. Communication is very straightforward, and both of you emphasize responsibility and are conservative regarding finances. The Conscientious person introduces some humor which allows you to utilize your logical, strategized manner while making this an enjoyable situation.

Patient—The communication styles are similar and neither of you likes confrontation; you both prize peace and order. Both of you also spend money wisely. The Patient person will not push you to reveal your strategy, allowing you to do this in your own time, and would never embarrass you.

Idealistic—Both emphasize responsibility, high standards, principles, and morals and both stick strongly to these values. The Idealistic person doesn't pry, which gives you the opportunity to disclose your strategy when you are ready. Respect is also important to both of you.

Sensitive—Many similarities exist here. Both of you think before you speak, are on the quiet side and are quite responsible. However, the Sensitive person is so aware of everything you do it might begin to make you uncomfortable.

Anticipating—While you enjoy the thorough planning abilities of this person, the need for reassurance and support wears on you. When you offer your opinion it may be seen as criticism, and it's hard for you to be right all the time in this situation.

Influencing—Responsibility, orderliness, and organization are important to both of you, but the similarities end there. You're rather conservative, while the Influencing person has expensive tastes. You do not like being forced to do things, while the Influencing person has a tendency to control situations and to make decisions for you. This individual is rather outwardly verbal, while you are much less verbal.

Persistent—Persistents want affection and togetherness, which is extremely difficult for you. They are daydreamers, while you're a down-to-earth person. You spend money conservatively, while they buy lavish gifts. Work for you is its own reward, while Persistent types want you to make a fuss over them for a job completed. They make many demands for closeness.

Perceptive—Compassion flows easily from Perceptive persons, but you do not share the same sense of immediacy. They are outspoken with you, which shows disrespect in your eyes, and your communication styles are direct opposites. You have little opportunity for privacy when Perceptive is around, and your emphasis on being right will be a source of conflict in this situation.

Accomplishing—This is a very difficult interaction. You are rather subtle, while Accomplishing individuals can be overt. You are respectful in all ways, while they are irreverent and can embarrass you. You want to be right, while they want approval, particularly for accomplishments; you feel that a job well done is reward enough.

Adaptable—Communication is the foremost problem in this situation. You tend not to disclose much information, while Adaptable persons thrive on hours of conversation. You want to be right, while they play devil's advocate which makes it hard for you to be right. You're a homebody and they like to socialize. You're a rather firm person, while Adaptables are extremely flexible; this makes for direct opposites.

Chapter Fourteen

THE ADAPTABLE PERSONALITY

PROFILE

- Great communicator; can make conversation with anyone, under any circumstances.
- Has a very flexible outlook; will listen to and consider all positions and opinions.
- Enjoys and can adapt to a wide variety of social situations.
- Enjoys leisure time and activities.
- Will play devil's advocate, take the opposing view just for the sake of communication.
- Likes to stay tuned in to whatever is current and fashionable.
- Likes to please; looks for ways to accommodate.

TV TWINS

- Steven Keaton—"Family Ties"
- Remington—"Remington Steele"
- Amanda—"Scarecrow and Mrs. King"
- Mary Brenner—"Mary"
- Phil Donahue

Imagine that you, the Adaptable Personality, have just walked in off the street to apply for the job of being the first earthling to visit a newly discovered planet inhabited by intelligent life. I ask, "What qualifications do you feel you have for this job?" You answer, "What qualifications do you need?"

For the Adaptable Personality, adjusting to any situation or social setting—even extraterrestrial—never seems to create much of a problem. You are a good listener and a naturally social being: gracious, charming, and able to react openly and spontaneously to whomever, or whatever, you encounter. You never find it difficult to mingle or strike up a conversation, which seems to put those around you at ease.

The Adaptable Personality is very open to others: communicative and responsive, affable and considerate, rarely overly aggressive, and seldom destructively competitive. No matter who's doing the talking—the executive in the boardroom, the derelict at the bus stop, the young homemaker in the laundromat—the Adaptable can respond and react openly to the presence, moods, and qualities that others display. He or she can laugh when you laugh, weep when you weep, get excited by your ideas, share silence comfortably, admire your successes, and soften your defeats. Communication is the Adaptable's greatest overall strength and it can carry him or her anywhere from the classroom to the assembly line to the White House.

With a sharp eye for the fashionable, and an acute sense for what is current and appropriate, the Adaptable Personality delights in a broad range of interests. He makes friends easily, blends well into almost any environment, and has a real flair for the dramatic and the eventful. Involvement is the key. The Adaptable does not want to watch; he wants to take part.

When the Accomplishing Personality does his dazzling best, who applauds? The Adaptable Personality, delighted to share in the excitement. Who warmly congratulates the Ambitious Personality as she steps into the winner's circle? Her Adaptable opponent. And who is attentive to the end when the Influencing Personality tells his tale? The Adaptable listener.

However, should the Adaptable Personality have to decide whether to listen to the Influencing story, or to play opposite the Ambitious challenger, or to watch the Accomplishing performer, he might falter. Decisions—having to choose among all the offerings—are the bane of Adaptable existence. The Adaptable doesn't like to give anything up. "No decision is a decision," is an aphorism that aptly suits the Adaptable Personality when he's faced with a choice.

Rather than pursue the decision, he may let the decision pursue him. This Hamletlike hesitancy, however, is not always what it seems to be. The Adaptable Personality often forms a tentative decision but, if his confidence is on the low side, he may hesitate to voice it. Instead, he will invite others into the process, soliciting other points of view, sampling various attitudes and proposed solutions. He is shopping for a consensus. If the Adaptable finds himself in a position where he needs to make a responsible decision, he may not like it, but he can, and will, make it. It's not that he is incapable, it's just that he prefers to keep all the doors open: His sense of well-being comes from knowing that he can continue the flow of communication from all sides. Thus, "What do you think?" is a typical part of his conversation, as are, "It seems to me . . ." and "I may be wrong, but I think. . . ." The forum is always open.

MEET YOUR TV TWINS

It shouldn't take you long to recognize and identify your Adaptable TV Twins. They are open, affable, and charming communicators, just like you, and they share your need to tell all to whomever happens to be listening or watching.

Your TV Twins will be easy to identify because they are:

- Open and great communicators.
- Flexible and adaptable.
- Often the devil's advocate.
- Able to listen well.
- Aware of what's current.
- Interested in the practical and achievable.

You and your TV Twins are so open and flexible that some people may think you can be easily swayed and manipulated. Not so. You are more like stainless steel—flexible, yes, but with strength and resiliency, with a well-polished surface that resists corrosion while reflecting the world around. You are naturally social beings. You like people and people like you. You accept people as they are, all the time drawing out their best qualities. You're able to talk to almost anyone because you truly believe that everyone has some valuable contribution to make.

Adaptable **Steven Keaton** on "Family Ties" is the father of a contemporary American family. With four children ranging in age from preschool to college, and both parents working, the Keaton household tends to be somewhat hectic. But Steven does his best to keep all lines of communication open and adapt to whatever situation presents itself.

In one episode, daughter Jennifer is just beginning to experience the pangs of adolescence. In the past, Steven and Jennifer have been very close, sharing wishes, dreams, and secrets. But now Jennifer is more comfortable confiding in her mother. "We really haven't done much talking lately," Steven tells Jennifer. "Sit down, let's talk, buddy to buddy." Later, when Jennifer comes to her mother with a problem, whispering it in her ear, Steven is anxious to tap into the conversation. "What were you whispering about? I have to know," he pleads. "Tell me. I can't stand it. Please tell." For the Adaptable, being precluded from sharing in the communication, especially with his own children, is torture.

The Adaptable Personality makes it a habit to be aware of what's going on in the world of current events, sports, culture, and politics. For Adaptable **Phil Donahue,** it's a career. He always manages to keep the communication going on his TV show with a wide variety of guests and an equally wide, and controversial, variety of topics. His Adaptable skills come into play as he guides the interaction between studio audience, call-in viewers, and the day's guest or guests. And he does not hesitate to play devil's advocate if the action begins to wane, or if there's a question just begging to be asked or a comment pleading to be made.

On "Scarecrow and Mrs. King," Adaptable **Amanda** slips easily from the guise of homemaker to that of undercover agent with a top-secret government organization. Her skill in blending into any number of situations is equalled by her ability to communicate and draw people out, soliciting their opinions and gathering essential information.

Remington Steele, from the show of the same name, shares his detective duties with a female partner in a private investigation firm and shares the Adaptable Personality's chameleon-like qualities by being able to blend into any number of unusual situations. His suave, Adaptable charm helps get him through the usual scrapes and close shaves. He does have a tendency to ramble on a bit in his conversation. Of course, that's nothing more than the desire to effectively communicate what's going on in his mind without tipping his hand too soon or risking having the proverbial door slammed in his face.

Mary Brenner shows her Adaptable Personality on the show "Mary" by making the transition from writing for a chic, sophisticated fashion magazine, to writing for a slightly seedy, rough-and-tumble big-city newspaper. Her ability to associate and converse on all social, economic, and cultural levels is constantly put to the test by her blunt, audacious editor and the variety of eccentrics who form the newspaper staff.

As you follow your TV Twins' video lives, look carefully for examples of:

- Appearing reluctant to be forced into action or to be dictated to.
- Having multiple interests and different friends for different situations.
- Being nine-to-five persons who enjoy free time with friends and other nonwork interests.
- Possessing a soft approach and light-touch way of handling the anger or criticism of others.
- Appearing at times as the most dependent/independent persons in the world.
- Being less of a follower and more of a leader as he or she grow older.

You and your TV Twins function best when you establish a framework for your life and then build upon it. You benefit from communication and constructive criticism. You want and need to discuss possibilities, and yet you reach your own conclusion and position. You gain confidence when others cooperate with you and give you their vote of confidence.

COMMUNICATION IS THE KEY

If we could reduce the entire Adaptable Personality's world to one word, it would be *communication*. It is your key to the abundant and exciting life you see unfolding around you every day, so you try to keep it as clear and flowing as a mountain stream.

Communication is your ticket to what's going on at the desk next to you. On "Mary," Mary Brenner has just started her new job at the *Chicago Eagle*, a big-city newspaper. Her desk faces the tough-talking and slightly hostile Jo Tucker. Jo is not one to make friends easily, but Mary makes the opening move by inviting her to have dinner. "Why not?" asks Mary. "I mean, we work together and we certainly don't know each other. I was just thinking, I'd like to get to know you and some of the other people working here."

"I guess I'm like Mary," says one Adaptable Personality. "When someone new starts working in our office, I'll hang back for a little while just to figure out when there's an opening, some common ground for conversation, then I'll start the ball rolling. Most times, it really helps everyone to relax."

Communication is your ticket to what's going on at the dinner table, in your living room, and inside your children's, mate's, and friends' minds.

As we once again watch Steven Keaton, his efforts to communicate with his family, and his distress in suddenly being closed out of daughter Jennifer's adolescent trials and tribulations, the point is clearly made.

"I probably would feel the same way Steven's feeling about being cut off from the conversation," said one Adaptable Personality. "I know that it's very important to me that communication keep flowing in our house. Sometimes my wife or one of my children will be angry or have something on their mind and just refuse to talk about it. That can really drive me crazy."

"My husband would refuse to discuss a problem with me, just go upstairs and go to bed, leaving it to hang over me like some dark cloud in the living room," said another Adaptable Personality. "Then, together, we started watching Steven Keaton and the other Adaptable TV Twins. There was one show in particular where Mary, who writes a help line column for the newspaper, says, 'Most of the problems that come across my desk are caused by a lack of communication and understanding.' That really clinched it for me. Now my husband is beginning to understand my need to communicate, to get things out in the open and discuss what's going on. Otherwise, he knows he's going to get rolled out of the bed. Even a fight is better than being stonewalled."

THE NEED TO GET OUT AND ABOUT

The Adaptable Personality's love, and need, for communication is manifested in many forms. It may show up in the size of the phone bill. Or in your need to get out and about, to socialize. Mary Brenner very seldom thinks twice when friends invite her to dinner or to join in a poker game after work.

"I guess you could say I'm a 'social' person," says one Adaptable. "I really enjoy going to parties or to family gatherings. In the evenings, my husband will be content to just sit around the house and do nothing, and he expects me to be content with that too. But there are times when I really feel the need for social contact, to go out with friends, to go have a drink or listen to music; just to be around a lot of people. That used to cause a lot of problems; my husband would take it personally, or think I wasn't content with him or that I had something sneaky going on. But now that he and I both understand my Personality a little better and have watched my TV Twins, he is beginning to understand those times when I just need to be where the air is buzzing."

HERE'S PROBABLY NO ONE YOU CAN'T TALK TO

The Adaptable Personality is seldom at a loss for words, no matter what the social context or company. And where is all of this conversation going to take us? Well, if we're with the Adaptable Personality, it could take us to a steel mill, a country club, a yacht, or a bass boat on a still, green country pond. The topic of discussion could be mutual funds or parimutuel betting, upper respiratory ailments or the soybeans in the lower forty acres, postimpressionistic art or premature ejaculation. And the colloquy could be over a beer, communion wine, milk shake, or diet soda. The Adaptable Personality can shoot the breeze with just about anybody.

When the late Lillian Carter, mother of President Carter, was invited to appear as a guest on the Donahue show, she reportedly said, "I don't wear an IUD, I'm not a homosexual, and I don't smoke pot. What in the world am I going to talk about?" She had a valid excuse. She obviously did not know the Adaptable Personality. "She came on and we ended up doing two shows," says Phil Donahue.

"That's your opinion," is Donahue's response to a much more controversial guest. "All right, fine. This is America. You are allowed to say anything you want." The key, if I might add in the Adaptable spirit, is to just go ahead and say it.

When Mary Brenner interviews for a job at the slightly seedy *Chicago Eagle*, she is forced to communicate with the slightly seedy editor, Frank DeMarco. Mary has just come from a job at a sophisticated fashion magazine, so the communication gap would appear to be considerable. But Adaptable Mary soon gets into the swing of things. "Bottom line is, Mary, I don't think you're tough enough," says Frank. "I am tough enough," counters Mary. "So prove it," Frank challenges. Just then the phone rings, as it has done several times already, interrupting the interview each time. Mary reaches the phone first and yanks the cord out of the wall. "I'll try you," says Frank. "Sounds like fun," says Mary.

On "Family Ties," Steven has just been promoted at the public TV station where he works and is in Washington, D.C. on an important fund-raising trip. After a day of sophisticated conversation with potential sponsors and executives, he is sitting alone in his hotel room, waiting for his room service dinner. In walks a hotel waiter delivering dinner, and Steven immediately notices his name tag. That's good for an opening line. So Steven shifts conversational gears. "I see your name is Andrew," Steven begins. "I have a son named Andrew." "I do too," says the waiter. Steven pulls out his wallet to show a picture. "That's my Andrew," he says proudly. "Hey, yours is cute," says the waiter, "mine has purple hair." Steven laughs, tried to empathize. "Well, you know teenagers," says Steven. "He's thirty-two," is the waiter's reply. "He's a record producer in New York; that's what he says he's doing this week, anyway. Last week he was a carpenter. Next week who knows what he'll be, a shepherd maybe." What might appear as a hopeless conversation to other Personalities is an invitation and a challenge to Adaptable Steven. (Besides, this waiter's son is sounding just a bit like an Adaptable himself.) "It's nice he calls each week to stay in touch," says Steven. "Yeah," says the waiter, "he likes to reach out and nag someone." "Still, they're our kids, right?" Steven observes. "Blue hair, purple hair, spiked hair, we love them anyway, right?" The waiter hesitates for a moment: "Love is a strong word."

"That was an interesting scene," was one Adaptable Personality's observation after watching. "It showed how the Adaptable Personality can carry on a conversation with people from all walks of life; from executives to the people who wait on your table. I'm like Steven, I can usually find some way to open the discussion, whether it's a name tag, a book someone is carrying, or even a tune they might be humming. But it also showed Steven's concern for the communication between the waiter and his son. That was enough of a topic to keep the conversation going."

"My husband used to accuse me of being a 'fair weather friend,'" says another Adaptable Personality. "But you have friends at work, friends at the bowling alley, friends at the health club, and people you might talk to at the grocery store or run into on the street, and you can't always mix and match. They all have something to say and you want to be totally immersed in the flow of ideas, whatever each situation has to offer. So you become sort of a social switchboard through which all the information flows. Now that he has been watching Mary Brenner, Steven Keaton, and my other TV Twins, my husband has a better idea of why I can appreciate that each person has something unique to offer and that one or two special friends can't offer it all."

"My friend says it's like I always have a 'We are open' sign hanging in my eyes," is a viewpoint offered by one Adaptable Personality. "I guess people just sense that they can talk to me because there is always some common ground, even though it's not always obvious. But like Steven with the waiter's name tag or Mary showing her toughness by ripping the phone out of the wall, I'll find some way to break the ice."

THE ADAPTABLE CHAMELEON

The chameleon is well known for its ability to adapt and change to match its background. The Adaptable human shares the chameleon's ability to conform and blend into any number of situations.

Mary Brenner has gone from writing for an upscale women's fashion magazine to punching out copy for a downscale daily newspaper, but she is convinced that she can fit into the city room as easily as she fit into the salon. "I can write anything," she tells her new editor. "I've done all kinds of materials: short stories, novellas." OK. But the next question is: Can you write for this third-rate daily rag? "I've been rejected by some of the finest publishers in this country," is Mary's reply.

On "Family Ties" we once again tune in on Adaptable Steven who is anxious to maintain communication with daughter Jennifer, who's going through the trials of puberty. Jennifer has a Sunflower Girls meeting, which is a mother/daughter club, but mother Elyse can't attend. Steven volunteers, convinced he can fit in. "No, Steven, it's not for you, it's for girls," Elyse argues.

"Not so fast," counters Steven. "It says here, 'come one, come all.' " Elyse is unmoved, "Honey, I know how much you want a shared experience with Jennifer, but this is not it. You won't fit in." Elyse obviously doesn't realize that she has just issued the ultimate Adaptable challenge. "Oh, really?" says Steven. "Well, what do they do there? What's so special about the Sunflower Girls' tea that I can't be part of it?" "They sing songs," Elyse says. "What songs?" Steven asks. "Songs like 'I've Got a Mule and Her Name Is Sal,' " Elyse answers. So Steven proceeds to sing the song.

"I can usually fit into whatever is going on around me," says one Adaptable Personality after watching Mary and Steven. "You want to eat snails or frog legs? I'll give them a try. Do some impromptu barbershop quartet numbers? No problem. Hop in the car and drive to the beach for a midnight swim? Count me in."

"I guess I'm like Steven," said another Adaptable after watching the "Family Ties" segment. "I just like to share in the activities. I find it easy to walk in, start up the communication, and at least give things a try. So why not?"

The Adaptable Personality is rarely out of place. You could have been the first female sports writer admitted to an NFL locker room; the first male member of the National Organization of Women. You blend in well with others because you readily accept them and establish communication on their level. But even though you are a match on the surface, there may still be some discord deep inside.

On "Family Ties," Steven finds himself conforming to the demands of a job promotion. His boss comes into Steven's office to congratulate him on the promotion. "Well, you want to go out for dinner?" the boss asks. "We'll celebrate and talk about some new projects." "Well, I'd love to," says Steven, "except my family, they're expecting me." "Maybe tomorrow night," says the boss. But Steven is still not totally comfortable with the idea, although he hesitates to come right out and say so. He doesn't want to cut off the communication. "I usually try to have dinner with my family. Maybe. I'll let you know tomorrow." But the boss persists. "We'll order in," he says.

"We'll make it a working dinner." Steven then realizes that working dinners are a part of the position he'll have to fill, for better or worse. "Well, OK," he says with a little hesitation, but still enough enthusiasm to convince the boss of his sincerity. He is successful in his new job, but the cost to his Adaptable spirit is too high. In that same episode he resigns and takes his old job back.

"I know exactly how he was feeling," said an Adaptable Personality after watching the episode. "The problem is not in playing the role, or fitting in; you can always do that. As a matter of fact, sometimes it's almost involuntary. You don't want to cut off communication or disappoint anyone, so you find yourself doing what it takes to please and fit in. But sometimes the price is too high. It's no good to please everyone else if you're not pleasing yourself."

Another Adaptable Personality related Steven's dilemma to her own process of self-discovery. "I guess for Adaptable Personalities it's sometimes hard to pin down exactly who you are. But the more you figure yourself out, the easier it is to avoid going along with every situation, just because you can. You might get sucked in initially, be afraid, or unable to say no, like Steven, but in the end you blend in where you really want to."

And so, like a chameleon trying to match Liberace's wardrobe, you sometimes find the process of adapting as painful and complicated as it is satisfying. But it is your nature, and one of your great strengths. It's the mountain you climb, just because it's there.

For Phil Donahue, the mountain was laundryland. He has no problem showing his Adaptable skills on TV by adjusting and relating to an endless variety of guests, topics, and situations. But he revealed to an interviewer his utter despair at trying to conform to the demands of the laundromat, after separating from his wife and assuming custody of four sons and their dirty laundry. He found himself gearing his life, somewhat reluctantly, to being there exactly as the spin cycle ended on his machine so that some other customer wouldn't unload the unattended machine and spread Donahue's laundry to the four winds. Even chameleons have a tough time in the laundromat.

Donahue's final step in adapting to laundryland was to acquire a washer and dryer of his own.

Despite the occasional problems in conforming to conflicting circumstances, and the difficulties that might arise from the inability to be all things to all people at all times, in the end your flexibility remains.

Elephant polo, anyone?

ALWAYS WILLING TO LISTEN

How is it that, as an Adaptable Personality, you have little or no trouble talking to just about anyone you meet? Well, part of the secret might be that you are willing to listen to anything anyone has to say.

For the Adaptable Personality, communication is a two-way street. That means you'll listen, really listen, to what the other guy is saying.

Mary Brenner spends a great deal of her time at her job just listening. Her help line column is an outlet for readers who have a problem and need a friendly ear. When drama critic Ed LaSalle wants to talk about the play it has taken him twelve years to write, Mary is there. And when Jo Tucker wants to confide in someone about her relationship with her parents, Mary is happy to oblige.

Steven Keaton is a willing ear for the hotel waiter who laments about his thirty-two-year-old son with the purple hair.

"It's a way to maintain communication," says one Adaptable watcher. "But it's also a good way to learn. You never know when there might be some gem of wisdom buried in all that endless story."

"I always make sure my husband watches my Adaptable TV Twins," says another Adaptable Personality. "It used to be that I would listen to his ideas, judgments, and opinions, but he wouldn't return the favor. Now he understands that listening goes both ways. I will always pay him the courtesy of listening, but I need a sounding board also. Just because I'll listen to what you have to say doesn't necessarily mean that I always agree with what you're saying, or don't have an opinion of my own."

ALWAYS READY TO ENCOURAGE THOSE YOU ARE LISTENING TO

If you listen closely, and long enough, chances are you will hear some good in everyone. It's your flexibility and willingness to consider other points of view that allow you to communicate with such a wide range of people.

We can watch Phil Donahue as he listens quietly to countless guests, phone callers, and studio audience members. Part of his professional success and appeal is in presenting interesting topics, then letting the complete story get out, and encouraging the hesitant and self-conscious to go ahead and speak their minds.

On "Mary," Ed LaSalle has finished a play he has been working on for over a decade. Ed is an eccentric character and the other people at the newspaper are not thrilled by the prospect of attending his opening performance. But Mary is optimistic. "Why do you have to assume the worst?" she asks her reluctant coworkers. "Maybe it's going to be good. Ed is an intelligent, sensitive man. His reviews are well written, usually witty. Maybe the play's going to be a bit experimental, but Ed's a friend."

On another episode, Mary does some ego boosting for Jo Tucker. Jo has her eccentricities and they don't happen to coincide with the idea her parents have of how she should live. But Mary is encouraging. "Jo, your parents raised an original. If that's not good enough for them, then that's their problem, kid, not yours."

"There are times when I get accused of shallowness, or even of being crazy myself," says one Adaptable Personality of his tendency to listen to and encourage the most off-beat people. "But I watch Mary and my other Adaptable TV Twins and realize that it's just me. No one has the right way or the only way. Everyone should sing his own song, and I like to encourage that."

"I know from watching my Adaptable Twins that one of my strengths is my ability and willingness to listen to a whole room full of opinions and then bring them all together," says another

Adaptable. "I guess you just take the best of each. We all like to be heard."

There are times, though, when the Adaptable Personality might find himself listening to too many opinions and views. And the results might be that his own opinion never gets voiced.

"Sometimes I have problems expressing myself when I have a difference of opinion," said one Adaptable Personality who had come to me. "I don't really agree with what's being said, but I don't want to cut the other person off or offend. So I just go along and don't say anything."

We watched Mary Brenner as she paints herself into a corner with her inability to say no to her editor's request that she write a review of Ed LaSalle's play. She had been the only person in the office to encourage Ed and the only one willing to attend his opening night. So when the editor asked her, she just couldn't refuse.

On "Scarecrow and Mrs. King," we watch Amanda as she accepts cash from a man who has just crashed into her car, in response to his plea that they don't bother with insurance companies. She is obviously not comfortable with the arrangement but is willing to go along anyway.

On "Family Ties," one of Steven's old college friends shows up for dinner. The two worked together to publish a political magazine in college and the friend is planning to publish the magazine once again. He asks Steven to help and Steven, remembering the wonderful experience of the past, accepts. But there's trouble. His friend expects Steven's attitudes and views to be the same as they were in college, slightly anarchistic and left-wing. Steven tries to conform and fit into the reborn magazine, but finds that his present views are much different from his past and from his friend's views. They disagree and the friendship, as well as Steven's position at the magazine, is terminated. Steven's confidence is shaken. Communication with his old friend is broken. But in the end Steven is reassured, both by his wife's vote of confidence in his commitment to his present views, and in his knowledge that he is just being true to himself.

"I guess it's hard for some Adaptable Personalities to say no or to express their own opinions sometimes," said my Adaptable friend after watching Mary, Amanda, and Steven. "I guess you're afraid that you're going to alienate people, so you go along; you're flexible, you're adaptable. The urge to adapt is the urge to communicate. But being flexible and open at the expense of denying your own wants and needs is taking things too far. Sometimes you have to be like Steven; you have to have the confidence to know that even though the short-term effect of disagreeing or not fitting in might be a breakdown in communication, the long-term effect will be respect from others, and for yourself."

OUT OF HAND, BUT STILL IN THE GROUP

Mary Brenner is very happy because she is involved in her first office poker game. She is now officially a part of the family. But she has extraordinary luck, gets slightly carried away, and gets very loud and aggressive. She is cleaning out everyone's bank, enthusiastically scooping in the pot, and suddenly realizes that the other players are not having quite as much fun as she. Suddenly she gets very quiet and leaves the room. "The only reason I got into the game was so that I could feel that I was part of this place," she says to Frank DeMarco who has followed her into the next room. "I wanted them to get to know me, you know, and what did they see? A side of me that is so low and ugly. I just don't know how I'm going to face them tomorrow."

"I had a similar experience when I was playing bingo with my girlfriend," said one Adaptable Personality after watching Mary. "We had split the cost of the cards with the understanding that we would split any winnings. Well, I ended up winning $500, was real excited, and probably made my girlfriend uncomfortable because I reacted the way I did and because she thought I wasn't going to share. I felt bad in a way that I had embarrassed her, and because a part of me did want to keep the money since I had won it. But I also felt good sharing the winnings and making my friend happy."

After Mary has walked out of the poker game, afraid that she has alienated herself from her coworkers, they all file out past her on their way home. "Played like a champ in there, Mary. I'll get you next week," says one. "Thanks for livening up the evening," says another. "Mary, you know that lunch tab you owe me? I want it tomorrow," says a third. "What just happened here?" a slightly confused Mary asks Frank DeMarco after everyone else has left. "They know a lady when they see one," is Frank's answer. "You're smart, attractive, and you play a hell of a game of poker."

"I noticed that when she started to win, she kind of lost herself momentarily," said another Adaptable after watching. "She felt bad when she was winning. She wanted everything to go well and didn't want to turn her friends off or away by beating them. I used to go to parties and end up being loud, telling jokes, and acting up. I'd always ask my wife the next morning if I had turned everybody off by being so boisterous and talking so much. She would always tell me that the party would have suffered without me. Now that I'm become more familiar with my TV Twins and my Personality, I find it easier to believe her. I guess we just have to recognize that we may get out of hand once in a while, but people will still like us."

SHOPPING FOR OPINIONS AND A VOTE OF CONFIDENCE

With so many fresh ideas and different perspectives floating around, you may find yourself feeling a bit inadequate at times; your self-confidence might slide a notch or two. "I listen to so many people with so many good ideas that sometimes I feel less capable," is how one Adaptable explains it. "It makes me wonder if others don't have more to contribute than I do."

Even when you decide to act on an idea, you may still find yourself shopping for opinions, inviting others into the process, and soliciting other points of view. For the Adaptable communicator, that's only natural.

We can watch Mary Brenner as she fishes for Frank DeMarco's opinion on how everyone feels about her behavior at the office poker game. "That person in there, I don't know that person," Mary says, referring to her display of aggressive competitiveness during the game. "I've never met her before in my life; grabbing and clawing and clutching at that money." Frank reassures her that no one was offended. "I still don't feel good about it," Mary says, still looking for the convincing vote of confidence.

We see Mary shopping for opinions again when she seeks reassurance from Frank that she can handle her new job at the newspaper. "I'm a guy who plays hunches and I've got a hunch you're gonna work out," Frank tells her. "Well, thank you, Frank," she tells him. "To tell you the truth, I could use all the encouragement I can get."

On "Family Ties," Steven is up for a big promotion at work but he is not confident that the job is his. He gathers opinions from his family and coworkers on his chances, and still he isn't convinced. "I'm so proud of you," says wife Elyse as Steven prepares for his interview. "I haven't got the job yet," Steven replies.

"Sometimes I guess it's like you let the decision pursue you rather than you pursuing it," was one Adaptable Personality's comment after watching Mary and Steven shop for opinions and a vote of confidence. "You have already made your mind up to a certain degree on what the outcome is going to be, but you leave the final vote up to the people whose opinions you're getting. They are really just reassuring you."

"People can make you feel like you're being indecisive and wishy-washy," says another Adaptable. "But they never hesitate to give you their opinion because *they* see you as indecisive, and because *you* listen. So you take their advice and use it. Just watch Mary Brenner as she goes through the process. After she gets her reassurance from Frank that no one was turned off by her behavior in the poker game, she goes back into the other room where the money from the poker game is and you hear her say, 'Come to momma.' When you solicit opinions from people, it's not necessarily to have them solve the problem for you or make the decision for you. You just like to get different views. In the end, you usually abide by your own decision after all. Other people just get mad because you don't put as much stock in their opinion as they thought you were going to. But that's their problem."

A DASH OF THIS AND A LITTLE OF THAT

"To me, life is a canvas to paint as you wish," is how one Adaptable described her philosophy. To another Adaptable, a bit less artistic (maybe just hungry), life appears as "a big smorgasbord and I just can't seem to find a big enough plate."

For you, life does offer many appealing possibilities and you usually find it very easy to make contact, blend in, and become a part of the many interests and activities you choose. You might be the person who sits down at the piano and picks out a simple tune by ear, plays a passable game of racquetball with only a few lessons, or takes the stage on amateur night to try your hand at standup comedy. It's the appeal of a little adventure, of trying the next thing.

When asked about moving his show from Chicago to New York, Phil Donahue's response was, "We get something, the show gets something from moving to New York. We get scared again."

Mary Brenner's friends ask her if she is happy with her move from fashion magazine writer to newspaper reporter. "It's been kind of an adjustment," is her answer. "You know, a few things to get used to. But you know what? It's exciting at a paper. It's got an edge."

On "Scarecrow and Mrs. King," Adaptable Amanda is game for everything and will try anything from plumbing to piloting a boat. She enjoys being a homemaker by night, a danger-stalking secret agent by day.

"I like to try a lot of different things," says one Adaptable Personality, "I guess because of the challenge, and because I find it easy to fit in, learn, and adapt."

The Adaptable Personality likes to keep abreast of what's current and fashionable. That might be possible just by watching Phil Donahue's choice of guests.

But one of the real motivators of the ever-sampling Adaptable is the challenge. When Mary Brenner is challenged to fit into a rough-and-tumble newspaper job, she accepts the job and thrives. Steven Keaton is challenged to go all the way and become a Sunflower Girl, and he does, almost. Phil Donahue is challenged by the New York audience and his ratings climb.

"I can really relate to the notion of being motivated by a challenge," said a young Adaptable friend of mine after watching her TV Twins in action. "And I guess my father has been learning too. When I was having some doubts about going to college, he baited me like that. He challenged me, and I had to give it a try."

With all your various pursuits, interests, and answers to challenges, it may sometimes appear that you're spreading yourself thin. But it's not so much a matter of not being able to make up your mind as it is simply being yourself. "My direction is forward and I always wonder why others perceived my sampling of many things in life as a failure to keep moving," said one Adaptable Personality. "Now that I have become better acquainted with my TV Twins and my Personality I feel more confident about it."

Another Adaptable sums it up this way: "I don't want to watch, I want to be."

THE ADAPTABLE PERSONALITY AT WORK

"Sometimes it seems like everyone else has long-term goals and I ask myself, 'Why don't I feel the need to have long-term goals too?' " That is the dialogue many Adaptable Personalities have with themselves. The pressure is on, particularly in the working world, to commit to a long-term career and follow through. But you find yourself changing or mixing career and jobs in some strange assortments, especially early on. You usually don't have any trouble at all conforming to what the job requires, but it might take you a while to find the working situation best suited to your interests and talent.

Sometimes a situation is thrust upon the Adaptable. He tends to pursue a job or career that a parent or other significant person urges. Other times he will simply leave the situation open and flexible without the need to make a decision or to act assertively. Either way, the Adaptable Personality may have a tendency to change jobs or careers as opportunities present themselves. Even so, he will be diligent and responsible, efficient and purposeful at whatever he is doing, blending in with the tone and atmosphere of the working environment.

Mary Brenner's friends would certainly question her move from a secure, prestigious job at a fashion magazine to an uncertain future at a questionable newspaper. But if they followed her progress, they would see that she made the decision carefully, and when she finally committed herself to the new job, she made it a success. It was right for her.

Because of his openness to the ideas and opinions of others and his keen interest and enthusiasm, the Adaptable Personality will be well received by coworkers and superiors. His ability to soften disputes and to summarize varying points of view, coupled with his willingness to yield, make him persuasive in all sorts of confrontations and conferences. Despite the fact that he tends to be a nine-to-five worker who seldom takes the job home, he will be marked as promotable and promising.

"I've always said to myself that if I found the right job, I could really blossom and show my true value," said one Adaptable who had sampled every position but Indian chief. "People will put pressure on you and say you're crazy if you pull a move like Mary did, going from a job they think is better to one you think is better. But once you finally find a job that suits you, you can really buckle down and do your valuable best. And that's what's really important."

What term do we give this auspicious occasion when the Adaptable Personality finally digs in and commits? I call it "biting the bullet."

Because the Adaptable Personality thrives on sampling a great many of life's offerings and may, as a result, be shy of making hard choices, he may be a late starter. He may defer initiating his direction in life until the age of twenty-five, thirty-five, or even forty. But once he makes that choice, however late, he will stick with it.

We can watch Steven Keaton "bite the bullet" when he makes

the decision not to take a new position he has been offered. True, it involves more money, more power, and will let him push through many of the projects he's dreamed of. And he is fitting into the demands of the new job with astounding success. But it will also cut into his time with the family, jeopardize his communication with them, and keep him working nights and weekends. There will hardly be any time for other interests. So Steven decides that his commitment is with his family and with his old job. After he returns from a business trip, he informs Elyse that he is giving up the new job and going back to the old. Not able to comprehend Steven's decision, Elyse asks what happened on the trip. "Well, just like I said, it was a great big success," Steven answers. "So big that you want to quit?" is puzzled Elyse's next question. "Everything I care about, really, really care about, is in this house," Steven answers. "There's no such thing as success for me if it gets in the way of my life here. I don't want to be number one at work. I want to be number one right here."

This guy is a hopeless case, right? Wrong. When the Adaptable Personality finds the right fit in a job, he'll stick with it. For Steven, the right fit was in his old job and with his family. He made the commitment where it was best. Bite the bullet; pass on the money and prestige. But let's not forget the fact that Steven was also opting for the free time and flexibility that his old job offered.

"I guess you could say I'm a nine-to-five sort of person," said one Adaptable Personality. "I'll bust my butt for you and do what it takes to get the job done. But, like Steven, I would prefer a job where I've got plenty of free time to pursue my own interests. My work is definitely not my life."

Retirement would pose no problem for the Adaptable Personality; in fact, he might welcome it as an opportunity to pursue the many activities and interests that he finds so attractive. He could be expected to enjoy the shade in his backyard for long hours, going fishing, playing tennis, chatting with old friends about anything or nothing, taking that long-awaited trip to Paris that has intrigued him since his student days. He would love the luxury of leisure, feeling no pressure to do anything but what he wants. The rocking chair and the front porch were invented for the Adaptable retiree.

ADAPTING TO LOVE AND MARRIAGE

What's the secret to getting along with an Adaptable mate? Well, as we can see with Mary Brenner in the office poker game, keeping a secret is not exactly the Adaptable forte. Your life, and mine, are essentially an open book.

"I guess it's because I want to share whatever the environment offers," explains one candid Adaptable. "And to me, part of being involved in a relationship is letting the other person see exactly what makes me tick."

In the case of a potential suitor or mate, you will look for someone who can, and does, keep the communication flowing.

The Adaptable Personality is drawn to people who are physically attractive, socially appealing, assured and assertive, stimulating and exciting. If a person comes from a good background or displays a certain degree of affluence, it would not go unnoticed by the Adaptable Personality, although that would not be a primary consideration. Forcefulness—the other person's ability to give direction and offer support—would be more significant.

Remington Steele and his partner, Laura, have their differences, he is suave and easygoing, she is matter-of-fact and practical. But she is also physically attractive, assertive, and keeps him in line. And the appeal is obvious.

On "Family Ties," Steven is thinking about his college days, how involved he was with the peace movement and ecology, and how much his life has changed. Now the most important things seem to be family, home, and job. He feels as if he has sold out. But Elyse gives him some much needed support. "You're one of the most committed and caring men I know," she says, giving him the vote of confidence he needs.

In marriage, the Adaptable spouse would be content to accept the lead of a capable partner who has definite ideas and knows what he or she wants; the Adaptable spouse responds to the inclinations of that partner and would permit him or her to set the standards. The mature Adaptable spouse's willingness to yield would set a tone in marriage and home life that would be productive and contagious, soothing and settling for the entire family. He or she might be glorified as the unselfish parent who has so much to offer, who is responsible to the children as well as to the spouse.

For the less mature Adaptable Personality, marriage and parenthood may not be that simple and serene; rather, they may be anguishing. He or she would have a tendency to be too dependent too much of the time, too clinging or indecisive.

Learning to be resolute and more self-directed can be productive and liberating for the Adaptable Personality. One Adaptable woman told of being content to let her resourceful and assertive husband make all the decisions and assume all the responsibility in their marriage. But becoming familiar with the strengths and weaknesses of her Personality, and watching her TV Twins, helped her to discover that fine balance between flexibility and assertiveness, complacency and communication. After some time she began to recognize that she, too, had many good ideas and values to offer. At first, her husband found the emerging flow of her ideas uncomfortable. But the more he listened and observed, the more he appreciated what she contributed. "It's much better now," she said, "more like two persons who have differing ideas, different interests, making different decisions. The mix is better. It's been a lot more exciting for both of us. I now have my own ideas and I feel confident to express them."

When they purchased a new home, her mother-in-law, a professional decorator and a vigorous woman, offered to help select furniture, drapes, and color schemes. "I let her know in a nice way that I would rather she wait," the Adaptable woman said. "I told her I would rather she come to see it when the house was finished." The woman was able to handle her mother-in-law in an adroit, tactful way without offending. In the end, everyone, including the mother-in-law, was pleased with the finished house. And the Adaptable woman was pleased with herself, although refreshingly modest when she was praised.

KEEP THE PLACE HOPPING; PLAYING THE DEVIL'S ADVOCATE

I suppose you're about ready to take a vacation from reading this chapter? It's interesting and very valuable to learn so much about yourself and your Adaptable TV Twins, but sometimes all of this staying on top of things and conforming gets a person down. It's so much more comfortable to fit yourself into a pair of skis, a bathing suit, or a lounge chair. And the chance to travel always promises some scintillating scenery and conversation.

Well, what if every other Personality felt that way? Where would the world be? How would we ever get anything done? So you're the nine-to-five person? OK, why not nine-to-four, or nine-to-three? Or how about robots to do everyone's work? Then we can all retire.

Before you start taking all this personally and your confidence level slips, or you ask yourself, "Is this it? Has the doctor finally gone off the deep end?", just listen to one of your Adaptable Twins. "I'll take a side, any side, ask an embarrassing question, or make a provocative comment when things start to slow down. Phil Donahue does it all the time on his show. He's an incurable devil's advocate."

So you like to put a dash of pepper in the old conversational stew every once in a while. Well, you're certainly not alone. Just watch Mary Brenner as she gives Frank DeMarco a little conversational poke when he can't decide whether or not to stay with his poker hand. "Come on, you've gone this far," Mary taunts, "live a little."

In another episode, Frank is surprised to find Mary reading a rival newspaper at his desk. "You mean you read the competition first?" Frank asks incredulously. "Mary, you know I believe the *Eagle* is the finest newspaper in the city. What do you think?" Mary jabs at him again. "I think you actually believe that," is her answer.

Steven Keaton notices daughter Jennifer reading a magazine. He is feeling devilish. "What are you reading there?" he asks.

Seventeen, Jennifer answers. "You're only thirteen. You shouldn't be reading that for another four years," Steven quips. But Jennifer sticks with her magazine. "Well, let's see, what have we here," says Steven, reading over her shoulder. " 'Twelve Ways to Shape Up for the Prom.' Well, too late for me now."

"I don't like to encourage blatant argument or confrontation," says one Adaptable instigator after watching Mary and Steven, "but I do like to keep things stirred up."

BLAST OFF

Well, it's time to decide. You've read your chapter, met your TV Twins, and the bullet is between your teeth. Are you going to accept your job as ambassador to the newly discovered planet? Commit to all those lonely hours in space and the notion of facing the unknown? Yes, you say, you'll bite. It's an adventure.

Fine. I'm sure you won't have any trouble making friends up there and will be an excellent representative of all we have to offer here on earth. But I'm just wondering, what if you get there and the planet is deserted? Suppose all the inhabitants are Adaptable and have gone on vacation?

ALTERNATIVES AND OPTIONS

The Adaptable Personality, as discussed, is a very sociable person who is also open, flexible, optimistic, and interested in a broad range of ideas and activities. But his urge to conform, while it makes him attractive, can also limit his self-direction.

The Adaptable is inquisitive and impressionable, sometimes gullible, and sometimes on the edge of becoming a dilettante. He loves nice things but sometimes mistakes glitter for substance. His bright optimism can tempt him to overromanticize people and relationships, only to be disappointed or disillusioned when they turn out to be less than he had hoped for. His soliciting advice and opinions can build consensus, but it can also degenerate into dependency.

To enhance strengths so that they do not become weaknesses, the Adaptable Personality needs to be conscious of behavior patterns and prevailing attitudes. He needs to rely more on his own resources and less on the advice and consent of others. In sum, he needs to "toughen up," increase communication, and be more decisive. If you are an Adaptable Personality, here are some ways you can do that:

- Be aware that you often seek guidance to the point of arranging for others to set the stage for you. Be more independent. Listen when others tell you: "You can do it. You know what to do." You really *do*.
- Once you have made a decision, carry it out. Don't continue to shop around for other points of view. Just do it.
- Try establishing a framework or outline to build upon, then proceed with being more assertive.
- Listen to praise and compliments. Don't brush them off; don't minimize them with an offhand joke. People really are telling you that you are capable.
- You benefit from communication and constructive criticism, so look for those who provide it.
- You are interested in the practical and the achievable. If you can get seventy-five percent of what you want, take it. Then continue to try for the rest.
- Learn to say no and really mean it. Be firm. Become aware of what *you* want. Know what *you* stand for.
- Once you develop more confidence, you'll appreciate yourself much more. Your great social awareness will not diminish; it will be enhanced because you will be more adaptable—but with all your resources available to you.
- Genuine flexibility means being able to give a little and take a little, but with enough self-assurance that you know that giving and receiving are a matter of choice, not submission.
- Be willing to make short-term compromises but keep your long-term values in mind.
- You don't have to be sweet all the time. People won't desert you for having your own opinions and your own standards.
- Quit sending the message, "Don't expect too much of me." Wouldn't it be a nice change to say, "Look out! Here I come!"

- The greatest assurance is self-assurance.
- Work on being the right person rather than seeking the right environment or the right job or the right crowd.
- Take those chances. Test what happens when you let yourself communicate and commit. You'll gain confidence, which leads to further risks, further success, and further confidence.
- Your declaration of independence would be to make your own choices and then act on them. Know when to yield and when to fight. When that happens, you truly have something fine and wonderful to celebrate with all those people who love you so much.

SECRETS

The keys to a successful relationship with the Adaptable Personality are:

- Keep the communication flowing. There is nothing more frustrating to an Adaptable Personality than for you to clam up.
- Be supportive. A word of encouragement can do wonders for confidence.
- Understand that the Adaptable will play devil's advocate. So don't interpret every opinion, comment, or view as gospel truth.
- The Adaptable will solicit your opinions but don't be overly flattered, or offended if he doesn't follow them. He is likely gathering many other opinions also.
- Flexibility is not a sign of weak character or indecision. It is the Adaptable strength.
- The Adaptable needs social contact and activity, so strike up the band.

MATCH AND MISMATCH

Adaptable Personality matchmates:

Accomplishing—Both of you share an outgoing, spontaneous, socially oriented and optimistic approach to life. You enjoy a variety of activities, interests, and friends and are encouraged by the Accomplishing person to pursue these varied interests. You provide the approval the Accomplishing Personality needs because you are a great audience for their dazzling performances—never critical, always supportive. The communication flow is effortless between you two.

Anticipating—You naturally solicit opinions and ideas from those around you, which makes the Anticipating person feel important and valued. You have a great knack for building the confidence of others, as does the Anticipating Personality. Anticipating persons' tremendous planning abilities ensure that life runs smoothly; when praised or given credit, something you do so well, they do a tremendous job and their tendency to worry is kept to a minimum.

Persistent—Your flexible nature is put to good use with these dreamers. They tend to follow wherever their imagination leads, and you have no trouble going with the flow. You seek confirmation for your ideas and you'll get that and more from the Persistent person. Persistents will pamper you and make a fuss, which makes you feel special, and you have no trouble returning this special treatment.

Patient—Your need to communicate will not be stifled by the Patient person, who will gladly sit and listen to you. You are both easygoing and relaxed, and do not like arguments. Communication is a two-way street, however, and you may experience some difficulty getting feedback from the Patient Personality, although you do encourage the person to verbalize needs and wants.

Perceptive—Both of you are verbal and social people who enjoy spontaneity and recreation. Your open and up-front communication style is shared by the Perceptive person. Perceptives are very feeling individuals, and you encourage them to express themselves by being a good listener.

Conscientious—This person's tremendous sense of humor is sure to brighten any conversation and you enjoy his or her dry wit. However, your flexibility does not mesh well with the Conscientious Personality's tendency toward a fixed routine; you may have to maneuver around this. You're rather spontaneous, while the Conscientious person collects and examines much information before deciding.

Ambitious—Your openness and candidness is appreciated by the Ambitious person, as well as your ability to bolster confidence—giving good ratings. Your ideas and opinions are requested by the Ambitious, particularly if they offer some prospect of success. Your social nature may not be a problem here as long as it includes some potential business contacts. Your willingness to bend does not coincide with their goal-oriented style. They invented the eighteen-hour work day, while you operate on banker's hours. Leisure time is hard to come by with the Ambitious person.

Sensitive—The Sensitive person is a quality listener and will provide you with honest feedback and genuine reassurance, but probably not as often as you would like. Private time alone is very important to this Personality, while you would rather be around people. Your openness, social interest, and changing opinions may provoke some suspicion on the part of the Sensitive person.

Influencing—Both of you communicate directly and openly, but the Influencing person does not like to be interrupted or to have opposing views brought up. So much for the role of devil's advocate. Influencing individuals' perfectionist tendencies are difficult for you to deal with. More important, they want to control all situations, which directly opposes your flexible nature in pursuit of personal interests. Little freedom is available in this relationship.

Determined—You may find it easier to talk to yourself after hearing "yes," "no," and "not now" from the Determined Personality. Communication is your life line, but it is only a functional necessity to the Determined person, who remains undeclared until he or she is sure a decision is right. While you solicit many opinions before making a decision, Determineds tend to make decisions on their own. You have many interests and friends, they have few. You have great difficulty respecting someone you can't talk to, while respect is essential for Determineds.

Idealistic—This relationship is a confrontation between flexibility and inflexibility, open communication and a closed set of rigid standards. Your changing views or shifting of positions is seen as a personal weakness by the Idealistic person. You follow the latest trends, while Idealistics follow only their individual and independent standards, not standards dictated by society. Your efforts to draw them out meet with intense resistance.

EPILOGUE

Now that you've met your TV Twins and gotten to know yourself better, you're well on your way to developing a special and valuable insight into what exactly is going on on both sides of the screen.

Why do you see and feel about things the way you do? Why do friends and family, spouse or lover, boss or employees see, act, and react in the same, or completely opposite, way? It is no longer a mystery.

You have discovered not only the reason why there is a wide variety of viewpoints on such subjects as love, relationships, security, work, and play, but also how those different viewpoints can be appreciated and brought together to form the basis of our human family. Differences of opinion arise from different Personality Styles, but the strength of each comes in being aware of how and why that opinion or feeling arises.

Each Personality Style has its strengths and weaknesses. That is made even more obvious by the trials and tribulations of our TV Twins. Now that the motivation behind them has been made clearer, you will be better able to recognize and use the strengths in yourself and appreciate them in others. You will also be more comfortable with the weaknesses, seeing them simply as part of the whole Personality Style; you can be much more tolerant and understanding of them now, both in yourself and in others.

Before you met your TV Twins you may have seen a friend as simply a person who could never make up his mind, or as someone mired in detail and self-doubt. But now you can see your Conscientious friend as someone who shares **David Letterman** and **Dick Loudon**'s dry wit; whose self-doubting is no different from **George Utley**'s uneasiness about room decor; and who could easily share **Cliff**'s passion for fact and detail.

Where you once saw your neighbor as an incurable daydreamer—maybe even a little spacey, but definitely with a sort of charisma—you will now see your Persistent neighbor. You will know that he or she shares an imaginative and searching mind with **Kate**, a great sense of faith and perseverance with that angel **Jonathan**, and **Zach**'s obvious flair for relationships.

Your boss is no longer a workaholic overachiever. You now recognize your Ambitious boss as a person who simply thrives on the action, the competition, and the thrill of the game. He or she shares that desire to get to the top and to keep the action going with **Alex Keaton**, **J. R. Ewing**, and **Barbara Walters**.

Why is your spouse such an incurable ham and where does all that amazing energy come from? Now you know why your Accomplishing husband, wife, or companion pulls those crazy stunts and can manage to be in three places at one time. **Johnny Carson**, **Tony** the Boss, and the **Seaver** bunch would understand perfectly.

And whether you have found yourself sharing a sensitive moment—or a pair of sunglasses—with **Ray** and **Peter**, or patiently following the exploits of **Jeff Colby** and **Krystle Carrington**; whether you now find yourself in good Anticipating company, worrying along with **Allie**, or keeping a tight Influencing reign on the situation with **Blake Carrington**, you are now able to recognize and appreciate how it all seems to fit.

"I'm so happy because I've finally gotten my husband to start remembering birthdays and our anniversary," said a Perceptive Personality who has discovered the power of TV Twins. "He's an Idealistic Personality and doesn't think of special occasions and sentimental times the same way I do. He needed to find out how important those little things are to me. By the same token, I needed to learn to appreciate his independence and occasional aloofness. He watches **Mary** on '227,' I watch **Sam** on 'Cheers,' and we both watch 'The Cosby Show'; **Cliff** is Perceptive and **Clair** is Idealistic. We've definitely learned to read and handle each other in better ways. So far, it's a successful compromise."

An Adaptable salesperson I know uses *all* the TV Twins to help him in his business. "I've tried to study some TV Twins from every Personality Style and familiarize myself with how they operate," he says. "Now I can do a quick evaluation of which Personality Style I think a client is, then approach him or her in the best way. An Influencing client is going to be a perfectionist and want to master the situation, like **Blake Carrington.** An Accomplishing client, like **Tony**, will respond to some joking and joshing, whereas a Determined client, like **Frank Furillo**, will not. I'm not always totally accurate, of course, but it does work a lot of the time."

With the newfound knowledge of your Personality Style and the discovery of your TV Twins, a valuable tool has been placed in your hands. Whether you use it to improve your love life, your career status, your relationship with the in-laws, or your desirability as a party guest, is entirely up to you. It's just nice to know that somewhere out there in videoland you have Twins who are traveling a similar road, facing similar peaks and valleys.

Wherever that road may lead you, your TV Twins will be there as long as you take along your trusty TV set. But wait. What if the worst happens? The event that your TV Twins probably dread far more than you do: cancellation.

As I mentioned earlier, the shows that portray Personality Styles most accurately and consistently are the shows that seem to survive and succeed. Then there's always that chance for resurrection: reruns. And it seems that the actors and actresses who have really tuned in to their own Personality Style are always showing up somewhere on the tube. Even the dreaded cancellation does not necessarily spell the breakup of your video family. So don't touch that dial.

Besides, now that you have the means to refine your knowledge of Personality Styles, you can begin to spot your own TV Twins on the new shows. I always find some satisfaction in watching a character develop and finally assume a full-blown Personality Style. It adds an entire new dimension to my viewing time.

Finally, I would like to thank all the TV Twins of each Personality Style for being themselves, for sharing their video lives so generously, and for showing us just how far we can go if we truly find and know ourselves.

I would also like to sincerely apologize to those TV Twins whom we did not mention or include. Perhaps they just didn't spend enough time on the screen to let us make a definite decision as to which Personality Style they truly fit. Or maybe their writers and creators, or the actors or actresses portraying them, have not yet discovered the full potential of their own Personality Style. There's always next season.

And how about you? Now that you've discovered how to be all that you can be and the best that you can be, you are ready to become a star in your own right, on *this* side of the screen. Whether it's Hollywood, Wall Street, the White House, or your own living room, the choice is now yours. You have the wonderful gift of being able to decide just how far you want to go and just what route you want to travel.

So good luck, and stay tuned to those TV Twins. You're in good company.

INDEX

ABOUT THE AUTHOR

GREGORY G. YOUNG, M.D., a psychiatrist with a private practice in Dayton, Ohio, is also the Chairman of the Department of Psychiatry at the St. Elizabeth Medical Center, a former Associate Clinical Professor of Psychiatry at the Wright State University School of Medicine, and has been involved with psychiatric facilities throughout the world. His findings have been the subject of many magazine articles and television interviews. His articles have been published extensively in professional journals and he is the author of *Your Personality and How to Live With It.* His primary concern is the promotion of good emotional health through the use of Personality Styles and the medium of television.